THE BAKU
INHERITANCE

THE CITY OF WINDS SERIES

Anne M Kennedy

ANNE M KENNEDY

First edition published 2024 by WONKY CAT PRESS LTD.

ISBN 978-1-0686302-0-0

Cover design by Jessica Bell Design

Typeset in Adobe Garamond Pro by Heddon Publishing

www.thecityofwinds.com

*For the writing group that met on the 17th floor
of the Radisson Hotel in Baku.*

Baku بادکوبه *Bâd-kube*

Wind Pounded (Ancient Persian)

A place where the wind is strong and pounding.

CHAPTER ONE

Baku, Azerbaijan. South-west outpost of the Russian Empire.
November 1890.

KLARA KNEW TO BE ON HER GUARD BECAUSE NIKOLAI HAD warned her. He'd be carrying something valuable, the old man had said. Something men will kill for – it was why he'd given her the Smith 'n' Wesson revolver. The weapon felt heavy in her pocket, solid metal banging against her leg as she moved. *You are the last man in the world I want to meet, Anton Nikolayevich Sabroski.* She drew a shawl over her hair and draped it over her thin shoulders as she glanced about. The man who had been outside the house had followed her. Overweight, ill-dressed, lumbering along in her peripheral vision, a glowing red dot between his fingers. There were others, but she'd grown used to the masquerades: the Okhrana secret police, the gendarmes, the oil spies, pickpockets (she'd been one herself) and assorted villains. The man who caught her interest was tall and well-built and overly muffled – something about the way he held himself seemed familiar.

She took a deep breath. Dusk had crept over the Baku harbour, the crescent-shaped bay filling up with fishing boats and steamers making ready for the night. Being out at night was a risk for a young, unaccompanied, European female. But Klara was used to keeping to the shadows. The ancient city of Baku, on the edge of the Caspian Sea, was ideal for anyone who wanted to remain unseen, perfect for outcasts and runaways and those hiding from hunters. A call to prayer arose from a mosque, then another, then another, until the dusk was filled with the overlapping of songs.

Somebody poked her hard in the back and she spun round. A ragged child handed her a note and held out its hand. Klara took a kopek from her pocket. She read. A bold hand. Written in Russian.

The docks. Second cargo shed.

Her heart quickened. Was it a trick? She looked this way and that, but there was nobody obvious and no sign of glowing-red-dot man. Peddlers and merchants packed their wares. Wagons creaked, donkeys brayed, horses pawed the ground. Lights dotted the hillside and the ominous Maiden Tower loomed up from the walled fortress of Baku's old city, the *Icheri Sheher*.

She would risk it.

She secured the revolver, gathered up her dress and ran, darting and hurling herself into doorways and archways to draw breath and check. She ran until she reached the loading bays and found a hiding place. She took out the gun and stood still to catch her breath. Then she slipped between the shadows until she reached the second cargo shed.

The man she guessed was Anton Nikolayevich was sitting on a crate talking to a fisherman. He was wet through. He had no overcoat or hat, his jacket was ripped and a streak of blood ran down the side of his face. He was drinking from the fisherman's flask. Cautiously she emerged. 'Anton Nikolayevich?'

The man jerked his head up and one hand flew to his pocket but came away empty. He cursed. 'Who are you?'

Anton had brown deep-set eyes, too many lines for a young man, and long wavy hair tied back.

'My name is Klara. Your father, Nikolai Mikhailovich... he sent me.'

He scowled at her before handing the flask to the fisherman.

She motioned. 'Hurry. There might be... trouble.'

He stood at that. Awkwardly, as his right leg was bleeding. He picked up a battered travelling case. 'Why didn't my father come?'

'He can't. Nikolai doesn't go anywhere any more.'

'Why?'

'He's unwell.'

He drew closer, towering over her, dripping seawater and blood tinged with rum. 'Do you have a means of transport?'

'By the garrison. A gig... What happened to you?'

'I took a beating... from men who knew no better.'

He limped alongside her, his soaking jacket glancing her arm. It was completely dark now. The cargo area of the docks was heaped with canvas sacks, wooden barrels and long iron pipes to trip over. She felt a shiver up her spine. A bell tolled from the Armenian church on the hill.

'Give me your gun,' he said. 'We're being followed.'

'Where's yours?'

'Lost.'

Reluctantly, she gave him the revolver. Anton took it, checked the cartridges before taking hold of her arm. Despite his injuries, he moved at considerable speed, gathering her and his bag at a pace.

They hadn't gone far when they were ambushed by an explosion of street children in rags around them. Little hands snatched at the travelling case and pulled at the man's pockets and his belt. Klara batted them away. Anton raised the weapon, more for show than a threat, and the children shrieked when they saw the gun and scattered like mice.

'How did you find me?' he demanded.

'A note. From a child.'

'These ones, no doubt.'

She flushed. 'Just be thankful somebody came to get you.'

They reached the gig. Klara hooked up the horse, took the reins and drove along the embankment. She beat a path between wagons and donkeys, a Turk in a fez carrying a trunk on his back. Two shrouded women shouted as they sped past, spraying dirt.

'What are you carrying that's so valuable?' Klara shouted. 'A sack of diamonds?'

He ignored her as he looked left then right. Suddenly he grabbed the reins, forcing the horse to veer to the right.

'What are you doing!'

'Get down.' He pushed her into the well of the seat. Klara had just enough time to witness a covered wagon roll across their path before a grinding noise filled her ears. Anton pulled hard right on the reins, and the gig bumped as it scraped along the side of the cart. The horse whinnied and struggled to free itself.

Then came a blur of violence.

A man's arm in a fitted jacket; breeches tucked into black boots. An arc and thwack of a cane, then a cry, an animal snort. The gig rocked and screeched sideways but remained miraculously upright. The stranger on the horse reached down and snatched at the travelling case but Anton Nikolayevich was too quick. He wrenched it away and swung it hard into his attacker's face. The horse reared and the stranger fell.

'Drive,' he ordered, thrusting the reins into Klara's hands before slumping into his seat.

The residential streets were quiet. As they approached the grand house on Nikolaevskaya Street, a watchman unlocked the iron gates and guided the horse into the courtyard. Klara's head spun. Anton Nikolayevich was far more dangerous than she'd realised. He would draw attention to her, to Ivan, which would be the end of them both. The protective blanket that Nikolai provided had gone. She watched him climb out of the gig and limp his way to the door.

Why did you have to come back?

He hadn't said another word to her. It was as if she didn't exist to him. She knew he had dismissed her as a nobody, a servant, a paid messenger.

But oh how wrong he was.

CHAPTER TWO

ANTON SAT ON THE FLOOR IN THE LIBRARY WITH HIS LEGS stretched out, leaning against a cushion by the fire. It was less painful to keep his wounded leg straight. He'd been outnumbered on the boat. The cutthroats on the cargo vessel from the eastern shore thought he promised more and would have killed him if he hadn't managed to jump overboard. The fisherman had been a godsend, hauling him out of the water. Perhaps the cutthroats had done him a favour – arriving in such an unexpected manner had saved his life.

He massaged the mutilated finger on his left hand. Smashing the spy with the travelling case had bent his fingers back activating a memory of a brawl in a Shanghai bar. He flexed his fingers and pushed back the pain. Whatever was going on in Baku was far more dangerous than he'd anticipated, even though he knew the frontier city on the edge of the Russian Empire had a reputation for volatility.

Anton took stock and reflected. He had hidden the secret documents and hired another guard while he decided what to do next, but his pursuers were unlikely to give up so easily. *I should have paid more attention in Shanghai. Taken the warnings more seriously.* He sighed. What did he really know about the specifications he was carrying? *Deliver the documents to your father,* the merchant had said. *Nikolai Sabroski will know what to do.*

Only his father didn't know anything any more.

He closed his eyes and took a steadying breath as he recalled the images of the night two days ago. His father in a dirty four-poster bed surrounded by blood-red curtains. His emaciated body, wisps of white hair, the smell of sweat and urine. The fire burning in the grate, suffocating stale air. And the girl. *Who the fuck was she?* Standing in the shadows, untamed dark hair, twig thin with wild eyes like a cat about to scratch. His father had called over to her, clawing at the bedsheets to pull himself up, 'What do you think of him, Klara?'

'He seems… old – older than you said,' she'd answered.

His father had given a scratchy laugh as he looked Anton up and down. 'That's true. You've aged, my boy. I don't think the Orient has looked after you. And already I see you've been in trouble. That wound needs attention. Klara – fetch the medicine box!'

The memory was hazy except for the end, when his father had clutched his hand with fevered strength. 'I'm sorry for what's happened, son. I've made life hard for you. All those years ago, we had such dreams, all of us. Your mother and me. Fabian and Olesia. Now you have to do this on your own.' He had trembled. 'You must be careful, son. You must be as watchful of the past as you are of the present. Remember that, Anton. Nobody ever forgets. Not completely.'

Anton didn't know what his father had meant by that, but it didn't matter now. Nikolai Mikhailovich Sabroski was buried on the hillside overlooking the bay and nobody came to the funeral except himself, the lawyer and the girl.

He clenched his fists and felt every joint in his body lock tight. *I'm sorry, Father. If only I'd known.* He gasped out loud, shuddered involuntarily and closed his eyes as he forced deep breaths. He stayed like that for a while, aware of horses trotting past, the cloying scent of lilies somebody had arranged in a vase, and the warbling pigeon on the windowsill. The clock on the mantelpiece struck the half hour. He snapped from his reverie, rubbed his eyes and massaged his forehead.

He lit a cigarette and took a deep drag. After the funeral, the family lawyer, John Seigenberg, had returned to the house and read the will. Calmly, John had informed him of his father's misfortunes, peppering each sentence with *bankruptcy, accounting fraud, ill-judgement, dried-up oilfields and rash decisions.* 'I wrote and told you, but it appears you never received my telegrams,' he said.

'That is correct. Father gave no indication in his letters.'

'I see.' John pushed a pair of gold spectacles up onto the bridge of his nose. 'There are a couple more matters.' He reached into his attaché case and produced a package. 'Your father left you this – I've had it locked in my safe.'

'What is it?'

'I don't know – you'll have to break the seal to find out. The only instructions I have is that you are its guardian, and it cannot be sold – Nikolai was very insistent. You are to open it on your own.'

Anton took the package. It fitted into the palm of his hand. It was wrapped in brown paper, plain and unmarked. 'How very mysterious of him.'

John Seigenberg cleared his throat. 'Also, your father made a codicil to his will. It states that Klara Darkova is to be retained as your assistant. Given board and lodging and employed.'

'That girl?'

'Yes. That girl.'

'You mean as a servant?'

'No, as an assistant. With your work.'

Anton spread his hands. 'I don't have any work. Sabroski Oil is bankrupt. What do I need an assistant for?'

Klara sat cross-legged on the floor outside the library while the lawyer read through the will. She listened to Anton Nikolayevich's protestations of disbelief and silently raged at his rude comments about her. John Seigenberg was a good sort: he had defended her, told Anton he had no choice. The old Jewish lawyer had been in Baku for nearly fifty years. He knew everything and everyone, saw the good and the bad. He had a daughter about her age – Julia – though Klara had never spoken to her.

She drew up her knees and hugged them to her body. *What am I going to do about Ivan?* She rubbed her forehead with the heel of her hand. Rasoul was keeping an eye on Ivan on the oilfield, but how much longer could that go on? What would happen when Anton Nikolayevich found out?

Dread swirled in her stomach. What if the Okhrana found him? If the gendarmes were alerted? If the trackers discovered her? Should she reconsider and return to Kiev?

No.

If she did, she risked *him* finding her. Being a woman made things so much more complicated. The only way for a woman to secure herself was to marry, she'd been told. The dread in her stomach expanded and rose into her throat. It made her want to retch.

Imagine saying that to a man. Imagine his response.

Chapter Three

It was tempting to escape into an opium haze, but Anton resisted. He had to see the loss for himself, to prove it was true. On the fourth morning, when his leg injury had improved, he saddled the horse and rode south on the coast road that skirted the Caspian Sea. It led down to the plains known as *Bibi-Eibat*, where the major oilfields lay. The fields had been farmland, but they were now a mesh of churned-up oil, trenches, pipes, wooden huts and towers.

Anton didn't know what he was hoping to achieve. John Seigenberg said most of the fields had been sold off, so he had no right to trespass and ask questions, but he didn't care. He read the names on the company signs: Mantashev, Lianozov, Taghiyev, the Nobel Brothers, and then, to his distaste, Brakov Oil. *Damn you, Fabian Brakov. You were supposed to be my father's friend.*

One field lay empty. A rusty Sabroski Oil sign lay on the ground, thrown aside like a discarded toy. In its place, new signage: *No Trespassing*. He pulled up his horse and drew breath, heart hammering in his throat. It was incredible to think that two years ago Sabroski Oil had owned fifteen oilfields producing thousands of barrels of oil for the Rothschild refineries on the Black Sea.

Anton tethered his horse and peered through the iron gates. He hesitated, then climbed, swinging his legs over, and lowered himself gingerly to the ground. It had been a long time since he'd set foot on an oilfield. What struck him most was the lack of noise: a silent, eerie quiet lay about the place like a battlefield after the fighting had finished and all that remained were the dead. Hundreds of derrick towers dotted the landscape. Doors hung open and broken equipment lay scattered about. Anton saw a squat office building in the distance. As he made his way over, a figure flitted across the window and disappeared. He heard a shout. Three rough-looking men approached – one with a rifle slung across his shoulder, the other two carried iron bars.

'*Ostanovka!* Stop!' the one with the rifle shouted.

Anton raised his hands. 'Gentlemen – my apologies. I'm just taking a look. I heard these fields were for sale.'

'You heard wrong. This land is private!' A tall man in a woolly cap poked a rifle butt in his ribs. Half the man's teeth were missing, and he had a red scar that looked like a scald mark down one side of his face. Anton flinched but kept his hands up. 'I came to assess these fields. I heard they were empty. Open to bids.'

'These fields are the property of Zenovitch Liquid Fuel. You are trespassing.'

'My name is Anton Sabroski. These fields once belonged to my father.'

The man spat. 'Sabroski? Never seen you before. Besides, I don't care who you are. Get going!'

'Is there somebody I can speak to? Someone from Zenovitch Liquid Fuel?'

'There's nobody.'

'What's happening with these fields?' pressed Anton. 'What are they going to do with them? Are you guards?'

'None of your fucking business. Move yourself!'

Anton did as he was told. He heard the men muttering as they tramped behind him. 'One last question,' said Anton as they approached the gates. 'What happened to Sabroski Oil?'

'You say you're his son – you should know.'

'I've been away.'

'Spent too much. Didn't know what he was doing.' He tapped his head. 'Not right in the head.' He gestured to the oilfield. 'They say it's no good.'

Anton rode away. Once he was out of sight, he pulled off the road and sat staring across the Caspian. The water gleamed silver in the pale sun. *What did the man mean, 'not right in the head'?* His father hadn't lost his wits – he was coherent until the end. His business sense and knowledge of the oil industry had held him in stead for nearly two decades, so why would he make such an error of judgement? Anton flicked the reins and rode along the Bailov road until he saw the sign for Brakov Oil. His chest tightened. He recognised that field; it had belonged to Sabroski Oil and was where he'd spent his childhood, mucking about with his friend, Rafiq.

He rode through the gates. *Let's see what you have to say, Fabian Brakov.*

As he approached the main office, a bear of a man stepped out. Fabian Brakov had put on a great deal of weight since Anton had last seen him, his hair was grey and grizzled, his face jowly. He wore thick cotton trousers tucked into long boots and a stained shirt stretched over a fat belly. 'Well, well. Anton Nikolayevich,' Fabian growled. 'At last. You are back. Welcome.'

'I buried my father two days ago. On the hillside over there.' Anton gestured. 'You didn't come.'

'I am a busy man.'

'Too busy to pay respects to a friend? An old business partner?'

Fabian raised an eyebrow. 'What do you want, Sabroski?'

'Answers.'

'You already have them.'

'No, I don't.'

'Then ask your crooked accountant, Dmitry Ivanovich.'

'He's gone.'

'Well, doesn't that just say something?'

'How could this have happened?'

'Nothing to do with me,' Fabian said. 'I warned your father, but he wasn't the type to listen.'

'That's a lie!'

Two Cossacks on horseback trotted over. They wore fur caps and silver swords hung by their sides. 'Sabroski's not staying.' Fabian indicated Anton with a dismissive flick of his hand. 'Come and see me once you've calmed down, boy. If you intend to stay in Baku, you'll need help. I may even have a job for you.'

CHAPTER FOUR

STEFAN BRAKOV RELAXED IN A WARM GLOW OF SATISFACTION. He had learned that only this morning Anton Nikolayevich had stormed onto his father's oilfields demanding explanations. So typical of him. Oh, how Stefan wished he'd been there to see his childhood tormentor getting his comeuppance. He would have savoured the scene… though he doubted misfortune would hold Anton down for long. Anton had an irrepressible core that connived to endure, regroup and bounce back. When he left Baku all those years ago, a hypnotic beacon went too, one that Stefan had tried his hardest to stop staring at, but had never succeeded.

'It must have been a terrible shock for him,' he heard his mother say, picking up a serviette and dabbing her mouth. Olesia Brakov looked pale and taut, sheathed in indigo-blue, with touches of grey snaking through her thick hair. It was the first thing she'd said all evening.

'What did he say to you, Father?' asked Stefan.

His father ignored the question. 'If he hadn't got involved with those university types, Olesia, he'd never have had to leave. God knows the mess he got into to have the tsar's secret police after him. If he kept his nose clean, he could have stayed in Baku and might have prevented Nikolai from making rash decisions. Don't give me that look, Olesia. As I have always said, it doesn't do to fill young heads with political ideas. Foolish ideas of worlds that can never be. And I was proved right, wasn't I? No one is going to forget *that*, are they?'

'Why do you always jump to conclusions?' his mother said. 'We know nothing about what really happened in St Petersburg. Anton was just in the wrong place at the wrong time.'

Stefan's father snorted and gulped down his wine. Stefan watched his mother finger the lace embroidery around the collar of her bodice. His father was right: no one would ever forget. Ten years ago, the assassination of Tsar Alexander II in St Petersburg had been in every newspaper from Vladivostok to New York. He had been fourteen when the world reeled from shock. Every newspaper carried vivid illustrations of the atrocities. He had collected pictures and pasted them into his scrapbook. There were horses, maimed and dead, Cossack soldiers lying in the snow, the tsar bloodied and battered. If the illustrations had been in colour, the snow would have been red.

Afterwards, the new tsar had vastly expanded the size and power of the Okhrana. The secret police had crawled over the empire like maggots, burrowing and breaking down anyone with a different viewpoint.

His father continued. 'The truth is never pleasant. Not that I wish to speak ill of the dead, but Nikolai let a lot of people down. The Sabroskis were an odd family. I see now that it was a mistake to go into business with them.'

'I think a gesture of friendship wouldn't hurt now that Anton's back. It was a mistake not to go to the funeral.' His mother's violet eyes had narrowed to slits.

'So, it was a bad decision, was it?' his father said, wiping his mouth. 'And you, madam, never make mistakes.'

Silence stretched across the table. Stefan felt sure that his mother was about to say something, but she sat straight-backed with her hands in her lap and stared across the room. Stefan caught his wife's eye. Miranda Aleksandrovna pulled a face and gave him a small smile. She was wearing his favourite gown, the one he'd had commissioned in Paris. It was a flame-red silk bodice and matching skirt, covered with black sequinned net. The light from the candelabra spilled shades of gold across her dangerous almond eyes, dark lashed and half closed. She had a way of pursing her lips together in a façade of coy submission, but he knew better.

'I heard there was a fire on one of Taghiyev's fields,' Miranda said lightly. She raised her wine glass and a servant darted forward to refill it. 'People said it set off a spouter and the fountain of oil reached over two hundred feet!'

Fabian appraised her over his wine glass. 'You are right, my dear. A bad business. The oil's still spraying over Bibi-Eibat. Luckily for Taghiyev, the Nobel Brothers are sending their engineers who will have it capped in no time.'

Miranda blinked her long lashes. 'Is it as powerful as the spouter Brakov Oil had last year? I understand you personally supervised the cap on that one.'

Stefan's father relaxed in the chair, his yellow poplin waistcoat straining over his stomach. 'That was a vicious beast. Let's hope it never breaks free again, else we may lose the field.'

They finished the rest of the meal in silence as cutlery chinked against porcelain, claret splashed into wine goblets and kitchen staff came and went, carrying and clearing plates.

Eventually his father looked up. 'Albert Prankman is joining us later, Stefan.' He barked at the servants lining the wall. 'Make sure the gentleman is shown into the library and that we're not disturbed.'

An hour later, Stefan followed his father across the mosaic-tiled hallway into the library. The room smelled of cigars and leather with candle wax. A ceramic fireplace with olive and peach tiles dominated the corner of the south wall. The walnut desk in the opposite corner was equipped with several new fountain pens from Philadelphia. Four upholstered, blue-striped chairs and a low table were positioned in the heart of the room. Stefan inspected his manicured fingernails and picked a long dark hair from the sleeve of his tailcoat. 'Why is Albert Prankman coming tonight?' he asked, keeping his voice even. *Fucking Albert Prankman. The know-it-all oil consultant from Philadelphia.*

His father threw down his newspaper. 'Idiot kaiser. What was the man thinking… sacking Bismarck? That chancellor is the only man in Germany with any sense.' Stefan opened his mouth but closed it again as his father waggled a finger. 'This is what happens when you don't keep people in their rightful place. The kaiser had some nonsense idea about giving workers better rights and conditions. Bismarck called it a fool's policy and I agree.' He cursed. 'Now, what did you say?'

'Nothing.' Stefan felt himself shrinking as if his skin had become too big for him.

His father retrieved his newspaper and glanced over the top of it. 'You dislike Albert, don't you? I can tell by the way you behave whenever he's around – like you've got a board up your arse with that superior look on your face.'

Stefan reddened. 'I think he has too much control of our company.'

'Indeed? So, you think an oil expert from Philadelphia is of no use to us? After the bad decisions that Nikolai Sabroski made, we need somebody with experience!'

Stefan shuffled his feet. *Breathe slowly. Don't let him rile you.*

'He's the best there is. He gets results and that's what matters. Prankman may be brusque, but he's a clever man and we need him. Don't you forget that. Try listening to him for a change. You might learn something.'

I listen to you all the time, Father. And all you do is criticise.

There came a knock at the door and a short man in his early forties entered. He was wearing a dark brown tailcoat with matching trousers, a mustard waistcoat, and a starched white shirt. Cropped hair and dark circles under his eyes gave him a skeletal appearance.

'Good evening, gentlemen,' Prankman said, handing his top hat and cane to the manservant. He pulled off a pair of white linen gloves and dropped them inside the upturned hat, then adjusted a tortoiseshell monocle that nestled in his right eye. Stefan murmured a greeting and avoided shaking his hand. The American's skin was always too smooth, and he smelled of Hoyt's cologne. He automatically drifted to the drinks cabinet as his father and the American started to talk.

There was discussion about the Rothschilds and contracts and the possibility of new business and expansion. Stefan brightened at that. Expansion meant new positions and new responsibilities, which could mean he'd be given a section of the company to run. Prankman did most of the talking as usual. He had a deep red groove carved into his cheekbone, beneath his right eye where his monocle lodged like a glinting orb. He reminded Stefan of a stoat he'd stepped on as a child that sprang from the snow baring its teeth.

'I hear Anton Nikolayevich came to see you,' he heard Prankman say at last.

Fabian scoffed. 'The boy worked himself into a fury. Wanting answers of course.'

'He can ask away. The only one who knows what happened is Dmitry Ivanovich, the accountant, and he's long gone.' Prankman crossed his short legs. His lacquered boots had a fleck of dirt on the toe.

'Where did Dmitry go?' said Stefan as he refilled his glass and moved closer.

'Odessa,' said his father.

'How do you know?'

'The landlady. The old trout demanded we pay his rent, can you believe? Owed her three months. He sent a note requesting she pack all his belongings and put them on the train bound for Tiflis.'

Stefan frowned. 'People are strange, aren't they? He steals all that money and yet doesn't pay his rent. Whyever not?'

His father sighed. 'Because he didn't have any money. Not in the end. He owed too many debts and angered the wrong kind of people.'

Stefan said, 'I wonder if Anton's seen his Muslim friend yet.'

'Rafiq Hasanov? He's not been around for years.'

'His father, Talat, comes to the club,' said Prankman. 'The Hasanovs own Caspian Shipping. The boy's a talented engineer, so I'm told. Worked on one of the Nobel Brother's tanker designs.'

'His wife died, didn't she?' said Stefan sitting down. 'I wonder if Anton knows that.' He stretched out his slim legs and admired his patent leather pumps. The last time he'd seen Anton was seven years ago at the funeral of his mother, Emma Sabroski. Stefan's own mother had taken the loss of her friend badly, not that he remembered his mother and Emma Sabroski spending much time together, but then women were always so emotional. Father had been in a wild mood, drinking too much as usual, whereas Anton's father, Nikolai Sabroski, had watched the coffin be lowered into the ground in silence before shutting himself away in his library. Anton had stayed in Baku for less than a week with scarcely enough time to show his respects. He'd been abrupt and distant and had hardly spoken to anyone. It was unbelievable that a man with such education and experience could be so uncouth.

Then again, Anton always had been strange and thought nothing of consorting with the Tatar workers on the oilfields.

'No doubt the lawyer will acquaint Anton with all he needs to know,' Fabian said glancing at Prankman. 'Seigenberg appears to regard himself as the boy's guardian.'

The lights in the room flickered and Stefan looked up at the ruby glass lamp. Its crystal prisms twinkled in the light. Few of the mansions in Baku had been installed with the new lighting phenomenon. Stefan reflected that the Sabroski house would still be lit with gas, or even candles. Each time he passed the house, it seemed more neglected and desolate; Anton would never have the money to repair it now.

His father cleared his throat. 'You can leave us now, Stefan. Albert and I have matters to discuss.'

Stefan hesitated. Once again his father was dismissing him like a child. He forced a tight smile. *Fuck the pair of you.* The pressure in his chest returned and a familiar throb of pain started in his temples.

An hour later, Stefan sat on the bed and watched his wife undress. Miranda pulled the pins from her hair and studied herself in the long mirror. 'What was that man doing here tonight?'

Stefan tugged at his bow tie and yanked it off. 'Persuading Father to do business with the Rothschilds.'

'Sounds sensible. Your father agrees?'

'Father agrees with everything Albert Prankman says.'

She glanced over. 'Come. Help me with this.'

Stefan sprang up. She had changed after dinner into a demure cream silk gown embroidered with green flowers, a paradox of chaste sexuality. He undid the tie fastenings and gently slid the bodice from her shoulders, bending down to kiss her neck and run his hands over her skin. A hot rush spread through him. She smiled and pulled away. 'Don't let that man intimidate you,

Stefan. If the company does expand, it may be a good opportunity for you.'

Stefan sat down and kicked off his patent leather shoes. 'Father still doesn't trust me to do anything important. Just now he dismissed me like some schoolboy because he had private matters to discuss.'

Miranda sat at the dressing table and picked up her hairbrush. A pink corset trimmed with black lace sculptured her body, dipping in at her waist. She started to brush her hair, running her fingers through individual strands to coax them into shape.

'Ever since that damned American arrived, Father's been impossible,' said Stefan unbuttoning his shirt.

Miranda put the hairbrush down. 'Tell me about your friend.'

'Who?'

'This Anton Nikolayevich everyone's talking about.'

'He's the son of Nikolai Sabroski, Father's old partner.'

'I'd like to meet him.'

'Why?'

Miranda laughed. 'Because everyone keeps talking about him and it provoked your mother and father into such a temper.'

Stefan took off the rest of his clothes and lay down on the bed. The room was stuffy, and his head was starting to ache again.

A few minutes later the light clicked off, casting the room with shadows. Miranda slunk over, sat down next to him, and ran her fingers through his hair. He could feel her sharp nails against his scalp.

'Did I say something wrong?'

He closed his eyes. 'You never say anything wrong.'

She bent low and kissed his cheek, a waft of orange blossom mingling with her unmistakable aroma. He pulled her down and kissed her, sliding his fingers around to unhook the stud fastenings of her corset. Miranda stood up and slipped off the rest of her clothes. Stefan remained very still, watching her as she lay on the bed before turning on her side to face him. The curve of her body gleamed silver in the night. Slowly he traced a path with his hand down the slope of her breasts into the dip of her waist and over the sweep of her hips. She looked like a wave of silk.

His heart was beating fast. Miranda was all his and he could enjoy her any time he wanted. But he wanted to prolong the moment, savour the desire as it flooded his body, swamping all thoughts and anxieties. A strand of hair fell across her breasts, and he stroked it away.

Then he folded her into him.

CHAPTER FIVE

I⊤ WAS LATE AFTERNOON BY THE TIME ANTON RETURNED home. He'd spent the day visiting the different oil regions of Baku – *Bibi-Eibat, Balakhani, Saboonchi* – questioning those who had been willing to speak. He strode into the house and slammed the front door. He flung off his overcoat and went to the library to get himself a drink.

It had been a depressing and desperate day. He'd found it hard to marry the two images of his father: the frail old man in the sick bed and the man who had brought the family from St Petersburg. The hardworking businessman who had built Sabroski Oil out of nothing. He could still picture his father striding around the oilfields like a Cossack warrior commanding armies of Tatars while drills thudded, steam engines whistled, and fountains of oil flowed. The Sabroski empire had been an efficient, slick machine that ran day and night since he'd been a child.

Anton rubbed his eyes and sat down, cradling a glass of whisky. The grief at his father's death would have to be borne, there was no escaping it. The last time he felt so lost was when his mother died, as he'd been too young to remember his sister's passing. He took a large gulp of whisky. *So, it's just me now.*

Ironically the last time he'd been in Baku was to attend his mother's funeral seven years before. But his father had warned it wasn't safe to stay, so he returned to Vladivostok and then onto Shanghai. He sighed. *I should have stayed in the city and brazened it out.* Baku was a long way away from the reach of the tsar. It was unlikely they'd track him there. If he had stayed, would his father still be alive?

He cursed at a knock at the door. It would be the girl, but as much as he craved solitude, he couldn't avoid dealing with her any longer. 'Enter,' he called.

When she appeared, he noticed her eyes were red-rimmed. She was wearing a dark brown day dress buttoned up the front which dwarfed her slim frame. Her muddy brown hair had been scooped in a bun, but she looked wrung-out and unwholesome. She walked into the centre of the room and stood straight with her shoulders back. 'I should like to know your intentions, sir, regarding my position.'

Anton took a slow breath. 'My father's made provision for you in his will. But I'm sure you already know that. You will be allowed to stay and work in the house.'

Her eyes bored into him. 'I'm not a servant. I was Nikolai's assistant at Sabroski Oil, not his housekeeper.'

He threw out his hands. 'Don't be foolish, girl. What do you know about oil?'

'Probably a great deal more than you do.'

He blinked. 'How exactly are you going to assist me? There is no company. There is no money. I have nothing to offer you. Just a house in serious need of repair.'

'You have your army pension. We won't starve.'

He almost laughed. *The nerve of the girl!*

She clicked her tongue. 'A man like you will survive. Your type always does.' She paused. 'You need staff. A housekeeper, a stablehand, a cook and a valet. I will also collect your father's papers,' she said, as if ticking off a list in her head. 'He kept documents all over the house. You'll need to go through them.'

A prickling sensation started at the back of his neck. 'My father's papers are not your business. I'll see to that.'

'You don't know where he keeps them or what the documents mean.'

'Your help will *not* be necessary.' He stood up.

She regarded him coolly. 'As you wish. I will continue to use the bedroom at the back of the house. It is adequate. I only have a few belongings, so do not require any more space.'

'I'm glad to hear it. Anything else?'

'Are you hungry?'

'Yes.' He waited for new terms to be dictated. Maybe she'd ask him to prepare the meal.

'I'll organise some food later.'

'Oh, so cooking's acceptable then?'

'I like cooking.'

After she left, Anton lit a cigarette. What strange ideas had his father put into the girl's head? An assistant at Sabroski Oil? She must have been a secretary, running errands, filing, helping out in the office. And at the end, his father's nurse and companion.

He blew out a plume of smoke. His father's library had always been a peaceful retreat. It was situated at the back of the house and overlooked the courtyard. French-style doors opened onto a leafy space with a solitary mulberry tree where doves cooed and fluttered. Two faded oriental rugs covered the library floor, a roll-topped writing desk stood to the left of the fireplace, and in the centre sat two overstuffed armchairs separated by a low coffee table. Walnut shelves with cream-papered volumes smelling of vanilla ran the length of two walls from floor to ceiling, equipped with an access ladder. There was a floor globe beside his chair. He reached out and touched the waxed surface, watching as oceans and land masses swirled round.

It was sunset and a call to prayer rose from the Icheri Sheher. Anton wrenched off his boots, unbuttoned his waistcoat and was about to lay his head back when he caught sight of a package lying on the writing desk – the one John Seigenberg had given him after the funeral. He'd forgotten about it and went to retrieve it. The package was four inches long, wrapped in brown paper and bound many times with string. He broke the wax seal and unwrapped it.

For a very long time he stared in disbelief.

Inside was a glittering, jewelled egg: enamelled, translucent, rose-red and encrusted with diamonds. It had a hinged top decorated with a trellis of green-gold orchids. He held it up to the light. The egg sparkled and glistened, a shimmer of reds and greens like a magnificent gem from an ancient temple. He turned it around and noticed a tiny clasp, which he tried to open, but it was jammed. Bewildered, he retrieved the packaging lying on the floor and unwrapped each piece of paper, tissue and string, but there was nothing more to find.

John Seigenberg must have made a mistake; the jewelled egg couldn't possibly belong to him. How had his bankrupt father possessed such a treasure? *You are its guardian, and it cannot be sold*, the lawyer had said as he stood before him in this very room, wearing a black frock coat, black silk top hat and a starched white collar. A ripple of unease ran through him. He must hide it.

His father had a secret safe concealed behind the bookshelves. He secured the egg in his pocket, positioned the ladder and climbed up, running his fingers across a stretch of leather spines examining the spaces behind, but there was nothing except for a desiccated beetle and a layer of dust. There was a line of oversized books on a shelf at the top of the far wall. Anton repositioned the ladder and climbed up, pushing aside a five-volume series of Nikolai Aleksandrovich Naidenov's Imperial Russia plate books.

He felt around until his fingers touched something metallic. He pushed a lever and a compartment clicked open and he stowed the egg inside. As he climbed back down, he banged his wounded leg. Cursing, he made his way to the kitchen.

The basement under the kitchen stretched across the back part of the house. Half-moon windows peered up towards the street, where a dirty light filtered through and rested on a wooden cupboard. A stone sink stood on his left, a large, scrubbed table in the middle and two broken chairs piled up in a corner. Anton removed his jacket and rolled up his sleeves and sloshed water over his face. He caught sight of himself in a dusty mirror propped up against the wall. The girl was right, he did look old, even though he was not yet thirty. A mass of dark hair curled the longer it grew and his face was lined from too much sun. His arms were a startling blue and red swirl of designs that curled up his arms like serpents – courtesy of Zhou-Dan's tattoo parlour. Anton dried himself, opened the doors of the medicine cupboard and rummaged around until he found a bottle of iodine. Rolling up his trouser leg, he removed the soiled bandage, cleaned the wound, and put on a fresh dressing.

What did you do, Father, to come by such a treasure?

CHAPTER SIX

THE OILFIELD ON BIBI-EIBAT BURNED. A MASSIVE explosion ripped through the boiler room hurling a steam engine into the air. Wooden derricks cracked in a blur of orange, spitting sparks of boiling oil.

In his downtown office, the oil spy known as the Pallid Harrier smiled. He could almost smell the smoke and feel the burn as the flames licked his imagination. It was so easy to do. An accidental spark during an oilfield spill, or the deliberate triggering of a blowout which sprayed a cocktail of chemicals for miles. Enough to destroy an oilfield and put a producer out of business for ever.

His men had done well. Rockefeller would be pleased.

The Pallid Harrier leaned back in his chair, picked up his customary glass of milk, and re-read the cable from New York:

NY to Pallid Harrier October 10th 1890

Locate and deliver specifications carried from Orient by Anton Nikolayevich Sabroski.

34

The documents from the Orient were a mystery. John Rockefeller had given no explanation as to why they were important. The president of Standard Oil had always taken his chief agent into his confidence. But not this time.

The oil spy drank hard, gulping down the creamy white liquid until the bottom of the glass was visible. Then he wiped his mouth and set the glass down.

Anton Nikolayevich. *What did you bring back from the Orient? Whatever could have sent Rockefeller into such a spin?* There was nothing there but foul-smelling spices, slit-eyed locals and filthy practices. Certainly no oil, and no prospect of oil ever being found.

He put the cable down and scratched at a mosquito bite. *Christ, I must get out of this stinking place!* He was stuck here because of that infernal railway. *Damn you, Rothschilds, and your fucking refineries.* That new railway meant thousands of barrels of Russian oil poured into Europe like a great black tide flowing up from Baku all the way to the Black Sea. A serious competition to John Rockefeller's Standard Oil company. Cheap Baku sludge sloshed up and down the railway inside hundreds of tank cars, and even though Sabroski Oil was dead and no longer their chief supplier, it would not be long before the Rothschilds found a replacement.

He considered his next move. He had to get his hands on those documents by any means necessary. There were two people close enough to Anton Nikolayevich who could be useful: the girl, Klara Darkova, and the lawyer, John Seigenberg. Both had their weaknesses. The girl had a chequered past, while John Seigenberg was vulnerable and adored his daughter far too much – Julia Seigenberg, protected and indulged, who knew nothing about anything.

*

Klara made her way across the Bibi-Eibat oilfields. A blanket of sand and ash shrouded the land, and even though the fields had only been closed for a year, the unforgiving wind had hastened their decline. She shielded her eyes against the stinging sand and looked around. A group of men sat around a small brazier playing dice. Further away, plumes of smoke rose from a neighbouring field which had been on fire for days. Klara's head ached and her body felt heavy. The funeral and discussions with Anton Nikolayevich had weighed her down. The replacement of one Sabroski with another was unhelpful: the son was not of the same mind as the father. As she approached, Rasoul Kazimov, the drill manager, hurried over. Rasoul was a stocky man with thick strong arms. He had straight brown hair tucked behind his ears and a small moustache. He greeted her eagerly. 'At last. What kept you?'

'He's dead.'

Rasoul shuffled his feet. 'I'm sorry. I know you admired him.' He paused. 'I heard yesterday – the son was here. On the oilfield. Climbed over the gate.'

'Jesus! Did he see Ivan?'

'No. Mehmet managed to stop him. Sent him packing, but he'll probably be back. I heard he went on to the Brakov fields as well.'

'We'll have to move Ivan. I knew it wouldn't work, hiding him out here.'

'I'll find somewhere else. There are places near the docks.'

'As long as it's safe. Ivan won't survive another bout in prison. Every time he coughs, I think his bones are going to snap.' She sighed. 'I must go and see him.'

Klara made her way over to the office and tapped on the door. 'It's me, Ivan.'

Immediately the door flew open and a very thin fair-haired man with grey eyes flung his arms around her. 'Ivan, I can't breathe,' she said laughing.

'I'm so happy you're here.' He covered her face with kisses.

Klara gently disentangled herself. 'I brought you some food.' She put her basket down on a stool and unpacked it. Then she held his eyes. 'Nikolai Sabroski is dead.'

'I heard.'

Klara took his hand. 'You'll have to move. It's not safe. Nikolai's son is back from the Orient. I don't trust him.'

'But where is safe?'

'The gendarmes are watching for you. The son's been asking questions. He may well come back here. He's not the sort of man who gives up easily.'

Ivan coughed. 'It has to be somewhere I can write, somewhere I can still see you.'

She stroked his hair. 'Rasoul knows a place near the docks.'

'The docks? It's grim down there.'

'There are places that are not so bad. I'll make sure they're safe.' She looked over to the table and noticed it was covered with papers. 'What have you been writing?'

'The oilfields. You know – conditions, bad treatment, housing. I'm going to print names this time. Shame those oil barons.' Ivan pulled her close. 'But I don't want to talk about politics now. I want to talk about you.' He kissed her and led her towards the little camp bed.

Klara left Ivan sleeping and went to find Rasoul.

'How is he?'

'Not good.'

'Walk with me.'

They trekked across the field. A watchful silence surrounded them as they wove around pools of treacle-like sludge, stagnant water and rocks. Some of the wooden derricks were padlocked shut. Others gaped open, their doors banging in the wind.

'God, I hate to see such waste,' said Rasoul. 'Do you have any food left?' They had stopped at the base of one of the towers. The arched door was hanging off, its hinges revealing a dark, shed-like room cracked with light. Ladders led up to a series of platforms. Klara entered and climbed to the first level. Rasoul followed her.

'Why do you always like coming up here?' he asked as he took her basket and set it down on the boards. The wind had dropped. They sat cross-legged leaning back against the wooden supports. Rasoul took off his cap and Klara untied her bonnet and dropped it into her lap. She closed her eyes and tilted her face into the pale sun. She felt Rasoul's eyes on her and she heard him drawing back the cheesecloth covering the basket, tearing off hunks of flatbread and white cheese.

'Here...' He handed her some.

'I find the view restful. It helps me think.'

Rasoul finished his food, opened a bottle and drank. 'What's he like? The son. Anton... whatshisname?'

'Nikolayevich. Anton Nikolayevich... Too soon to tell. Full of himself as men like that are. Older than I expected. Doesn't like me.'

'I've heard something.'

'What?'

'Sabroski brought something back. Something that's worth a great deal of money. Documents.'

'Where did you hear that?'

'You don't need to know.' Rasoul paused. 'I want you to find them. See where he keeps them. I know someone who'll sell them for us.'

'That's crazy. I'd be the first to be suspected.'

'No, you won't. This man, he'll arrange for the house to be burgled. Make it look as if the documents have been stolen.' Rasoul's eyes gleamed. 'There's oil here, Klara. I know it. I can smell it.'

'So you keep saying.'

'If we could get money to buy this oilfield back, we could turn it into a workers' cooperative.'

'And how do you explain it all?' Klara snapped. 'Suddenly we have money – money that's miraculously rained down from the heavens. Enough to buy back these oilfields. It's ridiculous. You haven't thought it through, have you?'

'Yes, I have! *We* won't be buying the fields. It'll be an unknown oil producer.'

'And who will this unknown oil producer be?'

'I know men in the city who have the resources to take this on. Men who believe in our cause.'

She looked away. *I wish I had your faith, Rasoul, but I don't.*

'So, you'll do it?'

'I'll think about it.'

Rasoul got up. 'Good.' He retrieved his cap and stood holding it with both hands. 'Thanks for the food. You coming?'

'No. I'm going to stay for a bit.'

'Suit yourself,' Rasoul said, shuffling his feet. 'Let me know as soon as… right?'

Klara nodded and watched him leave and stared out across the oilfields. There was something about the savagery of the landscape, the crudeness of it that appealed to her. There was no pretence out here, no gloss to camouflage the truth, no fine manners to hide the corruption.

The gentle warmth reminded her of her mother's house with the orchard and the blooms of spring with glass jars full of bluebells and daisies. *I miss you, Mama. I wish you were still here.* She had been so innocent then, not knowing the truth, but that is the way with children. Her life had taken a different direction after arriving in Baku. Meeting Nikolai Sabroski had given her a purpose and had channelled her anger into something worthwhile.

So how could she think of betraying him.

CHAPTER SEVEN

BAKU HAD CHANGED IN THE YEARS ANTON HAD BEEN AWAY. Newly erected telegraph poles stood like troops along the street. Some of the buildings had electric lights. The roads and the pavements crowded, and the city bustled with the population increases every year. Baku was no longer a small town on the edge of the Caspian Sea, the sleepy Persian settlement that his mother and father had moved to thirty years ago. Now, street cars clanked, horse-drawn gigs creaked, and men in top hats and morning suits strode in and out of imposing sandstone offices. Investors poured into the city hoping to make fortunes in oil, tempting thousands of Muslim Tatars from the countryside to come looking for work.

A distant ridge of brown hillside rose from the desert and fed down a dusty wind. Baku was famous for its winds. His father once told him the word *Baku* had been derived from the Persian *bâd-kube,* meaning *city of winds*, or a place where the winds strike hard.

'I'm sorry for your loss, Anton Nikolayevich.' The Armenian bank manager from the Apsheron banking house ran an ink-stained finger down the page of a cash ledger, his face rumpling into a frown. 'If you wish, I'll find the details of the company liquidation.'

Anton nodded, realising how little he knew about Sabroski Oil – like memories of his father – more of an impression than any real knowledge. The bank manager pulled a ledger towards him, opened it and examined several documents. He pulled out a silver snuff box with a blue topaz embedded in the centre and took a pinch, throwing his head back and sniffing several times. Then he massaged the end of his nose and sneezed. 'Excuse me, sir,' he said, pulling out a handkerchief and looking back down at the documents. 'Ah, here we are – Sabroski Oil assets: three major groups in the Bibi-Eibat oilfield – numbered eighteen, nineteen, twenty – and twelve groups in the Balakhani region. Fifty tank cars, eighty steam engines and miscellaneous drilling equipment, down-tools and sundries. There are more details if you care to read them for yourself.' The man looked up, his waxed moustache daubing his face like a smudge of charcoal.

'I heard a company called Zenovitch Liquid Fuel bought the assets,' Anton said.

'Zenovitch Liquid Fuel was Sabroski Oil's supply company. They bought most of it and then passed on the more profitable resources to interested buyers.' The bank manager swivelled the ledger around for Anton to see.

'For how much?'

'Fifty-six thousand, one hundred and forty gold roubles.'

'What happened to the money?'

The bank manager sighed. 'Your father had many creditors.'

'So it is as John Seigenberg predicted.' Anton swallowed hard and got up and lit a cigarette. *Fuck – I really am bankrupt. No company. No money. A slur on the Sabroski name.*

The Armenian cleared his throat. 'There's the trust fund of course. It's not much, but it will help.'

Anton turned to look at him. 'Trust fund?'

'Didn't Seigenberg mention it?' The man hesitated. 'But then I suppose there's no reason for your lawyer to know.' He turned to another page in his ledger, running his eyes down the pink columned lines. 'Ah yes, here we are: account number 153, Anton Nikolayevich Sabroski: two thousand seven hundred roubles.'

The words resonated around the room. *Two thousand seven hundred roubles.*

'Are you certain?'

The manager sniffed. 'And a deposit of fifty roubles is paid into the account every month.'

'A deposit? From whom?'

'I don't know. The donor is anonymous – at least there's no name recorded. I assumed you would know. A relative perhaps?' The manager's gaze rested on him as if he were trying to assess Anton's credibility.

'I don't have any relatives.' Anton spoke quickly, his heart speeding. 'Not that I know of.' *It must have been Father... but how did he hide the money?* 'I can't think who it could be.'

The bank manager closed the ledger. 'Then count yourself fortunate, Anton Nikolayevich. At least somebody is looking after you.'

Anton ignored the calls of the hansom cab drivers and walked back. On the way he bought slices of lamb wrapped in thin lavash bread, savouring the smell of onions and cumin that made his mouth water. *A trust fund! What extraordinary luck.* Whatever had transpired, those three words had changed the colour of his day. Now, he could afford to repair the house, and, with his army pension, eke out a living of sorts. It would be a simple life, but he'd known worse.

The house lay quiet and still except for the ticking of the grandfather clock. Peeling off his coat and hat, Anton wedged his cane into the coat stand and sought out the kitchen. A cast-iron range warmed the room and a scrubbed wooden table stood in the centre surrounded by six stick-back chairs. A brass samovar, perched on the edge of a marble-topped counter, dispensed a continual supply of hot water. It hissed steam as he filled a tea glass and sat down and stretched out his long legs.

The kitchen door opened, and the girl appeared, lugging a basket of fresh sturgeon. Her face, flushed from the wind, turned to a frown. 'Oh. I didn't expect to see you here.'

He sat up. 'There's no need to leave.'

He watched her put the basket down and unwind her black shawl. She looked different today: tidier and cleaner in a brown serge bodice and skirt. She was not as young as he'd thought – her eyes appeared older, as if she'd seen too much. She went over to the pantry and poured herself a glass of lemonade.

'How old are you?' he said.

She drank, wiped her mouth and put the glass down. Then she picked up the basket and headed towards the scullery. 'Why do you need to know?'

'I'm interested. I'd like to know something about you. Where do you come from and what brought you to this house?' The words came out more pompously than he intended, grating against her thin shoulders as she disappeared down the steps to the basement, so he picked up his tea and followed.

He watched her step onto the duckboard beside the stone sink and fling him a look. 'My background is very ordinary.'

Anton shrugged. 'That doesn't matter.'

'Why do you care?'

'You looked after my father. I'm grateful for that. I'd like to know how you came to be his… assistant.'

'You don't believe that, do you?'

Anton spread his hands. 'I don't know what to believe.'

43

'I don't like people prying into my private affairs. Asking questions.'

'I'm not prying. Surely your age and how you came to know my father cannot be such a secret? Are you in trouble with the authorities?'

'No.'

'Then why the secrecy?' Anton put his tea glass down and lit a cigarette. He smoked in silence and studied the line of her rigid body. The scullery smelled of wet clothes and he noticed a trail of rat droppings under the table.

Klara took the fish from the basket, filled a pan with water and immersed one. 'I'm nineteen… nearly twenty', she said, 'and I come from Kiev.' She finished washing the fish, sharpened a knife and used it to slit through its belly.

'And your family?'

She held the knife still. 'I don't have any.'

'There must be somebody.'

'They're all dead.'

'Oh… I'm sorry.'

Silence hung between them. Klara cleaned the rest of the fish, stripping out the backbones and started cutting the flesh into small pieces.

'What are you cooking?'

'Fish.'

'I can see that.'

'The dish is called kulebyaka.'

'Fish pie with eggs.'

'It was your father's favourite,' she said.

'Mine too.'

'I know. He said you liked it.'

Anton finished smoking his cigarette and let the stub drop to the floor. She frowned at him, and after a moment he bent down and picked it up.

*

The wind dropped the following evening. The night sky sparkled blue-black beneath a canopy of brilliance and the bitter cold released its grip. Anton had made several efforts to question Klara, but they had all ended in failure. She was suspicious and hostile, and whatever he did say seemed to irritate her. Now he sat in the drawing room and listened to the crackling of the fire. It had been eight days since he'd arrived in Baku. Eight days of grief, bitter disappointment, and frustration. Nothing made any sense and yet he had to make sense of it. The company had been bankrupted by a man everyone trusted; his father was left penniless yet owned a fabulous jewel, and a strange girl lived in the house with an attitude his father would never have tolerated. Meanwhile, someone was secretly supporting him financially.

Anton lay his head back and closed his eyes and by the time he opened them again the fire had gone out and the candles had burned down. The house creaked in the wind, but even in the short time he'd been home, he'd become familiar with the groans of the house: the scratching and settling of wood against sandstone. He sat up. Something banged in the distance. A cat yowled. But as he listened, there was nothing but the dead sounds of the night. He lit a candle and went out into the hallway. It seemed unusually cold. A draught coiled around and blew out the candle, leaving him standing in darkness.

A creaking noise came from the library followed by a rapid succession of thuds. Adrenalin coursed through him as he grabbed a cane from the umbrella stand and stole across the hallway.

The library door was slightly ajar. Slowly he edged it open. He could see and hear nothing now, just inky blackness, a cold breeze and silence. Possibly someone had left a window open, and the girl had come down to close it. He thought about calling her name, but the words froze in his throat. He tightened his grip on the cane, his body taut and fired up. Reaching inside, he felt along the wall until he found the gas light. He turned it, kicked open the door and flattened himself against the wall.

The French windows were wide open and crumpled papers scattered the floor. He whirled round, cane angled, ready to strike, but there was nobody there. Books had been pulled from the shelves. Several pressed-glass inkwells lay overturned dripping dark blue liquid. Fountain pens lay strewn across the rug like spent arrows and the large floor globe had been tipped onto its side. Anton shot a glance up at the hidden compartment, but the large books had not been moved and the ladder remained leaned against the opposite wall.

Whoever it was had gone.

Anton spent the next day fixing strong bolts to the doors and securing the windows. He couldn't afford to hire more guards, so he put a lock on his bedroom door. He had hidden the secret documents between his mattress and the bed slats that first night – more of a spontaneous decision than a calculated one. He knew he should hand them over to the Rothschilds and forget about them. *So why don't I? Why not get rid of the infernal papers?* He stretched and massaged his neck. *Because I want to show them to Rafiq first.* He gave a wry laugh out loud. *Why do I always do this? Get myself into trouble?* Especially as Rafiq was in Tehran and not due back until next week, according to the turbaned footman at the Hasanov house in the Icheri Sheher.

Later that week, he turned his attentions to the house, which was in a poor state of repair, and set about mending what he could. The roof leaked, the chimneys needed cleaning, many windowpanes were cracked and two in the parlour had been smashed. Some of the timbers had an infestation that was so bad that he was able to pull away the sodden wood with his fingers. The back rooms reeked of mould. It would be months of work, but in a way he relished the physical labour. It redirected the melancholy that seeped through him.

'So, this is what your night-time visitor was after,' announced John Seigenberg, holding up the jewelled egg for inspection. 'I'm not surprised.' He twisted the egg around to watch it catch the light, before handing it back to Anton. 'I'd no idea your father possessed such a treasure.'

Anton had let the lawyer reach his own conclusions about the motive for the break-in. John knew nothing of the documents and Anton wasn't about to tell him. *Keep them secret and trust no one.*

'Are you sure Nikolai left no explanation?'

'No. It was wrapped in the package just as you gave me.'

John stroked his beard, which had been oiled with Macassar oil infused with cedar. 'He must have bought it some time ago before the money ran out.'

'You must know something, John. It was in your safe.'

John shook his head. 'Your father gave me the package to give to you. I assumed it was a family heirloom. A keepsake of your mother's he didn't want the creditors to take.'

'Do you know why I can't sell it?'

'Unfortunately not. They were the instructions left in his will.'

'There's something inside. If you shake it, you can hear. Once opened, we might learn more.'

John raised a warning hand. 'Don't be hasty. I know a silversmith in the Icheri Sheher who may be able to open it properly. He also might know something about its background.'

'There's something else. Another mystery.' He told John about the trust fund.

John tugged at his hair. 'All I can think of is that your father used some of the company funds before the creditors arrived. Crafty old Nikolai… he kept that very quiet.' He drummed his

47

fingers on the back of the chair. 'What other secrets shall we find, I wonder? But I advise you not to tell anyone about this fund. Even though your father has passed away and his creditors paid off, questions could still be asked.'

Anton nodded, but he wasn't convinced.

Somebody, very much alive, was still paying into it.

CHAPTER EIGHT

JULIA SEIGENBERG LET THE BEDROOM DOOR SLAM AND flung herself onto her bed. *Hateful woman! Why do you always find fault!* She lay still for a while before sitting up to study her silk slippers. One of the rosettes was dirtied from where her brother, Alfred, had stood on her foot. She pulled the slipper off and rubbed it with her fingers, but the black mark smudged even more. Julia threw it across the room and slumped back with a sigh. Outside, the wind rattled the shutters and a splat of rain hit the window.

Julia concentrated on the dance of flames in the fireplace. Dinner had been like a dull church service. Father had been serious and stern, Diane preachy and pompous. Ever since the funeral of Nikolai Sabroski, Julia's father had sunk into a gloom. He'd been hard hit by the death of the old man, but then, she supposed, it was only natural as they'd been friends for thirty years. He'd barely mentioned Anton Nikolayevich, which disappointed her. She was ten years old when Anton went away, and she was eager to know more about the exotic son's return from the East.

Julia went over to the dressing table. Pulling the pins from her chignon, she let a curtain of brown hair spill down while she stared at her reflection. If only her nose were smaller and her mouth less wide, someone might think she was beautiful. Years ago, her mother said her eyes were her best feature: long-lashed and emerald-green. Her stepmother, Diane, never said things like that. *Nagging old witch!* She tugged at her mother's gold locket which she never took off. It was warm and smooth like the touch of her mother's hand. Her eyes stung. Smoke coiled out from the fireplace and floated across the room. She leaned forward until her nose nudged the mirror and contorted her face into a grimace.

The door opened.

'Be careful the wind doesn't change, miss. Your face will stay like that for ever', said her maid, heaving a bucket of coals.

'It wouldn't make any difference if it did, Sveta.'

'Oh, we *are* in a bad mood tonight, miss.'

'I'm trapped here day after day with nothing to do. You've no idea how dull my life is.'

'I'm sure I don't, miss. But I wouldn't mind trying. I'd like the chance to spend a day doing nothing.' She launched the contents of the bucket into the fire.

'I'm not afraid of hard work. Just boredom.'

'I don't know what you mean, miss.'

Julia looked at her thoughtfully. 'No, I don't suppose you do.'

'Now, do you want me to help you undress?'

'No thank you.'

The maid left. Julia picked up a book lying atop the marble-topped dresser. She sank into the chair by the fire and ran her fingers over the sleeve of the Gothic thriller *The Midnight Bell* by Francis Lathom. A melancholy young man with long dark hair and brooding eyes stared back at her. Alphonsus Cohenburg, her hero. She sighed again. *How will I ever find love?* Her heroines lived such thrilling lives, experienced unimaginable passion and excitement. The only men she ever met were friends of Alfred's, who were so dull. There was Leo, of course, but Leo didn't count.

Julia thought about Anton. At least *he* would be different. From the little she'd gleaned from her father, Anton was older and more worn than her father had expected, which must have been because he'd been in the Orient for seven years. Such a mysterious and dangerous place. She'd heard stories of opium dens and decadent bars and establishments that offered exotic services. Not that she believed all of them, but some of them might be true. She hoped. It was possible that Anton's presence in Baku would make life more interesting. He didn't fit in and could disturb the natural order of things, and a disturbance would be very welcome. She must engineer a way to call on him, because if she waited for Father to organise a visit it would be months. Her friend Leo would help her. She flicked to her bookmark and started to read.

An hour later a crash of wind battered the house. Julia closed the book and went to the window. Opening the shutters, she leaned out into the night. The wind whipped her hair, jerking it in several directions. A beech tree dripped in the road, water droplets clinging perilously to each leaf. Distant lights winked over the oilfields and legions of distillation towers trampled the horizon. The landscape looked as if it had been ravaged and stripped of life. It was unthinkable that men could live there, wallowing in grime like animals. *What made you come to this place, Father?* It was something he never talked about; the bad air had sapped her mother's strength until she died.

A soft tapping on the door sounded like the rain entering the room. 'Who is it?' She closed the window.

'Just me.' Her brother appeared. 'Sveta said you're in one of your moods, so I've come to cheer you up. Goodness, what have you done to your hair?' Alfred Seigenberg stood in the doorway, dressed in his gold silk smoking jacket.

Julia raked her hair as she crossed the room and dropped into

51

a chair. 'Baku's so tedious when you're a woman. I can't do anything without Diane checking up on me and Father's refusing to let me out unchaperoned.'

Alfred strolled to the fire, a waft of cigars and patchouli following him. 'It's not much better for me.'

'At least you do something.'

'Working in an office is not exactly interesting. All I do is file papers and check accounts. I'm sure Father set that up deliberately to keep me busy.'

Julia smiled. 'Maybe I should go to work instead, and you can stay here and read novels.'

'Goodness me, Julia. Why would you want to work?' He sat back in the chair and linked his hands across his large stomach, squeezing Julia's fingers as she stretched out and took his warm hand.

'What you need is a husband, Julia. It's what all women want: a house of their own, babies, servants to order about.' Alfred leaned forward. 'Why don't you marry Leo Rostov? He adores you.'

Julia laughed and pulled her hand away. 'Don't be silly. Leo's just a friend. He's not what I want.'

'How do you know what you want?'

'Well, I know what I don't want – Leo.' She shot him a look. 'Have you seen Anton Nikolayevich yet?'

Alfred rolled his eyes. 'He's too old for you, Julia. And far too uncouth.'

'So, you *have* seen him.'

'Only briefly. Anton came into the office.'

'Zenovitch Liquid Fuel? Why?'

'Asking lots of questions. Wanting to look at some papers. It must be hard for him, losing the company like that.'

An hour later, Julia turned off the ginger-jar lamp so only the light from the fire remained. She unbuttoned her bodice, stepped out of her skirt and stood looking at herself in the mirror. Strapped into her satin corset and white stockings she looked vaporous, almost ghostly and wanton – not that she was sure what that word meant, except she thought it was something she'd like to be – like the women in the art book Alfred kept hidden in his bedroom. It had intimate paintings of men and women with entwined limbs and showing their private parts.

She ran her fingers over the silk braid trimmings contouring her breasts, feeling her skin tingling beneath. Slowly, she unhooked the metal studs, took off the rest of her undergarments and pulled on her nightgown.

Oh, how she longed for something exciting to happen.

CHAPTER NINE

On Friday evening, Anton met John Seigenberg in the foyer of the Hotel Continental. As they greeted each other, John murmured to Anton, 'See who's over there?'

Anton followed John's gaze. A young man had sauntered into view with a beautiful woman by his side. *That can't be... damn... it is. Stefan Brakov.* Apart from a small moustache, Stefan had hardly changed. He was slim with blue eyes, possessing that sleek, chiselled look that women seemed to like. He was dressed in a black dinner jacket, a black bow tie, and a crisp white linen shirt, and he wore a pair of excessively pointed, patent leather button pumps. Stefan's eyes were fixed on the dark-haired beauty gliding alongside him. He looked up and flushed, then whispered something to the woman and steered her towards them.

'Anton Nikolayevich! What a pleasure. Welcome home,' Stefan said in a smooth voice with a bow. 'My condolences on the loss of your father. I'm so very sorry for your misfortune.'

'Thank you, Stefan. It has been a long time. You are looking well.'

'Please allow me to introduce my wife, Miranda Aleksandrovna.'

'Enchanted, madam,' said Anton dipping his head. *God, she's beautiful. How did he manage that?*

'Good evening, gentlemen.' Miranda appraised them, her gaze lingering on Anton for longer than he anticipated, but her regard did not appear critical, but curious. Anton wondered which stories Stefan had told her, and which ones he had chosen to leave out.

'I expect we'll see you at the club soon, Anton,' said Stefan. 'I assume you will be taking up membership. I can vouch for you if you wish. You will need a reputable backer.'

'That won't be necessary, Stefan, thank you. Seigenberg has already arranged my membership.'

'Has he? Excellent.' Stefan produced a gilt monogrammed leather pouch from his pocket and lit a cigarette. 'I hear you spent much time in the Orient. A fascinating part of the world, so I've been told.'

'Indeed it is.'

'With Count Sergei Witte. Ministry of Transport. I've read about the new railway: the Trans-Siberian Express. The Baku *Vedomosti* has published many articles about the design and the money involved... going to cost the tsar over a billion roubles.' A cloud of expensive smoke drifted between them.

'It's a very ambitious project and one that the count is staking his reputation on.'

'Then I gathered you moved to Shanghai. Another position with the ministry?'

'I can see you've been following my travels, Stefan.'

'The Sabroskis have always been an interesting family. You've been missed.'

'I'm sure I have. And I suppose people talk.' The mutilated finger on Anton's hand started to ache. He flexed it slowly.

'They certainly do.' Stefan laughed and ran a hand through his fair hair. 'You've been away a long time. There were those that wondered why... especially when your father became ill.'

'The bankruptcy of my father must have been an enormous source of speculation.'

Stefan frowned. 'I didn't mean any disrespect.'

'I am sure you didn't.' *Yes, you did. I know you, Stefan.*

'My husband meant no offence, Anton Nikolayevich,' said Miranda. Her voice was deep and rich like her hair, but her wide, heavy eyes were cold. She closed her tortoiseshell fan and looped it around her wrist, her fingers resting on a golden snake bracelet curling down from her elbow over the top of long white gloves.

'Of course, madam. Please forgive me.'

Stefan pulled a silk handkerchief from his top pocket and dabbed his forehead. 'If you will excuse us, gentlemen, my wife and I have a dinner reservation. It was a pleasure.'

Anton bowed as Stefan turned and escorted Miranda through the hotel crowds.

John clicked his tongue. 'After seven years I thought you two could be civil to each other.'

Anton flushed. 'I was perfectly civil.'

'It didn't sound like it to me.'

'Stefan never thinks before he speaks.'

'He's not the only one.' John sighed. 'Well, thank goodness for Miranda. She's a cool-headed beauty, isn't she.'

'How on earth did Stefan manage to marry a woman like that?'

'He's a good-looking boy. Charming, well dressed, and rich. Isn't that enough?'

Anton frowned. 'Not always.'

They exited the hotel and crossed the street. Two arched gateways heralded the entrance to the Icheri Sheher: the walled citadel of the Muslims, where cinnamon, musk and the tang of tobacco lingered in the air. A cobbled square sloped down towards the market and overlooked the sea. John nodded at the gatekeeper as they passed beneath the arch. Two men with brush-like moustaches, curved daggers and leather papakhas approached them from the shadows.

'The gochus will escort us,' said John. 'It's not wise to travel alone after dark. These bodyguards come from the leading clans in the city and will offer protection.'

Anton pulled up his collar as the shades of the evening deepened. A soft strumming drifted down from an open window and echoed round the square. The night hung still and watchful as it swallowed the haunting sound. Anton saw a shrouded figure reach out to close the shutters.

'Where does this silversmith live?'

'Next to the Maiden Tower.'

It was pitch-black as they wove through the winding lanes: a warren of whitewashed houses cramped side by side. Some of the houses had balconies encrusted with vines that dangled down into the street with sinewy roots reaching deep into the ground. Anton cursed as threads tickled his face and he stumbled in the dark. Behind him, the gochus' chamois-leather boots thudded accompanied by the clank of their weapons.

Anton was still smarting from Stefan's comments and cursed himself for over-reacting. Stefan *had* probably meant nothing, as his wife so clearly stated, and was trying to make conversation. But it was typical of Stefan to make light of the Sabroski name and talk a lot of nonsense. Except it was probably true that people were discussing Sabroski Oil and the shameful bankruptcy. Anton felt himself burn as he thrust himself forward.

They rounded a corner and an ancient stone structure loomed high above: Baku's famous landmark, the Maiden Tower, stared at them moodily, its patchwork of chipped stonework glinting in the moonlight. The tower had stood there since before anyone could remember, rising up from the edge of the sea, the highest building along the shoreline. A curve of two-storey houses, built into the city wall, stood under its protection. John walked up to one of the houses and knocked on the door while the gochu bodyguards dissolved into the gloom.

Melek Grashi, the Armenian silversmith, swivelled the rose-enamelled egg between his fingers and scratched his beard with a long fingernail. He picked up a magnifying glass and peered through it. Anton saw Melek's enlarged, watery eye fixed upon the egg.

'Fascinating.'

'Have you seen one like this before?' said Anton, loosening his collar. The workshop stewed in a claustrophobic haze of firelight, gas lamps and a smouldering sandalwood incense. The silversmith didn't answer. He handed the egg back to Anton and began rummaging through a pile of newspaper cuttings. Bottles with assorted nails, hinges and metal fasteners competed for space on shelves with receptacles full of brightly coloured stones, smelting tools, hammers and glue. Above his head sat a collection of silver drinking vessels with handles shaped like swans.

Suddenly the man exclaimed, drew his wild hair from his face and seized a piece of paper. He hurried across to a table cluttered with half-finished objects and pushed them aside, flattening out the newspaper and tapping it. It was the front page of the Russian *Vedomosti* newspaper dated March 1887.

'See here,' the silversmith said, stabbing his fingernail at the central photograph with a caption underneath. '*The Third Imperial Egg* presented by Alexander III to Tsarina Maria Fyodorovna.' This is a photograph of a Fabergé egg. See how similar it is to yours. If you don't mind, sir.' He reached across and took the egg from Anton and turned it around. 'My word, it really is exquisite. Such ingenious engineering.' The silversmith stared with such rapture he seemed to forget they were there.

'What is a Fabergé egg?' Anton said.

The silversmith blinked out of his reverie. '*Surely* you have heard of these fabulous jewels, sir? Carl Fabergé is the most famous jeweller in the land. He's the tsar's court supplier.'

'And this egg was made by him?' John asked.

'Certainly. It has his hallmark.' Melek screwed up his eyes and examined the egg's rim. 'Hmm. A shame it's been damaged. Someone's tried to force it open. These eggs have a hidden release mechanism.'

'You mean there's more than one of them?'

'Oh yes. There must be… let me see now.' He began counting off grubby fingers. 'A total of six.'

'And this is one of them?'

He clucked his tongue. 'No, no, no. The original six are in the royal palace. This is a different one. One I have never seen or heard of before. Utterly incredible! I never thought I'd see one of Carl Fabergé's creations.' He held the egg with both hands, hunching over it like a protective mother hen.

John cleared his throat. 'Maybe if we opened the egg, it might tell us more.'

The silversmith started. 'Oh, but we must be careful. Very, very careful. Let me see what I can do…' He stared around the workshop, tapping his chin, before seizing an object that looked like a silver toothpick. He sat down and examined the egg's rim through his magnifying lens.

Anton pulled up a stool. 'Why were these eggs made, and why are they so special?'

'Ah ha. There's a story to tell and I can see that you do not know it.' The silversmith twisted the egg around, humming to himself, as he ran his fingers over the egg's surface.

'And what is this story, sir?'

'What? Oh yes.' He picked up the silver toothpick and gently applied it to the rim. A long grey strand of hair fell over his face. He cleared his throat and began to speak in a singsong, melodious voice. 'The story of the Fabergé egg started soon after the tsar's marriage. Tsar Alexander was worried about his wife, the tsarina,

Maria Fyodorovna. She was homesick for her native land of Denmark. So, in 1885, he planned a surprise. The tsar commissioned the House of Fabergé to make the tsarina a special Easter egg that would remind her of the kind of eggs she received as a child. Carl Fabergé made his first egg from white enamel with a gold band around the middle. It was two and a half inches long, about the size of a duck egg, so that it looked just like an ordinary eggshell.' The silversmith paused and turned his large watery eyes onto Anton. 'But, when Maria Fyodorovna opened it, there was something inside: a perfect golden yolk. And when she opened the yolk, she found a golden hen sitting on a nest of golden straw. And when she opened the golden hen, she found a diamond miniature of the imperial crown. Inside that was a tiny ruby pendant.'

'Like a set of Matryoshka dolls,' said Anton.

'Indeed,' the silversmith agreed. He sucked his teeth and gazed back down at the egg. 'Of course, Maria Fyodorovna was delighted with the gift and Tsar Alexander was so pleased that he ordered Carl Fabergé to create a new egg for the tsarina every year. Each year the eggs are different and each year they contain something special inside.'

'What were they like? These other eggs?'

'Ah, let me see now,' Melek said using the silver toothpick to scratch the end of his nose. 'The second egg was quite similar. Inside was a golden hen in a wicker basket with a sapphire pendant. The third egg was the one we saw in the newspaper: The *Third Imperial Egg* contained a lady's wristwatch. The fourth egg, the *Cherub Egg*, held a miniature golden chariot.' He paused. 'Then there was the *Nécessaire Egg* with a set of thirteen ladies' toiletries inside: tiny golden manicure items. Beautifully carved.' He stared across the room as if he could actually see the manicured items floating in the air. He pushed wisps of hair from his eyes and looked at Anton. 'This Easter, Carl Fabergé presented the *Danish Palaces Egg*. It was exquisite, with a miniature ten-panel screen showing pictures of the tsarina's homes and the imperial yachts. What do you think of that?' The silversmith leaned forward and jabbed the silver toothpick at Anton, his eyes bright with expectation.

Anton didn't know what to say. It was bewildering that he should own such a treasure. Maybe the silversmith would report its discovery to the authorities and the tsar's secret police would come looking for him.

'Do they always have something inside?' said Anton.

'Yes. It is called the egg's surprise. The tsar never wants to know what the surprise is. It's a carefully guarded secret.'

'So where has this egg come from? If it is not one of the tsar's collection, then who was it made for?' said John.

The Armenian picked up his magnifying glass. 'I would guess this egg has been commissioned by a member of the royal court.'

Anton stood up and stretched his legs. He walked over to the window and leaned his head against the glass pane. *What does this mean?* Such a valuable jewel could not have belonged to his father. And such a valuable jewel would be coveted by many. Smudging his fingers over the condensation, Anton looked out through the blurred porthole. Two camels sat outside the caravanserai inn, their legs tucked beneath them, their knees poking out, their long shaggy necks motionless as merchants untied their packs for the night. They looked serene and untroubled.

'Ah ha,' said the silversmith. 'Here we are.'

Anton turned. The man twisted the metal instrument and the egg popped open.

'Hmmm,' frowned the silversmith, as he carefully extracted the contents and handed it to Anton.

It was a miniature scroll.

Anton unrolled it carefully. Gold lettering, gossamer-like, threaded across a silken surface revealing a poem.

Now that I have gone
remember the essence of what we were.
Soft breathing inside the envelope of night,
half-closed eyelash gaze,
an errant lock of hair,
interlocked fingers and souls,
perfumed spirit and salt-sweet skin.
Do not grieve, for nothing has been lost.
Just an expectation of what should be.
The present is not changed, the past cannot
be taken, the future is all illusion.
As I kiss you for the last time,
remember to keep our Treasure safe.
For the jewel is priceless beyond measure
and will, one day, be reclaimed.

'What does it mean?' Anton said.

The silversmith poured himself a glass of tea and dropped a cardamom pod inside. 'I have no idea. But I'll try and find out.'

CHAPTER TEN

THE MYSTERY OF THE FABERGÉ EGG OBSESSED ANTON. Returning home that evening, he kept retrieving it from the safe, examining it and then putting it back again, as if by sheer determination he could shake out its secrets. The company was bankrupt, the Sabroskis were penniless, yet his father owned one of the finest jewels in the empire.

Anton read the poem over and over until he knew the words by heart, thinking about the lines and who might have written them. He had noticed that the word *Treasure* was written with a capital letter, and he wondered what it meant. The miniature scroll had tiny pink-purple orchids embroidered down the sides of the silk. He twisted the egg round in his hands, re-examining every inch of the decorated surface before returning the scroll, closing the egg and stowing it in the secret compartment.

At first, he thought his father might have written the poem, then dismissed the idea – the romantic words didn't mesh with the man he remembered – he'd never heard his father recite or read anything, let alone poetry. He considered questioning the girl, then thought better of it. There was no point drawing attention to such a valuable item secured in the house; the fewer people that knew about it, the better. Who knew by what means the egg had fallen into his father's possession? It was a dangerous charge, glinting in the dark, locked inside the library safe, like a giant eye watching him.

Anton's throat tightened at the stray comment Stefan Brakov had made in the Hotel Continental: *People talk*.

Two days later, Anton was busy pulling out a rotten window frame from one of the front bedrooms, when he heard a loud banging on the front door. He poked his head out of the open window. Down on the steps, in a quilted red gaba and pantaloons, stood a young man with long dark hair. Anton's heart leapt. He laughed and shouted down. 'I thought you were in Tehran?'

Rafiq Hasanov looked up. 'How could I stay there when I heard you were back?'

Anton tore down the stairs. Klara had already opened the door and was staring at Rafiq curiously.

'*Salam*, my friend. It's been so long.'

'Far too long. My God, it's so *good* to see you.'

They clapped each other on the shoulders and embraced.

'You just arrived?' said Anton.

'The steamer this morning. How long have you been here?'

'A couple of weeks.'

Rafiq slipped off his shoes and removed his jacket and adjusted the cummerbund around his waist. They fell silent as the years of separation melted away. Rafiq Hasanov had aged since Anton last saw him. Silver threads streaked through his shoulder-length black hair and his handsome face had lost its carefree look. The small scar on his left cheek had faded, but he was thinner and his eyes were dull. Anton put a hand on his friend's shoulder. 'I am sorry to hear about your wife. John Seigenberg told me.'

'My poor Leyla. They tell me it was God's will, but I'm not

sure I care for this God any more.' Rafiq's face darkened. 'But let's not dwell on unhappy memories. You must tell me what you've been doing all these years. You look like you've seen life. A lot of it.'

Anton led Rafiq into the drawing room where, over glasses of tea, they shared stories from the past. Rafiq sat cross-legged on the floor and chain-smoked. Barefoot, dressed in a white open-necked shirt and a yellow striped waistcoat, he looked wild and outlandish. As they reminisced, a vital warmth flowed through Anton. The past seemed like an exotic story, his childhood one long adventure under a hot sun and a blue sky. He could practically taste the desert, the salt of sea air and hear the shriek of gulls.

'So, you were called home by your father's ill health?' said Rafiq eventually, lighting his fifth cigarette and turning the burning end round into the palm of his hand.

'I didn't even know my father was unwell until I arrived.' Anton paused. 'My father wanted me to deliver some secret documents.'

'Secret? What are they?'

'When I was in Shanghai, I met a Jewish merchant from London's East End. Name of Marcus Samuel. He's wealthy with powerful friends – Baron Rothschild for example. He's connected to a string of trading houses in the Orient. They backed his textile company – Samuel Samuel & Co.'

'Don't tell me you're moving into the textile business?'

'Nothing like that. Marcus is a businessman. He can turn his hand to anything. Some years ago, he met Baron Rothschild and my father in Baku. They made a plan to export oil to the Orient – there's a huge market for oil in places like Malaya and Singapore which nobody has tapped into. Baku has so much oil to sell at a decent profit. It's a brilliant export opportunity.'

Rafiq cocked his head. 'The Orient is thousands of miles away. Transportation costs would outweigh any profit.'

'We would have to build a tanker, rather like the Nobel Brothers use. The sort that you're familiar with, but better. Because we will have to take a short cut through the Suez Canal.' He raised his hand to stop Rafiq interrupting. 'It's the only way this plan will work. It will save over four thousand miles.'

Rafiq looked at Anton in astonishment. 'Build a tanker to go down the Suez Canal?' He gave a wry laugh. 'The Egyptians took ten years to build it and you want to send dangerous, inflammable tankers. One explosion and the canal will be out of commission for years.'

'Just hear me out.'

'You haven't changed, Anton, have you? Still full of wild ideas.'

'They are not *my* ideas. They're Father's and Marcus Samuel's.'

'It doesn't matter – they can't possibly work.'

'Are you going to listen to me or not?'

Rafiq waved his hand. 'As you wish. What are these documents?'

Anton jumped up and ran upstairs. He flattened himself on the ground, crawled under the bed and retrieved the papers from between the mattress and the bed slats. Then he ran down the stairs and handed them to Rafiq. 'Tell me what you make of these.'

Rafiq bent his head to study them. 'These are tanker specifications from the Suez Canal authorities! How did you get them?'

'Marcus.'

'Are they real?'

'Of course they're real.'

'What will you do with them?'

'Design a tanker. Well... not me... you.'

'Me?'

'Yes, you. That was my plan all along. I suggested you to Marcus in Shanghai because I knew you could do it. Father told me how you'd designed the *Zoroaster* tanker for the Nobel Brothers.'

Rafiq frowned. 'The Nobel Brothers have excellent engineers.'

'So that's why they commissioned *you* instead of their own Swedish engineers? You're creative and different.'

Rafiq gave a theatrical flourish with his hand. 'That is very true, my friend. I'm not a stiff-thinking Russian. I'm a Muslim. A Tatar. I live in the Icheri Sheher, where Europeans fear to tread.'

Anton laughed. 'You've always underrated yourself, Rafiq. I know you can do it. If you design the tanker, Marcus will build it and the Rothschilds will fill it with oil from their refineries on the Black Sea.'

'Do the Rothschilds know about this?'

Anton looked away. 'Not yet. I'll make a proposal once the designs are complete.'

Rafiq fingered the scar on his cheek and then pulled out a chewed pencil and a squashed black notebook from his pocket. He unrolled the specifications, squatted on the balls of his feet, and began to read.

He said nothing for half an hour, and as the light started to fade, the only movement he made was to scribble something down. Outside, a trolley bus clanked past and children shouted and laughed in the park opposite. Anton stoked the fire and turned on the gas light. Rafiq's presence was a reassuring link to a happier past. He had shared more laughter and adventures with Rafiq than anyone he had ever known. He looked across at his friend's dark expression staring down at the specifications. It was odd how life changed. Just like a pendulum swinging backwards and forwards, tugging happiness and sadness behind it. He had met Rafiq on the day of the Spitting Devil oil spouter seventeen years before. An oil well had erupted, spurting two hundred feet into the air. His father had allowed him to travel in the gig to the field where a hundred men had gathered to watch the spectacle. Nikolai had jumped down to speak to an important-looking Muslim. 'Hasanov! Thank God. Are your men here yet?'

The man pointed. 'Over there. They have the cap in the wagon.'

A wagon pulled by two horses was struggling up the hill. Inside, sitting cross-legged on top of a cast-iron plate, was a small figure wearing a bright yellow turban. He looked like a temple boy sitting on a ceremonial elephant.

'Rafiq! Get down!' shouted the man before turning to Anton's father. 'Apologies, Sabroski. My son thinks this is a game.'

'Anton, take Rafiq and keep him out of mischief,' said Nikolai. 'Stay at a safe distance and wait until I call you.'

'Yes, sir.' Anton ran over to the wagon and shouted up. 'Hello. You've got to come with me.'

The boy jumped down and wiped the sleeve of his shirt across his face. 'This is fun, isn't it? I wish we could see more.'

'We can climb that derrick over there. The view's great.'

'Are we allowed to?'

'No. But nobody will notice. Come on.'

They sped off, slipping and skidding in the rivers of oil that ran down the hill. Anton had helped the boy up to the drilling deck where they had settled down to watch. It had been such an exciting afternoon, finding out about each other and watching the events, and it would have been even more perfect if Stefan hadn't spoiled everything by sneaking on them. Stefan Fabianovich Brakov, the son of his father's partner, sly and unpredictable, a telltale and a cry-baby. It had been odd to see him so poised and confident, and so very favourably married the other night.

Rafiq rolled up the specifications, put the pencil back in his pocket and lit a cigarette.

'What do you think?' said Anton.

'I agree this *might* be possible. But what good would it do you? Sabroski Oil no longer has the Rothschild contract.'

'With these specifications you could build the greatest and

safest of tankers. That would be such an achievement for you, Rafiq. The Rothschilds will get their oil from another producer.'

'You don't expect me to believe that, do you? I know you too well.'

Anton shrugged. 'I don't have a choice. Sabroski Oil is finished.' He paused. 'Besides, it's irrelevant. You can still *design* the tanker with, or without, Sabroski Oil. I can still make that happen, at least.'

'This merchant, Marcus Samuel, what else does he want from you?'

'To oversee a contract with the Rothschilds on his behalf. It was supposed to be my father doing that, but now… it's just me.'

'Taking on John Rockefeller and Standard Oil is dangerous. America's Standard Oil is the most powerful oil company in the world.'

'I know. I've already come up against Rockefeller's agents.' Anton told Rafiq about the waterfront fight and the break-in.

'Don't underestimate these men, Anton. Once they realise the value of what you have, they'll be back. Why would you risk such trouble on top of everything else?'

'I made a promise to my father and to Marcus Samuel.'

Rafiq frowned. 'A promise can get you killed. Your father wouldn't have wanted that. Not after what happened before.'

'Which is why I want you to take the specifications back to the Icheri Sheher. Study them and see what you think. They'll be safer in the Hasanov house with your gochu bodyguards.'

Rafiq stroked his beard. 'That is true, my friend.' He leaned back on his elbows and stretched out his legs. 'When do you plan to meet with the Rothschilds?'

'January. Their new business manager, a man called De Boer, will arrive then. He's having a new mansion built on Sadovaya Street.'

They fell silent. A horse cantered past and somewhere a dog

barked. Rafiq pushed his hair back from his face. 'I don't wish to pry, but how bad are your circumstances?'

Anton refilled their tea glasses. 'Curious things have happened since I returned.' He related the details of his inheritance.

'Strange stories indeed,' Rafiq said, 'but Baku is a strange city. My father used to say that fortunes could be won and lost in a day here. I'll wager that jewelled egg has a story or two.'

'A gambling debt?'

'Could be. It's Baku's favourite pastime.'

Anton agreed. Men would come back from the saloon bars and play long into the night with his father. Before Anton left for university, he played many games under his father's tutelage. It was a valued skill in Vladivostok and Shanghai, but not one his mother had approved of.

Rafiq took his tea and added four spoonfuls of sugar. 'And what about your… situation?'

Anton paused. He hadn't discussed the past for a long time, but Rafiq knew everything. 'I heard the Okhrana's presence in the Caucasus was being reduced. The tsar's been recalling his secret police back to St Petersburg.'

'Yes, I'd heard that. I wondered if it would make a difference to you. I reckon the imperial government's got far more pressing issues to worry about than chasing you.'

An hour later the doorbell rang. A young woman in a nut-brown coat trimmed with fur stood on the doorstep with a fair-haired man. Anton stared at the grown-up girl whom he hadn't seen for years.

'Anton Nikolayevich,' said Julia Seigenberg, gushing into the room in a sweep of orange taffeta, the young man trailing behind. 'I gave up waiting for you to call so I thought I'd come myself.' She screwed up her eyes. 'Let me look at you. Much taller and grimmer than I remember, and your hair is so long. No moustache or beard. Very modern. Gracious, what's that on your wrist?' She held his arm up for inspection and his coat jacket fell back.

'It's called a tattoo, Julia. The Chinese symbol for eternity.'

'Really? I've never seen one before. Do you have any others?'

Rafiq caught Anton's eye and grinned.

'No.' Anton felt hot and cleared his throat. 'Rafiq, this is Julia Seigenberg, daughter of John Seigenberg, my father's lawyer. I don't suppose you remember her. Julia was just a child when I left. Julia, this is my friend, Rafiq Hasanov. His father owns Caspian Shipping. He also has a caviar shop in the Icheri Sheher.'

'A pleasure, Miss Seigenberg,' said Rafiq, taking her gloved hand and kissing it. 'And I do remember you. Once you came to my father's shop. I showed you the sturgeon we kept in the tanks outside.'

Julia looked at him curiously. 'Did you? You have a very good memory, sir. I don't remember at all.'

'I never forget anyone or anything.' Rafiq bowed.

Julia fidgeted with a charm bracelet that hung over her gloves. 'You remember Leo Viktorovich, Anton?'

'I do,' said Anton, shaking the young man's hand. Leo had grown up too. He looked dapper in a dark blue morning coat braided with velvet and a blue spotted waistcoat.

The four of them talked for the next half hour and Anton took the chance to study Julia. She must have been ten years old when he'd last seen her with freckles across her nose and hair braided with ribbons. The Seigenbergs had attended his mother's funeral: John Seigenberg, his second wife Diane, his daughter Julia, and her older brother, Alfred. Julia had clutched her father's hand, not letting go for a minute, anxiously fingering a golden locket around her neck. John had kept her close. With a hand on his son's shoulder, he looked like a defensive force around his family, as if he feared someone might tear them apart. Now that Julia had grown up, there was something striking about her, but it was hard to determine why. Was it her chestnut-brown hair, her green eyes or that distinctive mole on the left side of her cheek? Perhaps it was her smile that made the difference. It transformed her face from being quite ordinary into an impression of vitality. It made you want to keep looking at her.

Anton noticed Rafiq's eyes sweep over her face more than once.

*

The Pallid Harrier took tea with the beak-nosed man in a dim teahouse near Parapet Square. The man wore a striped brown sack suit, a cream necktie decorated with stars and a pale lemon shirt. His hands clenched and unclenched to reveal a silver signet ring bearing an eagle with outstretched wings. Sweat glistened on the man's forehead and a sour smell encircled him.

'The specifications have been moved, Fretwell. Your task just became a lot harder.'

'Sabroski's being tipped off. Somebody's warning him.'

'The Hasanov family are powerful. Their house will be guarded. It's unwise to challenge the gochus.'

'I have a watch on the house. It's a matter of time before he brings the papers out again. Hasanov and Sabroski are joined at the hip.'

'Make sure you get them. This is your last chance.'

The Pallid Harrier sipped his tea. Hamilton Fretwell was one of the few subordinates he met with in Baku. Beneath him, a network of men and women spied for Standard Oil. There were clerks in offices, labourers and railway engineers. Even tribesmen in the mountains had their uses since raiding on trains made Russian oil less competitive. A brilliant idea to buy up raw materials needed to make oil barrels was proving a great success. Rockefeller had commended him and had authorised a bonus.

He looked at the reports that Fretwell had delivered, licked his lips and ordered another tea. It had been a very good month.

Chapter Eleven

That night Klara was awoken by a man shouting. She got out of bed and followed the cries to Anton's bedroom. Quietly she opened the door. Anton was twisting and turning, winding the bed sheets around himself in a strange torment. At last he groaned, pulled himself up, and sat on the edge of the bed with his head in his hands. A moment later, Anton stood up and grabbed his robe, but before he did, she caught a glimpse of his body: lean and taut and covered in scars. But they were not all scars – some were inky designs coiled around what looked like wounds from the past. She looked away quickly knowing she had no business to be looking. Then she looked back. Anton had taken something from a drawer and sunk into an armchair by the window. She stayed watching until he became a silhouette submerged in a blur of blue smoke.

You have almost as many secrets as I have, Anton Nikolayevich. But now I know one of them.

*

Anton stood by the Catherine Canal in St Petersburg. A snowy mist settled across his face and droplets froze the end of his nose. As he swayed with the unwelcome current, terror immobilised his limbs. In the distance, a clump of hooves carried on an icy wind. Five Cossacks protected the tsar inside the bulletproof carriage while a sixth sat next to the coachman. Two sleighs of military police followed, but as they approached the Pevchesky Bridge a figure ran out clutching a white package. Anton shouted but nothing came out. When the bomb went off, a man with blood-soaked hair turned to face him. It was Yuri Bulganin.

Anton's eyes jerked open and he shivered. He was sitting in the chair by the bedroom window covered in a cold sweat. His head swam, his skin itched, and he felt nauseous. It was early morning, and the sun was rising above the Caspian streaking red gold across the surface. He hadn't seen the face of the Okhrana for a very long time. He went to the washstand and sloshed water over his face. *It must have been that conversation with Rafiq.* The discussion of why he'd come back.

He pulled on his clothes and went downstairs. Olga, the new housekeeper was supervising the new cook and giving orders to the new stable hand. She was a middle-aged woman with a fan of hennaed hair and a starched black dress. The hiring of staff had settled Anton's concerns as now the house would be taken care of.

Anton spent the rest of the day reading his father's papers huddled next to the library fire. The mild weather had swung back into winter. Lines of plane trees bent and swayed in the wind, their black branches whipping from side to side. After the heat of the Orient the cold seeped into his bones and seemed to thicken his blood.

It was proving a long task, reading through the company documents, but he needed to understand the circumstances of Sabroski Oil's final years. He also looked for clues to explain the Fabergé egg. Here were surveyor reports, accounts, purchase orders, invoices and a stack of miscellaneous notes. He searched for bills of sale and purchase receipts, read through letters, but there was no reference to jewellery or gifts that sounded like a Fabergé egg. He remembered Rafiq's suggestion that it might be a gambling debt, so he looked for a record of an IOU, but found nothing.

He read about the setting up of the Sabroski Oil partnership between Fabian Brakov and his father in 1872. Dmitry Ivanovich Rabinovich had been hired as their accountant. Apart from Fabian and his father, Dmitry was the only person who had been with the company from the beginning.

Klara appeared and stacked the last of the documents on the library floor. 'Shall I sort them?'

'There's no need.'

Her face fell. She was wearing an old-fashioned day dress with a flat laced collar. It was faded maroon silk, tiered with bands of lemon embroidery, and might have been an expensive dress many years ago, though it was too big for her.

'Actually,' Anton said, 'it would be helpful if you separated the invoices and purchase orders from the general reports.'

Klara's eyes brightened. She sat cross-legged on the rug, brown buttoned boots sticking out from under her dress, and began sorting the papers into neat piles. For a moment, Anton watched. It was hard to imagine her working as his father's assistant. 'How well did you know the accountant, Dmitry Ivanovich?'

'We worked together.'

'What happened to him? Where did he go?'

'Odessa,' Klara said. 'His sister's house. That's what they said.'

'Did anyone try to contact him?'

'They sent constables, but there was nobody living at the address.'

'So... he didn't want anyone to find him.'

'Maybe.'

'Didn't you suspect something was wrong?'

Klara lowered her papers. 'Dmitry became very secretive. I don't think he trusted anybody. Even me.'

'So, he *was* embezzling money. That would explain the secrecy.'

She shot him a look. 'Dmitry never stole anything.'

'That's not what I was told. Everyone holds him responsible.'

'Well, they're wrong. I knew what he was like.'

Anton frowned. 'Then why run away and hide? If he was innocent?'

'Sometimes you have no choice. There are many reasons for running away. It doesn't mean you are guilty.'

Fair point. 'What do you think happened then? Dmitry must have said something.'

'He was very troubled towards the end. Some bad people were after him.'

'Did he owe money. Gamble?'

Klara hesitated. 'I saw him in the Devil's Bazaar a few times.'

'A gambling debt – easy to fall into if you don't know what you are doing.'

'I don't think it was that.'

He shook his head. 'It's absurd. A company as powerful as Sabroski Oil, failing overnight.'

'It didn't fail overnight. It was a gradual decline over years.'

'That's even worse. Why didn't anyone notice… do something about it? I don't understand.'

'Of course you don't! You weren't here.'

Anton scoffed. 'And you think I could have prevented it?'

'Possibly.'

'I'm flattered you think so highly of me.'

'Well, you're wrong there. I don't think highly of you at all.'

'I beg your pardon?'

She stood up, letting the papers fall from her lap. 'Why didn't you return home earlier? Nikolai waited for you. He wouldn't let himself die until you came home. That's how important you were to him. Every day he asked if a letter had arrived.'

'I wrote many letters.'

She placed her hands on her hips. 'Not often enough. And it still doesn't explain why you stayed away. He talked about you all the time. He loved you. What sort of a son are you?'

Anton stiffened. 'I would have come if I had known he was ill. I would have come if I'd known about the company. But I didn't.'

'But you did know! I wrote you a letter myself – Nikolai was too weak by then. I took it to the post office and posted it.'

'I never received it.'

'And I know he asked you to return earlier because he showed me a letter you'd sent. You said you had important work to do for Count Witte and Admiral Possiet.'

Anton looked away. He remembered the letter delivered to him at the offices of Admiral Possiet.

'Letter from home?' the admiral had said, while tugging at his moustache, which was long and bushy and had bits of food stuck in it.

'Yes. From my father in Baku.'

'In the oil business, isn't he? My daughter said your father was in some sort of trade.'

'He owns an oil company. Baku is one of the largest oil producing regions in the world.'

'Is it indeed? Not as powerful as Philadelphia, I assume. I can't imagine John Rockefeller tolerating that.'

'I don't suppose Rockefeller has a choice.'

The admiral raised his eyebrows as if he regarded Anton's comment as impertinent. 'Is that your intention, Anton Nikolayevich? To return to Baku and join the oil business with your father?'

'I haven't made up my mind yet, sir.'

'Rough business. Oil. Not a gentleman's pursuit.' He studied

Anton. 'How's that daughter of mine been treating you? Keeping her out of trouble? She's a bit of a handful. Needs a lot of entertaining and attention. You'd better watch out.' He chuckled as if he'd made an amusing joke.

'I will certainly watch out, sir.' Anton wondered if the admiral knew he was already intimate with his wilful daughter. He decided that the revelation might not be good for his health, his or the admiral's.

March 2nd 1888

My dear son,

I hope this letter finds you well and that your work with the tsar is drawing to a close. Certain matters have quietened down recently, and it may be possible for you to return. If so, I would welcome your swift return to take up a position at Sabroski Oil. A new opportunity has arisen which I am sure will be of great interest to you. I will explain more upon your arrival. I look forward to your reply.

Your attentive father
Nikolai Mikhailovich

'Surely you remember that letter?'

Anton started. He could feel the girl staring at him. 'I wasn't able to return. I was committed to a project with the admiral. Father gave no indication there was anything wrong.'

The girl's eyes widened. 'I don't believe you.'

Anton threw up his hands. 'You understand nothing! I don't care whether you believe me or not.' He pulled at his tie. The heat from the fire had trapped stale air in his throat. 'Are you going to help with these papers or not? Because if not, I suggest you go and do something else.'

'Such as?'

'I don't care as long as you leave me in peace. Why don't you go off to the Devil's Bazaar and find yourself another old man to prey on? The tavern should be open by now.' Anton massaged his forehead. *I shouldn't have said that.*

'I know that's what you think,' Klara said, nostrils flaring. 'I heard you talking to John Seigenberg after the funeral. You're the sort of man who thinks all woman in saloon bars are prostitutes. No doubt you met plenty in the Orient and that's what kept you there. You probably lost that finger in a bar brawl.' She backed away. 'You didn't stay because of duty, but because you didn't want to face the responsibilities of home.'

Before Anton could digest what she'd said, Klara had run from the room, slamming the door behind her. He heard footsteps on the stairs and a door crash in the distance. Anton closed his eyes and swore. The door opened and the housekeeper appeared. 'Is anything wrong, sir?'

'Everything is wrong, Olga.'

'Can I do something to help?'

'You can make me tea and take a glass to Klara. Add plenty of sugar.'

CHAPTER TWELVE

ANTON RECEIVED A MESSAGE THE NEXT MORNING FROM Melek Grashi, the silversmith. He headed straight for the Icheri Sheher, calling for Rafiq on the way. He had a mind that Rafiq with his different way of thinking might help to unravel the puzzle.

They found Melek in his local cayhane, drinking tea and smoking a tall shisha pipe. Braziers burned and the teahouse was crowded with shaggy, moustachioed men in fur caps and fezzes, all congregating inside clouds of pungent smoke.

'*Salam,* Anton Nikolayevich.' The silversmith's large watery eyes rested on Rafiq. 'Tariq Hasanov's son, if I am not mistaken. Rafiq, isn't it? *Marhaban.*'

'*Marhaban bik,*' Rafiq said.

'Let me order pipes. They have tobacco mixed with aniseed and herbs.' The silversmith's eyes reflected the burn of the coals. 'But if you'd like something stronger…'

Anton pulled up a stool. 'Just tobacco, thank you. You said you had news?'

'I have. But first, let us smoke and drink tea.' A man appeared carrying tall pipes with water bowls, long silver hoses and brass trays piled with coals and tobacco.

'This business is very interesting,' said the silversmith lowering his voice. 'From my enquiries, it seems your egg has a royal background. It is rumoured to have been commissioned by the Grand Duke Konstantin Nikolayevich, a distant relation of the tsar. The grand duke had the same mistress for many years, even after he remarried. He had the egg made for her. They say he was very much in love.'

'Who was she?'

'Katharine Lapinski. There used to be several Lapinski families at the Romanov Court. Thus, she would have been a woman of breeding – not royalty, but of good pedigree. But much about the lady remains a mystery.'

'Why is that?'

'She disappeared.'

'Disappeared? You mean she died?'

'No, I don't think so. In eighty-four she disappeared from public notice. Nobody has seen or heard from her since.'

'She might have come to Baku with the egg,' said Anton watching Rafiq uncoil his pipe. 'Maybe she met my father, needed money and offered it for sale? He would still have been a very rich man then,' he paused, '... except, if she had been the grand duke's mistress, surely he would have provided for her?'

Rafiq shrugged. 'The lady might have been abandoned by the grand duke. Romances go sour. Even royal ones'

The silversmith scratched the side of his nose with his long fingernail. 'Especially royal ones, which accounts for the many mistresses littering the empire. But it wouldn't be the first time a mistress has been paid off.'

'I know many men whose wives tolerate another woman, but only while they remained insignificant. The moment the mistress becomes important, she is dispatched.'

'You mean murdered?'

'Not necessarily, though that does happen. Usually it means paying them off – sending them to a different part of the country to a house far away.'

'If Katharine Lapinski was greatly loved she would have been a threat to Konstantin's new wife,' Anton reasoned. 'You said he remarried?'

'Yes,' said the silversmith. 'In 1882. She vanished less than two years later.'

'Paying her off to appease the new wife,' Anton said. 'But the poem inside. It doesn't sound like it would have been written by a man about to leave his mistress.'

The silversmith blew out a funnel of smoke. 'Sacrifices must be made by those with power and wealth. Konstantin was probably ordered to give her up.'

Anton lowered his tea glass. 'Suppose Katharine Lapinski brought the Fabergé egg to Baku. That means my father *must* have known her.'

'Not necessarily,' said Rafiq. 'The egg may have been stolen and brought here to sell.'

'How old would Katharine be now?'

'Konstantin was with her for fifteen years, which would make her… thirty-five… forty.'

'She might have married.'

The silversmith hummed as he sank back in his chair. Anton watched a man on the next table clean his fingernails with a dagger.

'How did you come by this information?' Anton asked.

The silversmith laid down his pipe and stirred sugar into his tea. 'I read the newspapers… follow the court gossip. I know how to trace jewellery back, as do my friends in the guild.'

Rafiq leaned back against the wall deep in thought. Beaded tassels hung down to his shoulders from under his skullcap and his face fell into shadow.

The day was darkening by the time Anton left the teahouse. The call to prayer from a nearby mosque rippled through the crooked alleyways. Anton bade Rafiq farewell and wound his way through the market square where the Maiden Tower loomed above. Many of the stalls were packing up. Dogs were scavenging through piles of rubbish. A boot cleaner sitting on an upturned box shouted across at him and pointed. Anton looked down at his boots, dirty and mud-splattered. He made his way over.

The conversation with the silversmith looped though his mind. Had his father known Katharine Lapinski? If she had sold him the Fabergé egg, there must be a record of the sale, though he'd found nothing so far. Surely his father's long-trusted friend, John Seigenberg, would have known about her? And what about the missing accountant, Dmitry Ivanovich? He'd have known too.

The boot cleaner tapped his leg and Anton shifted his weight onto his other foot.

So many secrets and so many puzzles. From the moment he arrived, Anton felt he'd been captured inside a city full of rumour and half-truths. He looked over at the spice stall where the last sales of the day were taking place. Dark spectres sheathed in black were gliding past: anonymous women in red slippers with turned-up toes and golden heels clicking along the dusty paths. He knew the women could be fifteen or fifty, a goddess or a gorgon, draped in their dark tent of secrets.

It would be easy for a woman to hide in a city like Baku.

*

Klara sensed somebody watching them. The house was attracting attention, whether it be from passersby who looked up more frequently, carriages that slowed on the hill, or tradesmen who called repeatedly. It could be a coincidence, as the Sabroski house had fuelled a great deal of gossip: the funeral, the arrival of the long-lost son, the appointment of household staff, to say nothing of past misfortunes – which would remain a riveting topic until some other poor soul was ruined, or worse.

Klara stared at the pickle jar on the table in her bedroom. It was full of dried grasses and poppies she'd pressed in the summer, but now the redness had faded, and the grasses were like straw. Her worries turned to Ivan. *You mustn't get caught again, Ivan. You'll never survive.* She'd never forget the stench of the prison or the decaying round tower with thick walls and arrow-slit windows. Perched on the top was a small turret where the guards looked out, rifle butts protruding like feelers. The bribe had bought them a time slot when the guards changed. They had found Ivan lying in his own filth. Rasoul picked him up as easily as a child and covered him with a blanket as they stepped over the other prisoners. But the plan went wrong. A different guard, misjudged timing, or maybe it had always been organised that way – she would never know. Rasoul slashed the guard with his dagger, but the alarm had been raised, and if it hadn't been for the uproar caused by the prisoners realising the cell door was open, they might never have escaped.

She sat down on the floor and looked at the documents surrounding her. The old man was always asking her to fetch this and that, an invoice here, a file there. There was correspondence between the Baron Rothschild and a merchant called Marcus Samuel. This must have been what Rasoul was talking about. Secret documents connected to Anton. Gone now, locked safely in the Icheri Sheher. She was glad she hadn't been tempted to intervene.

Klara gathered the letters, went downstairs to the library and placed them on the desk. The house was quiet. Anton had left that morning in a hurry and the housekeeper had gone to the market. She went over to the bookshelves, repositioned the ladder and climbed up. She pushed the books aside, felt along the wall and clicked open the safe. Inside, the egg sat in its dark protective cave. She rested her chin on the top rung. It would be so easy to take it and disappear. Anton would never find her. She could sell it, smuggle Ivan away, leave everything behind.

All she had to do was to take it.

She reached out and touched it, then wrapped her fingers around it. The egg's brittle surface began to warm, making an impression on her skin – like holding something vital and alive. She hesitated and then slowly opened her fingers and put it back. She'd been through this before, and she knew it wouldn't work.

CHAPTER THIRTEEN

JULIA SEIGENBERG LOOKED DOWN FROM HER WINDOW AS someone knocked on the door. A man with long hair tucked under a red and green skullcap stood hunched on the doorstep. He flicked his hair back and looked up. Immediately Julia drew back. It was Anton's friend, and the third time he'd visited this week.

She watched him put a cigarette into his mouth, struck a match and cupped his hand against the wind to light it. A tiny point glowed orange. Footsteps echoed in the hallway and Julia heard the front door open. She inspected her face in the mirror, tidied her hair and hurried onto the landing.

'I'm afraid Mr Seigenberg's not at home, sir,' she heard the housekeeper say.

'Do you know when he's expected back?'

'Not until—'

'My father will be back soon,' said Julia feeling a twinge of excitement as she walked down the stairs. 'Show Mr Hasanov into the drawing room.'

'If you say so, miss.'

'And bring us some tea please.'

Rafiq's dark eyes flickered. 'I don't wish to intrude, Miss Seigenberg.'

'You're not intruding.'

A breeze blew leaves into the hallway. Rafiq threw the butt of his cigarette outside, removed his skullcap and handed his coat to the housekeeper. He wore a cream sash around his waist and a red-and-yellow-striped waistcoat fastened with loops and buttons. He looked exotic and mysterious.

Julia led the way to the drawing room glowing with light from the fire. 'Please sit,' she said, indicating with a sweep of her hand.

Rafiq sat with his back to the window. His face disappeared into the shade while the sun lit the back of his head picking out strands of silver. The room fell still and silent and even the sounds of the street faded away.

'Tea will be coming soon,' she said.

'I won't stay long.'

'Oh, but you must. Father will be disappointed to have missed you.' *I have to make him stay.*

'As you wish.' He fidgeted as he looked around the room. 'Your mother, she is well?'

'Oh, yes. Playing vint this afternoon. She enjoys her card games.'

'And Alfred? Is he—?'

'I don't know. In town somewhere. I think. But, also, very well.'

Rafiq stared across the room, his eyes fixed on a space somewhere between the fireplace and the pianoforte. He pulled out a cigarette case and caught her eye. 'May I?'

'Please do.' Julia fiddled with her bracelet. She felt as if she were in the room with something intense and unknown, something trapped. She'd been determined to speak to Rafiq alone, and now she'd succeeded. It was the most excitement she'd had in months.

He took a drag from his cigarette and smiled, his eyes creasing with fine lines running down from the corners. A strange scar, shaped like a dimple, cut into his left cheek. *How did you get that?* She wanted to lean forward and touch it. 'Anton Nikolayevich said your father owns Caspian Shipping and that you are some sort of engineer,' she said. 'Do you make boats? Or does that mean you simply make the designs? Oh, I didn't mean *simply*, I meant…' She felt herself burn. *Oh God, why do I say such foolish things?*

Rafiq smiled. 'I know what you meant. I design many sorts of craft. But somebody else builds them.'

'What are you working on now?'

'Something new.'

The flicker of conversation died. Julia looked over at the door. 'I can't imagine where this tea is.'

Rafiq gazed at her. It was a bold look, his eyes running over her face as if he were inspecting her thoughts. He looked over at the pianoforte. 'Do you play?'

'A little.' She pulled at the cuffs of her dress. *Why didn't I change?* It was an old dress with dull blue flowers; the lace collar was ripped and one of the sleeves had a stain on it where Alfred had spilled a glass of port.

'I was surprised you remembered me from your caviar shop.'

'I never forget people. Do you like caviar?'

'I'm not sure… I don't think so.' *It made me sick last time.*

'Then you've not tasted beluga caviar,' he said. 'The beluga sturgeon produces the best caviar in the world. Next time you visit the Icheri Sheher, I'll show you how we make it.'

'That's very kind.'

The housekeeper entered carrying a tray. She set it down and began moving everything onto the table. The cups chinked, the teaspoons clattered, and the teapot clunked down spilling tea onto the surface. Three sugar cubes tumbled from the bowl. The housekeeper looked at Julia. 'Shall I serve?'

'No thank you, Chinara. I'll do it.' Julia waited for the door to close. 'Lemon?' she said, picking up a pair of silver tongs.

'Please.'

'Sugar?'

'Thank you. Four.'

She hesitated.

'I have a very sweet tooth.'

She wasn't sure whether he was mocking her. She jumped as a pigeon fluttered against the window, its wings beating against the glass pane. It hovered for a second before taking off into the fading light.

Julia handed him the tea. Rafiq stirred and placed it on the table between them. 'You need more coal. The fire's burning low.' He went to the fireplace, took the scuttle and shook a heap into the flames. Sparks leapt into the air, crackling and spitting as he stabbed the coals into place with a poker. It was almost dark in the room and Julia knew she should turn on the light, but she didn't want to. Rafiq stood up and leaned one elbow on the mantelpiece. She wasn't sure whether he was smiling or not, his face was painted with shadows.

'Your tea will get cold,' she said.

He sat on the floor and reached for his cup. It surprised her than she didn't feel uncomfortable in the settling silence. Perhaps it was the lack of light, or the absence of expected conversation that always existed in the drawing rooms of her stepmother's friends. She had no desire to speak and sensed he didn't either. He seemed the sort of man who didn't waste time on unnecessary words. And it wasn't as if she had nothing to say. She had many questions, but felt no desire to know the answers. It was enough to watch him lean back on his hands and cross his legs with his back to the fire. It was most unconventional and shockingly casual, but she liked it.

Muffled voices, footsteps and then a wedge of light spilled through the door from the hallway.

'Julia? Goodness – why is it so dark in here?' A switch clicked and bright yellow light flooded the room. A wave of damp, cool air rolled towards her. Leo Rostov stood in the pool of light removing his top hat and suede gloves. Her father, John Seigenberg, stood behind him.

As Rafiq got to his feet, Julia organised a smile. 'Leo. What are you doing here? I thought you'd be away for weeks.'

'So did I, but there was a problem.' Leo's eyes widened. 'Hasanov! Didn't expect to see you here.'

Julia cut in quickly. 'Mr. Hasanov has been waiting for you, Father. I think you had a meeting planned.'

'Apologies. I was delayed by this young rascal.' John slapped Leo on the back. 'Telling me all about his trip to Tiflis.'

Rafiq fingered his cigarette case. 'Thank you for your hospitality, Miss Seigenberg.' He turned to John. 'I was telling Miss Seigenberg, our shop in the old city sells the finest beluga caviar.'

'Beluga caviar is my favourite extravagance,' said John. 'I must order some more.' He laid a hand on Rafiq's shoulder. 'Come, let's get down to business. I have already prepared the papers for your new patent.'

After they left, Julia smoothed her skirt folds and ran her hand over the chintz covering of the divan. She sensed Leo staring as he sat opposite her.

'What did Hasanov come to see your father about?'

'Some new shipping project,' said Julia tracing the outline of a flower pattern with her finger. 'I felt it only polite to offer him tea while he waited.'

'He seemed very interested in you.'

'I didn't notice.'

'He couldn't take his eyes off you.'

'Don't be silly, Leo. You must have imagined it.'

'I always notice when men look at you, Julia.'

She forced a laugh. 'Always my protector, Leo. What a good friend you are.'

'I brought you something from Tiflis.' Leo reached in his pocket and produced a small box covered in crimson velvet and placed it in her hands.

Immediately a pang settled in her chest. 'That's very thoughtful of you. You spoil me far too much.' She opened the box and smiled: inside was a golden cat charm.

'I know you like to collect them.'

'It's lovely. Thank you so much.'

Leo clutched her hand. 'It gives me great pleasure to find things you like, Julia.'

His skin was cool and smooth, fingernails clean and cut short. Julia imagined Rafiq's hands would be calloused, work-worn yet strong. They would be warm in her hands.

'Give me your bracelet. I'll fix it now.'

She unhooked the clasp and gave it to him. Leo had grown a small moustache and he looked quite handsome in his dark blue morning coat. But apart from that he was just the same. The same good-natured look. The same dimple in the middle of his chin. The same sleepy blue eyes.

She made an effort. 'What happened in Tiflis? Why did you return so soon?'

Leo pulled out a pocketknife and began to manipulate one of the links. 'Some of the railway tank cars were damaged. Father thinks it was deliberate. Somebody trying to derail the shipment.'

'Why would they do that?'

'The price of oil is low, there's too much of the stuff. Export markets are already flooded. There's a lot of competition for customers.' He held out the bracelet. 'Here, I've fixed it. Let me put it on for you.'

Julia held out her arm. 'You must be careful, Leo.'

'Don't worry about me. I'll stay out of it as much as I can. I've no love for the oil industry. If I had my way, I'd have nothing to do with it.'

'And then what would you do, apart from play poker with my brother?'

'I'd paint.'

'Who would you paint?' Julia smiled because she knew the answer.

'You, of course. Well, that would be my first painting. Then I'd have to paint Alfred, otherwise he'd feel left out. Then I'd hire myself out to all the families in Baku who wanted their portraits painted. Everyone wants to be immortalised. I'd make millions of roubles and be richer than any oil baron.'

Julia laughed. Leo was such a dreamer.

The events of that day stayed with Julia for the following week. Images of Rafiq Hasanov kept appearing at the most inconvenient times. During afternoon tea the next day while her stepmother and friends were exchanging gossip, and while she was having measurements taken for a new promenade dress. It wasn't until the seamstress accidentally jabbed her with a pin that Julia focused on her stepmother's exasperated expression. 'What is the matter with you, Julia? Stand still and pull your shoulders back.'

She enjoyed having somebody to think about. It meant she could spend hours sitting in the window wondering what he was doing and what new craft he might be designing. She couldn't remember whether that strange scar had been on the left or right side of his cheek. She wondered how he had come by it and whether it had been won in a fight over honour, or even a woman. Rafiq seemed so brooding and dark. Anton said that his wife had died two years ago, which had to be why he was so melancholy and strange.

CHAPTER FOURTEEN

ANTON HADN'T BEEN TO THE BAKU GENTLEMAN'S CLUB before. His father had been a member, as was the custom with the city's wealthy oil men, so he knew that's where he'd find John Seigenberg. He remembered his father recommending the club's first-class restaurant, its wood-panelled bar and gaming rooms. It wasn't the sort of place he liked, being the preserve of the wealthy who harboured ideas that kept other sections of society in their place, but it was vital to keep digging, and the oil men were his best source of information.

He looked through his wardrobe. The only formal clothes he possessed, apart from funeral attire he'd borrowed from John, had been made in Shanghai. He selected a dark blue mix of satin and wool with ornate enamelled buttons. The collar and cuffs were embroidered with ivory symbols that smelled of patchouli. He tied his hair back and studied himself in the mirror.

It would have to do.

An hour later, Anton found John in the club restaurant and told him about Katharine Lapinski.

'This business becomes even stranger,' the lawyer said, studying Anton's attire with amusement. 'I never saw such a woman with Nikolai.'

'She must be in Baku somewhere.'

'I'll make enquiries. See what I can find out.'

Anton ordered a drink in the saloon bar. The club was an old-fashioned establishment, smelling of polish, leather and cigars. The rooms were festooned with potted palms and metalware, including long-spouted brass teapots, silver tankards, and sets of silver shot glasses monogrammed with various initials. The marble floors were covered in oriental carpets and the walls hung with tapestries. Long-hosed shisha pipes filled the air with mint and fruits.

Anton heard a gruff voice behind him. 'Well, if it isn't Anton Nikolayevich. We wondered when you'd grace us with your presence.' It was Fabian Brakov, whom he hadn't seen since their encounter on the oilfield.

Anton heard murmurs and felt eyes on him. He raised his glass. 'Greetings. Your very good health, gentlemen.' *Look them all in the eye and stand straight.*

The saloon bar fell silent. Prehistoric-looking fish with elongated snouts glowered out from mounted displays. Anton shook proffered hands, made polite conversation and accepted condolences from those around, but he sensed the oil men looking him up and down. *I know what you're thinking. You're wondering how I could have let my father down. Why I stayed away so long and what have I got to hide.* He squared his shoulders and held his head high.

Some faces were familiar. There was Stefan, who despite their tension of the previous meeting greeted Anton enthusiastically. Beside him sat a short-haired American who'd been introduced as Albert Prankman. Then there were the millionaire Tatar oil barons: Zeynalabdin Taghiyev and Musa Naghiyev both with black beards, moustaches and fezzes; and the Armenian oil baron,

Alexander Mantashev. He deduced that the fair-haired man sitting nearby was one of the Nobel brothers – Emanuel Nobel – owner of the Swedish Branobel oil company. He sensed Taghiyev studying him. The Tatar millionaire, dressed in a long dark jacket buttoned all the way down the front, had raised a tea glass to him the moment he'd entered the room. He remembered the oil baron owned land in the Bibi-Eibat oilfield region next to his father's oilfields.

The American, Prankman, put down his newspaper and took out his monocle as Anton joined them. 'So, Sabroski, what brings you back to this forlorn part of the world?'

Anton cleared his throat. 'I happen to like this forlorn part of the world. This is my home and I'm glad to be back.'

'If that's the case, what kept you away so long?'

'Business… and other matters,' said Anton. 'And what about you, sir. What keeps you here?'

'Business.' Prankman smiled. 'And other matters. It seems we have much in common.'

'Indeed.'

Prankman drummed his fingers against his walking cane. Anton saw it had a handle fashioned in the shape of a dog's head with small glass eyes. 'I'm sorry about your father's estate. Most disappointing for you. You come back from the Orient full of expectations and now you have nothing.'

Anton noticed the room had become very quiet. Everyone seemed to be concentrating on reading, drinking or smoking, but with such stillness that not a single newspaper twitched, nor a whisky glass chinked. 'I wouldn't say that. Baku is full of opportunity. No doubt I'll make my way.'

'Bravo. Such determination – just the sort of man I admire. But you'll need plenty of nerve and luck to survive here. And friends. The right sort of friends. Men to give you advice.'

Anton rested his hand on the smooth leather of the armchair. 'I'll bear that in mind.'

Prankman produced a mother of pearl card holder and flipped open the top. 'I can help if you need to raise capital. I have many contacts, not just here, but overseas as well.'

Anton took it. 'I'm much obliged.' *Not in a million years would I trust you.*

The American signalled the attendant to refill their glasses. 'You need to develop a hard shell here, Sabroski, but I expect you've already realised that. Oil is a mucky business and not one for the fainthearted.'

Is that why you're in it?

'Don't misunderstand me,' Prankman continued. 'I'm just giving you advice. I tried to give your father advice once, but he wouldn't listen.'

'With respect, it must have meant he didn't think the advice worth taking,' said Anton, picking up a periodical from a nearby side table and flicking through it.

'Fair point. I can see you're just like him.'

'I take that as a compliment, sir.'

Prankman smirked. 'Yes. I imagine you would.'

There was a long moment of silence before a buzz of conversation started. A red-faced man whose mouth had been ajar for much of the exchange, closed it briefly before turning back to his audience. Cigars were relit and drinks replenished. At one point, a man exclaimed from his newspaper. 'My word! Have you seen this? The tsar's going to sign an entente with France.'

'France?' said Prankman swirling the drink around his glass. 'I don't think that's likely. Russia already has an agreement with Germany.'

'I know, but that cannot last. The new kaiser is a bombastic idiot. He's already dismissed Bismarck and refuses to listen to his ministers. The tsar can't stand him.'

'There'll be war in Europe soon,' growled the man with the red face. 'The countries are lining up: Germany with Austria-Hungary and now France, Russia and England.'

'Look on the bright side. War is good for business,' said Prankman.

'And where would America stand, sir, if such a situation arose?'

'New York is six thousand miles away. I doubt we'd be involved.'

'Come, sir, no need to be pragmatic,' said the red-faced man. 'Your government must have a standpoint.'

'I expect they'll ask Rockefeller,' chuckled Prankman. 'Business must go on, and he's the best man to know about that.'

The debate continued.

Prankman downed his drink, retrieved his cane and stood up. The tails of his brown morning coat reached down to his knee bend, making him appear shorter than he was. 'Game of poker, gentlemen?' Prankman eyed Anton. 'Sabroski?'

Anton shook his head. 'Please excuse me.'

'Another time then.'

Anton watched the American leave and sipped his wine. If he'd returned to Baku earlier, he might have had to work with that man. How long would their relationship have remained cordial. A few days? A few hours?

Stefan drew up a chair and lowered his voice. 'Prankman used to work in Philadelphia with John Rockefeller. Knows a lot about oil.'

'You mean he wasn't employed for his charm?'

'Quite. Not the most tactful of men. Can't abide him myself.'

'I'm not surprised.'

'Father thinks he's invaluable. Gets things done. Fortunately, I have little to do with him.' Stefan hesitated. 'I'm in charge of a different section of the company now.' He sank back into the velvet cushions of a studded leather chair and crossed his legs. His tailcoat fell open to reveal a blue patterned waistcoat and a red ascot tie.

Stefan signalled the waiter. 'Have you seen Hasanov yet?'

'Yes.'

'I hear his father has done well in Caspian Shipping. Hasanov is some sort of engineer, isn't he?'

Anton blinked. Stefan had a way of speaking about people as if they weren't eligible members of the human race. 'He's a marine engineer. He designed one of the Nobel tankers.'

'Impressive. Considering his background.'

'Why do you say that?'

'The Nobel Brothers' engineers are usually Scandinavian, like the rest of the family. Hasanov's not their usual sort. You know, being a Muslim.' Stefan pulled out a red handkerchief and dabbed his forehead. It was the exact same shade as his tie.

Across the room, a group of Tatar oil barons were refilling their tea glasses from long-spouted teapots, and in another corner four men were playing backgammon.

Anton lowered his voice. 'Stefan, what do you know about Dmitry Ivanovich?'

'The accountant who disappeared? Why do you ask?'

'I want to speak to him.'

'He went to Odessa to stay with his sister. That's where his landlady sent his belongings.'

'And where does the landlady live?'

'Somewhere on Chadrovaya Street. A German woman. Why do you want to know? Dmitry's not going to be there now, is he?'

The afternoon had brightened by the time Anton left the club. It was unfortunate that Fabian Brakov had chosen a man like Prankman as a consultant. Anton wondered what special role Stefan had at Brakov Oil. *You are a fortunate man, Stefan. You have everything, yet you can't see it.*

Anton kicked at a stone and stepped off the kerb. It landed at the feet of a tall man in a grey-belted overcoat who had paused to light a cigarette. The man glanced over. He had brown hair swept back from his face, gold-rimmed glasses and a pointed beard.

Anton looked away and continued down the hill. The discussion about war had disturbed him. A war, which might pitch Russian against Turk, or French against Austrian, would be a disaster. He had no wish to see military action again, he'd seen plenty of that in the Afghan territory.

A blue sky and a cold December sun beckoned. Anton's stomach growled. If he wasn't too late, he'd buy a piece of grilled sturgeon from the fishermen.

Anton quickened his pace. Four camels ambled by, heads held high, coats stiff with tar to prevent mange. Blocks of indigo-blue bulged out from packs strapped round their bellies while two barefooted Indians trotted in pursuit. As Anton waited for the camel train to pass, he noticed the tall man in the grey-belted overcoat glance away and pretend to consult his pocket watch. Anton's spine prickled. He shoved his hands into his pockets, put his head down and made towards the harbour.

The bay of Baku boasted one of the most magnificent harbours in the region. Crescent-shaped, stretching seven miles across, it played host to thousands of crafts plying their trade between the Volga River and Persia. Anton dodged a medley of peddlers and naval personnel until he reached one of the landing piers where the fishing boats bobbed up and down. He bought a piece of grilled sturgeon wrapped in bread and leaned back in an archway to eat it.

As he watched the passersby, he considered his situation. The Okhrana secret police had hundreds of spies across the empire. They operated in secret offices under the supervision of the gendarmes of police and had the power to arrest anyone at any time. They were bound by no laws and answered to no one but the tsar.

I was foolish to think they'd forget me.

The tall man reappeared. He stopped, scanned the crowds,

shielding his eyes from the sun, and then climbed up the stone steps, where he rested his gloved hands on the railings. The sun glinted off his spectacles as he looked left and right. A moment later, he descended the steps and headed along the embankment. Anton discarded the remainder of his sandwich and followed.

The tall man picked up pace and developed a determined stride. As Anton propelled himself forward, an old man bent double with a trunk strapped to his back blocked his path. Anton dodged, promptly colliding with a stout Turkish merchant. Muttering an apology, Anton bounded forward.

Minutes later, the tall man stopped and turned as if somebody had said his name. Anton slipped into a doorway. Beads of sweat ran down the side of his face. His stomach clenched.

A Tatar, with a thin face and long sideburns, joined the tall man.

They talked, the Tatar mostly nodding while resting one hand on a curved dagger tucked into his belt, the taller man gesticulating. Finally, they parted. The Tatar walked through an archway into the Icheri Sheher. The tall man disappeared into a teahouse.

Anton hurried out of the archway as a figure moved in front of him, blocking his way.

'Can it be Anton Nikolayevich?' A woman in a dark brown mantle fastened with a moonstone brooch appeared. She cocked her head and held out a gloved hand.

Anton instinctively bowed and kissed the glove reeking of violets. Breathlessly, he composed himself. 'Indeed, it is. My pleasure, madam.' The woman looked familiar, but he didn't know who she was. His eyes strayed to the entrance of the teahouse, a wave of frustration rolling over him.

'My goodness. You've changed so. Do you remember me, Anton Nikolayevich?' he heard the woman say. 'I'm Stefan Fabianovich's mother, Olesia Romanovna.'

Anton tried to withdraw his hand, but she had curled her

fingers around it. 'We didn't think you'd ever return. What have you been doing?'

'For the last month, I've been busy attending to my father's estate, ma'am.'

'Of course. How thoughtless of me. Please accept my condolences.' She scrutinised him from under a green hat crowned with a feather and a rhinestone buckle. 'You look so much like him. It's like looking into the past.'

Anton pulled away as behind them a shout rang out and a wagon laden with hessian sacks creaked forward.

'If you'll excuse me, ma'am, I have an urgent appointment. It was a pleasure to meet you. Good day.'

Anton raced towards the teahouse and glanced inside. The tall man was still there, drinking tea and consulting a notebook. Anton loosened his collar; he was boiling hot. How foolish to think the Okhrana would ever forget.

As soon as Anton got back to the house, he went upstairs, took out the Smith 'n' Wesson revolver and reloaded it. He selected six spare bullets and secured them inside his pockets. He looked out of the window at Nikolaevskaya Street, but apart from the usual itinerant flow of people, there was nobody who matched the tall man's description.

CHAPTER FIFTEEN

ANTON ROSE LATE THE NEXT DAY HAVING WOKEN FROM A solid dead sleep. He had arranged to meet with Rafiq to look over the first draft of the tanker plans that afternoon, but first he had something to do.

He saddled his horse and rode to Chadrovaya Street, where Dmitry Ivanovich's landlady lived. He reined to a halt, beckoned a street boy over – who in turn collected a number of other urchins – and waited while they argued and bargained information. Now, many kopeks lighter, Anton continued up the road with a number and a name.

It was a busy street; the lower section had been turned into a market. Boxes of onions, muddy potatoes and red peppers were strewn across makeshift tables. Pyramids of cabbages balanced in doorways and gourds hung from hooks like decapitated warrior heads. The landlady's house had a wrought-iron balcony on the second floor. Red and gold rugs dripped onto the street below. The gargoyle above the doorway grimaced down at Anton as he pulled the bell.

A middle-aged woman poked her head round the door followed by a waft of camphor. She wore a blue-and-black-patterned dress buttoned up under a series of chins, and a navy woollen shawl draped across her shoulders. A black cap clung to the back of her hairpiece.

'Please forgive the intrusion, madam, but would you be Frau Kalian?'

She leaned on her cane and looked him up and down suspiciously.

'My name is Anton Nikolayevich. I understand Dmitry Ivanovich lodged with you some time ago. He was the accountant for my father, Nikolai Mikhailovich Sabroski. Might I speak with you? I'll not take much of your time.'

The woman's face softened. 'I'm afraid Dmitry Ivanovich doesn't live here any more, but if you're Nikolai Mikhailovich's son, I'm happy to talk. Please come inside.'

The hallway was well lit, with stone steps leading upstairs. The smell of baking bread hung in the air and saucepans clattered nearby. Anton followed Frau Kalian to the second floor to a spacious room full of long-tongued plants, copper plate-ware and a blaze of tapestries covering the walls and floor. Lavender pomades hung from hooks and perfumed the musty air.

Frau Kalian hobbled across the room, eased into a faded chintz armchair and rearranged a cushion behind her back.

'Well, Anton Nikolayevich, this *is* a surprise. I never thought to hear from Sabroski Oil again. You're the son that lived in the Orient? Dmitry thought you'd never return.'

'I'm not sure if you know, Frau Kalian, but a short while ago, my father passed away.' Anton could see by her expression that the information was not new. 'Dmitry was a friend to me when I was a child. There are several matters that are unclear, but they are of a sensitive nature.'

Frau Kalian linked her fingers. 'I'm very sorry to hear about your father, sir. Dmitry thought highly of him.' She indicated a chair with her cane and tucked a sprig of grey hair under her wig. 'Please sit.'

Anton removed his hat and sat. 'I need to find Dmitry. It is of the utmost importance. I would be grateful for your help.'

'He is gone, sir. To Odessa. To his sister's.'

'There is speculation about why he left.'

Frau Kalian drew her finely plucked eyebrows together. 'Dmitry was troubled by the way things turned out. There was a lot of bad talk... but what they said about him was lies.' The old woman leaned forward. 'He always paid his rent on time and kept his rooms clean. He was polite and thoughtful, not like some I've had in my time. Each week he'd treat me to a bottle of good vodka. "Frau Kalian," he'd say, "come and have a drink with me, I'd like your opinion on this or that." He trusted me with his confidences. So, you see, Anton Nikolayevich, he wasn't the type to be dishonest. If you've come to find fault with him, you'll not find it here.'

'I haven't come to condemn him.'

Frau Kalian relaxed and picked up her fan. It was made of long golden feathers from a bird of paradise. 'How do you like my carpets, sir? I expect you're quite surprised to see such a collection?'

'I am,' said Anton looking around. 'You have good taste, madam. I believe some of these are antique from Persia?'

'You are correct, sir... carpets keep such secrets. Did you know Muslim girls used to express their love to young men by weaving secret messages into them? Love knots, they were called. See the one over there.' She pointed to a large blue-and-cream tapestry hanging on the wall. 'The winding and intertwining loops represent everlasting love. My late husband, Gerhard, bless his soul, bought that back from Tehran. It was our anniversary present.'

'You are fortunate to have such a collection.' He paused politely. 'Frau Kalian, did Dmitry leave any papers? Documents? Letters?'

She shook her head. 'There's nothing. He asked me to pack his belongings and send them to the railway station.'

'Do you remember when?'

She scratched one of her chins. 'About two years ago. Around the time of the tsar's visit. When the Romanovs came to lay the foundation stone for the new cathedral. I remember now. It was a public holiday.'

'Did he have friends? Someone he might have confided in?'

She waggled a fat finger. 'Now that you mention it, there was someone. A lady friend, although I don't think she was a lady, if you understand me.' She gave Anton a wink and lowered her voice so that he had to lean forward to listen. 'Dmitry used to drink.' Her warm breath was sour against his face. 'Not too much, mind you, and not half as much as my poor Gerhard. But he *did* frequent saloon bars, especially the one out along the Bailov road: the Devil's Bazaar. He liked one of *those* women. You know the type. I only found out because one night he drank so much she had to bring him home. You should have seen the state he was in. Covered in blood, mud all over his clothes. His hat trampled as if a score of horses had run across it. All this at three o'clock in the morning, would you believe? Lord save us, I thought.' She clutched her cane, her eyes bright. 'I thought it was those Mohammedans who had done it. You know how it is with the Armenians. Bad blood between them. And always will be with all that fighting and cursing, and I think the situation's only going to get worse. Soon it won't be safe for any of us to go out.'

'You were telling me about Dmitry, Frau Kalian,' Anton said softly. A canary fluttered its wings in a cage. It hopped onto its perch and began preening itself.

Frau Kalian touched her hairpiece. 'Where was I? Ah, I remember now... I just happened to be looking out of my window and there he was, lying in the road as if half dead. The woman was banging on my door shrieking like a demon, shouting for me to call a doctor and setting all the dogs off barking and howling.' Frau Kalian stopped for breath. 'I hurried down as quickly as I could, and we carried Dmitry upstairs. He was in bed for a week.'

'What was the woman's name?'

Frau Kalian scratched her nose. 'Not sure I can remember now. Grace, was it? No, not Grace – that's the market man's daughter. Mind you, she looked a bit like Grace with all that hair. I expect it'll come back to me soon enough.' She studied him, her wrinkled grey eyes brightening. 'I'd like a drink, sir, if you don't mind. Will you join me?'

'It would be a pleasure.'

Frau Kalian beamed a set of yellow teeth. 'I've got a nice bottle of Pertsovka flavoured with pepper and honey. My favourite.' She fumbled behind her cushion and pulled out a bottle. 'If you'd be so kind as to fetch two glasses from the cupboard.' She pointed to a tall wooden cabinet with greasy glass doors. Anton got two glasses and filled them.

'Your good health,' said Anton.

'Another?' said Frau Kalian, briskly refilling hers.

'Not for me, thank you.' She finished her second, then splashed another brimful. Her hairpiece lay on top of her head, lifeless and dull like something dead.

'Do you think Dmitry was in trouble?'

The landlady frowned. 'Dmitry was troubled rather than *in* trouble. All was not well with the company. Something was wrong with the accounts.'

'What do you mean?'

'All those bills. That last oilfield. He knew it wasn't right. There was an argument.'

'Which oilfield? On Bibi-Eibat?'

'Oh, I wouldn't know that, but Dmitry said he'd been cheated.' She paused. 'It was the last one, I think.'

Anton took the vodka bottle and refilled their glasses. 'Did he ever mention a bill for an expensive jewel? A present for someone?'

'A jewel? You mean for a woman?' Frau Kalian shook her head. 'Not that I can recall. But there were too many bills. Everything was so expensive. Dmitry said the company couldn't afford it.'

'Do you remember anything in particular?'

She tapped her head. 'My memory is not that good now. There was something about a new steam engine.' She paused. 'And then he left without so much as a farewell. Very disappointed I was, but I'm sure he meant no disrespect. He knew there would be trouble. He packed all his belongings and went to a meeting in the Black City – you know – where all the refineries are. He asked me to send his trunk to the train station.'

A clock on the wall chimed twice. A small door opened in the casing and a wooden bird sprang out.

'He left nothing behind. You are quite sure?'

'Absolutely. I had his room cleared and cleaned. I had to relet his rooms.'

Anton could have sworn that she hesitated before replying. He waited for her to say more but she didn't. Eventually he stood up. 'I must take my leave now, Frau Kalian. If you remember anything else, will you send me word?'

She took the calling card and patted Anton's hand. 'Thank you, sir. I've thoroughly enjoyed myself. It's not often I have the company of a gentleman.'

As Anton retrieved his horse, he sensed somebody watching. Casually, he glanced around and saw the Tatar with the thin face and long sideburns standing in a doorway. The man looked up at Frau Kalian opening her balcony door to check the sodden rugs. Then, quite deliberately, he sliced open a pomegranate with his dagger and bit into the blood-red pips.

Anton rode to Rafiq's house, his mind churning. *Too many bills. An argument over an oilfield.* How much could he rely on the old woman's recollections? Yet there was a sincerity to Frau Kalian and he could well imagine Dmitry taking a drink and confiding in her. She'd packed his belongings and sent them on, but it was unlike Dmitry not to say goodbye. Did he even board the train? If not, where was he? And what about the business with the woman in the Devil's Bazaar? On thing was clear. Dmitry had got into trouble and had not confided in Klara or his father. Anton remembered something his mother had said. *Corruption and temptation in Baku is too much for most men. Too much money, too easily made and too easily lost.*

Had Dmitry been seduced by such wealth?

Anton rode through a sprawling bazaar off Chadrovaya Street. Makeshift workshops and stalls besieged an open space cratered with potholes. It was busy with merchants in thick goatskin coats unloading donkey carts. Everywhere stunk of dung and rotting debris. He clicked the reins and drove a path through the crowds. Stray dogs barked and chased so closely he thought the horse would trample their paws. He glanced at his pocket watch. Half past two. Late. He had promised to meet Rafiq hours ago.

Rafiq Hasanov crouched on the floor of an upstairs room surrounded by sheets of paper. He was wearing a blue velvet waistcoat with three-quarter-length sleeves lined with red silk. His long hair was tied back, and his feet were encased in slippers embroidered with oriental designs.

Anton made his apologies, which proved unnecessary since Rafiq had no idea of the time. Anton sank into a low divan and helped himself to Turkish delight that lay heaped in a bowl of powdered sugar. The tanker plans were far from Anton's thoughts, but he forced himself to focus as Rafiq spread a drawing in front of him.

'This is the first draft,' Rafiq said, pushing up his sleeves. 'As the Suez Canal authorities stipulate, none of the individual tanks should exceed two hundred tons and the pumps must be able to discharge oil at three hundred and fifty tonnes per hour.' He grinned. 'I've adapted the design of the Nobel Brother's *Zoroaster* tanker.'

'Did you get to look at their plans again?'

'No need. I remember the details from years ago.'

Rafiq's exceptional memory had maddened Anton at times. He was impossible to beat at chess.

'I've also improved on them. Look.' Rafiq jabbed a slim brown finger at the diagram. 'I've used the actual skin of the ship as the wall for the oil tanks.' He leaned forward on his knees, pushing a cigarette into the side of his mouth. 'And I've added tanks to allow for the expansion and contraction in different temperatures.'

Anton asked questions as Rafiq punctuated his comments with swift movements of his fingers. Rafiq's face was animated and alive with enthusiasm and it bolstered Anton's spirits to see his friend so focused and happy.

'You've done a remarkable job, Rafiq. Marcus Samuel will be delighted.' Anton grinned. 'But John Rockefeller won't. Standard Oil will be furious if we get to the Orient before they do.'

Rafiq laughed. 'These drafts are almost ready. Another few weeks and you can take them.' He started to roll up the plans. 'Now tell me what's on your mind. I can tell something's bothering you.'

Anton recounted his discussion with Frau Kalian. 'Dmitry thought there was something amiss with the company accounts.'

Rafiq stretched out his legs and leaned back on his hands. 'It's probably nothing. Just an old woman gossiping and elaborating on stories from the past. If Dmitry thought something suspicious was going on, why not say so to your father or Fabian Brakov?'

Anton had no answer to this.

'What did John Seigenberg say?'

'That Dmitry was at fault.'

'Then probably he was. Maybe what happened to him that night had nothing to do with Sabroski Oil. Sounds like he got himself mixed up in bad company if he arrived home covered in blood. A debt would explain why he falsified the accounts.'

'The landlady was convinced of his innocence.'

Rafiq shrugged. '*Allah Barif*, only God knows. He was probably very charming and spun her a tale. What would she know anyway?'

A manservant in a blue turban brought a silver tray with a long-spouted teapot and fresh tea glasses. He bowed and left. Rafiq poured, releasing a swirl of cardamom into the air. Anton looked out of the window over the rooftops. A tangle of alleyways led down to the sea. He could see the silversmith's workshop, and in the distance the foundations of the new Alexander Nevsky Cathedral.

A framed photograph of a young woman in one of the wall niches caught Anton's eye. He looked away quickly, but Rafiq's eyes had also strayed to the picture.

'My wife. Leyla… I wish you could have met her.'

'She was very beautiful.'

Rafiq's face darkened. 'It's been two years since my Leyla died. Time enough for a man to get over such things, so my father tells me. But my father believes women have no souls. Many Mohammedans believe women turn to dust when they die and have no worth.'

'Do you believe that?'

'I don't know what I believe any more.'

Anton studied Rafiq's face and remembered how he'd looked at Julia. But then how often had he appreciated a woman's beauty even though he had wanted somebody else?

CHAPTER SIXTEEN

JULIA SEIGENBERG DUCKED INSIDE A DOORWAY AND RAISED the hood of her cape as she peered into the market square of the Icheri Sheher. The newly appointed house guard stood hands on hips alongside her maid. After a few minutes they said something to each other before heading in the opposite direction. Julia watched, her heart fluttering like a frightened bird. *This is madness!*

It was early morning, but the Icheri Sheher was wide awake. Julia had never seen so many people in one place. At one point somebody had grabbed her shoulder and shoved her aside to allow a mangy camel through the jostling crowd. Its matted fur brushed against her leaving a greasy mark on her sleeve. But it didn't matter. Her spirits were soaring. At last she was alone and unaccompanied inside the ancient walled city.

Nobody took much notice of her, with the exception of a man who leered, making her pull her cape more tightly around her. Several women standing at the bread stall stopped chattering as she passed. One woman's face was covered in transparent muslin. Julia felt their eyes upon her, but their gaze was more curious than hostile. She had covered her hair and her orange taffeta dress to conceal her foreignness, but it was obvious she was no woman from the old city. She imagined her paleness seeping through, singling her out as an impostor, one of the privileged from the outside.

The path opened onto a wide square. Merchants sat huddled in the archway shops, gathered around small braziers. Some smoked shisha pipes while others sat legs splayed around low tables, concentrating on their chequerboards. The click and snap of the board pieces cut through the air.

Julia hurried on. The creature inside her chest started fluttering again and the palms of her hands felt clammy. She was almost there.

It was insane to come here, of course, but her feelings for him amounted to insanity. She was filled with thoughts of him, consumed with his image, rerunning scenes when she last saw him. He had called on her father several times since the day they first met. He'd told her more about the family caviar house and the mysterious sturgeon fish that lived in the Caspian.

The alleyway between the caravanserai inns was dim and a funnel of wind. Two gatemen in thick fur caps paced. She rounded the corner. A shiny blue sign swung from a high wooden plinth bearing the words *Hasanov House of Caviar*. She hesitated. She could always turn back now and forget this foolishness. She could go home and tell her stepmother she'd got lost.

The sign creaked in the wind and a lone gull cried overhead. It circled and landed on the plinth, its webbed yellow feet protruding over the edge. She could hear someone approaching, footsteps padding along the path behind her: a step, a sharp click, then another step, a scrape. But it was just an old man, head covered and cloaked, his cane tapping the way forward. She looked up at the shop sign and shivered.

Suddenly, a hand gripped her shoulder, forcing her round. The old man's face was upon her, except it wasn't an old man at all, it was a young thin face with long sideburns. The eyes were black like raisins, the teeth chipped and yellow.

'Miss Seigenberg, I believe?' He touched her face, and she shrank back.

'You're a pretty thing.' He came closer. 'Tell your father that we're waiting.'

'Please let go of me,' she managed to say. *Oh, dear God. Save me.*

He shoved her against the wall and held the top of his cane under her chin, pressing the bone handle into her windpipe. 'Tell your father that *he* doesn't like to be kept waiting. Do you understand?'

She nodded. Her throat was so dry she couldn't swallow, let alone speak. She could hear her stepmother screaming in her face. *You stupid, stupid girl. What did you expect?*

'Good.' He pulled the cane away and let his fingers drift down her cloak. She started to shake as his hand felt her breasts. That same moment the shop bell jangled and the door opened. Immediately he darted away.

'Miss Seigenberg! What are you doing here?' Rafiq bounded down the steps and into the street, his long black hair loose under a blue-and-brown-striped turban.

She couldn't move. She couldn't speak.

Rafiq looked aghast. 'Who was that man? Was he bothering you?' He shot a look down the empty alleyway.

'I… yes.'

'*Ya Ilahi!*' Rafiq exclaimed. 'Come inside. Where's your maid?' He took Julia's arm and guided her into a dark shop. He shouted orders for tea to be brought and said something to an assistant behind the counter as he brought Julia to a chair.

Julia breathed slowly. 'My maid. We were separated. It was so crowded.'

'You must *never* come here on your own. The Icheri Sheher is no place for an unaccompanied woman.'

'I came to buy caviar… for my father. As a surprise. You said… you said you'd show me.'

'I didn't mean for you to come on your own.' A saffron sash hung around his neck and his multicoloured waistcoat was unbuttoned at the chest, revealing a V-shaped patch of honey-brown skin.

'I'm sorry. It was a mistake. I realise that now.'

Rafiq sighed. 'I didn't mean to sound sharp. Your maid should keep a closer eye on you. Come, I'll take you home.'

'I'd like some tea, first.'

'As you wish.' He shouted to his assistant. A moment later a tray of perfumed tea arrived. Rafiq poured her a glass.

Julia drank and composed herself. 'I'm feeling better, thank you. I do not wish to return home yet. I'd like to see the famous sturgeon you told me about.' Rafiq started to object but she cut him off. 'I'm not a child, Mr Hasanov.'

His expression softened. 'As you wish.'

Julia followed him to the back of the shop, which opened onto a courtyard with an enormous tank containing the biggest fish she'd ever seen. The creature was grey with a wave of sharp crests running along its spine and sides. Its sloping snout ended with fleshy lips that appeared to be located under what she assumed was its chin. Its head seemed out of proportion to the rest of its body and four fat whiskers dangled down. It looked ancient and terrible.

Julia sometimes bathed in the Caspian and had never considered a fish this large might be swimming there too. She glanced at a row of deep baths in the distance. A man leaned over and hauled out a struggling fish. He laid it down on a bench, slit open its belly and pulled out a huge sac of eggs.

Julia gasped. 'Oh! That's so cruel.'

'It's not a pleasant sight, but you cannot make caviar from dead sturgeon.'

'Now I've seen that, I'll never eat it.'

'You eat meat, don't you? I assure you that chickens and lambs don't enjoy being killed for your dinner table.'

Julia let herself be guided into another area of the warehouse where a man in a turban rinsed the eggs and added a layer of salt.

'Do you eat it?' she said.

'I do, but strict Muslims will not as the sturgeon is deemed an unclean fish.' He smiled at her expression. 'Now you must taste some.'

He brought her to a room which looked like a place where clients were entertained. There was no fire burning in the grate and the shutters across the high windows were closed. Now she was alone with him, she wasn't sure what she wanted. But it was too late for that now. She felt too silly to make an excuse and leave.

Rafiq moved to a marble counter containing several jars packed in blocks of ice. He picked up two porcelain spoons. 'Never eat caviar with a metal spoon. It spoils the taste.'

Julia sat down. She felt as if she was on the edge of something and that there was no going back. Rafiq sat next to her clutching the jar of caviar. The proximity of him made her tingle. She could smell the type of cigarettes he smoked, the oils he used in his hair. Rafiq scooped out a mound of grey eggs. He put the spoon into his mouth and swallowed. 'Delicious. Now your turn.'

'Just a tiny amount. I might not like it.'

'Just try a little. If you don't like it, I'll eat the rest.'

Julia took the tip of the spoon in her mouth. At first the glistening beads repelled her, but after a moment a buttery, savoury flavour filled her mouth.

'Not as bad as you thought?' He stared at her seriously. 'Now you can tell me why you came here.'

'I told you – to buy caviar.' She avoided his eyes.

'No. You could have sent your housekeeper to do that.'

She looked at him, his face inches away from hers. She touched the scar on his cheek.

Rafiq frowned. 'Julia, I'm no good for you.'

'Why do you say that?'

'Because the joy has gone from my life. I'm not capable of making anyone happy.'

Julia's heart was racing. 'That's not true. You've made me happy today.'

'Have I?' He hesitated. Then he cupped her face and kissed her. It was so fleeting that by the time she registered he was actually kissing her, it was over.

Immediately he stood up. 'Please forgive me. It was very wrong of me to do that. I apologise. You must leave.' He sighed. 'You are a beautiful woman, Julia. Far too good for me.'

She reached out and put her hand on his arm. 'Please don't say that.'

The taste and pressure of his lips had put a stamp on her that couldn't be erased. Like thick red sealing wax on an envelope – it couldn't be broken open without damage.

It was too late.

CHAPTER SEVENTEEN

THE FIRST WEEK OF DECEMBER HAD PASSED WHEN ANTON received a note from Frau Kalian containing the name and address of the accountant's sister. He ran the old woman's words through his head. She probably *had* been exaggerating, as Rafiq suggested. Yet there was a motherly, comfortable safeness and Dmitry might have felt relaxed enough to speak his mind. Anton was intrigued by the mention of a particular oilfield and wondered if Klara might know about it. He showed her the message.

'The gendarmes visited Dmitry's sister,' she said. 'But he wasn't there. There was a police report.'

Anton decided he would send a letter to the sister in secret. It could do no harm, and it could reveal a different outcome.

'The very last oilfield my father bought caused a dispute,' he said. 'Do you know why?'

'That would be the Group Twenty field. Nobody wanted it. They said it wasn't profitable enough.'

'Zenovitch Liquid Fuel own it now, don't they?'

'Yes. They bought up the resources that didn't sell.'

'I visited that field a few weeks ago. The welcome wasn't as warm as I had hoped.'

'Well, you shouldn't go trespassing.'

Anton regarded Klara. 'Word gets around quickly, doesn't it?'

'If you want information you should speak to Rasoul Kazimov,' she said. 'He was Nikolai's chief drilling engineer. He's also my friend. He knows everything about oil. Let's see if I can arrange it.'

They took the gig to Bibi-Eibat. Klara had dressed for the oilfields in a thick canvas skirt, stout boots and a jacket with her hair tucked under a blue headscarf. As they reached the oilfield, she ran over to the gates and shouted through the bars. A man appeared and unlocked them. It was the man with the red scar down his face. 'Back again. With a protector this time,' he mocked.

Anton felt his fingers close over his revolver. Perhaps trusting Klara had not been wise. The field was deserted. Then movement caught his eye, as men emerged from behind oil derricks. Somebody appeared from what looked like an old boiler house. He stiffened, his limbs taut and ready.

They reached a hut that looked like a makeshift office. A well-built older man with thick arms and straight brown hair stepped out. He wore a leather cap, a stained shirt and shabby trousers.

'Who is this?' said Anton.

'Anton Nikolayevich meet Rasoul Kazimov,' said Klara.

Both men exchanged surly greetings. From the look of him Rasoul was a man who'd seen action.

'Rasoul, what's your view on these fields?' Klara asked.

'There's plenty of oil here.'

Anton frowned. 'That's not what the bank told me.'

'What do bankers know?'

'You were one of the men who advised my father to buy it?'

'That's true.'

'It's part of the reason my father went bankrupt,' Anton said testily. 'Why would he listen to someone like you?'

Klara cut in. 'Rasoul's been drilling oilfields for fifteen years. Nikolai trusted him.'

'Didn't do my father any good though, did it?'

Rasoul swore. 'I told you, Klara, it was a waste of time bringing fancy boy here. Look at him. He knows nothing about oil.'

Anton braced himself. 'I'll wager you gave my father false information for your own gain and profited handsomely at his expense.'

Rasoul threw down his cigarette and charged towards Anton, head down like a bull. Anton readied himself, but before they came to blows there was a shriek. 'Stop it, the pair of you!' Klara threw herself at Rasoul and grabbed his arm. 'We will get nowhere if you fight.'

'I've walked over every inch of this fucking field,' growled Rasoul. 'Inspected every well. Climbed down them all. I know their worth.' He jabbed a finger at Anton. '*You* don't.'

'Listen to him,' urged Klara.

Anton spread his hands. 'Then why were these fields deemed worthless?'

'Because somebody wanted you to believe that.'

'If that's the case, what do you expect me to do about it? I'm bankrupt. I don't own the fields any more. They belong to Zenovitch Liquid Fuel.'

'Buy them back and I'll prove there's oil here.'

'Are you deaf, man! I'm bankrupt. Besides, it's not just a case of buying the fields. It's the money needed to invest in them. Look at the damage that's been done. It would take a fortune to get the fields working again.'

'The men could work for less money,' Rasoul countered. 'A small wage is better than nothing. You could set up a worker's cooperative.'

Klara spoke in a rush. 'It's an agreement between the owner and the workers. A share in the profits…'

'I know what cooperatives are, but it doesn't make any difference – you still need money, and I don't have any.'

Anton strode away, skirting around puddles of oil covered in dust which had formed a crepe-like skin across their surfaces.

'Where are you going?' shouted Klara.

'To look round.'

Klara ran after him speaking in a rush. 'It was my job to look after the workers. I oversaw the payroll for the fields. Welfare was part of their wages: seventy kopeks a day, rent paid and food for the family. I also persuaded Nikolai to get Doctor Levon to check their health each year.'

'And he agreed?'

'Not at first. Not until I came. None of the oil barons care, except maybe the Nobel brothers and Taghiyev.' She stumbled. Anton caught hold of her shoulder and steadied her.

'Leave me be. I want to think,' he muttered.

Anton continued on, stopping at the base of a wooden derrick. He tested the rungs of one of the ladders before climbing up and onto the platform. The drilling floor was a tangle of wheels, pumps, pulley systems and chains that stretched up to the top of the derrick tower and then down inside the well. In the early days a Tatar would climb down into the darkness to bail out the sediment from the bottom. Once Anton had climbed down while Rafiq kept guard. It was claustrophobic and smelled like a sewer.

He took out a cigarette and he gazed over the oilfield.

There was devilry here. A great deal of it. The situation stank. *Where do I begin to get to the bottom of this?*

He thought back to his meeting with the merchant, Marcus Samuel. They had met in Shanghai at the merchant's hotel on the Bund. Marcus Samuel was a stocky, agreeable-looking fellow with large bright eyes who spoke in broken Russian with an English accent.

'My interest lies in the Caucasus and in oil,' Marcus Samuel had said. 'Baku is becoming one of the most powerful producing regions in the world, almost equal to America. I don't think many men realise how much oil lies in this ancient city. My father visited your hometown thirty years ago when he was trading silks.'

The merchant cleared his throat. 'Your father and I have plans which he wishes you to be a part of.'

'So my father says. You have a document for me to deliver.'

'It must be guarded with the utmost secrecy. It is dangerous information and I want you to be aware of the risks in transporting it. Are you prepared for that?'

'It will be delivered safely.'

'Excellent. Welcome to my coup against John Rockefeller.'

'Rockefeller? The American oil baron? Are we going to war with him?' said Anton.

Marcus Samuel clasped his hands together. 'I'm a simple merchant, used to trading commodities such as rice, trinkets and shells. Oil is a new field of study for me and one which I find fascinating. For the past year I've made it my goal to learn everything I can about it. There are few places left in the world that have not been monopolised by Rockefeller's Standard Oil. The Orient is one of them. The most expensive cost is transportation from the refinery to the consumer. A new company can only compete by halving its transportation costs.'

'And how do you propose to do that?'

'By taking a short cut, Mr Sabroski. From Europe to the Orient through the Suez Canal.'

Anton blinked. 'The Egyptians will never allow that. One explosion and the canal will be out of commission for years.'

'Ah ha! But I have an advantage. I have the exact specifications to build a tanker that cannot explode. These are the documents you'll take to Baku.'

'Where did you get those from?'

'Egypt. From the Suez Canal Company.'

'That's very valuable information. How much baksheesh did you pay?'

'None at all,' Marcus cut in icily. 'That's not my style. I know bribery is common practice in the oil world, but I will have none of it.' He paused. 'I have contacts. Let's just say Lord Salisbury was invaluable.'

'The British Prime Minister?' Anton whistled. 'You do have useful friends... but who will build this tanker? Do you have an engineer in mind?'

'No, but your father has. It appears there are many skilled marine engineers in Baku.'

And when Anton had told him about Rafiq, Marcus had clapped his hands. 'This will be such a coup, Mr Sabroski! Rockefeller will not know what has hit him.'

'He certainly won't,' Anton said. 'But why do you need my father? Why not deal with the Rothschilds directly?'

'I need a man in Baku who understands the industry. The Rothschilds are bankers, not oil men. They do not understand oil like your father does. Money must be raised to build tankers. Sabroski Oil could be key investors.'

'Tankers? You need more than one?'

'Of course,' beamed the merchant. 'My new company will build a whole fleet.'

A steamer boomed in the distance, snapping Anton from his reverie. He gazed at the silent fields. If Rasoul was speaking the truth, then all around him, deep within the earth, lay thousands of barrels of oil, untouched and unspoiled.

And thousands of miles away, a Jewish merchant with a bold plan waited for news.

CHAPTER EIGHTEEN

KLARA KNEW IT WAS A RISK, ESPECIALLY AS IT HAD TAKEN A while to pick the lock, but Anton had spent all week on the oilfields, leaving the house in the morning and not returning until dusk.

According to Rasoul, Anton asked endless questions about each well and its history, recording the answers in a green, cloth-covered notebook. He shared nothing with her, and even when she demanded information, he grunted a few replies before shutting himself in the library. The secrecy angered Klara as she had been the one who had set up the meeting with Rasoul, alerted Anton to the untapped oil resources and made him aware of possibilities.

You have no idea how much your father valued me. If you did, you wouldn't treat me like this!

It was the same whenever she challenged him about his life in the Orient and why he'd stayed away for so long. She didn't believe any of that nonsense about having important work to do. It must mean he had something to hide.

Anton's bedroom looked over the city park and the walls of the Icheri Sheher. Minarets, domes and the Maiden Tower stuck up from beyond the walls, all arranged against a backwash of blue-grey sea. The room was smaller than Nikolai's, but twice, or even three times the size of her own. It was full of books, paintings, boxes and papers. A marble washstand stood against a wall with a porcelain bowl and jug, a folding razor with an ivory handle and a shaving brush. The bed was unmade with pillows and sheets strewn on the floor. An old armchair sat in the window with a gold cushion on the seat and a blanket thrown over the arm. His clothes hung in an open wardrobe fronted by a large mirror which needed resilvering.

Klara closed the bedroom door quietly and began.

She started with the boxes containing childhood items: jars of pebbles and shells, an old leather kaleidoscope and a broken red kite with the face of an eagle. She flipped through his books and journals: engineering and mining works, novels and art books.

She rubbed her eyes. *What am I trying to prove?*

She pulled a wooden box towards her and turned the key in the lock. Inside lay a silver medal pinned onto a red and white ribbon. A portrait of Tsar Alexander III was engraved on one side, the other had letters arranged in a circle saying *For Zeal*. At the bottom of the box lay a piece of paper: an imperial document of military service. She sat back on her heels. So that was how Anton had got his scars: he'd been at Panjdeh in the Afghan territory. He'd taken a bayonet in the shoulder and sword slashes across his back.

She spent the next hour reading and examining the contents of various cupboards and drawers, but the only other item of interest was a photograph taken eight years ago showing Anton standing with final year engineering students in front of a St Petersburg University building. She studied it. Anton's face was unlined and he wasn't as lean as he was now. He was surrounded by six other students. The signatures on the back were mostly illegible, except for one clear signature: Yuri Bulganin.

The room fell into shadows as the afternoon light faded,

casting a veil of gold over the city park. In the window beside the armchair, Klara noticed a leather travelling case, clipped with a bone handle. She opened it and felt inside. It seemed empty at first. Then she felt a long smooth object: a black lacquered box with a crack across the lid. She gazed at its decoration, her eyes snaking along a dragon's fiery tail. Then she unhooked the silver clasps and flipped it open. Inside lay a porcelain pipe decorated with Chinese motifs. Fifteen inches long, it had a jade mouthpiece and a ceramic pipe bowl. She ran her fingers over the smooth surface. *Beautiful.* Beside it lay a ball of cloth protecting a brown, cake-like substance. She rolled the stuff between her fingers: it was rough and warm and familiar. She had suspected this; it explained so much, but it was very bad news.

Suddenly the door flung open. Anton Nikolayevich stood in the doorway, his face like thunder with a revolver in his hand.

*

Anton could hardly breathe, he was boiling hot. Klara had jumped up clutching something to her chest. Panic froze on her face, and she stood like a petrified silhouette in the window. Anton forced himself to take a long slow breath. 'Pack your things and get out of this house.'

'It's not what you think—'

'I don't want to hear any of your excuses. You're untrustworthy and deceitful. God knows why my father made me keep you.'

'I was only trying to—'

'Spy on me?' Anton lowered the gun. 'That's what you've been doing ever since I arrived home. You fooled my father, but you won't fool me.'

'I don't want to go.'

Anton strode forward and took hold of her shoulder.

She twisted and kicked. 'Get your hands off me.'

'With pleasure, once you're out of my room and out of my house.' He marched her across the room and shoved her onto the landing. She stumbled back, breathing heavily, before turning and running down the corridor.

Anton went back into the bedroom and shut the door. He bent down and returned his books to the shelf, closed the lid on the box containing his army medal and retrieved the photograph on his bed. He gazed at it with a surge of emotion. Then he picked up the opium kit which Klara had dropped onto the floor. Fortunately, nothing was broken. Carefully he put the pipe back inside, snapped the silver clasps shut and put it back in his travelling case. Then he sank down into the armchair in the window and drew the blanket around his shoulders.

The December wind blew hard and rattled the shutters. Later he would call the housekeeper to make up the fire, but for the moment he wanted to think.

He would call John Seigenberg in the morning and explain what had happened. He would file a police report if necessary, anything to get rid of her. As for the will, he'd worry about that later. Whatever codicil his father had been tricked into writing, he'd have it overturned.

He laid his head back and closed his eyes. *What a fucking mess.* He was no nearer to making sense of things than the day he arrived. He'd spent the best part of a week on the oilfield listening to opinions. He'd visited the offices of Zenovitch Liquid Fuel to make enquiries but was regarded with suspicion: the son of the bankrupt owner, as if he were trying to accuse them of malpractice.

And now he had Klara to deal with. He groaned. He was sorry it had happened, having seen a softer side to her on the oilfield regarding her touching enthusiasm for worker's welfare. Her naivety had reminded him of how he'd been in those heady days in St Petersburg. *What were you looking for, Klara?* Finding her in his room and seeing the photograph brought memories flooding back.

He'd joined the Faculty of Physics and Mathematics at the Imperial University to study engineering. His fellow students had been an eclectic set from many different backgrounds: Alexander Isayev with his premature greying hair, Serge Avdonin who couldn't see anything without his thick black spectacles, inseparable Peter Bodrov and Ivan Vornovo who had joined some political organisation. Michael Goncharov, the real brains of the group. And Yuri Bulganin, the softly spoken one with the pretty girlfriend.

A prickle of fear coursed through him. What would have happened that night if he hadn't returned to his rooms unexpectedly?

A splatter of rain hit the window and he shivered again. It was no good dwelling on the past when it was the present that needed his attention. He threw off the blanket and went downstairs to the library where he knew a fire would be burning. The housekeeper stood in the middle of the hallway. The look on her face told him she'd heard everything.

'This came for you sir,' she said, handing him an envelope. She seemed to want to say something else, but he turned and went into the library. He closed the door, poured himself a drink and pulled a chair close to the fire.

The envelope bore his name but had no address. He pulled out the contents and unfolded what appeared to be a newspaper cutting from the Baku *Vedomosti* newspaper and then another sheet of plain paper. He stared at the coloured illustration. It was a picture of the first Fabergé egg: a golden hen and a white enamel shell lined with gold. Underneath the caption read:

The Hen Egg presented by Alexander III to Tsarina Maria Fyodorovna 1885.

Anton stared. It must have come from Melek the silversmith – he had found more information. But how odd that he'd sent him a note rather than asking to see him. He read the other sheet of paper, a single sentence:

Compare surveyor reports for the Bibi-Eibat Group Twenty fields.

It was signed with the initials K L.

His mind blanked as he stared at the letters: K L – who was that? Anton groped through the fog of his brain for names: *Konstantin, Konrad, Katya, Kyril, Klara, Katarina, Katharine.* Then he realised. The only person he knew with those initials who was connected with the Fabergé egg was the mistress of Grand Duke Konstantin.

Katharine Lapinski.

Immediately he dropped the paper and tore out into the hallway shouting for the housekeeper.

When she appeared, her eyes were wide. 'Whatever is the matter, sir?'

'This letter. Who delivered it?'

'I don't know, sir. It was just there... on the mat.'

'When did it come?'

'I'm not sure, but it wasn't there an hour ago.'

Anton flung the door open and raced into the empty streets. He crossed the road, ran to the entrance of the city park. There was a man walking a dog and a courting couple sitting on the bench near the pond, but there was nobody else. Could Katharine Lapinski have delivered the note? Surely she wouldn't have delivered it herself – she'd have got an errand boy to do that – but if it *had* come from her, then she might be waiting for him. Whatever her reasons for secrecy, a woman like that wouldn't be skulking in the trees in a park. More likely she'd be sitting in a carriage nearby.

Anton hurried out of the park and looked up and down the

road as rain blew into his face. A lone hackney cab waited outside the gentleman's club. He ran along the road, splashing into puddles and wiping the dripping water from his face. He reached the carriage and called up to the driver. 'Excuse me, are you waiting for someone?'

The man looked down. 'Where you are going, sir?'

'Nowhere. I'm expecting someone. A lady.'

'Well, she ain't here, sir. More's the pity. Hey, what are you doing?'

Anton had wrenched open the cab doors, but there was nobody inside. 'Sorry,' he muttered and slammed the door shut.

The rain had become heavier, and thunder rumbled in the distance. The gas lights on the street flickered, casting oily shadows to light his way as he trudged back to the house.

The library was still warm when Anton returned and orange embers were glowing in the fireplace. He was wet through and freezing cold. The housekeeper bustled about with towels and glasses of hot tea.

'Whatever were you thinking, sir, going out without your hat or coat in this weather?'

'I don't know, Olga. But next time a letter like that arrives, let me know immediately. And see if you can spot who delivers it.'

'Of course, sir.' She hesitated. 'I thought you'd like to know that Klara's gone.'

Anton said nothing.

'She hasn't packed all her belongings. They're still in her room.'

'No doubt she'll be back for them.'

Olga looked troubled. 'I don't mean to speak out of turn, sir, but Klara's a good girl. I don't know what she was doing in your room, but I wouldn't think too badly of her.'

'I must be able to trust my household, Olga. And I can't trust her.'

As soon as Olga had raked up the fire and taken his empty tea glass, Anton picked up the newspaper cutting signed with Katharine Lapinski's initials.

He wondered why Katharine Lapinski would send him a message about the oilfields. It had to be a mistake. Why would a woman like that be involved in oil matters? She had been the mistress of the Grand Duke Konstantin Nikolayevich, a relation of the tsar, a member of the aristocracy, so what was she doing hiding in Baku sending secret messages? All he could think of was that she had become involved with his father and had given him the Fabergé egg. But why? To save the company? But then why hadn't his father sold the egg? And why, now that his father was dead and the company liquidated, did Katharine Lapinski wish to remain anonymous?

Anonymous.

The anonymous donation.

Was *she* paying it? Was KL his secret benefactor? It had to be somebody alive. Fifty roubles were paid into the account every month. Only last week, the bank confirmed that another donation had been deposited.

He threw more coal onto the fire and went to the stack of papers and ledgers on the bureau. Riffling through the bundles, he found a wedge of parchments and pulled them out. The rest of the papers crashed onto the floor. He pulled up a chair, unfolded each piece of thick paper and spread it across the low table.

The first one had the coat of arms of the Russian Empire stamped at the top with the title: *Imperial Russian High Court of Justice.* The words *bankruptcy, plaintiff, debtors, action* leapt from the tobacco-yellow surface. A glistening red seal of the double-headed eagle dominated the bottom of the page. Anton pushed it to one side. The message from KL said to find the surveyors' reports and in particular the reports for the Group Twenty fields.

He unrolled other bundles and thumbed his way through. It wasn't until he opened one of the drawers to the desk that he found what he was looking for. Klara had organised the invoices chronologically with date dividers held down by a metal clip.

The surveyors were called Kaplan and Kaplan. A man called Gregory Kaplan and his brother Vadim Kaplan had been employed by Sabroski Oil from the late seventies. But in late 1886, the surveyors changed to a different company called Humberts. The format of the later reports was different. Instead of the heavy hand they were typed, but the newer entries were far more cautious, even suggesting that previous recommendations had been too optimistic.

Anton stared into the fire. Is this what Katharine Lapinski meant? Had the surveyors been incompetent or even fraudulent?

And if so, which ones?

CHAPTER NINETEEN

THE OFFICES OF KAPLAN & KAPLAN SURVEYORS WERE ON the second floor of a European-style building off Parapet Square. Handsome arched windows were overlooked by a stone monogram bearing the letter K. Vadim Kaplan was a thin, tired-looking man with long whiskers and straggly grey hair. He wore a dark grey frock coat, and his black necktie displayed a hexagonal gold tie pin with an amethyst stone. He was studying the surveyor's reports Anton had spread on the table

'Your father and Gregory knew each other from the early days. Nikolai used to say that Gregory could smell oil... but that was a long time ago.' Kaplan produced a pair of spectacles. 'What is it you want from me?'

'Your opinion. Why do you think the predictions changed so much? I thought your brother was very accurate, yet the later surveyor reports dispute that.'

Kaplan looked hard at Anton. His wrinkled grey eyes had flecks like marble. 'Gregory was more accurate than most. You make judgements by looking at the lie of the land and using your gut instinct. No man ever lost money drilling where Gregory advised.'

'Why did Sabroski Oil change to Humberts?'

Kaplan stiffened. 'Gregory had been ill. I took over some of his work, but it was difficult to keep all our clients. I'm not as skilled a surveyor. I took on the paperwork while Gregory went out in the field.'

Anton watched the man closely. 'The Group Twenty fields never sold. It is strange seeing as your brother recommended them. The later reports from Humberts said the fields were exhausted, yet the previous drill manager says this isn't true.'

'You can't listen to men like that. They want work at any cost.' Kaplan considered. 'Even so, I'd be surprised if those fields were completely exhausted. I remember your father purchasing land recently.'

'He did. I found a bill of sale for 1886.'

'It might have been for sale around the time Humberts took over. They might have done the survey instead.'

'But I thought you said your brother looked at the field?'

'If we did, we'll have a copy.'

The surveyor went across to a roll-topped desk and pushed up the lid. Numerous papers and files fell out. Kaplan gathered them up and placed them on the table, opening and closing at least a dozen before hesitating with one in his hand. 'Eighty-six, you say?' He stood turning the pages before shaking his head. 'Nothing here. I must have been mistaken.' He placed the folder back inside the desk, picked up the others and crammed them back inside. 'I'm sorry. My memory is not as good as it used to be. I must have been thinking of a different field.'

Anton left Kaplan & Kaplan and went to the waterfront to see Humberts: *Surveyors from Philadelphia*, as the bright sign displayed. John Humbert and his son were out of town, but an obliging secretary found an old report that she thought nobody would miss.

'Plot thirty-three, Group Twenty fields on Bibi-Eibat, purchased in 1886,' Anton had said in his most charming voice. She had patted her chignon, fiddled with her hair grips and said she would see what she could do.

The secretary seemed puzzled as she read the report back to him. 'The land had potential but was high risk. The samples had air bubbles, similar to lava rock, and showed little evidence of carbonated rock.' She looked up to explain. 'Air bubbles are a very bad sign.'

Anton took the report and slipped it into his pocket. Yet again he had come up against a dead end.

CHAPTER TWENTY

JULIA HADN'T BEEN ALLOWED OUT UNACCOMPANIED SINCE the day of the kissing. As predicted, her father had been angry – not that he knew anything about the kissing, but because she'd been out on her own. He became even angrier when she conveyed the strange message from the man who assaulted her. She had considered confiding in her friend Miranda Aleksandrovna before telling her father, but then thought better of it. Telling Miranda would mean explaining why she went to the Icheri Sheher in the first place, and that would never do.

Her father made her repeat every word of the message over and over until she wanted to scream. He had run his hands through his hair, removed his spectacles and put them back on again at least three times, but it was his despondent expression that worried her most. His face sagged and his eyes took on the haunted look as when her mother died. Julia trembled and felt for her locket. No doubt it was something to do with that horrid American with the monocle who visited the house.

She wondered how she would ever escape the guard and her housemaid and her father again? And her stepmother who prowled the house like a gaoler?

But escape she must.

In the end it was easier than she expected. On the appointed afternoon, while the rest of the house were resting, Julia climbed out of the parlour window. She wore a black cloak, a black scarf and a veil – mindful of keeping herself dark and invisible, even though she felt she was dressed for a funeral. By the time she reached the Icheri Sheher, she was able to slip through the archway like a local.

Rafiq was standing near the entrance, his hair loose under a blue-and-white turban. He appraised her disguise with a grin. 'Where would you like to go?' he said, a cigarette dangling from his lips.

'I don't mind. Anywhere.' It didn't matter as long as she was with him.

'We'll go to the tower. You'll like the view.'

He guided her across the main square and through the crooked streets. Each stone house had a courtyard containing a mulberry tree and a water well. Their gnarled balcony vines reminded her of withered arms clutching at the stonework. They threaded their way through alleyways where the Dagestani armourers and gunsmiths dwelt. She was assailed by blasts of hot air from the forges, a rhythmic clanging and an acrid cordite smell. A troop of merchants from the Bazarlar cloth trade hurried past carrying rolls of muslin and silk on their shoulders. Rafiq pulled her to one side, holding out the other arm to shield her from the swinging loads. He quickened his pace as if possessed by a sense of urgency.

'I'd appreciate it if you'd slow down,' Julia called after him. 'I feel like some package you're trying to deliver.'

'My apologies. I want you away from these crowds.'

She made to speak but was silenced when the call to prayer began. She watched a man in a long white robe roll out a small prayer rug and kneel down. 'Do you pray like this?' she said.

'Not any more.'

They wound through narrow streets, passing a mosque and a parade of carpet shops and a domed bathhouse with steam rising through its roof vents. They stopped at the base of a tall, dark tower.

'Here we are,' said Rafiq. 'Baku's enigmatic landmark – the Maiden Tower.'

She looked up at the tower with fresh eyes; she'd never taken much notice of it before. The tower had a strange shape with one tall cylindrical section and an elongated buttress that protruded from the eastern side making it look like a distorted figure six. Everyone knew the Maiden Tower – you could see it for miles, whether you were on land or sea. It had always just been there, part of Baku, standing forlornly on an outcrop of rock at the water's edge. Julia could hear the surf on the rocks and the slap of water against the piers. A flock of swallows swooped above.

She asked. 'Are we going inside?' It looked eerie and forbidding. 'Are we allowed to?'

'Yes, the military only use the tower as a beacon. The soldiers know me. We can climb to the top and enjoy the view.'

She followed him up the steps. Rafiq knocked on the door. Immediately a small, barred window flew open. The face behind the bars spread into a smile and the door creaked open.

Julia stepped inside. The tower was windowless and smelled of mould. Water trickled somewhere deep beneath, reminding her of a crypt.

'Come,' Rafiq said, taking her hand.

Through the gloom she saw an iron railing that ran around the perimeter. Far above, faint flecks of light bounced off the glistening walls. The twisting stairs were uneven and narrow. Every level was punctuated by deep niches slit into the south wall causing the sunlight to flicker and bounce like a shadow puppet show. Rafiq sped ahead like a mountain goat. Julia had to pause for breath and lean against the wall.

'Stay there. I'm coming back down,' he called out. His

footsteps echoed on the steps and a few moments later he reappeared and caught hold of her hand. 'Come. The view is magnificent.'

He pulled her up the winding stairs, laughing until they reached a wide flat roof. The wind ruffled her hair and her ears burned with cold. She saw a conical stone structure that supported a round glass and metal case and a cluster of electric lights facing out to sea.

'It's a beacon for the ships,' Rafiq shouted, as he peered inside. 'My father said they used to fly a flag in the old days. But the new electric lights are much better.'

'Why was the tower built?'

'Nobody really knows. Some say it was a Zoroastrian temple.'

'The ancient fire worshippers?'

'Yes. They laid their dead on the rooftop for vultures to strip the flesh from the bones.'

Julia peered over the perimeter wall. Winding lanes of the old city scored the landscape. In the distance, she could see the ruins of the old Shirvanshah's Palace. Further up the hill, high above the city walls, sprawled the foundations of the new Alexander Nevsky Cathedral.

Rafiq suddenly appeared at her shoulder. 'I knew you'd like it up here. There's another story they tell about the tower. One of the city's rulers fell in love with his own daughter. To stall his advances, the daughter demanded he build a tower from which she could see the whole of his lands.'

A thrill started in the pit of Julia's stomach and rose up through her chest.

'Each time the stonemasons announced the tower was finished, his daughter demanded another storey be added, for she did not want to give in to his demands.'

The light dimmed as dark clouds rolled across the sky. Her scarf fell back.

'When the tower reached its full height, the daughter knew she could prevent his advances no longer.'

Rafiq trailed the back of his fingers down Julia's face.

'Did she give in to him?'

'No. She climbed to the top and threw herself into the sea.'

Rafiq was so close now that she could feel the warmth of his breath as he spoke. There were dark shadows beneath his eyes that she'd never noticed before and the scar on his cheek looked like a white chasm. He took her hand, locked his fingers between hers and put his arm around her waist. She laid her head against his shoulder and breathed him in.

He kissed her.

She stroked his hair and the back of his neck. He tasted of salt and something exotic. She felt her body connect as heat sparked through her.

She was lost in him.

*

Miranda Aleksandrovna watched Julia duck through the Shamakhi gates of the Icheri Sheher. So, her suspicions were true.

Julia, dearest, what are you doing?

She called to the driver and the brougham carriage jerked forward. Julia was walking quickly, darting in and out of the peddlers heading into the old city. Miranda had known Julia for five years, long before she'd married Stefan. They had always confided in each other until recently, and now she knew the reason why.

She watched Julia walk past the Hotel Continental and into Parapet Square. Miranda knew she must do something quickly or the moment would be lost.

Miranda never liked acting without thought, but ironically it was one of the reasons she liked Julia, because that's exactly what she did. Julia acted impulsively and impetuously like the present day was all that mattered. Miranda would consider Julia's ideas and explain why she thought it was good or not, and Julia would laugh and kiss her, and say what good advice she gave.

But this was something new.

Miranda knew that Julia always imagined herself in love with dangerous men, heroes from her novels, dashing melancholy souls that needed the right woman to come along. It made Miranda smile as Julia read aloud chapters from *The Midnight Bell*, her eyes bright, her voice breathless. It was all make-believe and safe. But this was the first time Julia had actually met someone like that.

She opened the window of the brougham as Julia passed by. 'Julia!'

Julia stopped. A wary smile formed on her face. 'Hello, Miranda. Out for a drive?'

'Yes. Come and join me.'

'I was on my way home.'

'I'll drive you. Come on, get in. It's cold.'

Julia hesitated as Miranda opened the door. Then she gathered up the hem of her cloak and climbed inside. The brougham pulled away.

Miranda watched Julia unwind her scarf and spend a long time unbuttoning her cloak.

'I thought I saw you coming out of the Icheri Sheher a moment ago,' Miranda said softly. 'I don't think black suits you.'

Julia fiddled with her charm bracelet. 'I've been there a few times. Father likes the caviar...'

'I've heard it can be quite dangerous. I wouldn't like to go unchaperoned. Did you take Sveta with you?'

'Usually I do.'

'But not today?'

They fell silent. Miranda took Julia's hand. 'Do you remember how we used to write to each other after I met Stefan? Before we were married?'

Julia nodded.

'I knew nobody in Baku, had no idea what to expect of a place with such a fierce reputation. My friends told me that it was an uncouth backwater, a place where men abducted woman and forced them into marriage. Abductions were commonplace in those days and reported in the newspapers. The Mohammedans had a frightful reputation with their harems of concubines, bitter blood feuds and fights with curved daggers.'

Julia smiled. 'Some of it is true. But not as common as people make out.'

'My mother is Georgian so she knows the truth about the Caucasus, else she would never have agreed to the marriage.'

'Your father had been here on business, so he knew it wasn't true.'

'I know. But it was still a comfort to receive your letters in Moscow. Baku seemed such a long way away.'

'And now. What do you think?'

Miranda leaned back in her seat. 'I think what my friends said is true. Baku is wild and uncouth and dangerous, but that's what makes it fascinating.'

Julia laughed.

Miranda frowned. 'But that is also why we women have to be careful.'

The smile left Julia's face.

'I wish you would tell me, Julia.'

'Tell you what?'

'There's been gossip.'

'It's unlike you to care about gossip.'

'I'm worried because I think it's true.'

Julia held up her chin. 'There is nothing for you to be worried about.'

'If that's the case, tell me about him.'

'I don't know what you are talking about.'

'Rafiq Hasanov.' *Don't lie to me, Julia.*

Julia flushed. 'There's nothing to tell.'

'You've been meeting him.'

'He's just a friend. That's all.'

'Women like you and I don't have friends like that. Not men friends that we meet unchaperoned in the old city.'

Julia's green eyes flashed. 'You're not going to talk about class again, are you? It's the sort of thing my stepmother would say.'

'Why do you like him so much?'

Julia stared out of the carriage window as it slowed down to negotiate two camels sitting in the road. A moustachioed lime-seller rapped on the window brandishing a handful of small green fruit. His shaggy eyebrows and thick black fez seemed to merge into a single mass of woolliness.

Miranda waved him away. 'Is it because he reminds you of one of your Gothic heroes.'

Julia looked away as the carriage started up again, jerking in and out of a pothole.

'Don't be silly. Of course not.' Julia felt for the locket at her breast. 'I can't help it, Miranda. I can't stop thinking about him.'

'Well, he is very good-looking in that dark Persian way.'

'I think he's beautiful. And so sad. His wife died and he lost his only child.'

'So I've heard… What do you want from him?'

'I don't know. I just want to be with him. For a while anyway. Until this passes.'

Miranda sighed. 'He'll make you unhappy, Julia. Men like that always do.' *And I know this so well.*

'Please don't disapprove, Miranda. I need you to like him.'

'I don't know that I can. He used to bully Stefan. He and Anton.'

'That was years ago. They were children. He's not like that now.'

'I don't think people really change.'

'Stefan probably deserved some of the treatment he got.

144

Children can be cruel and thoughtless. You've said yourself how tiresome Stefan can be when he gets into one of his pompous moods.'

Miranda frowned. 'But it's not only that. Rafiq is different. Different from Anton. Different from Stefan.'

'You mean because he's a Muslim? A Mohammedan?'

'Yes. That makes a big difference.'

'Why? Mixed marriages don't matter here. Your father's Russian and yet he married a Georgian woman. My father is Jewish, and he married an orthodox Russian, and Rafiq's wife was European. I heard she came from Germany.'

'It's more about attitude. Mohammedans see women differently.'

'Surely you don't think he's going to abduct me?'

'Mohammedan women don't have the same rights. Look at the women who come here from Tehran. Sheathed in black with their faces covered, walking several paces behind their husbands. They would never be allowed to wander about unchaperoned and have a male friend. From what I've heard women can't even be in the same room with a man unless he's a blood relative or her husband. They have to be *obedient*. That's a word I don't think you recognise, Julia. I can't see you putting up with that.'

Miranda paused as two men on donkeys raced by, splattering mud against the window.

'Rafiq's not like that,' insisted Julia.

'How do you know? The Hasanovs are a very traditional family – a respected family in the old city stretching back generations.'

'Where have you got all this information from?'

Miranda paused. 'Stefan's mother, Olesia, told me. Stefan used to tell me about Rafiq as well. The old stories from the past. Rafiq is eccentric and not the same as us. You and he will never fully understand each other. He's too different.'

'So, it comes down to class and religion?'

'Don't try to deny it doesn't matter. Because it does.'

'Oh, Miranda. Whatever am I to do with you? I know you mean well, but this is something I must work out for myself.'

CHAPTER TWENTY-ONE

ANTON HOPED ANOTHER LETTER FROM KL WOULD ARRIVE, but the following days brought nothing. He showed Rafiq and called in on Melek, but the silversmith seemed as surprised as he was.

The following week, leading up to the New Year holiday, passed with much feasting and celebration. Anton spent much of his time with Rafiq, where they drank and ate and played countless games of nard. There had been no sign of Klara, though he suspected she came and went, as Olga, the housekeeper, became flustered if he arrived home unexpectedly. He hadn't said anything to John Seigenberg. Even though he decided Klara was untrustworthy, he had no desire to get her in trouble with the authorities, especially as she seemed to be living elsewhere. Besides, nothing had been stolen. He had checked thoroughly and concluded that she must just have been inquisitive.

On New Year's Day Anton had been invited to the Seigenberg house for a celebration dinner. Now the remains of a huge feast lay on the dining room table. Crumbs of a plum pudding lay strewn across the tablecloth and a heap of macaroons covered a silver tray.

Anton leaned back in his chair, stretched out his legs and studied the company. Julia's brother, Alfred, was already drunk. His black dinner jacket stretched across his back, his waistcoat buttons straining with the effort of not pinging themselves across the room. He lazed about the room stuffing macaroons into his mouth and refilling his glass of punch. Diane Seigenberg was busy directing the jug of Roman punch away from Alfred. Diane, John's new wife, was a pretty woman, but held herself with such stiffness that her beauty seemed frozen. Anton wondered if she was happy and what Julia thought of her stepmother. Their characters couldn't be more different.

Later that afternoon, Leo Rostov arrived. Immediately he looked around for Julia.

'Happy New Year, Leo. Have some punch,' said Julia, hurrying over to greet him.

'What's it got in it? Something strong I hope.'

'Rum, rum and more rum,' said Alfred. He held out his own to be topped up.

'Excellent.' Leo sighed. 'I've been on the fields since dawn.'

'What's happened?' exclaimed Julia.

'More problems with transportation. Our pipelines were damaged last night.'

John frowned. 'Same thing happened to Emanuel Nobel's pipelines a month ago.'

Leo nodded. 'The last few months have been awful. There have been fires, explosions, deliberate damage to drilling equipment and pipelines. One of the Taghiyev refineries was targeted two weeks ago, and someone is buying up all the components needed to make oil barrels. There's a real shortage. We've had to use old fish barrels. Taghiyev's making do with wine caskets.'

Alfred Seigenberg refilled his glass and stared out of the

window. 'Oh look, we have a visitor. Isn't that Rafiq Hasanov? I didn't know he was joining us.'

Anton noticed Julia become alert. She twirled a coil of hair between her fingers and smoothed down her pink silk dress. Leo was staring at her as well. Julia sipped her drink too quickly and began pulling at the locket around her neck.

For a long while the room lapsed into a soft hum. Snippets of conversation lapped at Anton and washed away. He sat in silence, watching everyone while enjoying the intoxication of a cigar until a chair scraped by his side and Leo sat beside him.

Leo lowered his voice. 'What do you know about this American who works for Fabian Brakov?'

'Albert Prankman? Odd chap. I met him at the club a few weeks ago. John says he was taken on to streamline Brakov Oil's operations. Why do you ask?'

'He's just bought all the tank cars from Apsheron Oil. They went bankrupt last month. Seems very fortuitous in light of recent events. Brakov Oil are now the third largest owner of tank cars after the Nobels and the Rothschilds.' Leo looked up as laughter echoed across the room.

'What else have you heard?' Anton threw the end of his cigar into the fire but noticed Leo was only half listening. His attention had strayed to the other side of the room where Julia had thrown back her head with laughter at something Rafiq had said. She looked flushed and beautiful in a profusion of silk and lace with white flowers woven through her hair. She kept flipping her fan open and then closing it, displaying a gauze of cats' heads nestling together. Rafiq looked eccentric in a black dinner jacket and a yellow neck scarf with a multicoloured waistcoat.

Suddenly the door to the drawing room flew open.

'I need to speak to Anton Nikolayevich.'

Anton groaned. Klara stood in the doorway, her hair wild and boots dirty. Her coat hung open to reveal her faded blue silk dress, its hem coated in mud.

Anton glared as she tramped over. 'What on earth are you doing here?'

'A message came to the house,' she bent down and whispered. 'It's about Frau Kalian.' Her hair was wet, and a sodden lock touched his forehead. She smelt of damp leaves and lemonade.

'Surely this can wait?'

'No,' she said. 'It has to be today.'

Anton glared. 'Why?'

'Because tomorrow she may be dead.'

Chapter Twenty-Two

It was raining as Anton followed Klara into a hackney carriage. Cold droplets sprayed in his face dispelling the dull-wittedness from his mind where too much food and drink had settled down for the night. Anton slammed the carriage door shut and shouted orders to the driver before turning to face her.

'What happened?'

'A message came from one of the neighbours. Frau Kalian's been hurt in an… accident. They've called for a doctor, but Frau Kalian keeps asking for you.'

Anton leaned back in his seat as a chill touched him.

When they reached the house on Chadrovaya Street, Anton saw a sodden carpet draped over the balcony, rainwater streaming from its tassels.

'Stay here. I'll tell the driver to wait,' said Anton, opening the carriage door. He jumped down and crossed the street. He heard the other door slam and Klara darted across the road.

'I thought I told you to stay inside.'

'Yes, but I don't want to.' She pulled down the brim of her hat, casting her face into shadow.

The street was empty and the house stood in darkness. The front door was ajar. Anton pushed it open and stepped into the hallway.

'Hello!'

Nobody answered.

They climbed the stairs. Cautiously, Anton opened the door to the living room. The room lay dark and silent. He switched on the gas lights and a sickly yellow fell across the space. Klara gasped. Drawers from a chiffonier lay upturned, their contents scattered. The cuckoo clock had been pulled from the wall and the canary cage lay broken on the floor, the bird gone. Cushions were torn, the curtains pulled from their runners. The armchair had been tipped over, the underneath webbing slashed. A clump of brown ringlets lay on the floor. He could hear Klara's rapid breathing and sensed she was about to step forward. He put out a warning arm. 'Frau Kalian?' he called again, pulling out his revolver. 'It's Anton Nikolayevich.'

There came a sound and a young girl appeared in a doorway on the opposite side of the room. She was wearing an orange dress with a lace collar. She couldn't have been more than ten years old.

'Where's Frau Kalian?' Anton said.

She pointed behind her.

'Are you here on your own?' said Klara, walking over, shards of glass and crockery crunching under her feet.

The girl nodded. 'Ma said I was to wait until the doctor came.'

Anton entered the small side room. Through the gloom he made out a figure lying on a divan covered with a blanket. Frau Kalian stirred. He hardly recognised the swollen face framed with grey wisps of hair. He pushed his revolver back inside his jacket and sat beside her. 'Frau Kalian.'

'Anton Nikolayevich. Is that you?'

'Yes. What happened?' Anton found a glass and filled it with water from a jug on the bedside table.

She spoke slowly. 'They came back.'

'Who did?' Anton held the glass to her lips. 'Try and drink.'

She coughed as the water dribbled down her chin. 'The first time, he wanted to know what I'd told you. Pretended he was a friend of Dmitry's.'

'I'm so sorry. This is my fault.'

'I should have given it to you straight away, but I wasn't sure. You seemed a nice gentleman, but you never know.'

'What should you have given me?'

'Then he came back with another man. Asking for it.'

'Asking for what?'

'I sent you a message, but you never came.'

'I didn't get a message, Frau Kalian.'

'He must have taken it,' she wheezed.

'Lie quietly. The doctor will be here soon. Drink some more water.' He held the glass to her lips, but she brushed it away.

'Dmitry left it behind. I hid it in case he came back. I knew it was important.'

Klara touched Anton's shoulder. 'How is she?'

Frau Kalian stared up at her.

'Find out what's happened to the doctor. And call the gendarmes.'

Frau Kalian clutched Anton's wrist. 'Dmitry gave me a key and told me to look after it.' He bent closer to listen. 'A secret.' She pointed to the drawing room and then closed her eyes.

'Where did you put it, Frau Kalian?'

She didn't answer. Anton drew another blanket over her. The room was bitterly cold and he shivered in his damp clothes. He pulled off his wet overcoat, pushed up his sleeves and set about lighting fires in both rooms, working a pair of bellows until the flames roared.

Klara appeared in the doorway and spread her arms. 'The

153

neighbour didn't call the gendarmes because she didn't want any trouble! I gave her a piece of my mind! I sent her husband to get them. He wasn't happy, but I told him the attacker might be back.'

'The men who attacked her were looking for a key.' Anton gazed at the devastation. 'But it looks like they didn't find it.'

'We should clear up first. We won't find anything amongst this mess.'

They set about sweeping up the crockery and glass. Klara collected piles of books, newspapers and journals and stacked them on top of the chiffonier. Anton gathered up the torn curtains and examined each one. Afterwards he pushed the drawers of the cupboard back into place while replacing and inspecting their contents.

Twenty minutes passed. Klara went downstairs to look for the doctor. Anton pulled an armchair upright, pushed the cushions back in place and sat to examine the contents of Frau Kalian's sewing box which had been emptied over the floor. His foot kicked against something hard. It was an empty bottle lying on its side: Pertsovka vodka, the old woman's favourite. Her refuge lay in that bottle along with memories, gossip and secrets. Anton hesitated.

Secrets.

Frau Kalian had mentioned something about secrets. Secrets and carpets. *Did you know Muslim women used to express love to their young men by weaving messages into carpets? Love knots, they called them.*

A charge went through him as he surveyed the room. There were four rugs lying on the floor and several others hanging on the wall. Anton knelt to examine them.

Klara reappeared. 'What are you doing?'

'The rugs. I think they might tell us something. Frau Kalian kept talking about secrets in rugs. I'll wager she's hidden the key inside one of them.'

'How can you hide a key inside a rug?'

'I don't know. It was something she said.'

'Let's check on her first.'

They went into the bedroom. Anton sat and took her hand. It was cold and marble-like, and dread touched him. What could Dmitry have done to provoke an attack on this defenceless old woman who gossiped too much and loved to show visitors her carpets? What had she known that was so important? He thought of Dmitry: his distinctive red hair and fair freckled skin. It seemed impossible that Frau Kalian lay dying, Sabroski Oil had been bankrupted and his father destroyed, all because of him.

Anton pulled the blanket around Frau Kalian's shoulders. 'Stay with her,' he told Klara. 'I'll carry on searching.' He returned to the living room.

Secrets and carpets – what can she have meant?

He examined the carpets in the room. The first rug was from the Dagestan region of the northern Caucasus. It was old and patched and covered in red and cream medallions. He ran his hands over it feeling round and underneath the patches, but there was nothing. The next two rugs were red kilims. He wondered if the key could be a message woven into one on their designs. Columns of motifs depicted the tree of life, but nothing looked like a message or a key. The next rug was a blue-and-white soumak, but he could see nothing remarkable about it.

Frustrated, Anton walked over to the window. No sign of the gendarmes or a doctor, not that he could see clearly. The rain fell relentlessly and the streets glistened. Out of the corner of his eye he saw something move. He cleared a patch of condensation with his sleeve and peered through the window. A large carpet flapped in the wind.

With a surge of energy, he wrenched open the balcony doors and dragged the sodden carpet inside. It had an orange-red background decorated with navy medallions and long cream tassels. He knelt down and ran his hands over the drenched surface. Then he heaved it over and did the same.

Nothing.

He stood up, lit a cigarette and circled it, crouching at intervals to examine it from different angles. Finally, he stood back and stared at the carpet as a whole. The design was regular and unremarkable, but the balance was wrong. Something didn't match. One of the tassels looked different – it wasn't as wet and straggly as the others. He felt it, turning it round in his fingers. Instead of being made of wool it consisted of several loops of string and the knot was fatter and elongated, as if someone had tried to repair it and had run out of thread. Anton grabbed the scissors from Frau Kalian's sewing basket, cut through the tassel, and slowly extracted a piece of paper.

He ripped it open and out dropped a silver key.

He snatched it up just as voices arose from the street. He heard Klara run down the stairs to open the front door. Anton slipped the key in his pocket and hurried into the bedroom. 'Frau Kalian, can you hear me? I found Dmitry's key,' he whispered urgently.

The old woman opened her eyes. 'Anton Nikolayevich. I'm so glad you found her.' She tried to lift her head. 'Where is she? The girl you brought with you?'

'Klara?'

'Yes, that was her name. I remember now. She's the one from the Devil's Bazaar.'

Anton eyes widened. 'Klara?'

Frau Kalian gave him a vacant look as a trickle of blood seeped from the side of her mouth.

It was fully dark by the time they returned home but Anton had no desire to turn on the light. He poured himself a drink. It had stopped raining and the sky had cleared. Pinpricks of lights dotted the sky, and he could make out Orion's Belt. He kept his back to Klara.

'It's time you told me the truth,' he said.

'If I tell you what I know, can I come back?'

'You're in no position to bargain.'

'But I can help you.' She spoke in a rush. 'That day in your room. I wasn't taking anything or spying on you, well not in the way you think. I wanted to find out more about you. You never tell me anything. You're so secretive and difficult.'

Anton swivelled. 'Me – secret and difficult?'

'Yes. I wish you were more like your father.'

'What's that supposed to mean?' Anton refilled his glass and eyed her carefully. 'Frau Kalian said you were with Dmitry the night he was attacked.'

Klara sat on the floor by the fire, her faded blue silk dress tucked around her legs, a style of dress Anton remembered women wearing ten years ago. 'I met your father four years ago in the Devil's Bazaar, when I first came to Baku.' She pulled at the lace on the end of her sleeves. 'Dmitry was in the bar one night, playing poker and losing. Getting drunk. He was never any good at drinking and worse at playing poker. He had the wrong kind of face. I could see he was in trouble… I felt sorry for him.'

'What happened?'

'I poured my drink over him. He thought it was an accident.'

'And?'

'He went to clean himself up. I followed him and told him the game was fixed. Those tables always are.'

'You seem to know a lot about this bar.'

Klara scowled. 'Sometimes in life you have to do things you wouldn't do if you had a choice, but it wasn't such a bad place. There were as many good and bad people there as you'd meet in any gentleman's club. In some ways it's more honest. In a bar like that nobody pretends to be something they're not.'

'I thought you said many of the games were fixed. I wouldn't call that very honest.'

She snorted. 'And you really think nobody cheats at the gentleman's club? Because men dress in dinner jackets and wear expensive cologne doesn't make them trustworthy.'

Anton thought of Prankman's Hoyt's cologne.

'It was the same night I met your father. Dmitry said your father owned Sabroski Oil. I needed work. I'd spent months listening to men in bars talk about the oil business. I reckoned I had a pretty good understanding of it. I'd also picked up some interesting rumours. I thought I could be of use to Nikolai, so Dmitry introduced me.'

'Was that the night you helped Dmitry home after he was attacked?'

She shook her head. 'That was another time. Later. Dmitry was upset about something that night. He kept asking questions about Nikolai's "Orient Project". I know he'd argued with Albert Prankman, and he wanted to know why Fabian had replaced the surveyors. He disapproved of the way Nikolai was keeping secrets about a new project from Fabian.'

'Sounds like he didn't trust anyone.'

'One night your father asked me to find Dmitry as he wanted to speak to him. I took the gig and rode to the Devil's Bazaar. It was late, must have been two in the morning, but the bar was full. There were Georgian musicians playing who'd come down from Tiflis. It was wild in there, more drunken and crowded than I'd seen for a long time. Fabian Brakov was playing cards with Albert Prankman. Dmitry was having an argument with a couple of men I'd not seen before.' She paused. 'I hoped the two men would go away so I could talk to Dmitry, but they dragged him outside. They started punching him. Pushed him to the ground and kicked him. One of the men had a knife...'

'Go on.'

'I jumped on the back of the man who was kicking Dmitry. I

bit his ear really hard – a piece of it came off in my mouth. It was disgusting – God, there was so much blood. The man started howling. When the other man tried to pull me off, I screamed and the doormen came out with their curved daggers. People gathered around. There was chaos.' She paused. 'That's when I got Dmitry away. I got him into the gig and drove.'

'What did those men want with Dmitry?'

'I don't know.'

'What did my father want to talk to him about?'

'He never said and I didn't ask.'

They looked hard at each other.

'You should have told me this before!' he said.

'I didn't trust you… I knew you didn't like me. Besides, you never asked.'

'Do you trust me now?'

She pulled a face. 'I don't have a choice.'

Anton studied her. 'Did Dmitry confide in you?'

'He used to.'

'Did he ever mention a silver key?'

'No.'

Anton pulled out the key. 'So you've never seen this before?'

CHAPTER TWENTY-THREE

THE DEATH OF FRAU KALIAN HAUNTED ANTON THAT WEEK. Statements were taken, witnesses interviewed, but it was clear the police had no idea who killed her. Anton kept silent about the silver key. Whatever Dmitry's reasons for hiding it, he doubted police involvement would help. The key was small and flat and could fit any number of locks, which he tested around the house. Once the fuss had died down, he would see if it unlocked anything in Dmitry's old rooms.

He had mixed feelings about Klara. She was around, mostly out of sight, but Anton felt her presence despite her efforts to keep out of his way. She was waiting – he suspected – for his hard feelings to soften.

The following week, he received a note from the Rothschild business manager suggesting a meeting for the coming Monday. He rolled up the note and tapped it against the palm of his hand.

The moment had come. The most important game of poker he would ever play.

On the morning of the meeting, Anton took the Fabergé egg from the safe and stowed it inside a protective leather pouch with a drawstring tie. Then he checked the document holder containing the first draft of Rafiq's tanker plans. Finally, he reloaded his pistol and placed spare bullets in his pocket. The journey between the house and the Rothschild residence was a short one, but that was no guarantee of safety.

The Rothschild house sat halfway down Sadovaya Street opposite the city park, overlooking the marbled terrace of the Baku Gentleman's Club. Anton's hands felt clammy, despite the freezing January air, and he realised he was sweating. He fidgeted in the saddle as he appraised the newly built mansion. It was a majestic house surrounded by towering pine trees and crowned with a blue-tiled dome. It radiated power and influence and authority.

When Anton rode into the driveway, a turbaned footman ran out to take his horse.

'So, you're the Sabroski heir?' A bulky man in a dark grey frock coat stood in the middle of a perfectly proportioned drawing room. De Boer had pale eyes that drooped at the corners and a mouth mostly hidden by a flourishing moustache. 'I never met your father, but people say you are much like him. The baron was saddened to hear of his death.'

The Rothschild business manager stared at Anton as if he were scrutinising a formal document.

Anton stood still and straight, trying to curb his desire to fumble for a cigarette.

De Boer pulled at his short beard and poured two whiskies into cut glass tumblers and handed one to Anton. 'I understand your father had a proposition for the baron? He represented a Mr Marcus Samuel?'

Anton nodded. 'Upon his death, I inherited the project.'

'Intriguing, considering you're supposed to be bankrupt.'

'Not quite bankrupt.'

De Boer's moustache twitched. 'And this man, Marcus Samuel, he's a Jewish merchant from the East End of London, I hear. Has a factory in Wapping making jewellery boxes?'

'Yes, that is correct.'

'From my understanding, this arrangement was made between your father and Marcus Samuel. The baron is only interested in a contract with a viable oil company. Marcus Samuel has no company.'

'Not yet, but he will.'

De Boer shrugged. 'The Rothschilds are not interested in stepping into your father's shoes. The baron has no intention of overseeing the building of a tanker or intervening in the political shenanigans that will undoubtedly follow with the Suez Canal authorities. We are bankers. Nothing more.'

'I understand. Which is why I need your support.'

De Boer's pale eyes narrowed. 'Sabroski Oil is finished – the contract with your father terminated.' He paused. 'However, as your father was a friend of the baron's, I agreed to meet with you – I'd heard much about Nikolai Sabroski and admit to feeling rather intrigued to meet the son who'd been in the Orient for so long. The baron was at a loss to understand how your father's company collapsed so suddenly.'

'Men say the accountant was to blame.'

'Surely the company had counterchecks in place to prevent such a thing happening?' De Boer raised his eyebrows. 'But I sense you do not accept this story?'

'No, I don't.'

'You have proof?'

'Not yet. But I'll find it.'

De Boer's smile showed crooked front teeth. 'Capital.' He refilled their glasses. 'What is it you want from the Rothschilds?'

Anton retrieved the document holder and pulled out the tanker blueprints. 'I'd be obliged if you'd take a look at these?'

Anton unrolled the plans and spread them out. 'The first drafts of designs for a new type of oil tanker. Designed by Rafiq Hasanov – his family are marine engineers. They follow the specifications given to Marcus Samuel by the Suez Canal authorities.' He swivelled the plans for De Boer to see. 'Lord Salisbury helped to obtain these.'

De Boer looked surprised for a moment. He produced a pair of spectacles from his top pocket. 'Help yourself to a cigar, Sabroski, and then come over and explain what these drawings mean.'

It took Anton an hour to explain the details. He watched De Boer's expression as he listened, nodded, frowned and scratched his chin. At one point De Boer paced the room, relit his cigar and bombarded Anton with questions.

Soon the light began to fade. Finally, De Boer ran a finger under his stiff white collar. 'Very interesting. Did the baron know of the British Prime Minister's involvement?'

'He must have. It was Marcus's plan all the time to obtain the specifications. Without such connections, I doubt he'd have been successful.'

De Boer looked thoughtful. 'The baron didn't mention this to me. This changes things. If successful, a chance to flood the Orient with Rothschild oil should not be missed.' He refilled the whisky glasses. 'I shall discuss this with him.'

'That's excellent news.'

De Boer cocked his head to one side. 'But what's in this for you?'

'What do you mean?'

'What drives you now that your father's company is dead?'

Anton shrugged. 'A promise made to my father, a commitment to Marcus Samuel. A chance for a friend to showcase his talent.'

'What else? I don't see a man like you standing in the wings.'

Anton held De Boer's gaze. 'There is something you can do for me. But it requires your backing… I want the Rothschilds to finance the reopening of the Group Twenty fields on Bibi-Eibat.'

De Boer's eyes crinkled. 'Why am I not surprised by this? You certainly have nerve. But you know that's impossible. As I said, the Rothschilds are bankers. We invest money, we don't throw it away.'

'You wouldn't. It's a good investment. Those fields have oil – a lot of oil. I've already investigated.'

'How can that be? The fields were valued, the best ones sold. The company that oversaw it, I can't recollect the name now—'

'Zenovitch Liquid Fuel.'

'They would have employed surveyors to investigate the fields. How could they miss such resources? I think you are letting sentimentality overcome your judgement.'

'The surveyors were wrong.'

De Boer looked sceptical. 'Indeed. And you have proof?'

'Yes. Not with me, but I can find it.'

'I see.'

Anton downed his whisky. 'Do we have an agreement? If I can prove there is oil in that field, will you back me?'

De Boer shook his head. 'There are plenty of successful oil producing companies in Baku – why invest in one that needs a great deal of money to resurrect it? Besides, Zenovitch Liquid Fuel may not wish to cooperate – they may have reasons for letting those fields lie fallow.'

'True, but the Rothschilds are influential and could make an attractive offer.'

De Boer frowned. 'Your father may have been a friend of the baron's, but he would not let friendship cloud his judgement.' He pulled out his pocket watch. 'I am sorry, Sabroski, but there's nothing more to be said. I'm afraid our meeting is at an end. I have another appointment, so you must excuse me.'

'Indulge me, sir. Allow me five more minutes.'

De Boer's face darkened. 'You are wasting my time.'

Anton took out the leather pouch and untied the drawstring. 'I have security that you may be interested in... bequeathed to me by my father.' He pulled out the Fabergé egg, holding it up so that it sparkled in the light. 'I will pledge this in return for your support.'

The air in the room seemed electrified.

'*How* did you come by this?' It sounded more like an accusation than a question. De Boer stretched out his hand and took it.

'It belonged to my father.'

'Is it real?'

'Certainly.'

'How can a man who owned such a jewel be made bankrupt?' De Boer took the egg to a cabinet, opened the drawer and took out a jeweller's loupe. He examined the egg, twisting it round and feeling the surface. Finally, he took out the eyeglass and looked up. 'Diamonds, rubies and emerald. Very fine quality. A magnificent piece. One of Carl Fabergé's, I believe.'

'That is correct.'

'Why haven't you sold it and raised the capital yourself?'

'I do not wish to.'

'And yet you are willing to sell it to me?'

'I will *pledge* it for a loan and your influence in reopening the Group Twenty fields. I want Zenovitch Liquid Fuel to return them to me for the price the fields were valued at. If I find oil and can turn a profit, you will return the egg to me. In return, I will supply your refineries, at some specified time in the future, with oil free of charge until the loan has been repaid.'

'De Boer laughed. 'I'd heard you were reckless, Sabroski. But not foolish. Once the baron hears about this egg, he'll want to possess it. I may even want it for myself. It is a dainty thing.'

'That's a risk I'll take.'

De Boer considered. 'A specified time in the future you say? I'll give you three months.'

'That's unreasonable. You must give me a sporting chance. I'll need at least two years.'

'Impossible... I'll set the date for just over eight months from now. The autumn equinox. That seems a suitable day for you to forfeit your treasure.'

CHAPTER TWENTY-FOUR

JULIA SEIGENBERG READ THE LETTER AGAIN. IT WAS ONLY A few lines long, but each word, every syllable and even the spaces between words seemed more significant with every reading. The strong black letters looped across the paper. She stared at the signature. She never thought his name would look like that.

Just looking at his name sent sparks through her. It was as if a tiny part of Rafiq was there in the room, encapsulated inside the signature. She allowed herself to stare at it for a few moments longer before folding the letter in half and slipping it inside her diary.

This is what true love feels like! It scares me!

She crossed to the window and pressed her nose up against the glass. It was ice cold and her breath fogged the windowpane. She traced his name with her finger, copying his sharp, deliberate strokes.

A chunk of ice fell down the chimney. She'd sat watching the snow fall and settle across the streets for hours while she thought about Rafiq. She hadn't realised how sensual she was until he'd kissed her. Sometimes she let Leo kiss her, but it wasn't the same. Being kissed by Leo was like sitting in the sun on a warm afternoon. It left you with a comfortable feeling but it was the sort of kiss that left no mark. She would never relive one of Leo's kisses, remember the detail of his mouth, the firmness, the smell and taste of him.

She pulled the letter from her diary and read it again.

January 12th 1891

Dear Miss Seigenberg,

I deeply regret that over the past month I have misled you as to my intentions. I feel very ashamed of my behaviour. When I saw you on New Year's Day, I realised how impossible our circumstances are. We live in different worlds, and I would only make you unhappy. Please accept my apologies and I hope you will not think ill of me.

Rafiq

It was ridiculous to think they lived in different worlds. In Baku, Russians married Muslims, Armenians married Tatars, and Jews married Armenians. Sometimes Jews married Muslims. There were no barriers here, which was one of the reasons people came to the city. It offered freedom from persecution. It wasn't just the oil industry that attracted people. It was why the Seigenbergs left Moscow and settled in Baku. The Jewish pogroms couldn't touch them here.

Julia stared at the blurred landscape. The world she knew had disappeared under a thousand soft-white mounds, all the way down to the sea. She closed the shutters and sat at her desk, pulling a crisp sheet of paper towards her. She picked up her steel-nibbed pen and dipped it in the inkpot. For a while she sat motionless with her eyes closed. Then she began to write.

*

The tellak at the bathhouse massaged the oil spy known as the Pallid Harrier.

I have to admire you, boy. You're full of surprises, I congratulate you.

It was a bold plan of Anton's to approach the Rothschilds and attempt to thwart John Rockefeller and eventually reopen the Group Twenty fields – the very same fields he'd taken such trouble to sabotage. Sabroski was proving a challenge. It was a shame he would have to be disposed of.

He waved the tellak away and turned over. Sunlight poured through tiny holes in the domed roof illuminating clouds of steam.

There were very few people who knew the truth: some were dead, others intimidated who would never open their mouths. He stared across at a man laughing so hard his belly wobbled like a jelly cake. It was impossible to know the identity of agents who reported directly to Rockefeller; it could even be that fat slob of a man next to him.

Anonymity was a deliberate policy. Many of his agents on the oilfields had moved on since the collapse of Sabroski Oil. He had placed them in more useful positions, so there were only a few left now who could do what was needed, but they would suffice.

He would get those tanker blueprints at any cost and relieve Sabroski of ever needing to breathe again.

*

Klara had been tiptoeing around Anton for weeks now, keeping out of his way and holding her tongue. Rasoul tried to persuade her to lodge with him, but she was reluctant. Rasoul's house was too visible from the road and a person's comings and goings would be seen by everyone. So even though Anton Nikolayevich could be tiresome, she preferred to remain at the Sabroski house on Nikolaevskaya Street.

It was also easier to remain in the background as Anton was preoccupied. Following his visit to the Rothschild manager, Anton seemed enlivened, busying himself with documents and discussions with John Seigenberg and Rafiq (naturally she eavesdropped on them), riding back and forth between the Icheri Sheher. She no longer saw him sprawled in the chair by the bedroom window engulfed in a cloud of smoke.

Meanwhile Klara was busy herself. Ivan had moved down to the docks. He had surrendered his writings to proofread and take to the printers. She had her reading and access to the Sabroski library when Anton was out. It was stocked with a host of literature – her favourite was Bebel who believed in the emancipation of women. She wondered if such a world could ever exist, where women were socially and economically independent.

In a world like that I'd be free.

Klara wondered what Anton thought on such matters. Initially, she assumed he was like so many men – condescending and selfish – but now she wasn't so sure.

A week later a note was delivered to the house. Klara picked it up off the mat and handed it to Anton as he came down the stairs dressed in thick wool trousers and stout boots for the oilfields. Anton read it and swore, threw it onto the hall side table and raced out of the door.

CHAPTER TWENTY-FIVE

AFTER THE MEETING WITH THE ROTHSCHILD MANAGER, Anton had felt his spirits bolster for the first time since he'd returned home. Admittedly, Zenovitch Liquid Fuel had prevaricated and made excuses and even locked the company premises. He'd banged on their door and peered through the window, but nothing stirred except for the *closed* sign that rocked in the wind. It looked like a neglected storehouse, not the powerful supply company that had managed the assets of Sabroski Oil. But after a week Anton received word that the paperwork had been completed and the fields were his – subject to various terms and conditions. All this came down to the power of the Rothschilds.

But now Anton cursed his complacency – good fortune always seemed to demand a payback.

And now this has happened.

He rode under the archways of the Icheri Sheher, slowing to navigate traders ferrying merchandise through the cobbled square. Children and stray cats scattered as he cantered along his path. Outside Rafiq's house, he tied up his horse, threw a kopek to a boy to mind it and bounded up to the front door.

'He's gone,' shouted a shrouded woman with a pannier of bread on her head. She pointed down the street towards the old caravanserai inn. 'There was trouble. A man. Ask the innkeeper. He saw them too.'

Anton tensed. 'Are you sure it was Rafiq Hasanov? From this house?'

The woman nodded, stepping back to let two camels plod past.

Anton sped down the alleyway towards the inn. *For Christ's sake, Rafiq, don't put yourself in danger.*

There were six caravansaries in the old city, where merchants stabled pack animals and found refuge for the night. The woman had pointed to the *Multani* caravanserai, which had a warren of underground rooms used for sleeping and storage. Anton was told the innkeeper was busy, but others had seen a man answering to Rafiq's description go inside the inn.

Warily, Anton descended the twisting steps into the damp gloom of the subterranean chambers. He slipped his hand in his pocket, felt the smooth surface of his revolver and clicked off the safety catch. The back of his neck prickled. Flickering candlelight revealed scores of multicoloured camel bags stuffed with cloths, along with silks and rugs heaped up outside rooms. Smoke from shisha pipes clung to the dank air.

Through open doors he could make out bunks and bedding. Figures lay asleep, but apart from some snores, the only other sound was made by a rat scratching a metal food plate on the ground.

Something felt wrong and Anton knew he should get help, but if Rafiq was in trouble, delay could be fatal.

A turbaned figure appeared in swishing gold and gave a small bow. He indicated a low vaulted corridor that led to a semicircular, iron-studded door. Anton followed the man, watching the shadows stretch and distort in the torchlight, his heart thudding and his instincts urging caution.

At the end of the stone passageway, the Persian pressed both hands against the studded door and pushed hard. It creaked open to reveal a long room with a low ceiling and a blazing fireplace. Thick rugs covered the stone floor and low, Arab-style mufrage seating lined the walls. Incense perfumed the air. The iron door clanked shut and Anton's heart crashed against his chest. He trained his gun into the darkness.

'Rafiq?'

An orange dot glowed on the other side of the room.

'Welcome, Sabroski. We've been waiting for you.'

Anton stared into the darkness. 'Where's Rafiq?'

'My men haven't seen him all morning. It's you we want to talk to.' The orange tip glowed again. 'Put your gun away. No need for any unpleasantness.'

'The note came from you.'

'You are so very trusting, Mr Sabroski. A few, well-placed ushers and you rush straight into my arms.'

The man stepped into the firelight with his hands raised. 'Hamilton Fretwell at your service. See how polite I am. No need for guns.'

Anton regarded the man with the beak nose and a brown check sack suit. The fire illuminated the right side of the man's face accentuating a thin white scar running the length of his neck. His forehead glistened with sweat.

Fretwell indicated a chair. 'Why don't you sit down?'

'I'll stand.'

'As you wish. But I'm going to lower my hands and sit... that's if you don't mind.' Fretwell crossed his legs, his patent leather boots reflecting the glow of the fire as he jiggled his leg. 'Let's not waste time. You have oil tanker blueprints for the Suez Canal authorities. I have a client who wants to buy them.'

Anton kept his gun trained on the man.

'You carried documents back from the Orient given to you by a Mr Marcus Samuel. You've also met with De Boer, the

Rothschild manager. We know what you discussed and what your marine engineer has designed. In fact, we know a great deal about you.'

'Who's this *we*?'

'A client. Someone who is prepared to pay a great deal of money. And you need money. From what I hear.'

'That's none of your business.'

Fretwell shrugged. 'Something that's of little use to you could make you very rich.'

'If you know so much, you'll know I don't have them.'

'True. They are with your marine engineer. So, we're going to need your help.'

Anton studied Fretwell. His mutilated finger twinged as memories flooded back of bars around the docks in Shanghai and rough characters, the type who slashed his finger over a card game. Anton flexed the remaining fingers of his left hand and took a slow deep breath. *You can talk your way out of this.*

He noticed a darker corner on the far side that led to a side room. There he sensed another presence, as if somebody had exhaled a breath. He stared into the darkness but could see nothing.

'What is it you expect me to do?'

Fretwell discarded his cigarette and stood. 'You will follow my plan. It is straightforward enough. You will tell Hasanov that the Rothschilds wish to see the tanker plans again. That won't arouse suspicion. En route you will be intercepted and robbed. A minor beating will make it look credible. You can think up a cover story. You will be well compensated. No need to worry about your future ever again.'

'Suddenly, I come into a great deal of money. Is that it? I inherit a fortune from a distant relative?'

'You disappoint me. I thought you'd be more inventive.' Fretwell spread his arms. 'A prize from the Orient. A princely gift from an exotic admirer. Investments in a little gold mine you had forgotten about. I'm sure you'll think of something.'

'And if I refuse?'

'Then you'd be foolish, and I don't take you for a foolish man.' Fretwell sighed. 'Why keep these tanker plans, Sabroski? You have no allegiance to this Jewish merchant. From what I heard, you only met him a couple of times. You'll gain nothing from this venture and profits from success will go to the Rothschilds and Marcus Samuel. Not you. And certainly not Sabroski Oil.' He paused. 'What have you got to lose?'

'When you put it like that, not much, I suppose.'

'I'm glad you see sense.'

Anton straightened up. 'I was never much good at seeing sense though.'

'You agree? Will you give me your word as a gentleman? We must shake on it.'

I can't do this. Anton narrowed his eyes. 'It would be of little use.'

'And why would that be?'

'Because you are no gentleman, so how could I honour such a promise?'

Fretwell clicked his tongue. 'You think a lot of yourself, don't you, Sabroski. What an arrogant fool you are.' He gave a nod to someone in the darkness. 'Open the door. The gentleman is leaving.'

Anton turned away. Something crawled up his spine and clutched at his innards, but he straightened his shoulders and forced the creeping thing down. He took measured steps forward, the soft rugs cushioning his tread. He fixed his gaze on the iron door that creaked open and the dancing torchlights outside that signalled his reprieve.

Anton wasn't sure what surprised him first: the blow across the head or the sight of a thickset man appearing out of the stonework. He was dragged backwards and frisked, and his gun was taken away. Someone grabbed a clump of his hair and whispered in his ear.

'You didn't think for a moment I was going to let you walk out of here, did you?' Fretwell's sour breath moistened his face. He examined Anton's gun, turning it round in his hand. 'Nice revolver. Smith 'n' Wesson forty-four.' He opened the chamber and emptied the bullets into his hand.

CHAPTER TWENTY-SIX

KLARA PICKED UP THE DISCARDED NOTE. UNEASE WASHED over her. Anton had dashed from the door as if the Devil was after him. The note had been hastily written, a scribbled signature on a smudged scrap of blotted paper. Klara grabbed a headscarf and coat and sped out through the front door.

She had never been to Rafiq's house before, but the Hasanovs were well known, and she'd heard they lived off the main square in the Icheri Sheher opposite the Shamakhi gates. Klara dodged through crowds of peddlers and women selling bread from panniers on their heads. Up ahead stood a row of fine houses with monograms carved on lofty stone plaques and her heart quickened when she saw Anton's horse tied up outside a house bearing the Hasanov initials. A small boy sat throwing pebbles at a cat.

Klara banged on the door. A disgruntled manservant informed her that Rafiq ibn Talat was out and not expected back before nightfall. There had been no other visitors, the man insisted, even after she had indicated the tethered horse. He regarded her disapprovingly before closing the door in her face –

her hair was showing; she'd not had time to pin it properly under the headscarf.

Feeling exasperated, she turned and looked at the sea of activity below her. The passage that led down to the Maiden Tower and the caravanserai inns was packed with camels spitting and flicking their tails, but there was no sign of Anton.

She ran down the steps to the boy by the horse. 'The man who owns this horse – where did he go?'

The boy shrugged and turned back to his pile of stones.

'Hey. I'm talking to you. It's important. I've got a message for him.'

The boy ignored her. Klara skipped forward and wrenched off his skullcap. The boy cursed. 'You give that back.'

'Not until you answer me.'

'I never saw. Give that back.' He jumped up as Klara held it high above her head and danced back.

'No.'

'He went down that way,' shouted the boy. 'Towards the inn. That's what the old woman said.'

'Which woman?'

'I don't know. She's gone. Give it to me!'

Klara threw the cap at him and ran down the cobbled streets, her thoughts in a hot muddle. She halted at the intersection of two caravanserai inns. A sign saying Multani caravanserai creaked in the wind.

What am I doing? Think! Where could he have gone?

She flattened herself against the wall as a ponderous camel lumbered past. The note said the tanker plans had been 'compromised'. If they had been stolen, Anton and Rafiq would be in pursuit, which meant they could be anywhere inside the sprawling inner city.

She stared into the courtyard of the caravanserai beyond its huge arched gates. Camels were settling for the night, huddled together like furry brown hillocks. Flies congregated around their huge eyes, but the beasts took no notice. A dark passageway to the left sank into the depths below the inn. She could almost feel a damp current of air rise out and touch her.

As she deliberated, a Persian in flowing robes appeared and gave her a gold-toothed smile. She backed away into the darkness of a doorway.

The daylight was fading now. The street had started to fill with a different crowd. The aroma of roasted meats, dried fruits and buttered rice seeped through the doorways from within the caravanserai courtyard. Klara's mouth watered, and she realised she hadn't eaten all day.

'Get away, woman,' shouted a doorman in a fur-covered hat.

'I'm looking for someone.'

'I'm sure you are, but you won't find them here.'

'I have a message for Anton Sabroski, a Russian gentleman. He would have passed by here an hour or so ago.'

The doorman ignored her.

'His friend is Rafiq Hasanov. And John Seigenberg,' she added decisively. 'You might know these people. They are important.'

'Everyone knows the Hasanovs, but they certainly wouldn't have business with a woman like you. Now be off with you.'

She looked around wildly. A man with a large curly moustache and a curved dagger in his belt was watching her. He was leaning up against a wall eating pistachio nuts, cracking and spitting the shells around him. He beckoned her over.

'John Seigenberg, you say. How do you know a man like that?'

'He's my... master's lawyer.' Inwardly she cringed. How it would amuse Anton to hear her call him *master*. She adopted a submissive posture and summoned a tear to trickle down her cheek.

'A man like that went down there a few hours ago.' He pointed to the dark passageway. 'I remember him from some months back. He was with the man you call John Seigenberg.' He put his hand on her shoulder. 'He probably won't be there now, and if he is, he must be on dark business. It's not a place for gentlemen from the outside and certainly not for a girl like you.'

The weight of his hand felt like a great claw. 'Let me go,' she gasped. He released her, but as she darted behind the doorman and into the courtyard, she felt his eyes in pursuit.

She stumbled down the twisting steps into a yellow gloom. The steps opened onto a wide cellar with a dozen smaller rooms leading off. Passageways led in different directions and to unwholesome smells. Men sat around sorting mounds of goods that had been disgorged by pack animals. Some were eating, others had glasses of tea and a few were smoking. The dialect was strange to her, these Persian merchants from the southern lands on their way to Samarkand. But their whole way of life seemed foreign to her. The silk road men treated women like the goods in their packs, as chattels that could be bought and sold, creatures that had no real worth other than for pleasure and the bearing of children. She shuddered. There wasn't a sign of another woman in the place. It was her against a score of fearsome men.

The only way was left, down a dark tunnel that flickered with torches. She felt sick as a wave of hysteria passed through her. She edged her way along the wall, slipping in and out of dancing shadows until she reached the tunnel. Fortunately, there was nobody about. Muffled voices arose from behind closed doors, and as she pressed her ear to them, all she could hear was the Persian tongue.

She crept further down the tunnel until she spotted a huge, semicircular, iron-studded door which looked like the entrance to a desert castle. She expected it would crash open at any moment and a cavalry of horses would charge out brandishing swords.

The man had been right. Anton wasn't here.

As she turned away a noise caught Klara's attention. It came from behind the studded door, and it didn't sound like the low conversational tones from elsewhere.

She pressed her ear up to the door, which was difficult as the iron studs were sharp and pointed. She could hear Russian voices. A man was speaking, movement and a groan. She held her breath, as if that would help her hear more clearly. She closed her eyes and focused her remaining senses on the scene behind the door, training her ears. A man was speaking in a threatening tone, while another answered so quietly she could not make out what he said. There came a scrape of a chair, a dragging sound, a thud, a cry.

Then a name.

Sabroski.

Energy charged through Klara's body. She examined the door, feverishly looking for a handle, a lever, anything that would open it, but it was solid and impenetrable. She considered banging and screaming. Somebody may come out and see who was causing the racket. She could slip inside and... *do what?*

I can't help him on my own. I must get out of here. I have to tell someone.

She turned and ran. A rat scuttled across her path as she clattered down the passageway. She gave no thought to the men squatting on the floor in the main cellar. Several rose to see what ferocity approached and were so startled to see a woman with flying hair that their mouths fell open before exclaiming out loud. One man opened his arms as if to catch her like a bird in mid-flight, but Klara leapt and twisted out of his reach. She took the stone steps two at a time and bounded out into the top courtyard.

Mercifully, the gates were still open, and she tore through them. The cobbled street was bustling with night-folk, but she propelled herself through the wall of bodies and ran, until she reached Anton's horse. She untied the horse, mounted it, dug her heels in and with her head down and body streamlined, she rode as fast as she could to the house of John Seigenberg.

Anton kept his eyes closed and focused on breathing through the pain. He had taken a beating, but he knew it was merely a taste of what was coming. They'd left him lying on the ground while they convened to a side room, as if they'd attended a show and the main feature had become tiresome. There were no windows or doors except for the huge iron door he'd come through.

Nobody had seen him come in.

Nobody knew he was there.

He'd be buried alive in this underground tomb, and nobody would ever know.

Anton lay there thinking of Rafiq. *You're dangerous to be around, Anton.* When they were sixteen Anton had nearly got them both killed, having persuaded Rafiq to sneak onto a rogue vessel bound for Astrakhan. The gang of sturgeon poachers hadn't taken kindly to stowaways. Anton escaped with a broken rib, but Rafiq had been slashed across the cheek and still bore a scar.

Anton heard footsteps approach. Someone crouched, enveloping him in a stench of sweat. A cream necktie dangled in Anton's face.

'Want some more of this, Sabroski? We'll kill you if you don't cooperate.'

Anton felt himself being dragged up and shoved into the chair. He could hardly see; his chest was on fire. A pen was pushed into his hand, but he flung it onto the floor. Immediately he took another punch, and a pair of hands wrenched him from the chair.

'You're going to kill me anyway and then you'd kill Rafiq if he came here.' He felt hot blood drip from his nose as he braced himself for the violent response.

But there wasn't one. Instead, he heard a tramp of feet and the creak of the iron door.

Then the hands that were holding him fell away.

CHAPTER TWENTY-SEVEN

WHEN KLARA FIRST SAW HIM, SHE THOUGHT HE WAS DEAD. John Seigenberg and two of the gochus carried Anton back to the house. He was dripping blood, his face so swollen his eyes had disappeared. His jacket was gone and his white shirt wet and red and ripped to pieces. John carried a single leather boot, the other had been lost in the attack.

The gochus carried him upstairs and one of them took out his carved dagger and cut off the rest of Anton's clothes while the housekeeper bathed his wounds and sent for the doctor. John Seigenberg gave each of them a bag of coins, and the gochus traipsed down the stairs and out of the house and melted into the damp, dark street.

It had been a terrible night. Klara thought he would die. Doctor Levon had arrived with a black bag full of bottles and instructions. They were to keep Anton's wounds clean and feed him chicken soup and change his bandages every day. The curly-haired Armenian doctor with his large white teeth and thick black spectacles visited each morning until the worst had passed.

The incident had filled Klara with dread. Even though Anton Nikolayevich could be irritatingly pompous, he had more in common with his father than she first thought. Even Rasoul had been forced to admit that Anton wasn't all bad, what with the opening of the fields and the resulting work for the men, though that statement had been quickly countered with a lecture about the evils of capitalism and the wicked bourgeoisie. Wasn't it possible that people who were rich could also be good? Rasoul thought not, but Klara didn't agree. It wasn't all black and white, she argued, no matter how much he fumed.

*

Anton could hardly see. It was difficult to open his eyes. Specks of light swirled round, fading and streaking into darkness. A door creaked and a cool stream of air washed over him. There came a fluttering of wings and then silence.

The silence was good.

He was happy lying there. Something must have happened, but he couldn't think what. He didn't know where he was, but it didn't seem to matter. It was comfortable and warm and safe.

Someone sat beside him and rested a cool hand on his forehead. Anton opened his mouth to speak, but words wouldn't come. His tongue was too big for his mouth.

'I think he's waking up,' said a woman. He sensed her lean across him and lift the weight from his face. The darkness faded. A blur of figures stood around him.

He closed his eyes as the strange dream started to play again. He was lying on the ground. It was cold. And so much pain. So much pain on a cold stone floor. Burning stabs were searing through his body. There were noises far away that sounded like gunshots. The door broke open and men with curved daggers and long-belted coats rushed in. But they didn't hurt him. The candles in the passageway flickered with excitement as they picked him up and carried him out.

Then he remembered a terrible scream. The semicircular door

swung back, its iron studs protruding like thorns. Hamilton Fretwell's body had been skewered to the surface like a wild beast.

Anton forced his eyes open.

'He's waking up,' the woman said again.

There was a lot of movement and a man with curly hair peered at him through thick glasses. He opened a black case and produced a bottle. Everyone in the room started talking and then melted away, except for someone sitting beside him. A door closed and he felt a soft hand touch his face.

'Don't worry, Anton. You'll be all right.'

It sounded like Klara.

Anton spent all of February recovering. The inactivity was as frustrating as it was boring, but Anton endured it with the knowledge that at least he had fared better than Fretwell.

When he felt better, he rested on the divan in the drawing room. Klara drew back the curtains and opened the window to encourage the early March sunshine to spill across the rug. Anton winced as he drew his smoking jacket around him. Beyond the window he could see two gochu bodyguards watching the house, appointed by John Seigenberg.

'It's for the best,' Klara said. 'You need protecting, if only from yourself.' She plumped up the cushion behind his head and picked up a spoon with a bottle half-full of a thick brown liquid. 'Now, don't complain. Take this. Doctor's orders.'

Anton manoeuvred himself into a sitting position. 'Seeing as I owe you my life, I'd better do as I'm told.' He swallowed the bitter liquid.

'Well, not just me. I couldn't have done much without the help of John Seigenberg. He was the one who organised the gochus. It's lucky he has so many connections.' She fell silent and cut him a slice of syrupy baklava. 'This will take the taste away.'

He took it and ate. It was true that without John's help there was no telling what would have happened. Hamilton Fretwell could have left him to die, or perhaps he would have devised some other way of luring the tanker plans into the dungeons. Anton liked to think he didn't have a breaking point, but that was easy to believe in the safety of his own home. He had seen many fine men falter during the Afghan war.

Klara busied herself stacking empty glasses and plates onto the tea tray and headed out to the kitchen. It was odd lying there, watching her fuss over him like a child. He was unsure how to behave. Too much had been said – bad things, things he regretted. The thought of being spied on had enraged him. But he couldn't bring himself to apologise. Not yet. It was all too awkward.

Klara returned and handed him a letter. 'This came for you. From Singapore.'

Anton opened it and began to read.

January 20th 1891

My Dear Friend,

Good news. I am leaving Singapore shortly. All is well with the Singapore Harbour authorities. I will take the steamer to Egypt and then a train to Constantinople. From there I shall take the steamer across the Black Sea to Batumi. I am scheduled to arrive in Batumi towards the end of April, where I plan to visit the Rothschild refinery. Wait for my cable then we can make plans for the goods to be delivered to Tiflis. I hope all is well.

Take very good care of yourself and give my regards to your marine engineer.

Your good friend
Marcus Samuel

'Is it from Marcus Samuel? What does it say?'

He didn't bother asking her how she knew. Klara seemed to know everything. He wanted to tell her to mind her own business, but he didn't. 'Yes. It *is* from Marcus Samuel. He's setting up agreements with the harbour authorities. Travelling back soon.'

'Will he come here? Will you meet him?'

Anton hesitated. 'I can't say.'

The energy left her face. 'You still don't trust me, do you?'

He looked away. 'I don't trust anyone, Klara. Besides, it's best you don't know anything. People get hurt around me.'

For the remainder of his recuperation Anton spent his time reading and moderating the pain of his injuries with the opium supply he'd brought back from the Orient. He allowed the sullen Rasoul to take charge on the Bibi-Eibat oilfields, to channel the Rothschild loans into buying equipment and resurrecting the wells. It was a start, but it would be months before any oil could be produced. And the Rothschilds had imposed a deadline of September 21st. Anton had tried to resist, but De Boer had insisted that the loans were to be repaid before autumn, else the egg would be forfeit. On some days Anton doubted his decision, remembering the damning Humbert's surveyor's report and thinking himself quite mad to have risked the Fabergé egg. But why would Katharine Lapinski be urging him forward, if not for a very good reason?

Rafiq visited most days. At first his friend wanted to abandon the tanker project, so horrified was he by Anton's condition and the implications. It took Anton a while to convince Rafiq to continue. Marcus was relying on them to meet him in Tiflis, the Georgian capital, to collect the finished tanker plans and take them to London. He would honour his commitment to Marcus, but the sooner the tanker plans were out of his hands the better.

'You have a stronger resolve than I do,' Rafiq said during one of his visits.

'Don't give up. By May it will be over.'

'Two more months,' Rafiq had replied darkly. 'But I shall make changes to the blueprints. They will be of no use to anyone but me.'

To Anton's consternation, he received an invitation to dine at the Brakov house. Olesia Brakov sent her condolences on behalf of the Brakov family saying they were concerned for his welfare, horrified at what had happened and wished him well.

Anton had put the invitation down and watched a flock of white doves congregate in the mulberry tree outside. Their cooing played around the courtyard and seeped into the house through the open windows. The last time he had visited the Brakov house was more than fifteen years ago, and the invitation left a bitter taste in his mouth.

CHAPTER TWENTY-EIGHT

RAFIQ HADN'T REPLIED TO JULIA'S LETTER FOR NEARLY TWO months, by which time she'd almost stopped eating. When the letter finally came, she was in such a frenzy that the words blurred into nonsense: mere curves and dots and lines on paper. She ran to her bedroom and locked the door. With trembling fingers she forced herself to be calm and read.

An hour later, Julia summoned her maid and headed to Parapet Square. The day was cold and grey, and the streets wet from rain. Julia shivered and pulled her mantle closer around her.

'Which shop do you want to go to first, miss?'

'The haberdashery on Bazarnaya. I shall buy some silk.'

Bazarnaya Street stretched out before her. On the left-hand side, spanning the whole length of the block, stood Firouz Haberdashery. It was awash with colour. Rolls of rich fabrics cascaded down the windowpanes, and banks of walnut drawers were full with all manner of buttons and buckles: gold and silver braid, diamante and beads, sequins, and tassels. The rectangular boards on shelves to her right were stacked with different types of lace.

Julia took the shop in as she wandered around. A river of

lavender greeted her – violet was all the rage in Europe. She ran her finger over a rich purple satin and decided it would look well on her.

The assistant looked over. 'Can I help, miss?'

Before she could answer, she felt a hand on her shoulder.

'Hello, Julia. Where have you been hiding yourself?' Miranda stood encased in a maroon tailored jacket. Her umbrella skirt clung tightly to her hips and flowed onto the ground.

Julia flushed. 'Hello, Miranda. I'm trying to decide what to buy. There's so much choice.'

'Take the purple silk. The colour will look lovely on you.'

'That's what I thought.'

'Why haven't you called?' Miranda asked. 'I visited last week and left my card.'

'Yes, I know. I've been busy.'

'What have you been doing that's taken so much time?'

'Oh, nothing very interesting. Some embroidery. Practising new piano pieces Leo gave me.'

Miranda frowned. 'Indeed? You must be a very proficient player by now.' She took Julia's hand and lowered her voice. 'Where have you been? Be honest with me.'

'Please don't concern yourself, Miranda.'

'You're still meeting *him,* aren't you?'

Julia looked away.

'Please don't lie to me, Julia.'

'Oh Miranda… You must let me be.'

'I will *not.* I care about you too much.'

Julia lowered her voice. 'I can't talk here.'

'Then when can you talk?'

'I'll call.'

'When?'

'Tomorrow.'

Miranda gave her a stern look. 'Promise?'

'Promise.'

Julia watched her friend leave. *I'm sorry, Miranda, but you don't understand!*

'Is Mademoiselle thinking of buying this?' asked the shop assistant.

Julia realised she was still clutching the purple silk in her hands. 'Yes. I'll take six yards, please.'

The assistant measured out the required length and folded the material and wrapped it in brown paper.

Julia took the package and handed it to her maid. 'Take this home, Sveta. I'm going to have tea with Miranda Aleksandrovna. There's no need for you to come.'

As Julia stepped outside the shop, four Cossack soldiers on horseback thundered by, kicking up mud and sending folk scurrying. Julia lingered in the doorway until their distinctive long-belted coats and shiny swords disappeared into the distance. Her father would prefer a Russian soldier as a suitor than a Muslim from the Icheri Sheher.

Mariyinskaya Street lay on the other side of Parapet Square, leading north towards the hills. Julia pulled her veil over her face, secured it under her chin and opened her parasol. She gripped hold of the wooden handle as the wind whipped beneath the black and green silk and tugged at the frilled border. A shop selling shisha pipes and tobacco stood on the corner of the square, its dirty white awning billowing and flapping. She looked into the distance at the barren hills that surrounded the west and northern part of the city, and beyond them, the sprawling oilfields and the desert.

Julia's heart was in her throat as she turned left at the top of the street and walked along until she came to a house with the number twenty-five painted above the doorway. It had a wooden balcony covered with a bare old vine hanging down into the street. She felt her fingers tremble as she rang the bell.

There was no answer at first. The branches scratched at the sides of the balcony and a couple of sparrows stared down. Julia rang again, feeling faint with apprehension. Seconds later she heard footsteps and the heavy wooden door swung open. Rafiq stared, then took her hand and pulled her into the darkness as he slammed the door. Without a word he led her up the stone steps, his hand gripping hers like a vice. At the top of the stairs, she put her arms around him and he held her tight.

'You shouldn't have come,' he said.

'Why not?'

'You know why.'

'You told me about this house.'

'I know… but I didn't mean you to come.'

'Then why did you send me that letter with your address?' Julia unwound her veil and untied her mantle and slipped it from her shoulders.

Rafiq regarded her. 'You can stay for ten minutes, then I'm calling a carriage. Ten minutes. No more.' He touched the spray of flowers under the upturned brim of her hat. 'Violets. Beautiful colour. It suits you.'

Julia smiled and pulled the hat pin from her hat and took it off. Rafiq took her hand and walked her into an adjacent room. 'Is this what you came to see?'

Two black-tiled fireplaces dominated a room that stretched the length of the house. A long table covered with drawings and mathematical instruments stood in the centre: charts, maps, protractors, rulers and other instruments she couldn't name.

'Why do you hide away here?'

'Because it's secret,' Rafiq said. 'Nobody knows I'm here. I come to work and escape.'

'Escape from what?'

He laughed. '*You.*'

She dug him in the ribs, and he clutched his side in mock protest as she snatched his saffron sash and wrapped it around her. Rafiq's eyes creased, his scar dimpling. 'It suits you. You must keep it.'

Julia felt a surge of happiness as she felt the satin next to her skin. 'How do you escape from the Icheri Sheher? I thought nobody escaped from there unnoticed.'

'There are ways. Many tunnels lead in and out of the citadel. But you have to be a Hasanov to know about them.'

'Secret tunnels from your house? That's so exciting. Will you show me?'

'No. Because they wouldn't be secret then, would they?'

She looked about curiously. 'Is this *your* house?'

'No. My father bought it for a friend a long time ago.'

'What kind of friend?' Julia let go of his hand and wandered down the length of the table, picking up instruments and looking at his work.

Rafiq hesitated. 'Just a… friend.'

'You mean a mistress?'

'I found letters. Years ago. Love letters. My father had hidden them, but I found them by accident when I went to clean out the fire.' Rafiq smiled. 'My father's summer hiding place.'

'Did your mother know?'

'She may have done.'

'What happened to this mistress?'

'I don't know.' He came over and kissed her forehead. 'Enough. Why so many questions?'

'I want to know all about you.'

'I'm not very interesting.'

'*I* think you are.' Julia turned to face him. 'Kiss me properly.' She cupped his face.

'No.' He pulled her hands away and stepped back. 'Your time is up. I'm calling a carriage for you. You cannot stay.'

'Please don't.'

'You do not understand.'

'You think you're incapable of feeling anything. You're feeling guilty.'

'It's more than that, Julia. I can't give you anything – not what you need anyway. Besides, it is not right that you are here, unaccompanied.' Rafiq turned and moved towards the door.

'Why are you doing this? Locking yourself away? Burying yourself in work? Why are you so fearful?' Julia retrieved her hat and began fixing it on her head. 'I think you need rescuing from your much-too-serious self.'

Rafiq picked up her mantle and held it out to her. As she moved forward to take it, he reeled her in. He put his arms around her waist and drew her into him and kissed her.

The noises from the street drifted into the house. His warmth wrapped itself around her and it seemed an age before he moved. Then he laid his head against her shoulder and sighed. 'What am I to do with you, Julia?'

CHAPTER TWENTY-NINE

ANTON DID NOT WANT TO DINE WITH THE BRAKOVS, BUT HE couldn't think of a good enough reason to refuse. He prevaricated until he finally agreed to a date in mid-March.

The house had changed since the last time he visited. The drawing room was palatial and very blue. Long sapphire curtains cascaded down the windows. The far wall was a patchwork of gilt-framed oil paintings. A pianoforte stood against the wall and overhead an opaline glass chandelier sent branches of light to the far corners of the room. It all looked very French.

Anton was sceptical about the reasons he'd been invited but assumed it was for curiosity, or a past sense of company duty brought about by his confinement. He was a thing of interest, an exotic object that had returned from the Orient to penniless disappointment and was now the subject of violence and intrigue. Such a source of entertainment would make fascinating dinner conversation for months.

Anton took the proffered glass of claret and glanced at his hosts. Stefan's wife, Miranda, glided around in a flame of red satin. Stefan looked stiff and awkward in a dinner jacket smoking a Sobranie cigar. Stefan's mother, Olesia, reclined in a wash of indigo-blue which matched the colour scheme of the room. There was no sign of her husband, Fabian.

'I'm very glad you appear well, in spite of your misfortune, Anton Nikolayevich,' Olesia said. 'I hope the gendarmes catch the men responsible.'

'I doubt they will be caught. But next time they will not catch me so unprepared.'

Olesia smiled. 'That's exactly the sort of remark Nikolai would have made. You are so much like your father... I hope you will settle and stay in Baku. Stefan often mentions you. I remember you spending so much time together when you were children – I would be happy if you two could resume that closeness.'

'Indeed,' said Anton politely. *We couldn't stand each other.* It was curious how parents so little understood their offspring. His father had encouraged their friendship too, given their closeness, and it would have made for easier family relations. But it was not to be. Anton sipped his wine and noticed Stefan, who had reddened.

'Did you go to see Dmitry Ivanovich's landlady?' Stefan asked quickly.

'Yes, but it was a wasted journey.'

'Nobody has seen Dmitry since the visit of the tsar in the autumn of eighty-eight,' Olesia said. 'It was such a grand occasion. They all came – the Romanovs: Tsarina Maria, the son Nicholas, five daughters, along with scores of the Okhrana.'

'Father was furious,' interrupted Stefan, 'because the tsar stayed at Emanuel Nobel's house, the new one out at Villa Petrolea. Nobody knows how the Nobel brothers were able to arrange that.'

'The Nobels have much influence at court, so I wasn't surprised,' said Olesia. 'Villa Petrolea is not just a house – it's an oasis, a beautiful, twenty-two-acre park. Have you ever visited, Anton? You should do. They say it has eighty thousand trees and shrubs, all imported from Europe. It cost Ludvig Nobel as much as an oilfield. So *that* is why the tsar stayed there. Besides, can you imagine the inconvenience if the tsar had come here?'

Anton's thoughts raced. 'Was a reception held? For prominent oil men or such?'

Olesia waved her hand. 'Oh yes, there were many. I went to the opening of the new hospital. The tsarina attended that one with her daughters.'

'Did many of the royal court come?'

'Indeed, but I didn't see a guest list. But I expect it was reported in the newspapers. Why are you so interested?'

'Just curious. It's a coincidence that Dmitry disappeared at the same time.'

Olesia frowned. 'Unfortunately, it was also a time of much violence and crime. Criminals take advantage of high spirits to make gains for themselves. Folk are not as watchful when they are making merry. Dmitry took his chances to escape while we were all distracted.'

Anton said nothing more. He was aware that Miranda had been very quiet since he'd arrived. She sat appraising him with tenebrous eyes and he wondered if she was still annoyed about the tense words exchanged with Stefan at the Hotel Continental. But that was months ago now. Miranda looked away as he caught her eye.

Anton turned to Stefan. 'You were telling me at the club how busy you've been, Stefan. How is your new role?'

Stefan cut in, speaking quickly. 'Yes – yes, many tasks to oversee. Yesterday, I supervised the laying of a new pipeline. Thirty men were digging a six-foot trench to house a five-inch pipe. And then there's the new steam pump – a magnificent beast. It has a twenty-seven-horsepower engine which they say can force the oil through at three and half feet per second...' Stefan continued but his voice had dulled to a monotone. Anton fixed an interested gaze and signalled for something stronger to drink.

Olesia looked from Stefan to Anton with a frown. Miranda

put a hand on Stefan's arm. The gong sounded for dinner and a throng of turbaned servants appeared. They stood up. Stefan escorted his mother, but Miranda drew Anton back and lowered her voice. 'Wait, sir. I have something I wish to say to you in confidence.'

Anton frowned. Surely she wasn't going to reprimand him for past misdemeanours? Miranda waited for the others to move away before turning to look at him. 'It is about my dear friend, Julia Seigenberg. I care for her a great deal; she is young and impetuous and given a little bit too much freedom, I think.'

Anton didn't know what she was talking about.

'Julia has a very romantic view of the world,' Miranda continued. 'It is unrealistic and childlike, probably due to the loss of her mother at an early age. I don't think she ever developed the closeness with her stepmother that is necessary for... delicate conversations to take place between a mother and daughter.' Miranda opened and closed a black silk fan embroidered with golden insects. 'She has recently formed an attachment which causes me concern.'

'What sort of attachment?'

She patted the small white flowers woven into a coiffure on the top of her head. 'A romantic attachment.'

'With who?'

'Your friend, Anton Nikolayevich. *Rafiq Hasanov*. You must put a stop to it.'

The conversation at dinner was forced and brittle. Anton felt he was under scrutiny; Miranda frequently glanced at him, and though Stefan was pretending to relax, Anton caught him snatching looks at him. Anton had little time to reflect on Miranda's words with Olesia watching and listening like a gracious ambassador.

After dinner Miranda played for them, gliding over to the

pianoforte, the train of her evening gown swaying behind like a long fiery snake. Discreetly, Anton followed the sweep of her hips before glancing over at Stefan. His eyes were fixed on his wife.

Anton leaned back in his chair. Miranda was playing a piece from Tchaikovsky, and for a few minutes he concentrated on watching her fingers dance across the ivory keys. He pondered Miranda's words. He recalled Julia's reaction when Rafiq joined the New Year's Day celebrations, and how Rafiq's eyes had followed her around the room the day they'd met at his house. Rafiq had said nothing about a courtship.

Rafiq and Julia. Would it be such a bad idea?

Miranda finished playing and everyone began to applaud. Stefan rose and flushed, clapped the hardest.

'Bravo, Miranda,' he exclaimed.

For once, the sight of Stefan's enthusiasm and passion touched Anton and he regretted their past hostilities.

It was an hour later when a tramp of feet cut through the room. There was a hush, and everyone looked up. 'Well, well, what have we got going on here?'

Fabian Brakov and Albert Prankman were standing under the archway that divided the drawing room in two.

Olesia stood up. 'Fabian. What a pleasant surprise. We didn't expect you back tonight.'

'Evidently. But no need to look so worried. I am glad to see everyone enjoying themselves.' Fabian regarded Anton. 'I am glad to see you, Sabroski, under more convivial circumstances. Welcome to my home.' He indicated Prankman. 'I believe you are already acquainted with my business consultant, Albert Prankman.'

Prankman eyed Anton, his tortoiseshell monocle dangling from his waistcoat pocket. There was a flicker of excitement in his eyes. 'I hear you took a bad beating, sir. Very unpleasant business.'

'I am mostly recovered, thank you.'

'What did these thugs want?'

'Money. Probably a debt owning from the past. I don't remember much.'

'Did you recognise these ruffians?'

'No.'

Fabian laid his top hat and cane across the walnut centre table, straightened his yellow poplin waistcoat and walked across to the floor globe at the side of the room. He rolled it open and picked out a bottle of vodka and filled two crystal glasses and handed one to Prankman. 'You should take care with whom you associate, Sabroski. Trust only those you have known for a long time.'

'You mean like my father did? He trusted a friend he'd known for years.'

Fabian paused. 'That was unfortunate. None of us expected the accountant to play false.' For a moment Fabian's face darkened and he stood with his glass pressed against his chest. Then he looked round the room, his eyes alighting on Miranda. 'I heard you playing earlier, my dear. Beautiful as usual. I hope you will play again this evening.'

Miranda inclined her head, prompting Fabian to stroll across the room and sink into a midnight blue armchair. 'I don't know why everyone is looking so serious. Relax. We have a guest. Let's enjoy ourselves.'

Prankman leaned against a marble column and lit a cigarette. He surveyed the room like a stalking cat. Stefan ran his hands through his hair. A blond strand had flopped across his face. 'How was your trip, Father?'

'Very satisfactory.' Fabian looked over at Anton. 'But business is not like it used to be. Not like the old days.'

Prankman tapped his cigarette into a crystal ashtray. 'Baku

needs new markets. A more efficient way of exporting oil. Any man who is able to do so can name his price. Wouldn't you agree, Sabroski?'

Anton shrugged. 'I wouldn't know, sir.'

Fabian snorted. 'I don't believe that – surely that's why you returned to Baku? It's in your blood, like your father, like all of us. They say most Bakuvians have oil in their veins.'

Anton swirled his drink around his glass. 'I just have the plain old red stuff in mine. Very dull, I'm afraid.'

Fabian eyed him conspiratorially. 'Then what's this we hear about the Group Twenty fields? Lot of money going into them – Rothschild money. You must know something we don't. Those fields are dead – at least that's what we were led to believe.'

'I'm investigating possibilities.'

'Bit of an expensive investigation, isn't it? What grounds do you have? You're not going on the words of a couple of drillers?' Fabian looked at Anton knowingly. 'But then my son tells me you like spending time with the workers. You understand they're exploiting your – shall we call it – your *social conscience?*'

'Desperate men will do anything to get their way,' interjected Prankman.

'That's for me to find out. If that's the case, it will be my problem.'

'Don't suppose the Rothschilds will be too happy. It's their money,' said Fabian.

'With respect, sir, that's none of your business.'

Fabian laughed and waved a finger at Anton. 'You know what, Sabroski? I have faith in you. Have you ever thought about joining another company? With your experience you could be of great use.'

'I've always been my own man.'

'I understand that. But if you expanded – loaned yourself out, so to speak – you might have access to unlimited funds and expertise.'

Where have I heard this before?

'Think about it,' Fabian continued. 'Brakov Oil could do with a man like you. Stefan could do with some guidance.'

Anton took a sip of whisky. 'I'm sure Stefan needs no help from me. I understand he manages a section of the company on his own.'

'Is that what he told you?'

Stefan reddened. 'Well not exactly on my own. More of a proposition Father and I have been discussing.'

'Have we indeed?' Fabian raised his eyebrows. 'I think Stefan's imagination runs away with him. He needs far more experience before he can run anything.'

'And how am I to gain that experience when you continually lock me out?'

Miranda put a steadying hand on Stefan's shoulder.

'I'm not locking you out. You need more time.' Fabian turned to Anton. 'How about it, sir? A chance to work in a thriving company. I'm sure you could teach my son a few things with your engineering knowledge from Count Witte and that railway project you worked on – the Trans-Siberian Express. And we could learn from you. Pool our knowledge, share our experiences and contacts. Brakov and Sabroski. Like the old days.'

Anton felt a chill run through his body, almost as if his father had risen up and clamped an icy hand on his shoulder. 'Thank you, sir, but no. I have my own plans.'

Olesia broke in. 'But you should give it some thought, Anton. I would be delighted to see you and Stefan work together. Don't dismiss the idea too quickly.'

Stefan rose to his feet. 'I don't understand. What do you all think Anton can bring to the company that I can't?'

Fabian waved him down. 'Sit down, Stefan. Sabroski would bring experience and a knowledge of a different way of doing things. He's been in the East. He has contacts. Just like Albert has been able to do.'

'I don't call mixing with a lot of foreign undesirables, experience.' Stefan started to rub his forehead. 'Get me another drink please, Miranda.'

Miranda took his glass with a frown and signalled a servant.

Fabian shook his head. 'Stefan's had enough.'

Miranda went to the piano and began looking through her music. She selected a piece and began to play.

Fabian regarded Anton and screwed up his eyes. 'Are these accusations true? Do you really keep the company of foreign undesirables?'

'It depends on your definition of undesirable,' said Anton, rising to his feet. He gave a small bow to Olesia. 'Thank you for your hospitality, madam, but now I must take my leave.'

Fabian frowned. 'Come, sir, don't let my son's bad manners drive you away.'

'It is not anyone's bad manners that concern me. But it is nearly midnight. I have business to attend to in the morning and several undesirable friends to meet.'

Fabian's mouth twitched. 'As you wish. But the Brakov door is open, Sabroski. Consider what I have said.'

CHAPTER THIRTY

THE EVENING AT THE BRAKOVS LINGERED IN ANTON'S MIND for several days. He decided that the offer of a position at Brakov Oil had been distasteful.

I pity you, Stefan, for having to endure such a father. Did Fabian seriously imagine I'd accept an offer of employment? Something's got you rattled, Fabian you old bastard, hasn't it?

Anton felt a flush of contentment. He did not understand how or why, but undoubtedly they were involved in his father's misfortunes. He could feel it in every particle he breathed, especially in the presence of Prankman. The man was poisonous. If Prankman had hired his attacker in the caravanserai, then, he reasoned, Fabian was not far behind. The letters between his father and Marcus Samuel made no mention of Fabian, and Anton wondered if the plan had been to cut him out somehow.

That would explain a lot.

The conversation about the Romanovs' visit had also interested Anton. A large section of the court had come. Might that include the Grand Duke Konstantin Nikolayevich? Perhaps he used it as an excuse to visit Katharine Lapinski? He might have brought the Fabergé egg and given it to her? According to Stefan's mother, Olesia, the newspapers said that it was a time of great distraction and celebration.

This had given Anton an idea.

The reading room at the Baku Gentleman's Club was empty except for a Tatar businessman in a red fez, who sat examining a book with a magnifying glass. A turbaned footman, with a square black beard, was standing by the door. The room smelled of incense – a mixture of peppermint and musk, and the mosaic floor was covered in rugs. The collection of books was modest – a few hundred leather volumes, but it was the journals, periodicals and newspapers that interested Anton.

He motioned the footman over and explained what he wanted and was led over to a section of tall leather binders which had dates marked on their spines. There were five weighty binders marked 1888. Anton extracted each one and carried it over to a table.

A variety of newspapers had been preserved: copies of the *Vedomosti* in Russian, *Kaspiy* and *Bakinskie Izvestiya* in Azeri, *The Illustrated London News* and a complete set of Russian *Ezhenedel'naia klinicheskaia Gazeta*. Anton made a start by turning to the October 1888 editions and paying special attention to the dates of the tsar's visit: the 8th, 9th and 10th.

For the next few hours, Anton read. There were scores of photographs of the Romanov visit, the laying of the Alexander Nevsky Cathedral foundation stone and the celebrations with fireworks over the Caspian. Thousands of people of all creeds had come to greet the tsar. Muslims stood shoulder to shoulder with Armenians, Jews, Georgians, Russians and Europeans. Photographs showed throngs of people lining the embankment, waving flags and hats, scarves and banners. But despite the happy mood, there had been a darker side to the visit. Hundreds of the tsar's secret police had flooded the city, rounding up anyone with a suspicious background, from students and agitators and members of political groups.

Anton turned his attention to the photographs. The tall, hulking Tsar Alexander III, with his receding hairline, bushy moustache, and beard, towered over his wife. According to the *Kaspiy*, it was rumoured the tsar dressed like a peasant in his own home and possessed Herculean strength. One photograph showed them at the Alexander Nevsky Cathedral site with all five of their children, flanked by scores of official-looking men in fur-collared overcoats. Anton examined the photographs carefully, but many of the faces were too small to see.

The old Tatar was still on the other side of the room, but he had put his book down and was smoking a shisha pipe. Anton went over and asked to borrow his magnifying glass.

Back at his table, he held the magnifying glass over the newspapers and scrutinised the photographs. The man standing behind the tsarina had a wispy beard and moustache, sandy grey hair swept back from his face and a pair of pince-nez. There was something about his face, a familiar expression, a look about his eyes, perhaps it was his mouth – it was hard to determine exactly what, but Anton had seen that face before. He proceeded to read the photograph captions, but they revealed little, other than to confirm that many members of the royal court were in attendance.

The visit had not gone smoothly. There had been a terrible crush on the embankment where scores of people had died. One of the wooden piers stretching into the bay had collapsed. Fifteen children were trapped underneath and had drowned. A speeding carriage had killed a whole family near Parapet Square, and it seemed that pickpockets, footpads and ruffians had taken advantage of the merry mood to steal and settle old scores. The hospitals reported many more casualties than normal and had appealed for volunteers to help.

Anton closed the newspaper and sat for a while, smoking a

cigarette. The visit of the tsar, the appearance of the Fabergé egg, Katharine Lapinski and the newspaper cuttings she had sent him were too much of a coincidence.

The newspaper cutting.

Anton jumped up and retrieved the binder for 1885 and opened the Easter copy of the *Vedomosti*. It was a thick volume, full of illustrations of Easter celebrations from around the empire. He flicked to the court news and stared.

A section of the page had been torn out. The photograph was missing.

All he could see was a column of type under the heading: *Carl Fabergé Creates Masterpiece for the Tsar.*

Anton returned the binders to the shelf and placed the magnifying glass near the Tatar gentleman who was now snoring in his chair. He made his way to the bar and found John Seigenberg, who was playing poker in the club's gaming room. To his frustration, the lawyer was sitting at a table with Prankman and Fabian Brakov and a man with a square jaw whom he'd never seen before. Except for the clatter of poker chips, the room was full of smoke and silence,

Somebody had torn out that newspaper article, but who? There were hundreds of members of the gentleman's club, all who had access to the library. There were attendants, footmen, bellboys, waiters, managers, cashiers and servants. The club also allowed gentleman's drivers to enter the main foyer to announce their arrival, so anyone from a hundred or so people could slip into the library and tear something from a binder.

Anton stared across at John, who was fanning his cards to examine them. He watched Fabian push two clay chips into the middle of the table. The game seemed to be taking forever.

As Anton moved nearer to watch, the square-chinned man threw his hand down. 'Fold.'

'Call,' said Prankman, a monocled eye fixed on the cards in his hand.

'Raise you two hundred.'

'Fold.'

'I'll see you,' said Prankman, taking two of his chips and adding them to the others.

John turned over his cards.

'Three queens and two tens: a full house,' said Prankman, slipping his cards amongst the discards on the table. 'Fortune smiles on you tonight, Seigenberg.' He snapped open his gold lighter and lit a cigarette.

Anton stood back as John scooped up his chips and a buzz of men flowed away from the table. He felt Prankman's eyes on him but avoided his gaze. He had no wish to get into conversation with him or Fabian Brakov, but he also didn't want to look as if he had something of interest to tell John.

Anton forced a casual manner and called across to the lawyer, 'I assume you're having a drink, John. You need something to spend that money on.'

John signalled an attendant to cash in his chips. 'I thought I saw you standing there. You been here all night?'

'No. I had dinner at home.'

John came over and looked at him up and down. 'You're looking a lot better than you did a few weeks ago. How are the ribs?'

'Mended. Almost.'

'Glad to hear it. Klara looking after you?'

Anton gave him a sideways look.

John smiled. 'I told you she's not as bad as you think.'

'Maybe not.' Anton looked around quickly. 'I'm surprised to see you at the tables with him… Prankman.'

John lowered his voice. 'It gives me great pleasure to beat him, especially as he cheats.'

'Now why doesn't that surprise me,' murmured Anton.

They made their way into the bar. John insisted on ordering cocktails. 'Ever had one of these? An Old Fashioned?'

Anton shook his head and watched the barman take two metal cups with bevelled edges and start to dissolve a lump of sugar in a glass of hot water. 'How do you know that Prankman cheats?'

'Instinct. I watch him.'

'What does he do?'

'All sorts of tricks.' John watched the bartender uncork a large glass bottle of bitters and shake two dashes into the mixture, followed by shavings of ice, lemon peel and a jigger of whisky. He indicated a corner of the room. 'We'll sit over there.'

They took their drinks and went and sat down. John sipped his cocktail. 'Sometimes Prankman puts a red chip on his cards. Other times he puts two single chips on top of them. I've seen him lay a hand over his cards in an odd way. In one game I saw him repeatedly touch his thumb to one of his four fingers.'

'A code? He must have a partner.'

'The last time I saw him do that was in one of those saloon bars along the Bailov road. But he changes tactics constantly. And be wary that he doesn't bottom deal.' John smiled. 'You've been warned.'

'You seem to know a lot about this.'

'Thirty years of playing. I know most of the tricks.'

'If you're so sure he's cheating, why don't you expose him?'

'Accusing someone of cheating is a serious charge.'

Anton frowned. 'My father taught me to play... to watch for cheats. It was useful. I played a lot in Vladivostok.'

'Cheating's a dangerous business. In this club, the worst that can happen is that you'll lose your membership. Cheat out in the oilfields, and someone will cut your throat.'

Anton changed the subject. 'Something curious has happened. It was the reason I came here tonight.'

'Nothing too dangerous, I hope. You don't want to get into any more trouble.'

'It's about a message I received and something Olesia Brakov said.' He told John what he had found out from the library newspapers.

'And this note from Katharine Lapinski – if indeed it did come from her – told you to look at the surveyor's reports?'

'Which is what I've done, but I haven't found anything helpful. What do you know about these surveyors: Kaplan and Humberts?'

'People said Gregory Kaplan wasn't particularly competent. He'd made some poor assessments of land, overestimating the potential of finding oil. Fabian had wanted to replace him for years, but your father resisted.'

'Why?'

'He and Kaplan were old friends. Known each other since the sixties.'

Anton pondered that. He looked round the room at the rich oil barons in their fine clothes sipping champagne and smoking fat cigars. 'So, it *is* all about old friends and the past.' Anton could almost feel the grip of his father's gnarled fingers on his hand. *Be as watchful of the past as you are of the present.*

John snapped his fingers and ordered more cocktails. 'The old days were volatile times. You lived on the oilfields during the day and in the saloon bars at night. It was easy to lose perspective when there was so much money to be made. Nikolai made enemies. We all made enemies. See the men in this room: Taghiyev, Mukhtarov and Naghiyev. They came from nothing. They were penniless Tatar peasants and look at them now. Oil baron millionaires. It's not easy to obey the rules when you live in such a world.'

For a few moments John looked regretful, but in an instant the moment had passed.

The house was in darkness by the time Anton returned. He unlocked the front door and made straight for the drawing room. He felt a burning pain in his shoulder blades. It was one of the areas the caravanserai thugs had paid special attention to and had made his back a torture. He unbuttoned his white waistcoat, pulled off his bow tie and massaged his shoulders, but the pain burned through his back and down his left arm.

He knew he'd never be able to sleep so he went upstairs, opened his travelling case, found the familiar box, and made his way back to the drawing room.

Throughout the years his precious opium travel kit had been a comforting companion. Anton understood the dangers and had seen the results with friends of lesser resolve, but he knew the quantities a man could safely imbibe. The hallucinations and sweats and prolonged sleeping were red flags threatening danger. But as soon as he was settled, as soon as his wounds were healed, he decided he would stop.

Anton set the box on the table, kicked off his patent leather pumps and slumped into a chair. He unfolded the compartments. Chinese motifs danced across their surfaces: two dragons, three herons and a phoenix. A section opened flat to make a black lacquered tray and another compartment contained two fifteen-inch bamboo pipes. He ran his fingers over the smooth pipe bowl which was coated with red glaze and a motif of bats. He'd been told bats were a symbol of happiness, which had been so important to him then. It was a true opium pipe, not like the cheap ones they tried to sell him in the opium dens, but one where the pipe bowl allowed the drug to vaporise, rather than burn.

Anton dug his fingers inside and slid out a long needle-like rod and instinctively felt the end with his thumb. There was a slight roughness – remains of a previous pill of opium where it had been skewered onto the end. He could almost see the pale green seed pods swaying in the wind, the pink-purple flowers four feet high. The first time he'd ever seen a poppy field was in Burma. Orange-swathed women harvested the immature seed pods by lancing them with a sharp blade to collect the milky secretions. As soon as the liquid oxidised it turned into a brown sticky gum: Opium. Or the *joy plant* as the ancient Sumerians called it.

'Are you thinking of stabbing yourself with that?'

Anton started. As usual Klara had materialised like a phantom. She stood holding a tray with a bowl of steaming hot borsch and a hunk of dark bread. He slid the needle back into its compartment and closed the box.

'Don't stop on my behalf,' she said, pulling a place mat from the centre of the table and lowering the soup tray.

Anton said nothing, instead picking up his spoon to dive into the thick red soup.

Klara pulled the opium box towards her. 'It's beautiful,' she said, turning the pipe with the red glaze around in her hand.

Anton stopped eating. The potency of the memory hypnotised him, almost as if he didn't need to smoke the pipe. It was enough to see a woman caress the pipe and twist the needle in an imaginary flame. 'Don't,' he said, quietly.

Klara packed the pipes back inside the box and made to leave, but he waved a restraining hand. 'There's no need to go. I'm not annoyed. Sit down.'

A flicker of a smile grazed her face.

'Have you ever smoked opium?'

'A couple of times,' she conceded. 'But a friend of mine from Kiev smoked a lot. He'd been injured and was in pain. Opium helped. Like it helps you. I used to make pipes for him, but they were not as beautiful as yours.'

'You can make pipes? That's quite a skill.' Anton paused. 'What happened to your friend?'

'He's... not here much,' she said looking away.

'I see. Is he... special to you?'

'Yes.'

She looked at him. 'How did you lose your finger? Was it in the army?'

Anton examined his mutilated hand. 'No.'

'How then?'

'In the Orient. In a bar. Over a card game.'

Klara regarded him. 'So many secrets, Anton Nikolayevich.'

'That makes two of us then, doesn't it?'

CHAPTER THIRTY-ONE

THE PALLID HARRIER HESITATED OUTSIDE THE SALOON BAR on the Bibi-Eibat road as a stream of people climbed the veranda steps. The Devil's Bazaar was Bibi-Eibat's most popular tavern, named after the famous gusher of '76. The ale (like the oil) never stopped flowing.

He pushed through the doors and let them bang shut. The gas lamps swayed in the current of air, illuminating tobacco-stained walls. A man was playing an out of tune pianoforte while a painted old woman clapped and sang. Out the back, familiar faces clattered chips across a faro table and an octagonal-shaped bar wheezed with ale pumps. His spine tingled at the discordant orchestra of frontier life as he jostled his way to the bar.

'The usual?' shouted a barman lumbering towards him, sweat running down the sides of his face. The Pallid Harrier pointed to a keg of ale and the barman sloshed a tankard full and slid it towards him. Scattering kopeks on the counter, he grasped the drink and found a seat. He ignored calls to join a poker table and pulled out the cables between himself and New York. The noise of the bar seemed to fade as he read.

Pallid Harrier to John D. Rockefeller, January 14th 1891

Rothschilds plan to export Russian oil to Orient via Suez Canal. Liaising with Anton Nikolayevich Sabroski, formerly Sabroski Oil. Hebrew merchant backer Marcus Samuel of Samuel, Samuel & Co London. New tanker blueprints developed. Marine Engineer Rafiq Hasanov.

John D. Rockefeller to Pallid Harrier, April 9th 1891

Marcus Samuel seen in Constantinople. Steamer booked Batumi April 20th. Rothschild refineries visit. Liaison with Sabroski– Hasanov Tiflis. Dates unknown. Intercept imperative.

The Pallid Harrier took a gulp of ale. The double life of a spy used to amuse him with its continual deceit and duplicity, but he had grown weary of it. Rockefeller demanded more and more of his agents and the current situation was getting tiresome. Sabroski had more stamina and luck than anticipated. But if the tanker plans were on the move, he'd have one last chance.

He lit a cigarette and glanced at two women fawning over a group of oil men. One woman, with a bright orange feather in her hair, sat upon a man's knee. A well-dressed man with dark sideburns put his hand down the front of another woman's gown and cupped her breast.

The Pallid Harrier's loins burned, and he shifted in his seat. He dragged his eyes away and looked down at the cable. The steamer from Constantinople to Batumi took three days, which meant the merchant would arrive around the 24th of April. Allowing for a few days to visit the Rothschild refineries and another day's travel to Tiflis, should mean the end of April would be the target. It was tiresome that there was no actual date, but his agent at the post office would let him know when the next cable for Sabroski arrived.

The Pallid Harrier took another gulp of ale as a woman in a gold-and-green-striped dress joined the group. He wiped his mouth and stared. She possessed the dark arrogance and vitality that reminded him of Stefan Brakov's wife.

The girl scanned the crowds and met his gaze, but he looked away. It would be so easy to have her in one of the cots for rent at the back of the tavern, but it might cost him, as several of his syphilitic friends had testified. There was also the chance of losing his purse to a pickpocket.

The table shook as the couple opposite him stood up. A Jewish man with ginger whiskers had finished talking roubles with a pasty-faced whore. Financially satisfied, she stood up and followed the man to the back of the bar, her shapely hips swaying. The Pallid Harrier watched her, his eyes straying back to the girl in the green dress. She flashed a smile and strolled over.

He hesitated and then moved aside to make space for her.

*

A month passed before Anton received more information about the downfall of his father's oil company. He'd slept late that day and sat for a long time in the kitchen eating blini pancakes topped with caviar and sour cream. It was during the afternoon that another mysterious letter arrived. The groom brought it in, announcing it had been pinned to the stable wall.

As before, it was a newspaper cutting with a coloured illustration of a Fabergé egg. Anton read the caption:

The Cherub with Chariot Egg presented by Alexander III to Tsarina Maria Fyodorovna 1888.

The illustration showed a golden egg decorated with diamonds and sapphires. Like before, the signature KL was there, but the paper attached was not a note from Katharine Lapinski. Instead, it was a formal document, displaying a bold hand in black ink.

Anton realised it was the missing surveyor's report from Gregory Kaplan for the Group Twenty fields in Bibi-Eibat, the report that his brother, Vadim, had been unable to find. But if that was the case, he now had two reports: same year, same field.

Anton pushed his plate away and took the letter to the library. He went to the desk and pulled out the entire drawer.

Klara appeared. 'What are you doing?'

'I'm looking for the Humbert's report. Ah – here we are.' He unclipped it and laid it side by side with the Kaplan report. Klara leaned over his shoulder and they both read.

'That doesn't make sense,' she said after a few minutes. '*Plot thirty-three – mother pool beneath the railway tracks*.' She looked up. 'Why did Humberts say the field was worthless.'

'Because they lied.'

'Can you prove it?

'Only by drilling in the recommended areas and seeing what's there. If we find oil, we can prove that Humberts were wrong.'

'Why would they lie about it?'

'They wanted to undervalue the field.'

'To sell it for almost nothing.'

Anton nodded. '*Or* not sell it at all.'

'Why?'

'Frau Kalian said "*All was not well with the company*". That's what Dmitry had told her.'

'What are you going to do?'

'Gather more evidence and present it to the courts.' Anton returned to the desk and took Dmitry's silver key. 'This key must open something incriminating, but I've had no luck in discovering what so far'

'You mean documents proving fraud?'

'Possibly.' Anton studied the key. 'Unfortunately, it has no markings on it, nothing to give me an idea.'

'I'm going to tell Rasoul.' Klara jumped up. 'He was right about the oil all along.' She raced out of the room, slamming the door behind her. Anton could hear her skidding across the hallway, shouting something to the housekeeper. He shook his head and on impulse went into the drawing room to watch her. The spring sunshine stroked the city park and coaxed it awake. Trees that had been stiff with winter relaxed under coats of blossom, and in the distance the Caspian glowed. A figure on the other side of the road caught his eye: a man, tall and fair with rounded shoulders that made him stoop. He wore a heavy, belted green overcoat and a fur cap, rather like the ones the Cossack soldiers wore. He was standing under a tree looking over at the house.

There was a bang as the front door closed. Anton watched Klara run down the steps of the house, tying her bonnet as she dashed down the street.

At the sight of Klara, the man became alert. He threw down his cigarette and followed her.

CHAPTER THIRTY-TWO

A STREET VENDOR SHOUTED AND RATTLED A BEAKER AGAINST his water jug. Rafiq's bare feet pattered down the stone steps. The bolt scraped and the door opened, allowing the sounds of the street to enter. Julia picked up a blueprint from the bench table, a tremor passing through her as she stared at his bold script. The document was covered with labelled drawings of what seemed to be a bird's eye view of a sea vessel. Across the top was written *Suez Canal Tanker Specifications*. Underneath, two cross sections had been annotated with incomprehensible figures and words.

She dropped the design onto the table and ran the tips of her fingers across the thick vellum until her eyes fell upon an old leather notebook held together with an elastic band. She pulled off the strap and opened it. Every page was full of sketches, notes, arrows, numbers and annotations.

All his work. All his ideas. All that he cared about.

She clutched the notebook; the leather was warm from where it had lain in the sunshine. Then she closed it, rolling the band back into place, and wondered why she had allowed herself to love such a man. His work was what he lived for.

Nothing else, and certainly not her.

They had been meeting in secret at the house for six weeks now and she wondered if her visits had meant anything to him. She dropped the notebook onto the table and hurried across the room and pulled open the door to the balcony. She stepped outside and took slow deep breaths. Below, she could see Rafiq talking to the water carrier, bowed and dark, almost sinister. A moment later, Rafiq picked up the water jug, handed a few kopeks to the man and re-entered the house. The front door banged shut. She gathered up her skirt and hurried back into the room, slamming the balcony door. A swirl of wind lifted the papers, sending one spiralling to the ground. She ducked down to retrieve it.

'Leave it,' Rafiq said, setting the water pitcher down on a side table.

Julia flushed. 'The paper had fallen onto the floor.' She placed the drawing on the table and moved away. It represented a part of his world that she was forbidden to enter.

'Sorry. I didn't mean to be sharp.' He poured two glasses of water and handed one to her. Rafiq emptied his glass and smiled at her.

The noises from the street filtered in. Birds chattered, a cart creaked up the road and far away she could hear the street vendor's advertising cry. She crossed the room and put her arms about Rafiq's neck, but she could feel his body tense.

He kissed her quickly on the forehead. 'I have a lot to do today. In a few days I'm going to Tiflis.' He pulled away and made to roll up the documents from the table. A mane of hair tumbled over his red-and-blue waistcoat.

Julia stretched out to touch him and then drew back as a dead feeling crept through her. 'What are you going to Tiflis for?' she said lightly, forcing the words out with difficulty.

He stopped rolling the papers. 'It's a business trip. With Anton Nikolayevich. We are meeting a client.'

She watched him roll the designs quickly and pull rubber

bands around them. The latex snapped against the vellum. 'When will you return?'

'In a few days, but my father has a new project he wants me to start. I'm going to be very busy over the next month.'

'I see.' She looked down into the street. Nothing moved. Even the birds had stopped chirping. She wondered where the water carrier was. Surely he couldn't have serviced the whole street so quickly.

Rafiq pushed the rolled-up plans into the centre of the table. Then he picked up a long leather document case and placed the bundles inside. 'What do you do each day?' Rafiq looked at her kindly, as if she were a child coming home from school.

'I read. I play the piano. I take walks. Sometimes I visit Miranda Aleksandrovna…' Julia trailed off. Her life sounded so trivial, so full of insignificant events.

'And what about Leo Viktorovich? Does he still call?'

'Sometimes.'

'Leo's an honourable man. I know he admires you, Julia.'

'I don't want admirers, Rafiq. What are you trying to say?'

'Nothing.' He turned back to the table, picking up the leather notebook and slipping it into his pocket. 'I'm just a poor engineer who's not very good with words.'

Julia crossed the room and stood by the window. The window ledge was cluttered with plants, some of which had grown out of control with too much sunlight. A silver frame nestled amongst the greenery. She picked it up. It was a photograph of a young woman with dark hair and laughing eyes, Rafiq standing by her side, holding her arm with a look on his face that she had never seen before. An expression of joy. She turned the frame over and read the name: Leyla.

'You seem troubled, Julia.'

Julia didn't dare speak in case her voice splintered. She put the frame down and turned round. He looked concerned. 'I'm sorry. I've not taken good enough care of you today.'

'I'm a little weary. I should like to go home now.'

'As you wish. I will call a carriage.'

She watched him leave the room, his bare feet pattering down the stone stairs. The front door creaked open, and she heard him shout for a hackney cab. She didn't want to cry but a salty burn streamed across the back of her eyes, seeping into her throat and her chest.

Julia let the carriage take her a few streets away. Then she got out and walked. She didn't know where she was, but she knew she couldn't go home. Not yet. Her stepmother would worry her with questions the moment she saw her face. Diane Seigenberg would know something was wrong. And she would be right.

Something was very wrong. *What has happened to me?* Since meeting Rafiq, Julia had lost the contentment she used to find in simple things. When they were apart, she was agitated, unable to concentrate, always thinking of him. When they were together, she felt anxious and unable to relax. To make matters worse, Alfred was forever remarking on how much Leo admired her and how she should marry *him*. Poor Alfred meant well, but if she heard anyone else say what a wonderful man Leo was, she would scream.

Julia blinked away the tears beginning to form. But she didn't want to cry in the street. She wanted to cry back in her bedroom, behind the safety of a locked door.

A carriage on the other side of the road pulled up. She quickened her pace.

The thought of Rafiq's touch sent a hot shiver through her. That first time, when he'd led her into the small bedroom where an iron bedstead stood, she'd trembled so much, she could hardly speak. She'd known in theory what could happen; she'd read enough romances to know the kind of thing her heroines experienced. Wicked men would seize and ravish them, but she didn't know what good men did. She thought of Alfred's art books and wondered if they would do the things those women did, and whether it would hurt. She worried she wouldn't look like they did, and she wouldn't know what to do.

But in the end, none of it had mattered.

The carriage on the other side of the road turned and drew up alongside. The door opened and panic gripped her. She was in the wrong part of town, on an unfamiliar road and it was getting dark. The man in the Icheri Sheher had threatened her; her father had warned her about bandits coming in from the countryside. Her mother's valuable gold locket was visible and Leo's charm bracelet was strung around her wrist. Quickly she tucked the chain inside her collar and pushed the bracelet up into her sleeve and sprang forward. But before she had a chance to get away, strong arms enveloped her and pulled her into the carriage. The door slammed shut and Rafiq's familiar dark eyes raked her face.

'Julia, I was worried about you.'

A mixture of relief and embarrassment swept over Julia. She wiped her eyes, pinched her cheeks, and tried to smile. 'I am perfectly well, thank you.'

'Then why are you wandering the streets on your own, two hours after you left my house?'

'I wanted some air.'

Rafiq took her hand. 'I upset you. I know I did, which is why I asked the driver to watch over you.'

'Why do you care what I do?'

Rafiq looked at her gravely. 'I care about you very much.'

'You don't have to say that.'

Rafiq dropped her hand. The trapped and unhappy expression on his face reminded her of that day in her drawing room when they had taken tea. She summoned her courage. 'I saw that photograph in the silver frame. A woman…'

'Leyla. My wife.' He said the words slowly as if he hadn't said them out loud for a very long time.

'You still love her, don't you?'

'Yes.'

The sick feeling in her stomach crept up her throat. 'I could tell from the way you looked at her. It was a very happy look.'

'I *was* very happy. But she's gone. I know that now. You made me realise that.'

'That's why you don't love me.'

Rafiq looked surprised. 'You remind me of her. Just in some ways, but not others.'

'I can't be Leyla, Rafiq. If that's what you want.'

'I thought I wanted that. But not now.'

'What do you mean?'

'I'm not sure. I need to think. When I come back from Tiflis, things will be clearer.'

'Why? How can they be?'

Rafiq cupped her chin. 'You must trust me, Julia. Everything will be all right.'

CHAPTER THIRTY-THREE

ANTON OPENED THE LATEST COPY OF THE *VEDOMOSTI* AND searched the personal column. He had placed a notice giving instructions to the newspaper offices that the message was to appear every day until further notice.

> *AS to KL. I am delighted to hear your news and would very much like to meet to discuss it further. Please arrange a time and place at your convenience.*

He scanned the column looking for a reply but there was nothing other than engagements and forthcoming marriage announcements, obituaries, funeral notices, missing people descriptions and special event broadcasts. There were no messages from Katharine Lapinski.

Anton threw down the newspaper and lit a cigarette. Yet again he was facing a dead end. To add to his irritation, he had received a letter from Miranda Aleksandrovna reminding him of his duty to protect Julia from the dubious intentions of Rafiq.

The matter of Rafiq and Julia had gone from his mind. Over a month had passed since Miranda had told him about their affair.

Anton's thoughts and time had been consumed with overseeing the oilfields, drawing up new workers' arrangements with Rasoul and Klara, and long discussions with the Rothschilds and Rafiq as well as visiting banks to see if the mysterious silver key fitted any of their safe boxes. Finally, a cable had come from Marcus Samuel with a date for the tanker plans to be delivered. Rafiq had put the finishing touches to the blueprints, train tickets had been bought and berths had been reserved for the journey. A few days from now they were to meet Marcus at the Hotel London in Tiflis.

Speaking to Rafiq about an affair of the heart was not something Anton relished. Even as close friends they had barely spoken of the death of his wife, Leyla, and Anton had told him little of the women he had known in the East. Rafiq was (and always had been) a very private person. Yet he was not unkind, nor intentionally callous, despite the stories Stefan must have told Miranda.

Anton's friendship with Rafiq had infuriated Stefan and maybe the age gap exacerbated the situation. Stefan was four years younger than Anton and had been keen to prove he was mature enough to join in, but his childish outbursts had driven them further apart. He remembered the morning the three of them had raced horses into the desert. Stefan was riding a white Arabian mare he'd been given for his thirteenth birthday, Anton rode a black stallion, and Rafiq a roan. A Bedouin camp had attracted their attention and Rafiq had ridden over; he knew many folks from the desert. Stefan remained watchful and had been reluctant to dismount, as if he expected a knife in his back. He refused offers of tea and sat apart eating pistachio nuts, spitting out shells with a dark expression. On the way home he confronted Rafiq.

'Why do you consort with these people? Most of them are ruffians. I'm surprised we didn't get our horses stolen.'

Rafiq narrowed his eyes. 'Don't be foolish, Stefan. They are honourable people and highly skilled. I like to buy their cloth.'

Stefan snorted. 'The cloth smells and those brash colours are only fit for circus entertainers.'

'Each to their own, Stefan. These are the colours of the desert. They have more spirit than your dark wools from Europe.' Rafiq produced a bright red scarf and waved it at Stefan. 'This colour would suit you. It would bring life to that sickly face of yours.'

'Get that smelly thing away from me.' Stefan kicked his horse and rode ahead.

Rafiq and Anton rode in silence. At length Rafiq drew up his horse and studied the sky. 'A sandstorm is coming. We need to take shelter.' He handed Anton a scarf. 'Wrap this around your face and protect yourself.'

They rode over to an outcrop of rocks and dismounted, wrapping the reins around the rocks. Then they stood to the leeward side of their horses and waited for the storm to pass. Anton laid his swathed head against the beast's belly and held the animal close. It had been a strange experience: solid velvet against a veil of stinging dust. The animal stood motionless, its long eyelashes protecting its vision; a beast bred for the ferocity of the desert.

Stefan had not been so lucky, as his horse had bolted and he had lost control and fallen. Fortunately, a passing camel caravan had invited him to take shelter. But once home, Stefan complained that Anton and Rafiq had abandoned him, and that Rafiq had deliberately alarmed his horse by waving a cloth in its face.

Anton read the letter from Miranda again. What would Stefan say if he knew Rafiq was courting Julia Seigenberg? If he knew his wife had written to him asking for his help? How would John Seigenberg feel about his daughter marrying a Muslim from the Icheri Sheher?

He would mention the matter to Rafiq on the train to Tiflis.

CHAPTER THIRTY-FOUR

AN EAR-SPLITTING WHISTLE JERKED ANTON AWAKE. THE train compartment glowed with the light from the curtained lamps. He heard Rafiq snoring somewhere in the gloom.

Anton pulled on his clothes and slipped into the corridor. A cool breeze snaked down the rocking carriage. He clutched hold of the handrail and pulled down the window and looked out at the passing countryside. In another twelve hours they would arrive in Tiflis, where Marcus Samuel would be waiting. In another twelve hours his part in the Suez Canal tanker venture would be over.

Rafiq had been subdued since they had boarded the train. He had adopted western-style clothes for travelling, but his long hair flowing from under his bowler hat gave him the look of a Parisian street artist. He seemed to be on the verge of saying something on several occasions, before changing his mind. Anton considered mentioning Julia, but the moment didn't seem right.

Anton finished smoking his cigarette and then threw it onto the track as the train pulled into a dingy station on the edge of the Karabagh Steppe. A bell clanged from the tender followed by a strident whistle, and the train shuddered forward. The heat of the early morning filtered through the window. Patches of marshes lay dry and dead in the distance, and despite the heat Anton shivered. The place had a malevolent air about it. Deep gullies ran the length and breadth of the land, which brimmed with mosquitoes during the rainy season, Before the railway was built, legend said the area was an impenetrable land, infested with poisonous snakes and deadly scorpions.

The carriage rattled and darkened as tank cars filed past with a tumultuous roar, tramping oil endlessly between Baku and the Black Sea. Anton steadied himself and made his way down the corridor towards the dining car.

A few people were sitting at a table set for breakfast. A fat man wearing a travelling cap and two men in cloaks and caps who looked Armenian. An effusive Englishman who sold ladies hairpieces (and spoke too loudly for this time of the morning) had opened his briefcase and was taking out wigs and coils of hair. Anton avoided his hopeful gaze and sat at the opposite end of the table near a man in a dark green uniform, who introduced himself as Narek Chorekian, an army surgeon.

Anton ordered a dish of eggs and pondered his next moves. Once he handed over the tanker plans to Marcus Samuel, he could banish threats of spies and agents with the knowledge that he had fulfilled his father's wishes. Marcus Samuel and the Rothschilds could take over the project and do whatever they liked. His role would be over.

He mopped his yellow egg yolk up with a slice of buttered toast. His next task was the oilfields – to get that field up and running and get to the bottom of whatever treachery had bankrupted his father. The enigmatic notes from KL remained puzzling, but in time he felt sure he would make sense of them.

He signalled the attendant and ordered a pot of tea. The wig man had closed up his briefcase and was brushing crumbs off his waistcoat as he stood up to leave. A glass of tea appeared before him. He picked it up and leaned back in his chair, but one more thought continued to bother him. What was he going to do about Klara?

He had never encountered such a woman before and didn't know where she fit into all of this. The women he'd known in the Orient had their own agendas, but Klara was different. She seemed to need nothing and no one – certainly not him. Did that bother him? *Yes – in a way it did. Why?* Was it because she had saved his life? *No.* It was more than that. She was mixed up in all of this. Without Klara, he would never find the whole truth. That's why she was in his thoughts, intruding on his plans and dominating his ideas.

That's all it was. Nothing more.

Anton finished his breakfast and made his way back to the compartment. It was getting light now. In the far distance, the snow-tipped Dagestan mountains ripped through the northern lands from the Black Sea to the Caspian.

When Anton reached the compartment, Rafiq had washed and dressed. His long-tousled hair fell over his shoulders and he yawned as he scraped it back into a ponytail. Anton studied his friend. Once this was over, they could relax in each other's company like the old days. He would find ways to lift his dear friend from his melancholy. If Rafiq wanted to be with Julia, then he would help him and be damned with the opposition. He'd persuade John Seigenberg and ward off Brakov disapproval, and whoever else might object. If the tanker plans were accepted, Rafiq's future as one of the best marine engineers in Baku would be assured.

Anton felt a rush of wellbeing. The future was bright.

The hours passed. Rafiq returned from breakfast and announced he wanted to go over the tanker plans one more time. Anton left him to his studies and returned to the dining car where he took lunch and sat with a newspaper. The train pulled into Elisavetopol, where several travellers alighted. A few minutes later, the train blew out a huge sigh of steam which drifted down the track. Anton decided he rather liked train travel. The rhythmic clanking and breathy chugging caused a billow of smoke to trail behind. It was rather like a beautiful woman sweeping through a room, leaving a hint of perfume.

The soporific motion of the dining car caused him to doze until he was startled awake. A door banged in the distance and shouts, muffled with the noise of the engine, floated down the carriage. There appeared to be a suspended moment of calm before a terrific grinding of brakes sent shock waves through him. The train screamed as hot metal scored the tracks spitting orange sparks against the carriage window. The train gave a violent shudder followed by a tremendous bang, as Anton felt himself being torn up and hurled forward into darkness.

CHAPTER THIRTY-FIVE

IT WAS STILL DARK WHEN ANTON OPENED HIS EYES. HE groped around and felt a hard surface above and realised he was wedged beneath an upturned dining table. He eased himself out, grabbed hold of the ledge and pulled himself free.

Nothing broken, I think.

Anton took a slow deep breath as he studied himself. Tables and chairs lay at odd angles. Tablecloths flapped in the early morning breeze like surrendered flags, and broken crockery and glass carpeted the floor.

Nearby, the fat man in the travelling cap lay motionless. Anton picked his way through and knelt beside him. The man's eyes were open and staring: a piece of glass had pierced his neck. Anton pulled one of the tablecloths over the man's face and stood. He saw one of the Armenians propped up by the window, his head at a strange angle and a trickle of blood running from the corner of his mouth. His eyes had a wide, surprised look, as if he had been looking out of the window and seen something extraordinary.

Beyond the window, a cloud of dust was slowly starting to sink to the ground. Anton pushed open a door and jumped down onto the track. His eyes stung and he could taste metal and smoke. He ran a sleeve over his face as other doors banged open, and shouts emanated from the rest of the carriages.

The army surgeon appeared. His military jacket was ripped and there was a cut above his eye. 'Sabroski, are you hurt?'

'No.' Anton stared down the track, his heart quickening. 'What happened?' The front part of the train, where the first-class compartments were situated, had ploughed into a pile of rocks and steam hissed from under the front carriage. The carriage doors remained closed and the windows were dark. Anton felt a surge of dread and raced forward. *This was no accident.* He reached the stricken carriage as one of the doors sprang open and Rafiq appeared.

'Are you all right?' shouted Anton.

'The door was jammed.'

'God, you had me worried.'

Rafiq patted his jacket as he jumped down. 'No harm done. I have everything.'

'We'd better be ready. I fear this is a set-up.' Anton looked down the track at the scores of passengers standing around shouting, screaming and squabbling with each other.

'Was it a landslide?'

'Must have been – how else would that rubble get there?'

'Doesn't look like a landslide to me. There's only a few rocks.'

'You think it was deliberate?'

'Bandits,' moaned a woman dressed in black.

A man spun round looking at everyone. 'Could it be bandits?'

'There are hundreds in these mountains,' said Rafiq exchanging glances with Anton. 'We must be prepared.'

The head guard and a few stewards hurried over. 'Gentlemen – arm yourselves and quickly. This was no accident. It's a delaying tactic. We may well be attacked. We have a store of weapons in the guard's van. Follow me.'

'God save us.'

'What chance do we have against bandits?'

Anton took charge. 'Women and children get to the carriages at the end of the train. Men – do as the guard said and arm yourselves.'

A buzz of excited voices erupted as the passengers mobilised. Some returned to their carriage to retrieve their belongings, while others hurried down the track to the third-class carriages. The head guard went to the guard van to supervise the distribution of revolvers and rifles.

Anton pulled out his six-shot revolver and scanned the horizon. The desert stretched away under a hot haze, but nothing moved. The train engine stood hissing, black and glowering like a metallic beast that had been caught in a trap. Some men were trying to lever rocks off the track, but Anton knew it would take hours to free the train. They were unprotected in the middle of the desert, the city of Elisavetopol miles behind.

A buzzard hovered overhead, its wings thrashing.

When it happened, Anton thought he'd imagined it – the sun played tricks in the lazy heat. Something glinted in the distance. Anton blinked the sweat from his eyes and squinted. Several more flashes winked from far away, followed by a blur of movement. He shouted to the men as a line of shapes formed on the horizon shrouded in a frenzy of sand. His whole body started to pump.

Horsemen. More than forty of them.

They were wearing heavily belted Eastern khalats with scarves protecting their faces. Stout boots kicked horses' rumps and their tunics bulged with curved daggers. The rifles, slung over their shoulders, bounced on their backs as they thundered towards them.

Anton shouted, 'Take cover.'

A bullet cracked past Anton's ear and a stout man with greasy hair opened fire. The passengers wrenched open the carriage doors and ducked behind the walls. Rafiq wedged his black document case between one of the folding seats and aimed his revolver through the window. Anton held his fire until the horsemen approached.

A bandit with an orange neck scarf and brown tunic pulled up his horse just out of range. He stood up in his saddle and looked down the length of the train while the rest of the men gathered round him. They conferred before galloping down to the third-class carriages.

'They're heading towards the women,' Anton said.

'It's a tactic to draw us out.'

'What can we do?'

'Do as they want,' said Anton. 'What do you think?'

'Play along until we see what they do,' Rafiq said.

'They'll shoot us,' the stout man argued.

Anton kicked open the door and looked out. 'They won't as long as you don't make any fast moves. It's valuables they're after, not bodies.' He shot a glance at the engine driver. 'Stay with your men. Get these rocks out of the way and get this train moving.'

Several bandits had reached the third-class carriages and were sitting on horseback, with their rifles trained on the passengers. Others proceeded to work through each carriage collecting travelling bags, purses and cases, emptying the contents of every bag onto the ground and sorting through valuables.

As I thought. It's bandits looking for spoils.

Anton turned to Rafiq. 'There's too many to fight. They're warriors from the mountains. If all they want is valuables, they'll go once they've got what they wanted.'

'Why not just stay here?' said the stout man. 'Shoot them if they come any closer.'

'And leave the women and children to be assaulted?' cried Rafiq.

'No. I didn't mean that.'

'Then follow me,' said Anton coldly. He put a hand on Rafiq's shoulder. 'Stay close.'

Anton led the way, hands itching to open fire, but he reined himself in – the priority were the women and children. They approached the bandit leader warily.

'Ah… the brave men have come to save their womenfolk.' He snarled. 'Drop your weapons. Stand over there and keep your hands up.' His eyes passed over them before resting on Anton and Rafiq. 'Your names?'

Anton hesitated. 'Seigenberg and Rostov.'

'Find your bags from that pile.' He jerked his head. 'Bring them over here.'

'Why us?' murmured Rafiq.

Anton felt uneasy. 'Probably because we're the only ones travelling first class. He thinks we're the wealthiest.'

'Taking the best for himself.'

'If so, he's going to be disappointed.'

Anton retrieved the travelling bags and carried them over. The bandit jumped down from his horse to search through the bags, pulling out Anton's spare evening shirt and scattering the contents of his travelling kit. He spat as he emptied the contents of Rafiq's modest travelling bag. Then he turned and poked Rafiq in the chest with the barrel of his rifle.

Anton's anger surged. 'There's no need for that. We're doing as you asked.'

The bandit licked his lips. 'I know what you're carrying. Find the documents.'

Anton's stomach lurched but he kept his expression even. 'I don't know what you're talking about. This is all we have.'

'Get those tanker plans, or I'll shoot you both.'

'Tanker plans?'

'They're in the carriage,' said Rafiq quickly.

The man pointed his gun at Anton. 'You! Go and fetch them. Five minutes or I'll shoot your friend.'

Rafiq urged. 'Go, Anton. It's all right.'

Slowly Anton backed away, hands held high. He could feel the revolver in his inside pocket. All it would take was one quick movement. Could he do it fast enough? *Not sure.* He would risk himself but not Rafiq.

At that moment a plume of white smoke billowed above the carriages. The tracks shuddered and with a roar the train engine shook itself free. The bandit leader jerked round and immediately Rafiq dived. A shot exploded in Anton's ears, and the rifle skidded across the sand. Rafiq and the bandit fell together.

Anton ran and hurled himself at the bandit. He kicked and lunged and wrapped his arms around Anton's torso. His strength was startling. Anton tore at his hair and gouged his eyes but the mountain man was too strong. His attacker punched him hard in the stomach and Anton's legs gave way as he fell.

Rafiq was pulling himself up from the ground, his face the colour of sandstone. The bandit pulled out his curved dagger and raised his arm to attack. A gunshot rang out and he coughed and fell to the ground.

The army surgeon raced over brandishing a revolver, 'Sabroski! Get onto the train. Quick.' As he spoke, gunfire cracked, together with a thunder of hooves.

Anton heaved himself up, hooked his arm under Rafiq, and staggered towards the train. He dragged Rafiq on board as shots ripped through the air and the train began to move. Countless bandits took aim with their rifles. Some thundered towards the moving train, leaping from their horses to clutch at the carriages.

Anton pulled out his revolver and shot two horsemen grappling with the doors. They fell backwards as the train creaked forward and gathered speed.

Five miles an hour. Ten. Fifteen. Soon the hot desert air was whipping through the open windows.

Anton shouted to Rafiq, 'I think we're safe.'

Rafiq clutched his chest. '*Inshallah.*'

Then he passed out.

Anton dropped to his knees and pulled open Rafiq's jacket. His waistcoat and shirt were soaked with blood. He shouted down the carriage. 'Someone find the surgeon. Quickly!'

Anton tore at the buttons of Rafiq's shirt. 'Rafiq! Can you hear me? Rafiq!'

'Anton…'

'You're going to be all right. I've got you.'

The surgeon appeared and crouched down. 'Help me get his jacket off.'

They worked together to ease Rafiq's clothes off his chest and shoulders.

'Press hard on the wound with a handkerchief or something,' the surgeon said. 'I'll get my bag.'

Anton tried to stem the blood as his mind raced. *It will be all right. The man's an army surgeon. Seen far worse than this in war.*

The surgeon returned and unfolded a leather bag with an array of sharp instruments. He felt Rafiq's neck. 'His pulse is weak and very fast. Let's get him onto the bed.'

Anton felt his throat and chest constrict. 'The bandit. He shot him. I didn't know, didn't realise Rafiq had been hit. They fell to the ground. I pulled them apart, but I didn't think to check Rafiq was unharmed. I…'

'You weren't to know,' the surgeon said gently. 'Help me get him onto one of those beds.'

Shakily Anton pulled the cushioned back of the seat down and lifted Rafiq onto the makeshift bed. He smoothed Rafiq's hair from his sweaty face and took his hand while the man examined him. 'There's no exit wound. The bullet is lodged somewhere in his chest.' He extracted a long pair of forceps. 'Hold him. I'll be as quick as I can.'

Anton nodded, unable to speak. He held Rafiq's arms and braced himself. The surgeon worked quickly, inserting the forceps into the wound. Rafiq moaned and struggled, but Anton gripped him fast.

'I can't see it. It must have gone deep into the chest.' He picked out a silver hypodermic syringe together with a slim vial. 'Morphine sulphate. It will ease the pain.'

'He'll be… all right, won't he?'

'He's lost a lot of blood. I can do nothing more until we get to Tiflis.'

'That's another two hours,' Anton said.

Presently the train pulled into another station where many passengers disembarked. Word had spread about the attack and the train was delayed while a group of gendarmes boarded the train to question everyone. Every moment's delay was torture. Anton closed his eyes, bit down his frustration, because if he interfered, the delay might be worse.

They were almost at the border when Rafiq groaned again. Anton crouched and felt his brow. Rafiq was restless, his breathing rapid and he had developed a bluish pallor. He vomited violently. Splotches of blood stained his lips.

Anton cried out in terror. 'Come quickly. There's something wrong.'

The surgeon hurried over and felt underneath Rafiq's body. When he pulled his hand away, it was soaked red. 'He's losing too much blood. I can't stop it.'

'We must be able to do something!'

'I fear the bullet has gone into his lung.'

'It can't have. He was sleeping a few minutes ago.'

'That was the morphine.'

'But when we reach the hospital, you'll be able to save him, won't you?'

The surgeon hesitated. 'I don't know. I'm sorry.'

Fear snatched hold of Anton's heart as he took Rafiq's hand. *Don't you dare die!*

Rafiq opened his eyes. 'Anton. Where are we?'

Anton cradled Rafiq's head. 'We're still on the train. You've been hurt but I'll get you to a hospital as soon as we reach Tiflis.'

Rafiq's eyes flickered. 'I'm going to die, aren't I?'

'No, you're not. Just rest.' Tears were filling Anton's eyes so fast he could hardly see.

'I've never seen you cry before.' Rafiq took Anton's arm. 'You've been the very best of friends to me, Anton. I never told you how much I missed you when you went away. I'm so glad you came back.'

'If I had stayed away, you'd have been better off.'

Rafiq held his eyes. 'You don't understand. Designing that tanker was the one of best things I've done in my life. It kept me sane. That and Julia.'

A hot lump stuck in Anton's throat. 'I know about Julia.'

Rafiq spoke slowly now and so quietly that against the roar of the train Anton could hardly hear him. 'I made Julia unhappy. I'm sorry about that. I saw something in her that reminded me of Leyla. But she's not Leyla. I know that now.'

Rafiq closed his eyes.

His breathing seemed quicker now, the rise and fall of his chest amplified in Anton's mind. He gathered Rafiq in his arms and laid his head against Rafiq's neck. *I'm sorry. So sorry.* He wanted to say so much to his friend, his dearest friend, but he could think of nothing.

The train rocked them in a distorted lullaby and Anton wasn't aware how long he held Rafiq. It might have been an hour. It might have been ten minutes. Maybe it was just a few seconds.

At the end his boyhood friend opened his eyes and squeezed his hand.

And then Rafiq died.

Chapter Thirty-Six

The train juddered to a halt and let out a long sigh. The doors swung open, and Anton climbed down and forged a path through the hundreds of curious eyes that followed the porters. He felt nothing. All was grey, cold and lifeless.

They carried Rafiq and the other victims out through the station office and then by carts to the local mortuary. Anton stayed by his friend's side, resting one hand on his stricken body. He imagined Rafiq's hand was still warm, as if his spirit couldn't decide whether to leave.

Attached to the Zakaria hospital, the underground morgue sprawled beneath the Mtkvari river, where the water kept the air cool. Anton descended the slippery steps, still holding onto Rafiq. They had found a plank of wood to carry him on and covered his body with sheets from the train-car beds. Anton pressed his sleeve to his face. The stench in the morgue was making his head swim. He watched the army surgeon direct the porters to place the bodies on stone tables and finally on the floor when they had run out of space. There seemed to be a lot of officials asking questions, writing notes, and a doctor examining each corpse. A choking dread gripped Anton. *Rafiq can't stay in this terrible place.* In anguish he called out to the surgeon.

'We have to get him out of here. He can't stay here.'

'That may be difficult,' the surgeon said.

'I don't care how much it costs. We must find a way.'

The surgeon frowned. 'There is a place. A private clinic. It has a cold chamber.'

'Take us there.'

It took an hour of official nonsense and bribery to deliver Rafiq's body to the clinic. And it took all of Anton's self-control to resist lashing out at the self-important bureaucrat who provoked and prevaricated until he was offered compensation.

The clinic was set in grounds close to the botanical gardens. The cold chamber, as promised, was clean, dignified and quiet. Anton made arrangements for Rafiq to be watched over, laid his hand on his dear friend's forehead, and then organised measures for the following day. He shook hands with the surgeon and expressed his gratitude – without the man's help he might have lost his senses.

The surgeon put a hand on his arm. 'I'm sorry for your loss, my friend. I'm also sorry I couldn't do more. They say death lies between the eye and the eyebrow. It's a fragile child and you never know when it will visit you.'

The Hotel London stood opposite the Vorontzoff Bridge. Anton collected his room key and followed the bellboy to a first-floor room. There, he lay down on the bed, curled on his side, drew up his legs and covered his head with his arms. He felt as if he were being sucked down into himself, his body imploding and shrinking.

At seven o'clock there came a knock at the door. Anton ignored it, but the knocking persisted. A bellboy shouted that there was gentleman waiting for him downstairs in the lobby.

Marcus. How am I going to get through this? Anton unfurled himself and took a deep breath. He snatched up Rafiq's black document case and made his way downstairs.

Marcus Samuel stood waiting for him with a look of concern on his face. 'I heard the dreadful news as soon as I arrived. Thank God you're safe.' He looked around. 'Your engineer. Is he here?'

'No.' Anton tried to keep his voice steady as bile rose into his throat. 'Rafiq Hasanov was one of those murdered by the bandits.'

Marcus froze. 'Oh, dear God. I'm so sorry.' He took Anton by the arm. 'Come my friend. You need a drink.'

They sat in silence in the hotel bar overlooking the Vorontzoff Bridge. Anton handed over the tanker plans while Marcus ordered a flask of strong Georgian vodka. Marcus rolled a cigar and handed him one. Anton took a long drag and waited for the alcohol to work as he related the terrible events on the train.

Marcus tapped his cigar against the ashtray. 'You realise the implications of this? The attack was no ordinary bandit raid. Somebody knew what was being carried on that train and intended to silence you both.'

'Well, they succeeded in silencing one of us.'

'The Caucasus is full of spies, working for different masters. There was probably a spy on that train tracking your movements. See the man over there? He's a Standard Oil agent. He's been following me ever since I left Constantinople.'

Anton noticed a very ordinary-looking man with brown hair, oiled back from his face. He reminded Anton of the irritating wig merchant. Now that he thought about it, he'd seen nothing of the man since the train had stopped at Elisavetopol. Had the man been a spy? Was that possible? Standard Oil had so many spies. Anton had seriously underestimated the task, and as a result he had paid a terrible price.

He ran his hands over his face and massaged his forehead. 'I can't eat, Marcus. You go ahead. I'll just drink.'

Marcus placed a hand on his arm. 'I cannot begin to understand your anguish. And I'm sure that if I had suffered such horror, I would feel the same. Your thoughts are with your dear friend, not with me and the project. But I will not lose hope.'

'I have lost all hope and I no longer care. I wish I'd never set eyes on those cursed specifications.'

Anton lay awake on top of his bed, fully clothed. He was glad to have seen Marcus and handed over the plans. He had never been so relieved to get rid of such a charge. He had wanted to get drunk, but the vodka hardly touched him.

He heard footsteps pad along the corridor. They paused and stopped outside. A knock sounded on the door. Had the train conspirators tracked him down? If so, he relished the chance to put a bullet in the person responsible for Rafiq's death. It would be of no consequence if they killed him too.

Anton jumped up, released the safety catch of his gun, and threw back the iron bolt of the door.

'Good gracious, man,' said Marcus. He stood clad in his dressing gown and slippers.

Anton lowered his gun. 'Apologies, Marcus. Come in.'

The merchant made straight for the table and spread out the tanker plans. 'I'm sorry to disturb you, and I appreciate that this is the last thing you want to think about, but I need your help.'

Anton slipped the gun in his pocket and examined the blueprints. There were three sheets of drawings: a bird's eye view of a tanker and two cross sections. Every part was labelled with terms that seemed unintelligible, a mass of indecipherable symbols. Across the top of each sheet was written *Suez Canal Tanker Specifications*. Rafiq's familiar writing covered the sheets, bold and decorative. The very sight of it made Anton want to weep.

Anton shook his head. 'I don't know what I'm looking at. I can't make sense of anything.'

'Exactly,' said Marcus. 'It's gibberish. Your man's written them in code.'

'Code?'

'It's not an obvious code either. I've just spent the last hour doing simple substitutions, but nothing works.'

Anton stared down at the plans as snapshots of conversation with Rafiq surfaced. 'I remember now. Rafiq made changes to the blueprints to make them more secure. After I was attacked. He must have redrawn them and devised a code.'

'The key to the code is surely written down somewhere?'

'He probably kept the key in his head.'

'In his head!'

'Rafiq had an excellent memory.'

Marcus's face sagged. 'That's very bad news. But there is little we can do about it now. However, I'll take the plans back to London. I know an experienced engineer who may be able to make sense of them.' He paused. 'But I fear time is running out.'

'I'll do what I can,' Anton said. But even as he spoke, he knew he had no interest.

The project had died with Rafiq.

The next morning Anton bade Marcus farewell and hurried to the clinic to supervise Rafiq's body being returned to the train. The body was wrapped in a carpet as was the tradition. For twenty hours the train rattled down the mountainside, through the Kur Steppe and finally to the shores of the Caspian. Throughout the journey, Anton's mind was oddly calm. Rafiq had been his main link with the past. Now Rafiq was gone, his father, mother and sister were dead, the company was bankrupt, and his investigations had reached a dead end. He felt he had accomplished nothing. He had even squandered the Fabergé egg on a foolish gamble with the Rothschilds.

It's time for me to move on. It was a mistake to return to Baku.

The train wound along the coast. It was early morning, the sun had barely risen, but armies of workers were already scurrying about the oilfields. The whistle of steam engines and the sound of thudding drills no longer thrilled him as it once did.

The last few miles of the approach to Baku were bleak. Dusty vegetation sprinkled the desert wilderness, and a dry wind blew across the plain. In the distance, the imposing façade of the railway station rose out of the desert. It was an oasis of architectural splendour that dominated the north-eastern outskirts of the city, but it filled Anton with dread.

CHAPTER THIRTY-SEVEN

SOMEHOW ANTON PULLED HIMSELF THROUGH THE following week. Rafiq's funeral was more painful than he thought he could bear. Rafiq's father, Talat Hasanov, spoke to no one as he stood by the graveside, staring at his son's shrouded body with such anguish that Anton didn't dare catch his eye.

I am responsible for this. How will I ever make amends?

The Imam's singing of the Koranic prayers echoed around the hillside and pierced Anton's heart. If he hadn't persuaded Rafiq to continue working on the tanker plans after the caravanserai attack, he'd still be alive. Rafiq had warned Anton about Standard Oil – he had known their tactics and understood the dangers. Anton had underestimated their ruthlessness and had overestimated his own invincibility.

After the funeral he sank into a melancholy that he had no desire to climb out of. Most nights he sat up smoking opium and staring across the Caspian. He slept through many days. Klara would appear now and again to bring him food, but Anton had little appetite. John Seigenberg called regularly, they had dinner and played poker, but conversation was an effort. It was early May but already the days were hot, as if someone had flicked a switch from winter to summer. The sun transformed the Caspian into a brilliant blue mirror reflecting hundreds of towering masts and white sails. Some days he would sit and stare out of the top window. Other days he frequented the opium dens near the railway. The sweltering cellar rooms were kept cool by an army of ceiling fans that scythed the air. He would lie underneath them, close his eyes and retreat into oblivion.

*

The Pallid Harrier was furious. The failure to acquire the tanker plans had been one of his greatest disappointments. If he had someone to blame, it would have been better. At least he'd have had the satisfaction of making someone pay for the mistake, but even that had been denied him. The bandit leader was dead, the greasy travelling salesman unresponsive, and his replacement for Hamilton Fretwell blameless. Rockefeller was incandescent now the plans were beyond his reach. Marcus Samuel had reached London and the British Prime Minister had already begun talks with the Suez Canal authorities.

His only satisfaction came with the death of the engineer, Rafiq Hasanov. Sabroski had taken his friend's death very badly and now spent most of his days lost to the poppy.

But he wasn't through with Sabroski yet. He would destroy the oilfields the Rothschilds had so foolishly financed. Those fields would be finished by the time Sabroski recovered.

*

One morning Anton had a visitor. It was Julia Seigenberg. She wore a drab cream dress buttoned up to her neck with seed pearls. Her face was pale and there were dark circles under her eyes.

'I will not stay long.' She fiddled with her hat pin and

248

adjusted her silk shawl. 'I'd like to talk to you about Rafiq. I know about the tanker plans.'

Anton flinched. 'I don't want to talk about Rafiq. If that's what you came here for you've wasted your time. I don't wish to be discourteous, Julia, but I'm very poor company at the moment.'

'Perhaps I will take some tea after all,' Julia said sitting down on the divan. She dropped a pink beaded bag with the design of an owl into her lap.

'My part in the project is over. Marcus Samuel has the tanker plans and he can do what he likes with them.'

'I think you need to find Rafiq's codebook.'

'What codebook?'

'The one Rafiq kept his notes in. The codes to the tanker plans.'

Anton clicked his tongue. 'How do you know about that? Not that it's important. The whole world must know about the tanker plans by now.' He stood up. 'I never want to hear about the Suez Canal again. I should never have got involved.'

Julia narrowed her eyes. 'I loved Rafiq and I know how much his work meant to him. If you are not going to do anything about it, I will.'

Anton lit a cigarette. 'If I had any idea where Rafiq kept those codes, I would find them. But I don't. It's unlikely they exist. You know Rafiq probably never wrote them down. Just kept them in his head.'

Her eyes flashed. 'But he *did* write them down. Rafiq had a notebook. A black leather one. It was full of drawings and numbers.' Julia blushed. 'I saw it when I was in his office. He must have taken it to Tiflis.'

'He couldn't have. I went through all his effects in the mortuary.'

'Then it must still be in his office.'

'The entire house has been cleared out. I helped his father last week. I looked through his papers to see if anything had been written down. I never saw a notebook.'

'Wouldn't it be worth asking his father, just in case he found it and put it somewhere? He may not have realised its importance.'

Anton shook his head. 'I don't want to disturb the family again.' He sat down beside her and took her hands. 'Look, I know you loved him, Julia, and doing this somehow keeps him alive. But he's gone. His work too. If there ever was a notebook and it did contain codes, he would have taken it to Tiflis to give to Marcus. Perhaps it was in his pocket and when we were attacked it fell out.'

She pulled her hand away. 'I won't waste any more of your time. I'm sorry to have bothered you.'

'Forgive my abruptness. Stay and have tea and I promise to be better behaved.'

'No thank you. I've changed my mind.' She picked up her bag. 'Look after yourself, Anton.'

*

Julia crossed the road and made towards the city park. She found a bench under a tree and sank into the shade. Now she would have to do this on her own.

Oh Anton, what a disappointment you are! How can you give up so easily?

She had felt certain Anton would rally at the news of the notebook. The old Anton might have, but he had changed – his strength had leeched away just like Rafiq's life had done. He seemed empty and purposeless in his grief like her father had been when her mother died. This is what death did to you: it wasn't just the victims who died.

She opened her beaded bag and took out the key Rafiq had given her. It was large and heavy and rusting slightly at the edges.

She closed her fingers over it and felt the hard iron surface. It was almost impossible to believe that Rafiq had gone from her life and that she would never see him again.

She closed her eyes and breathed slowly to compose herself. Then she stood up, opened her parasol, and strode down the hill towards Parapet Square.

Behind the Armenian church, on the corner of Mariyinskaya, she spied the familiar shop that sold tobacco and water pipes. A man in a turban was sitting in the doorway smoking a shisha pipe, the water bubbling in the bowl. She drew in the smell of charcoal and spices as she went inside and bought a slim gold tin with *Sobranie Black Russian* engraved across the top. Rafiq's favourites.

The upper part of the house was covered in a leafy vine. It had grown over the weeks and bunches of immature grapes dangled down.

Julia pulled the key out of her bag, unlocked the door and stepped into the cool darkness of the entrance hall. It was almost black except for a fan of light filtering through the half-moon lunette window. She climbed the steps to the upstairs room that stretched across the width of the house. It was green and bright and empty and she breathed in his space. The large desk that dominated the room had gone, as were his papers, books, maps and instruments. She walked the length of the room, her footsteps echoing in the emptiness. She saw remnants of his work on the floor: scraps of paper, a broken protractor, a pencil with a chewed end. She looked inside the bedroom. That was empty as well, except for an old broken chair pushed up against the fireplace. The iron bedstead was gone and the wooden cupboard and the marble washstand.

Where are you now, Rafiq? What version of heaven have you gone to? Or have you turned to dust like some believe?

She turned back to the main room. There was a pool of dappled sunlight in the corner. She returned to the bedroom, took hold of the old chair and dragged it into the ellipse of light and sat down. She opened her bag, pulled out the cigarette tin, a cigarette lighter that belonged to her father, and a small silver flask. She stared at the cigarette tin adorned with the Russian imperial eagle and prised it open. The cigarettes were smaller than she remembered: slim with a black wrapper and a gold foil filter. She put one in her mouth and tried to light it.

She had no idea how to smoke – it had amused Rafiq whenever she tried. He would light it for her, show her how to draw the smoke in and out through her nose, and then kiss her as soon as she started coughing, which usually happened within a few seconds.

She unscrewed the silver flash and drank in small gulps and felt the vodka burning her lips and throat.

The light in the room slowly began to fade as the sun moved, and she felt as though she were sitting in a leafy glade with sparrows chattering and flying in and out of the trellis to peck at grapes.

She wasn't sure how long she'd sat there, cocooned in a warm trance, full of disconnected thoughts. The silver flask had slid to the floor, but she didn't pick it up.

It was late afternoon when she opened her eyes. Her head hurt and she felt sick. She picked up the flask and pushed it down into her bag.

The room looked different in the fading light. Long shadows shivered across the floor as the vine swayed in the breeze. Only the two fireplaces stood immovable: solid, black, and glistening. She wondered how many women had been in this room. Apparently, Rafiq's father had kept love letters from his mistresses here. Had Rafiq kept her letters, or torn them up as soon as he'd read them? Maybe he'd laughed at them and found her love absurd? Ridiculous even. She would never know what he really thought of her. What decision had he come to on that train to Tiflis?

She thought about the love letters again. Rafiq said he'd found his father's letters by accident one day in a secret compartment. She could hear his words: *a summer hiding place.* Now that it was summer, the balcony was shrouded with green leaves and felt quite private. Julia opened the door, stepped out to pull at the stems, but the twisted boughs held no secrets. She went back inside and ran her hands over the walls, feeling for a loose brick, a fake section, the kind of secret chamber that her heroines found in novels. She stared at the fireplaces. Each one was made of stone and covered with black tiles and the front sections contained a small door that opened for coal. She crouched down and pulled each one open, but only ash spilled out.

Julia slumped with fatigue. Rafiq had probably burned her letters. He wanted to forget her and instead remember his wife. It was Leyla he loved, not her.

Julia looked up at the tiled column of blackness that stretched up to the ceiling.

And then she saw it.

The tiny metal lever below the mantelpiece was impossible to see from above. She closed her fingers around it and pulled and a letterbox section of the fireplace swung open. But there were no letters inside.

Instead, there was a black leather notebook fastened with an elastic strap.

CHAPTER THIRTY-EIGHT

KLARA WIPED THE SWEAT FROM HER FACE AND LEANED against the wall of the oil derrick. Wearily, she looked through the smoke to where she'd last seen Rasoul with an iron pipe in his hand, charging a gang of men.

There had been two raids already this week and this was the third. The attacks were increasing in savagery. She didn't know where they were coming from – trouble had been bubbling for weeks. At first it was mutterings about pay and complaints that wages were too low. Klara had defended Anton, explaining that reopening the oilfields was a risk and a challenge for everyone. But someone had planted the Rothschild name amongst the dissenters, spreading stories of great wealth and exploitation. Each new hiring bred voices louder than others. Arguments became more forceful, and some weak-minded newcomers listened too much.

Klara's heart leapt as drilling tools were hurled from the top of the derrick. The mangled instruments crashed into the mud and flung dirt high in the air. In the distance, three men wrenched open the boiler room to smash the steam engine inside. The twang of iron on metal resonated through the fog. She looked round in despair. *We're going to lose everything.* There was nobody to help and nobody could stop what was happening – least of all Anton.

For the past three weeks, Klara had said little to Anton as he slipped into melancholy. She understood the pain of death and loss, so bit her tongue and let things be. John Seigenberg had attempted multiple diversions to lift Anton's mood, but Klara doubted anything but time would work. She knew the soul had to sink down and lie at the bottom of the seabed while life bustled above. Anton would mend when ready.

Rasoul appeared at her shoulder. He had a black eye and a large cut across his forehead. 'They're leaving.' He indicated a score of men running and jumping on board a couple of wagons that splattered across the field.

'Who do you think is doing this?'

Rasoul swore. 'A rival company. Oil barons who fear more competition. It could even be the Okhrana who have heard of our plans to set up cooperatives. Cooperatives smack of revolution.'

'Those plans are a long way off. We're only trying to see how much oil these fields have.'

'The low wages are a problem. The Rothschilds need to do more.'

Klara threw up her hands in frustration. 'But they're not going to do any more. These are Anton's fields not theirs. It's only a loan and we have limited funds.'

'The men don't believe you.'

'Sometimes I think you don't believe me either,' she snapped. 'I'm going home. I'll see if I can talk sense into Anton Nikolayevich.'

Rasoul snorted. 'What's he going to do? Can't even look after himself.'

Klara left the smouldering fields and rode along the Bailov road. It was almost June, and the summer was looming. She could feel the heat building up ready to explode like a neglected stew pot. The lethargy of those stifling days would surely hinder them further. She seemed to have lost Anton Nikolayevich just when she needed him most.

Klara realised how much she depended on Anton's energy and determination, however infuriating he could be. It was as if they fed off each other: his recklessness and temper set a fire in her that at first she took for dislike, but she had been wrong.

She remembered the first time she'd seen him, dripping wet talking to a fisherman. *Jesus, how I cursed you! Coming back here to interfere in my life. I lay in bed praying for something to make you go away. And now it has.*

She spurred her horse and rode fast until she reached Nikolaevskaya Street. The grand old house looked strong and resilient with the sun glinting off its newly mended windows. All the broken panes had been replaced and the rotten sills and frames had been restored. Anton had painted the iron railings outside and fixed the hinges of the huge arched door. It was a shame he couldn't treat himself with the same care and attention.

Klara led the horse across the courtyard and pulled off her hat and gloves. Movement in the courtyard caught her eye. A figure was sitting under the mulberry tree throwing crumbs to the doves.

It was Julia Seigenberg.

*

Anton propped himself up on a cushion in the opium den and inhaled. An exhilarating rush coursed through him. The girl leaned forward into the light of the lamp. She twisted the raw sticky opium around a pin and held it in the heat, gradually turning it while it cooked. It bubbled and crackled as it hardened.

The girl handed the pipe to him. She had dark kohl eyes and full red lips, a low-cut bodice and her breasts partially exposed. He could have her if he wanted, but he had no desire.

The place seemed noisier than usual, and he sensed anger in the room. A girl shouting, a man speaking. A harsh familiar laugh.

*

The gig screeched to a halt and Julia and Klara climbed down. A crowd of men were streaming around the railway station entrance and others were lounging outside the dilapidated Hotel London. A man with an oversized flat cap approached them and grinned through tobacco-stained teeth. 'Can I help you ladies? Looking for some clients?'

'Piss off,' Klara snapped.

'Where is this place?' asked Julia. She'd never been to this part of town and never experienced such shabbiness. The Icheri Sheher was squalid and dirty, but here in the backstreets amongst the opium dens there was a feeling of menace and decay.

Klara pointed. 'Over there, underneath that laundry sign.'

A two-storey house beside the run-down hotel had a metal sign showing clothes pegged on a line. Klara held onto her hat and ran across the road, her maroon-and-white skirt billowing like a sail.

Steps led down from the laundry to a basement door with a metal grill. Klara knocked and the grill scraped back.

'What do you want?'

'We have an urgent message for Anton Nikolayevich.'

'No one by that name here.' The grill rasped shut.

Klara banged on the door and shouted. 'Anton Nikolayevich is expecting us. He told me he'd be here.'

The grill slid back. 'Wait.'

Five minutes passed before the door opened and a man in a

black cap with red tassels beckoned them inside. His skin looked like yellow paper that had been scored with a knife.

Julia's heart raced as a sweet smell hit her. She'd heard of these places and knew her brother, Alfred, had been to one, but she had imagined opium dens would be like the saloon bars on the Bibi-Eibat road, with drinking, smoking, card playing and prostitutes. But this place wasn't like that. The pungent, flowery smell made her head reel. The room was dark and hot, and parts of it had been sectioned off with screens. Dirty rattan rugs covered the floors and ceiling fans whipped the air. A yellow haze stretched like a gauze between the walls. Wooden pallets covered in cushions served as bed-like couches. Beside each bed, a low table had a lacquered tray of objects: pipes, needles, a small lamp and knives. Scantily dressed girls tended to each man.

Julia's eyes widened. One girl smiled and beckoned her over. Julia walked across – she didn't know why. The girl pulled Julia down on the couch and stroked her hair. She was very pretty with high cheekbones and a rosebud mouth.

'You are very beautiful,' the girl said. 'Are you starting today?' She kissed Julia's neck and put both hands on her breasts. Julia froze. The girl smelt of musk and sex.

'I've found him,' said Klara, appearing at her shoulder.

Julia stood up in a confusion of revulsion and fascination.

Klara pulled her away. 'Take care. These girls like European women. They are easier to please than men.' She gripped Julia's hand and guided her to the far end of the room.

Anton was lying flat on his back with his eyes closed. Painted dragons with long tongues and fiery eyes stared out from lacquered screens. The girl who'd been tending him stood up and slipped on her robe. A Chinese lantern with long red tassels swayed as she passed.

Julia noticed Anton's loose white shirt was open. Strange ink markings covered one of his shoulders – a criss-cross of lines and shapes, much like one she'd seen on his wrist.

'Anton,' Julia whispered. 'I found Rafiq's notebook.'

'Rafiq's dead,' he murmured.

'Come away from this place.'

'Why?'

Klara spoke. 'Please come home, Anton.'

'Klara? What are you doing here?'

Klara gently took the pipe away from Anton and handed it to Julia.

Anton's eyes opened, pupils like tiny dots. 'Are you going to make me another pipe?'

'The opium's finished. We'll find you some more later.' Klara leaned closer. 'You must trust me, Anton. You trust Julia, don't you?'

Anton nodded groggily.

'Then come with us. It's important. You can come back later.'

Anton didn't respond at first. Then slowly he nodded.

They hooked themselves under each of his arms and pulled him to his feet. Anton's legs shook and swayed, but they made their way towards the door. The man with the yellow paper face watched in silence.

To the left of the exit Julia recognised Albert Prankman lying down with his eyes closed, a monocle dangling round his neck. A girl appeared from behind a screen with a split lip and a black eye. She lowered her voice. 'Be careful of the American. He's vicious. Look what he did to me. Last week he did the same to another girl, but he'll get what's coming to him.'

'Thanks for the warning,' said Klara quickly. 'We'll take care.'

'Where are you taking him?' The girl looked at Anton with interest.

'He's our special client. We're taking him home.'

'Special treatment? Lucky man,' she said. 'And lucky you. He's a good-looking one and nice. Not like the creep in there.'

CHAPTER THIRTY-NINE

ANTON TURNED THE PAGES OF RAFIQ'S NOTEBOOK AND stared at the codes. It had been a week since Julia and Klara had found him in his opium hideaway and he burned at the thought. He rubbed his eyes and yawned. Even though he'd slept for hours after they'd found him, lethargy latched onto him like a leech. He craved a pipe but forced himself to push away the urge. Doctor Levon visited every day with an opium potion – a milder form of the drug, mixed with tobacco. Anton was to smoke only one a day and chew the leaves of a plant called *Mitragyna speciosa*. It had elliptical green leaves that looked like they'd come from a lime tree.

Anton knew this melancholy would have to be borne before it dragged him down further. The last few weeks had demonstrated how easy it was to be thrown off balance and lose sight of what was important.

How could you have let this happen? You know the dangers, you've witnessed it yourself enough times.

Rafiq would not have wanted this grief. In addition, Klara had told him what had happened to the oilfields. It shamed Anton to realise that while he had been wallowing in oblivion, the fields had come under attack.

Klara appeared in a cheap maroon-and-white print day dress with gathered sleeves and pearl buttons down the front. 'Shall I take the notebook to the post office?'

'No. I'll do it myself. I need a walk.'

It was nearly midday by the time he'd finished sending a cable to Marcus, followed by the package with the notebook and a letter. Anton didn't set foot anywhere near Telephonaya street. The post office would not be safe – undoubtedly monitored by Standard Oil spies. Instead, he engaged the services of a trustworthy courier recommended by John Seigenberg. The man was used to ferrying items of international security and was aware of the price of interception. The man's worn clothes and untidy beard and hair made him look unremarkable. The courier had one of those bland, average faces people found difficult to recall, which was exactly what was needed.

The thought of Marcus's pleasure at receiving the codes buoyed Anton, and he wandered through Parapet Square towards the saloon bar of the Hotel Continental. There he sat in the window nursing a whisky feeling a sense of release now the notebook had gone. It was up to Marcus now.

The reasons why Rafiq had hidden the notebook remained unclear, but Anton concluded the caravanserai attack had prompted Rafiq to separate the cipher from the tanker plans for added security. He must have been intending to send the codebook to Marcus once the plans arrived safely in London.

Anton stared out of the window into Parapet Square at people going about their business. The last month had been a painful blur, but he couldn't allow grief to disable him further. He could no longer help Rafiq, but he could still vindicate his father from the speculation surrounding Sabroski Oil. He was determined to set the matter straight though it would probably lead to more trouble, but he really didn't care.

Anton started as Stefan Brakov slumped into the seat opposite, drenching the air with citrus cologne. Stefan slurred his words, making his chiselled, handsome features twist with scorn. 'Anton. This is a surprise. Thought you'd given up on life. Heard you'd taken up residence near the railway station.'

Anton frowned. Despite the heat, Stefan was dressed in a grey cashmere morning suit, a silk waistcoat, and a floppy black bow tie.

'Aren't you hot in those clothes, Stefan?'

'You're not suggesting I go native, are you?'

Anton looked down at his own white cotton trousers and shirt as Stefan crossed his slim legs, better to admire his patent leather pointed shoes. 'Have you thought about my father's offer to join Brakov Oil?'

The steward handed Anton a whisky. 'No. Frankly, I want nothing to do with Brakov Oil.' He yawned. 'If you don't mind, I'd like to be alone. I'm in no mood for idle chatter.'

Stefan wrinkled his brow as if in pain. 'Is that how you see me? As idle chatter? That's the sort of thing my father would say.'

'It was just a figure of speech.'

Stefan leaned forward. 'Why can't you be more civil? We've known each other all our lives and yet you make no effort at friendship.'

Anton spread his hands. 'Why do you *want* my friendship? We don't even like each other.'

'Oh, I get it. Your travels in the Orient have made you a man of the world. And stay-at-home-Stefan is terribly dull.' Stefan sat back in his chair, his eyes glassy and unfocused.

Anton looked away. *Oh, fuck off, Stefan.* It was ironic how men saw their own fortunes. Stefan had wealth, a beautiful wife, and he was adored by his mother, but still he dwelt on the bitter side of life. It seemed to Anton that Stefan wanted something he had, or thought he had.

'Why do you think you're so much better than me? Why have

you always preferred types like Hasanov to the company of gentlemen?'

'Damn you, Stefan.' Anton pushed his drink aside and stood up. 'What makes you say things like that? And you wonder why I avoid your company. I pity you, Stefan. There's so much meanness in you. I wonder how your wife can endure it.'

Anton took his hat and cane and made his way through the bar. Over his shoulder he heard a chair scrape back and footsteps behind him. He winced at a sharp pain in his lower back.

'You dare speak of my wife like that.' Stefan was using his own cane to prod Anton's spine painfully.

Anton spun round and seized the end of Stefan's cane and twisted it away. 'Get home to her then and stop making a damn fool of yourself.'

Stefan swung a punch. Anton ducked and grabbed him, propelling him backwards into a chair. Stefan landed on the floor with a thud, knocking into a steward carrying a tray of drinks.

Anton strode across the bar and into the foyer and out through the revolving hotel doors.

By the time Anton arrived home his mouth was dry, and he was drenched in sweat. He strode through the front door and ran up the stairs and tore off his sticky clothes. Then he lay naked on the bed and closed his eyes. He opened them again when he heard Klara calling through the door. 'Are you all right?'

Anton pulled a sheet over himself. 'Yes. Leave me be.' He looked at the clock on the mantelpiece. *Seven o'clock.* He'd been asleep for three hours. He padded across to the washstand, sloshed water over his face and stared at his reflection. Dark shadows hung under his eyes and flecks of grey touched his hair. His skin had a dull pallor and new wrinkles had appeared. Life seemed to be seeping away as he languished in self-pity. Was this how Stefan felt every day – defeated and resigned?

He drank a glass of water and got dressed and went down to the drawing room.

Klara had prepared a bowl of okroshka cold soup and a dish of pirozhki. The crescent-shaped buns were filled with meat and potato and smelled of roasted onions. He forced himself to eat and drank a whole pot of tea.

Klara was apparently busy pouring over the accounts, listing the damages and losses from the oilfield attacks over the past weeks, but Anton could tell she was watching him. After he had finished eating, he pushed the plate to one side and looked up at her. 'I want a full list of names – individuals, whole teams. All those you think are troublemakers.'

'What are you going to do?' she said.

'Fight back,' he said.

CHAPTER FORTY

JULIA FELT SICK THE MOMENT SHE OPENED HER EYES. SHE could feel sweat trickling down between her breasts. Throwing back the bedcovers, she ran across to the washstand and vomited into the basin. She stood over the china bowl retching and pushing back damp strands of hair that dangled across her face until her stomach settled, and she began to shiver. Clasping her arms around herself, she padded across the room, climbed back under the bedcovers and closed her eyes.

This had happened every morning for a week.

She guessed two weeks ago – not because she'd hadn't bled for two months (although from gossip she knew what that meant), but because she wasn't the same any more. She pulled up her nightgown and ran her hands over the smooth tight skin than stretched from her belly button to the top of her pubic hair, and then across to the pelvic bones. Her stomach felt warm and soft. She rested her hand there feeling the tiny rise and fall of her body as she breathed.

She wasn't frightened, though the consequences would be hard being an unmarried girl with a baby. Her father would be disappointed, her stepmother furious. She was sad about that, but none of it seemed to matter. A part of Rafiq lived inside her, and even though she knew it was madness to feel pleased, she was pleased. Very pleased. But then she'd become a little mad with the obsession she'd had for Rafiq. His death had numbed her, until now. Elation – that she hadn't felt for so many months – leapt in her.

She would have to tell Miranda of course, and she also considered confiding in Klara. A few weeks ago that would have been unthinkable, but there was a non-judgemental energy about Klara that gave Julia energy and lifted her spirits.

There was a knock at the door and her stepmother appeared. 'Still asleep, Julia? Is something wrong? Sveta said you sounded ill.' Diane Seigenberg walked over to the window to open the shutters and gazed at the porcelain basin. 'How long have you been ill?'

'Just today. It must have been something I ate.' Julia pulled at the drawstrings on her nightgown.

'Why didn't you say before? Nobody else has been ill. We all ate the same thing.'

'It's nothing. I feel fine now.' Julia slid out of bed and stood up. Her stepmother stepped closer and felt Julia's forehead. She cupped Julia's chin and looked at her face. 'You're very pale. Get dressed and come downstairs. Leo's here.'

Leo was waiting for her in the drawing room pacing up and down. Julia felt a stab of guilt as she came in and he bounded over. 'Julia. I hear you haven't been well. I'm sorry to hear that.'

'It's nothing.' She held out her hand. 'It's lovely to see you, Leo. I'm sorry I haven't been very companionable lately.'

He beamed and kissed her. 'Not to worry. I imagine that tragic business of Rafiq Hasanov hasn't helped.'

Immediately Julia felt the familiar crushing sensation rise in her chest.

Leo's smile drained. 'I'm sorry. I shouldn't have mentioned it. Stupid of me.'

'No, don't be silly.' With a huge effort she forced a smile. 'It was terrible to...' Julia paused; she couldn't bear to say his name, '... to hear of his death. Dreadful for his family and for Anton of course. They were best friends.'

Leo was watching her anxiously. 'Let's not talk of such things, Julia. Shall we go for a walk?'

Julia nodded. It would be a relief to enjoy the morning air before the heat of the day became too overwhelming. 'I'll fetch my parasol.'

They walked in silence. Julia wondered what Leo would think when he found out. Leo was her oldest friend She had known him since childhood and confided in him about everything, but this was the one matter she couldn't discuss.

'Let's sit by the pond.' Leo took her arm and guided her down the steps between the trees to the benches arranged in semicircles a few yards away from the water.

Julia sat down and fixed her eyes on two boys in navy blue sailor suits clutching wooden sail boats. She hoped Leo didn't want to talk too much. Nearby, several tabby cats with watery eyes scavenged the ground looking for food.

'Julia.' Leo rested his cane against the bench. 'I have some news.'

She turned to look at him.

'My father's agreed to let me teach at the conservatory. He'll give me an allowance.'

'That's marvellous. You'll be able to give up your favourite study of oil!'

Leo grinned. 'Yes. Never was much good as a businessman, was I? I think my father's always known that.'

Julia touched his arm. 'I'm pleased for you, Leo. When will you start?'

'I'm not sure. I'm waiting to hear when I can go.'

'Go? What do you mean?'

'It's not the Baku Conservatory I'm talking about. It's the one in Moscow.'

She blinked. 'Moscow? Why not Baku?'

'There are better opportunities there. But I can always come back to Baku.' He paused. 'I'll miss you, Julia.'

A tremor ran through Julia. She assumed that Leo would always be there for her. 'I'll miss you too.'

'You will?'

'Yes of course. You've always been my dearest friend.'

Leo stared at her, and she looked away. The park was crowded. A large group of women passed them, their faces covered apart from two holes cut for their eyes. Domes of parasols nodded along the wide paths, many trimmed with ribbons and bows. One had a stuffed bird on top.

'I don't want to go, Julia,' Leo confessed. He began tracing a shape in the dust with the toe of his shoe.

'Don't tell me you'll miss the oilfields of Baku?' She examined the handle of her parasol. The knob was as large as a billiard ball and quite ugly.

'No. I think you know the reason why.'

'Do I?' *Don't say anything, Leo.*

'It's because I'll miss you too much.'

'Don't be silly. You'll soon forget me. I'm sure the women in Moscow are far more refined than I am.'

'You've always had a low opinion of yourself, Julia. I've never understood why.'

Julia looked down at her hands. An argument had broken out between the two boys at the pond. One of them had lost his sailor's cap in the water. A man strode towards them – probably the boys' father.

'I always hoped you'd think of me more than just a good friend,' Leo said. 'Because I love you, Julia. I've always loved you. I can think of no one else but you.'

Julia concentrated on the man who had picked up a stick and was trying to retrieve the boy's cap. *Oh, Leo. I'm not who you think I am. Not any more.*

'I want to marry you, Julia. My father will ensure we have enough money.' He took her hand. 'Could you marry me?'

Julia felt sadness sink over her like a veil. She felt like such a fraud. Leo loved a version of her that wasn't real any more. Once he knew the truth, he would think her tainted. He would regret his words and be embarrassed by his declarations of love. But for the moment, she was everything Leo desired. She would probably never experience such utter adoration from a man again.

For a few moments Julia tried to capture the passion. Then she pulled her hand away. It was a self-indulgent emotion and one that she must learn to do without. She turned to face him. 'I can't marry you, Leo. It wouldn't be fair.'

'I know you don't love me in… that way. But it doesn't matter. You are everything I want in a woman. As for the physical side of marriage, we can be like brother and sister until you get used to the idea. It needn't be something that's very important.' His eyes were pleading. 'I want you in my life.'

Julia wanted to cry because she understood his desperation. The pain of rejection was probably the worst pain of all. She couldn't bear the thought that she was about to inflict this on Leo. Her only comfort was knowing it would be short-lived.

'I'm not what you think, Leo,' she began, pulling away from him. 'You don't really know me.'

He laughed. 'Yes, you're right I suppose. I've only known you for the last eighteen years. We've spent every holiday together, every Easter, every Christmas. You're like a stranger to me.'

Julia didn't smile. 'I've changed. There are things about me that you don't know. Things I'm capable of doing that would shock you.'

'I'm glad to hear it. It makes you even more interesting. I like being shocked.'

'Don't laugh at me. I'm being serious.'

'What could you possibly have done that could be so terrible?'

She looked away. Should she tell him the truth? It was a thought that had been creeping up on her as she'd sat on the bench, watching the children. It would be the fairest thing to do, then Leo wouldn't spend days and weeks in anguish hoping she'd change her mind.

'I know about Rafiq,' Leo said softly.

She felt her stomach contract. 'What do you mean?'

'It was obvious you were in love with him. I could tell from the way you looked at him. Is that the reason you think you can't marry me?'

'Partly.' Julia knew he was staring at her. It was time to begin the unravelling. 'We used to meet.' She could feel the air thicken between them, folding his anguish inside.

A breath of air blew up from the sea and he sighed. 'I would have been a fool not to expect that. How can you love someone and not see them?'

'Rafiq had an office on Mariyinskaya Street.'

'Yes. Anton Nikolayevich told me.' He stood up abruptly. 'I think we should return to the house. It's getting very hot.'

Julia started to protest. She wanted to tell him everything, but he held up his hand.

'Don't say any more. It would make me very happy to marry you, whatever you think you've done. Nothing could make me not love and respect you. Remember that. Nothing.'

Leo held out his arm. Julia took it and stood up and they walked back through the park in silence.

A few days later Julia confided in Miranda.

'You *must* marry him,' said Miranda.

'I can't,' said Julia. 'As soon as he hears the truth, he won't want me.'

'Julia, listen. You can't have a baby and not be married.'

'I don't care what people say.'

Miranda sighed. 'You think you don't at the moment, but you will do later. You don't understand how hard it will be.'

Julia studied her friend. They'd been sitting in the courtyard of the Brakov house all afternoon, drinking tea and discussing her 'situation', as Miranda referred to it. Julia knew Miranda would suggest a sensible solution, but she didn't feel like being sensible. She hadn't been at all sensible over her affair with Rafiq, so why should she start being sensible now? Julia looked into her lap and played with the orange fringe of her sleeve.

'How many months are you?'

'Two or three – I'm not sure exactly when. I'm not going to do this, Miranda. I wouldn't be happy, and I'd make Leo unhappy. I want more for myself than this.'

'There isn't any more. You just think there is.'

Julia sighed. 'That feeling was so strong. I want it again and I don't have it with Leo.' She could feel the bow at the back of her dress digging into her waist. Surely she couldn't have put on weight already.

'You don't need that feeling to be happy. Be thankful you've experienced it at all and be thankful that it's gone. It's destructive and it's not real.'

'I don't think you like men very much.'

'I just want you to understand the reality of passionate love,' Miranda urged. 'It's a fickle thing and very fragile. Many women of our station never feel passion as you have done. Treasure the memory and don't demand to feel it again. Besides, Rafiq was sort of... damaged. And in the end he would have damaged you. I

271

think, ultimately, Leo will make you happier than Rafiq ever could.'

'But it still doesn't solve the problem. I'm pregnant with another man's child.'

Miranda took Julia's hands. 'Leo's very much in love with you. I think he'll accept the child. Rafiq is dead. You can't be jealous of a ghost.'

Julia looked away from Miranda at a tall, thickset man dressed in traditional costume standing on guard in the archway of the courtyard. He had powerful shoulders, huge hands and feet, a black beard, and a long, curled moustache. A shiny, carved dagger was tucked into his belt.

Miranda stood and paced, beating her fan against the palm of her hand. 'You won't show until you are five or six months, especially if you're careful with the gowns that you wear. Nobody will ever know if you encourage Leo to go to Moscow. You'll have to say the baby came early, but once you are married people won't be counting the months. Those that do will assume you and Leo couldn't wait until your wedding day.'

'Why do you need a guard?'

'I beg your pardon?'

'The man in the archway.'

Miranda looked over. 'Fabian insists… Julia, are you listening to me?'

'Why do you need so much protection?'

'You're not listening to a word I'm saying, are you?'

'He looks like an assassin.'

Miranda clicked her tongue. 'He probably is.'

It was warm in the Brakov courtyard, but a chill came across Julia. A drooping mulberry tree stood nearby, dark berries staining the ground purple like blood. Rafiq had probably been murdered by such a man. A hired assassin, paid by someone too cowardly to do the deed themselves.

Julia felt the familiar burn of despair settle and knew that once that corrosive knot had formed, it would eat away at her for days.

CHAPTER FORTY-ONE

WHEN THE NEXT LETTER CAME, ANTON WAS OUT ON THE oilfield reassembling a vandalised steam engine. A piston rod had been detached, and two valves had been smashed, but he reckoned he could salvage it. It was only as he returned to his office that he found the letter on the table. Yet again it contained an illustration of a Fabergé egg, along with a caption:

The Memory of Azov Egg presented by Alexander III to Tsarina Maria Fyodorovna 1891.

This time the egg was carved from a solid piece of jasper, or bloodstone as it was known, and decorated with rubies and diamonds. The 'surprise' inside was a miniature naval cruiser: the *Pamiat Azova*. The accompanying paper and signature comprised a list of oil worker employees and a message: *Hired ruffians*, it said, *groomed for violence and revolt.*

Anton frowned. Some of the names on the list surprised him as he believed them loyal from his father's time. He opened the desk drawer and pulled out the list of troublemakers Klara had compiled from her dealings with the workforce. Some of the names matched with those on Klara's list, others did not. How could Katharine Lapinski know about these men? And why insist on such secrecy? Every day he checked the personal column of the *Vedomosti* but there was never a reply.

Klara sat cross-legged on the floor studying the two lists of names. It was three o'clock in the morning. Anton hadn't been able to sleep so had risen to make a hot drink and found Klara in the library.

'What are you doing up at this time?'

'Who's been giving you this information?' She waved the lists in the air.

'I don't know. Anonymous letters signed with the initials KL. Somebody who wants to help me find the truth.'

'KL?' She looked puzzled. 'Can I see?'

He nodded to the letters and newspaper cuttings on the desk. She got up and went over to look at them. 'How very odd.'

'Mean anything to you?'

'No.'

Anton took a sip of cocoa. Klara came over and sat. 'Are you going to get rid of these troublemakers?'

'Yes, but discretely. I shall need backup and new stout gates to close the field. Then it won't be so easy for those wagons to break through. We'll lay everyone off, make it look like we've given in.'

'But then what? How are you going to defeat them?'

'By uncovering the truth behind that secret key that Dmitry hid. It's got to open something important.'

'Did you go to the bank?'

'Yes. It's not a safe deposit key. It fits nothing here and nothing in Dmitry's old room at Frau Kalian's house. There's only one place left – where Dmitry spent most of his days.'

'Of course. The Sabroski Oil offices!'

Anton nodded. 'I think it's all linked. The ruffians on the oilfield, the bankruptcy, even the tanker plans.'

Klara jumped up. 'The Sabroski Oil offices are locked up and empty. When the company was sold, nobody cared about the old paperwork.' She hurried towards the door.

'Where are you going?' said Anton.

'Getting my tools ready to break in. Isn't that what you meant?'

*

Sabroski Oil stood on the corner of Bolshaya Morskaya Street. It was usually a busy road leading down to Merkuryevskaya and the major banks, but this early in the morning it was silent and still. Two street cleaners in blue cotton headscarves looked up as they passed. Anton glanced back at Klara, who was holding onto her bonnet and half running to keep up.

The door to Sabroski Oil was padlocked with a rusty chain. Maroon paint peeled off the carved surface and the lunette window was broken. The sandstone columns on either side of the door were dirty and stained. Anton tested the chain and opened a bag of tools he'd brought with him. He selected a hacksaw with a pistol grip.

'Hold the chain tight and keep a lookout.'

He pulled the small blade backwards and forwards across the rusty surface. It rasped and scratched but made little impression.

'Here – let me try.' Klara dug into a brown leather purse that was hooked across her shoulder and pulled out two items: a flat, right-angled piece of metal and another that looked like a hair grip.

Anton stared at her. 'Where did you get those things?'

'I made them – a tension wrench and a lockpick. Here, hold the padlock up for me.' Klara pushed the pick into the upper

276

section of the keyhole, moving it backwards and forwards until she heard a faint click.

'Is that it?'

'No,' she murmured. 'Four more pins.'

Four clicks later, the padlock sprang open.

'That's how you got into my bedroom!' Anton remarked.

Klara unhooked the padlock and chain and tested the door handle. 'It's not locked!' she said as she pushed it open

Inside, the air was fetid and stale. Stone steps with a wrought-iron railing twisted upstairs towards a high arched window.

'Up there,' Klara whispered, as a mouse scuttled across the floor. She gathered her skirt and ran up the steps.

Anton looked round. He'd never been inside the building before. Sabroski Oil was always moving to larger and smarter venues as the company wealth grew in size. It was an odd feeling to be inside his father's old oil company, almost as if his father was watching.

A cat with a missing ear appeared on the stairwell, meowing. 'How did you get in here?' Anton cooed. It rolled on its back eyeing him hopefully, then jumped up and darted up the stairs. Anton hurried to catch up with Klara, who had stopped outside a door. 'Need another hair grip?'

She pulled out a bundle of keys. 'No need. I still have my keys. Let's see if they work.' She selected one from a brass ring and inserted it into the lock. It turned with a satisfying click.

The room beyond was tomb-like, with a musty, damp smell and wooden shutters clamped across the windows. A bank of narrow document cabinets lined the left wall and the three-drawer desk in the middle was cluttered with ink pots, fountain pens, a candlestick and a tarnished silver bell. A pedestal swivel leather chair lay on its side and a wicker basket full of crumpled papers had fallen over. 'This is where Dmitry worked,' said Klara. 'There's a storeroom in there.' She pointed to another door.

Anton took the silver key out of his pocket and looked

around. 'Let's get started.' He tested the key in a few of the locks, the drawers in the desk and the document cabinets and cupboards. Klara found a small carved wooden box hidden in the bottom drawer of the desk which looked promising but yielded nothing. A medicine box reeking of iodine, a locked compartment built into a shelf, and a tortoiseshell chest that looked like it had come from Persia all proved disappointing.

'Let's think about this,' said Anton. 'If you were storing documents somewhere, hiding them, what would you do?'

'I'd put them in a safe.'

'Does this look like a key to a safe?'

'Not really. Not the sort of safes I've seen.' Klara upturned the swivel chair and sat down. 'Maybe we've got this all wrong.'

'What do you mean?'

'You don't really know anyone... you don't. Not properly. I thought I knew Dmitry, but I didn't *really* know him. Maybe there are no incriminating papers after all.'

'Why are you suddenly doubting him?'

She sighed. 'That list of troublemakers you showed me. Those men have worked with Rasoul for years and were loyal to your father. It makes you wonder who *can* you trust?'

Anton regarded her. 'Most people have something to hide.'

'Like you,' she said. 'What happened to you in St Petersburg?'

'Nothing.'

'Something did. Something bad, which meant you had to go away.'

'Where did you hear that?'

'Your father told me.'

'What did he say?'

'That the Okhrana never forget. Once your name's on their list, you can never escape.' She fiddled with the ink pot on the desk. 'The day you found me in your room, I saw a photograph of you standing with your engineering colleagues at university. They had all signed the back. I couldn't decipher their names, except for one.'

Anton felt a chill sweep over him. Even after all these years, the images from that night haunted him. 'There were seven of us in all,' he began. 'Alexander Isayev, Serge Avdonin, Peter Bodrov, Ivan Vornovo, Michael Goncharov, Yuri Bulganin and me.'

'Tell me about them.'

'Alexander, Michael and Serge stayed in St Petersburg. I haven't heard from them for years.'

'And the others?'

'The others... Peter and Ivan,' he paused, '... they were arrested by the Okhrana. Nobody heard from them again.'

Klara stood very still. 'What did they do?'

'Nothing. But they liked to think out loud.'

'And what about the last one? His was the only clear signature.'

'Yuri Bulganin?'

Klara nodded.

'He's dead too.'

'I'm sorry.'

'Don't be. He deserved to die.'

'Why?'

'He was a spy for the Okhrana.' Anton fell silent. He hadn't talked about it for a long time. In the tomb-like office, the memory seemed even more oppressive. 'I don't want to talk about it.' He indicated. 'Why don't we try the storeroom?'

They came across four shelves of pigeonholes along the wall of the storeroom. The twenty slot storage unit was carved in walnut and fastened to the wall by two strong brackets. Each compartment was fifteen inches deep and bore a name engraved on a brass plate attached to a wooden lip. Anton held the flame of his cigarette lighter aloft, moving along the list of names, until he came to Dmitry Ivanovich Rabinovich.

He felt inside, but the pigeonhole was empty.

He ran his fingers across the name plates and asked Klara to bring the candles from the main office, the better to see more clearly.

'Do you know all these people?' he asked.

She studied the names, frowning. 'Most of them, except… that's odd. I don't remember Gerhard Kalian. In fact, I've never heard of him.'

'I have. It's Frau Kalian's husband.'

'Dmitry's landlady? Her husband never worked here. At least not when I was here.'

'He never worked here.' Anton grabbed a low stool and climbed onto it. Klara passed him the candle.

'I thought her husband worked in Tehran. He was a carpet merchant.'

'Indeed, which is why…' Anton reached into the pigeonhole. 'What have we here?' He had found a metal plate inside the pigeonhole. He took the key from Klara and inserted it into the lock and turned. A metal door swung open and bundles of papers fell out. Anton felt a thrill race through him as he gathered the papers and handed them to Klara.

They hurried back to the main room and threw them down on the desk.

Klara exclaimed. 'I still don't understand. What did Gerhard Kalian have to do with this?'

'Nothing.' Anton grabbed the first of the documents. 'But if you were hiding papers, you wouldn't use your own name, would you?'

'No, you wouldn't… but why Gerhard Kalian?'

Outside the room they heard the cat meow.

Anton stiffened and held up a warning hand. The cat was mewing constantly and then they heard a creak on the stairs. Klara flew to the door and quietly turned the key and beckoned him into the storeroom. Anton followed, feeling inside his jacket and cursing himself: in his haste that morning, he had forgotten his revolver.

Anton strained to listen. It could have been the cat playing on the stairs, but then he heard footsteps. Their tread was slow and heavy, as if the intruder was unsure of their footing. The candle crackled on the desk and went out.

The room fell into darkness.

Anton felt the warmth of Klara pressed up against him. She was clutching his arm, as if she feared he might run into the room and do something foolish.

The door handle turned, rattled and fell still. Then they heard a key being inserted into the lock. It jangled and fell short as it came up against the key on the other side. They heard more keys chink, and another one rattled in the lock before being withdrawn. Tense seconds passed. Eventually, the footsteps moved away.

'We're trapped. He knows we're in here,' whispered Klara.

'Probably gone for help.' Anton crept to the window and opened the shutters a fraction. He saw a man step out of the building. 'But there are two more coming up the road – he's signalling to them. Quick.'

Anton raced over to the desk and threw the documents into his bag. 'We must leave. Now.'

They sped out of the room and tore down the stairs. The main door was wide open and they heard voices and footsteps approaching. 'Too late,' Anton hissed. 'Get behind the door.'

'There's not enough space,' said Klara, and before Anton could protest she had run back up the stairs, her hair flying. Anton darted behind the door. There was just enough space between the door frame and the stone wall.

He heard three men stop outside.

'It's probably a vagrant. This padlock's rusted through.'

'No, it hasn't. Take a closer look. Someone's been at that with a hacksaw.' The chain rattled. 'There's somebody up in that room. It's been locked from the inside.'

'Probably jammed.'

'We'll take a look, but I can't imagine it's anything. Probably street children. There's nothing worth stealing. Place has been empty for ages.'

The third man swore. 'Best do as he says. We don't want trouble from the Yank.'

Anton heard a safety catch click off and saw a hand with dirty bitten nails grip the side of the door. 'I'll close this. If there's trouble, we'll need to keep it quiet. No point in alerting the authorities.'

Anton thought of Klara. He knew he only had seconds to act. Should he go for the man with the gun or smash the door hard against the other man? He didn't know what he'd do with the third. But before he had time to decide, he heard a loud smashing noise. Tinkling glass rained down the stairwell.

The men raced up the stairs. Anton listened, his heart banging in his chest. The men were opening doors, searching the rooms and shouting at one another. There was no indication they had found Klara. Desperately, Anton wracked his brains.

I must distract them to give her a chance to escape.

Then he heard horses trotting down the road.

Cossacks.

An idea shot into Anton's head. He tore outside and waved them down.

'What can we do for you, sir?' said one of the soldiers, slowing to a halt, a steel sabre hanging at his side.

'There's a robbery going on,' Anton gasped. 'Armed men broke the padlock and went in.'

'Indeed?' said the other soldier. They quickly dismounted and tethered their steeds.

Anton drew back, his stomach churning, as they drew swords and hastened into the building.

Anton lay in wait on the other side of the road, fighting the urge to go and see. He knew that if the Cossacks found her, it would prevent her from being harmed, but she'd be arrested for trespassing and property damage. Anton cursed. Alerting the Cossacks had probably made things worse.

He stared across the road, willing her to appear. The entrance door of Sabroski Oil gaped into the dim interior, but Anton could see nothing. The streets were waking up now, filling with gigs and carts. The day yawned and hot sunlight rose up from the sea.

Suddenly, Anton caught the glint of a Cossack sword, and a group of men emerged. Anton shrank back into the shadows. The tallest of the three men talked amiably with the soldiers as they padlocked the door and lingered in discussion. Then the Cossacks rode away and the men climbed into their gig and joined the traffic winding down to the waterfront.

Anton sped across the road, all senses alert for a sign of her. He didn't know how Klara would escape unless she knew a way to materialise through a solid wall. The door was locked, the courtyard barred by a solid iron gate. He paced the perimeter until something on the roof caught his eye.

Slithering across the roof tiles, brown boots stuck out like rudders, was Klara. Her maroon-and-white print dress billowed around her knees and her straw bonnet flew to the ground.

Anton threw off his hat and jacket and clutched an old vine dangling from the balcony. He began to hoist himself up.

Klara hissed from above. 'Don't be foolish, Anton. You'll injure yourself. I am perfectly capable. Get my hat.

'What?'

'My hat. Quick!'

Anton noticed at a strip of green ribbon waving in the air. An old woman had bent down to poke at it. Anton slithered down the vine and snatched it up. A thud followed as Klara's leather purse landed at his feet. A moment later, Klara had reached him, picked up her purse and hooked it over her arm.

Anton placed both hands on her thin shoulders. He didn't know whether to hug her or shake her. 'How on earth did you get out?'

'Through the skylight.' She grabbed her bonnet and pulled it down firmly on her head. 'It accidentally broke.'

CHAPTER FORTY-TWO

THEY HURRIED BACK TO THE HOUSE, EMPTIED THE BUNDLES of documents onto the floor, and set about reading them. Anton sent a message to John Seigenberg, who, expressing disapproval at what they had done, consented to join and help. The housekeeper provided plates of sweetbreads and meats which they feasted on late into the night.

Later still, Klara was sitting with a plate of apricots and lamb balanced in her lap unfolding papers and reading them. She looked up at Anton.

'Sabroski Oil had so many supply companies. Listen to this: *Aqua Terra Supplies – fifty yards of piping at sixty kopeks a yard. Kokoreff Manufacturers – feed pump and cylinder replacement for 180 roubles...* and there are many more. I've found eighteen different companies.'

Anton said, 'So, Zenovitch Liquid Fuel was just the parent company, overseeing scores of little supply companies.'

John took a sip of mint tea. 'That's why they're called supply companies. It's normal practice for big organisations.'

Klara clicked her tongue. 'And look at these debts. I'd no idea Sabroski Oil had so many. "*Apsheron Tool Company – invoice for fifty roubles for two-and-three-eighth-inch pipe drills and drill collars. Edward Stack and Son – invoice for a Davey Paxman Class B ten-inch-cylinder steam engine.* '"

They found many more as they continued to read.

Eventually Anton said. 'What's a deed of indemnity?'

John removed his glasses and rubbed his eyes. 'It's a legal document exempting someone from prosecution.'

Anton handed John a document. 'Here's one for a man called David Cherlin.'

'Can I see?' John smoothed down his hair and took the document. 'Could be an official at the Ministry of Finance.'

'Why would this David Cherlin need exempting?'

'He was probably asked to do something illegal,' John said. 'He may have bribed someone.'

'Which is what Dmitry was trying to expose.'

'Cherlin's name is on this registration document as well,' said Klara excitedly, handing Anton another paper. It was the original company registration for Zenovitch Liquid Fuel. Three Romanov coat of arm stamps were stuck on the bottom, franked by the official seal, and signed by David Cherlin.

Anton stared at the registration stamps. The inset showed St George on horseback killing a dragon. But the inset looked wrong somehow. Then he realised that the stamps were upside down. 'Look at this – the official stamps are invalid.'

Klara leaned over eagerly. 'Does it mean the registration is a forgery?'

'We must get it checked. John – you have contacts in the ministry. They would know.'

'Indeed, they would.'

'Do we have the addresses of these supply companies?'

'Yes,' Klara said, foraging through a pile of papers. 'A few of them are on the Apsheron peninsula near the Balakhani oilfields.'

The Apsheron peninsula jutted seventy miles into the Caspian Sea. Shaped like the head of an eagle, it spread its wings north and south to catch the wind sweeping across from the Caucasus. It took two hours to drive out to the tip where the Balakhani oilfields lay. They passed north from Baku through the refineries of the Black City, and then up the hill where the turquoise bay sparkled below. There, the road was nothing but sand and limestone track interspersed with clumps of spiky camel thorn.

Anton sat in the carriage in silence, churning over the events of the past few days. He wasn't sure what good would come of questioning the managers of the supply companies, except that talking to people with knowledge of the past might help him make sense of the present. He looked out of the phaeton window. Scores of pipelines ran down the hillside to the refineries and the land was pockmarked with iron reservoirs containing thousands of tons of oil.

Balakhani village was set alongside four hundred wooden derricks planted like a thick forest. A few hundred stone houses lay scattered over the hillside alongside wooden engine sheds.

The carriage squelched to a halt prompting them to open the door and step down. A group of men were standing around a cooking pot lodged in the rock. A metal pipe protruded from a crevice flaring gas. Anton stared at the phenomena. The whole peninsula was alight with flames that burned night and day. A man need only knock a hole in the limestone and hold a light to it for the gas to burn.

On the other side of the village an entire mountainside was burning. He'd first seen it as a boy – a mountain with flames shooting out from the hillside that had burned for hundreds of years. Rather like the flames in the Baku Bay fuelled by underground gas vents. As a child, Anton thought it was magic.

He looked towards the end of the peninsula where the Caspian swept across the rocks.

So much oil.

More than America. More than Russia and Europe. Probably more than anywhere else in the world.

And yet his father had been made bankrupt.

A bitter taste formed in Anton's mouth as he studied the ugly landscape. This is what greed had driven men to create and his father had been a part of it.

'Are we going over to the factories or are you staying to admire the scenery?' said Klara.

The factories were squalid, run-down areas with a fenced-off perimeter and some squat log cabins. Working men stood around an ugly limestone building that belched fumes from its chimney. One whistled at Klara and another laughed as she shouted an insult. A man dressed in a belted tunic and a fez sauntered over to them.

'This is private property.'

'We'd like to speak to your manager.'

'What do you want?'

Anton pulled out one of the invoices. 'I'm looking for the Kura Metals Company.'

'This is Blue Water Artisans. You're in the wrong place.'

Klara moved closer. The man eyed her with interest. 'We're sorry to ask so many questions but we wish to settle some debts. Is there somewhere we can talk? We realise you'll need to be compensated for your time.'

The man jerked his head towards one of the cabins.

The office interior reeked of tobacco and sweat. Flies circled a stack of dirty tea glasses and a bowl of grey sugar on a table. The man sat down and pulled out a packet of cigarettes. Anton gave him ten kopeks and spread the documents out on the table.

'Here's an invoice for Kura Metals, and another for Aqua Terra supplies. We need to know where to find these companies.'

The man lit his cigarette. 'Never heard of them.'

'How long has this factory been here? Could the names have changed?'

'I've worked here for ten years. Surankhani Tools and Blue Water Artisans are the only two companies here.'

'What about the other side of the peninsula?'

'Only oilfields over there. You've made a mistake. Whoever wrote these invoices got the addresses wrong.'

The next few days were equally as puzzling: Caspian Health Supplies proved to be a cowshed on the Seyidov family land; Kasparov and Son, the site of a disused pumping station; Kokoreff Manufacturers, a laundry house near the railway station, and Edward Stack and Son had no record of importing a Davey Paxman steam engine.

Anton knew trying to make sense of things would be hard, but it was proving a difficult week. Meanwhile, John Seigenberg had taken the registration certificate to the ministry and discovered that a few hundred incorrectly designed stamps had been issued in 1883. He told Anton that Zenovitch Liquid Fuel wasn't registered until March 1886, three years later. Such stamps had been recalled by then.

'So, we can prove the document is a forgery?'

'Indeed,' John said. 'If it was authentic, it would have stamps corresponding to the same year of registration.'

'We can prove the other companies are fraudulent as well. Whoever forged this charter is likely to have made the same mistake with the others.'

'Exactly. Not that we need much proof for the others. Few of them actually exist. But most importantly, Zenovitch Liquid Fuel is an illegal company. Which means you can apply to the courts for an investigation. The decision to liquidate Sabroski Oil may be reversed and the company returned to you.'

'But your son, Alfred – he works there. That's an odd coincidence.'

John agreed. 'Alfred will soon be looking for new employment!'

CHAPTER FORTY-THREE

KLARA HAD NOT SEEN MUCH OF ANTON AS HE'D BEEN BUSY with John Seigenberg preparing papers and statements for the court case. Everything had calmed down on the oilfield. She had done what Anton had asked and laid off the men. There had been a great deal of arguing and grumbling but, as she pointed out, they could not continue under the current threats of assault. Meanwhile, Rasoul had sturdy iron gates made and the old ones were taken down.

Klara found it hard to take her eyes off the troublemakers, the men she had thought trustworthy, as they stood in line waiting for wages. As she sat in the office ticking names off the ledger and handing each man seven and a half roubles and a basket of provisions. she looked long and hard into their faces.

By dusk, the field was quiet, and as Klara lit a lantern to go over the accounts, all she could hear was the hum of mosquitoes. Rasoul appeared, his hands stuffed in his pockets.

'How long can we stay closed for?'

She didn't look up. 'However long it takes.'

'What do you mean?'

'We don't have any money. It came from the Rothschilds.' She carefully blotted the last entry on the page and closed the ledger. 'We have bills for equipment coming in, so no wages for anybody, until we can reopen safely.'

Rasoul scowled. 'What are the men going to live on?'

'Fresh air.'

'What's the matter with you?'

She picked up her fan and cooled herself. 'The Rothschilds are not going to give Anton any more money. So, what do you suggest?'

'You could be more helpful. It's not the men's fault.'

'I'm sure a number of them won't go hungry. Sometimes you're so blind, Rasoul. It's always "them and us" with you.'

Rasoul spread his arms. 'Because that's how it is. There are rich and there are poor. There are those that exploit, and then there's the rest of us that get exploited. Anton Nikolayevich needs to persuade the Rothschilds to give us more money. He'll think of a way.'

'You don't care what happens to Anton, do you?'

Rasoul snorted. 'I don't care about the Rothschilds either. Oil barons are all the same – bloodsucking leeches.'

Klara lost her patience. She flung down her fan and wedged the ledger on the shelf behind her. 'I'm going to see Ivan.'

Klara rode down the Bailov road. She had told nobody about the court case or her knowledge of the fraud – not even Rasoul, who she'd known for years. There was no guarantee of justice, and many powerful men had connections to the law – this David Cherlin could well be one of them. Anton Nikolayevich had been buoyed up with the prospect of success, but she knew from experience the lengths rich men would go to protect their reputation and fortune.

A silver moon paved the way to Ivan's lodgings on the waterfront. Down near the docks, life couldn't be more different.

The salt in the air, the textures and smell – a vibrant contrast to the black and white of Bibi-Eibat. Here – despite the squalor and the dangers – Ivan could melt into the crowd. She stopped at the bakery, bought white cheese and flatbread and half a dozen kutabi pancakes filled with greens.

There were several large brigantines docked by the wharves surrounded by banks of soldiers. An official was nailing a public notice to one of the pier posts. She watched the soldiers move aside to let a familiar man with thick black spectacles pass. Clutching a black medical bag, Doctor Levon scurried down the narrow wooden pier towards the ships, both of which displayed yellow flags. She stared at the fluttering signals of distress and felt her heart hammer in her chest.

*

Stefan knew something was wrong. The atmosphere at home made his headaches worse, so much so that he'd spent the day lying down in a shuttered room. He wasn't sure what the problem was, other than it had something to do with Anton. His father stamped about the place, drinking too much and arguing with his mother. Many nights he wouldn't return until the early hours, or not at all. It was puzzling to think what Anton could have done. Thwarting his father always gave him pleasure, but he wasn't sure he wanted Anton to benefit, especially after that embarrassing scene at the Hotel Continental bar.

Stefan lay back on the couch and stared up at the ceiling fan buzzing over his head. He pulled out his Hunter pocket watch and clicked open the gold face to run his thumb over the engraving: *To my beloved son.* His father gave him the watch on his sixteenth birthday, passed down from father to son over the Brakov generations. The watch belonged to happier days... to the days before...

Stefan frowned. Before what exactly? Before Prankman

arrived? Before Sabroski Oil was ruined? Before Anton left for the Orient?

He snapped the watch face shut and slipped it back into his pocket. Years ago, he'd asked his mother what he'd done to anger his father. She had put her arms around his shoulders and cried.

It had embarrassed him, and he never asked again.

*

Anton struggled to sleep. Although he managed to resist the pipe and content himself with Dr Levon's *Mitragyna speciosa* leaves, his mind felt like an engine running at full speed.

Adjudicators were examining the evidence, the search for the mysterious David Cherlin was on, and questions had been put to Humberts, the surveyors, who had thrown up their hands in protest. A date for a court hearing was set for August 8th and an announcement placed in the newspaper.

Anton wondered if Dmitry might see it and what he might do. He also wondered if Katharine Lapinski would make contact now it had been made public. He continued placing the advertisement in the *Vedomosti*, and even though he'd given up expecting a reply, he hoped this might make a difference. Could the mysterious mistress and the presence of the Okhrana be linked, as if someone were playing a game?

Klara had been a godsend, though lately she seemed preoccupied. She had taken charge of the paperwork while he patrolled the oilfield with Rasoul, inspecting the damage and repairing what they could. They scrambled up ladders to the derrick platforms, shone torches down the well-shafts and checked the wheels and pumps. Rasoul talked politely enough, asking questions, making suggestions, while smoking thin, hand-rolled cigarettes. But all the time, Anton felt as if he were bargaining with an enemy.

During the second week of July, Marcus sent a letter to

Anton. The merchant had passed the plans onto a new engineer who would be able to proceed. It was hard to hear the news. Rafiq had died because of the tanker project. Rafiq had died because of him. But then Rafiq had died a little already, long before Anton's return. The project had given Rafiq new life and purpose and respite from a deep melancholy, and the thought eased Anton's heart.

Klara appeared, a basket on her arm. 'I'm going to the market. Do you want anything?'

'I have good news from Marcus Samuel,' Anton said showing her the letter.

She put the basket down and took it. 'When will they make their decision? The Suez Canal?'

'In a few months.'

'Will Rockefeller be able to stop it from happening?'

'He'll try. But now the fight will move to the courts and Parliament.'

'Rockefeller has powerful allies,' Klara said.

'So has Lord Salisbury. But this has gone beyond anything Marcus or I can do.'

As Klara picked up her basket and turned to leave for the market, Anton decided to join her.

The quayside baked in the July sun. There wasn't a gasp of air, almost as if the harbour was holding its breath. A Muslim lawyer in a tightly wound turban rode past on a mule, kicking up dung. Soldiers patrolled and many ships in the bay flew yellow warning flags for cholera.

Anton bit into his baked sturgeon sandwich, waving away a water carrier who held out a metal cup. Anton looked across the market to Klara, who was in mid argument with a fish trader.

Anton noticed two men nearby. One of them had fair hair with a slight stoop and a translucent pale face and seemed

295

familiar. His gaze was fixed on Klara while he spoke to his companion. The second man was dressed in a military uniform with a high-necked jacket, lapels, and tassels in the style of the Okhrana.

Anton threw away the rest of his sandwich.

Klara was standing with her back to them while the fish were being wrapped. A throng of passengers surged onto the quayside, momentarily blocking the men from view. Anton hurried over and grabbed her arm and propelled her into the crowd.

'What are you doing?' she exclaimed, snatching up the fish package and clutching it to her chest.

'Don't argue.'

Klara stiffened but allowed herself to be steered around into a packed teahouse. Anton pushed her into a chair and scanned the surrounding crowds – the men were nowhere to be seen.

'I think a man has been following you. I've seen him before watching the house. He has a companion with him.'

Klara blinked. 'Why would they be watching me?'

'I don't know. You tell me.'

She looked away.

'What's going on, Klara? Are you in some kind of trouble?'

Anton sat in the teahouse for over an hour after Klara had left. She had refused to say anything more and sat toying with the wrapping of the fish parcel. She allowed her glass of tea to go cold and after a while she made her excuses and left. Anton watched her blue-and-white dress blur into the harbour landscape, and it troubled him.

Why were the Okhrana so interested in Klara?

CHAPTER FORTY-FOUR

ANTON WATCHED KLARA FOR TWO WEEKS AND KEPT AN EYE on the streets outside the house. But he saw no sign of the men. Klara was distant and disappeared for hours at a time, but whatever trouble was brewing would make itself known one way or the other. So Anton spent his days overseeing the oilfields while he waited for the arrival of the court case. He would while away many evenings at the gentleman's club, drinking and watching the gaming tables.

On the last Saturday in July, Anton wandered into the gaming room and ordered a drink. An old grandfather clock with a glass case beat time in the corner, and the air was thick with tobacco and Macassar hair oil. There was a mixed crowd and plenty of games to choose from, but Anton had no desire to play.

Leo Rostov slouched in an armchair reading a newspaper and nodded at him. Anton saw no sign of the Brakovs – he hadn't seen them for weeks, but Albert Prankman was in attendance. He was playing poker with a sharp-faced man with a bald head. Anton watched the reflection of the American in the grandfather clock's glass tower. Every so often Prankman would take out his monocle and twist it between his fingers. Anton felt like leaping up and seizing the American by the throat and accusing him of corruption and fraud, but he knew it would be madness.

I have no proof. But I'll find some, you bastard. Just you wait.

Prankman scooped a pile of chips towards him. 'Sabroski. Why don't you join us?'

'Thank you, but no.' Anton forced a curt nod and distracted himself by reaching for the copy of the *Vedomosti* lying on the counter as the grandfather clock chimed the quarter hour.

Instinctively he flicked to the personal section, but as usual there was no reply from Katharine Lapinski.

Anton turned back to the headlines. In London there were mass demonstrations for an eight-hour working day and a new Factory Act prohibiting the employment of children. He raised his eyebrows. Whatever would the Reformists think of the working conditions on the Baku oilfields? He skimmed through the rest of the stories and then opened the business section. An article at the bottom of the page caught his eye.

It has been rumoured that a powerful group of financiers and merchants, of possible Hebrew influence, are attempting to take tankers through the Suez Canal. So far it has not been possible to establish the composition of this group and its objective...

Anton's heart quickened. The rumours were starting, as Marcus had predicted in his letter. He wondered if Rockefeller's power was greater than Lord Salisbury, the British Prime Minister. What a battle there would be.

Anton folded the newspaper and turned back to the game.

Prankman had removed his monocle again. Anton saw that darts of light caught the lens and speckled the wall. Chips clattered onto the card table and coils of cigarette smoke rose like wraiths. Anton studied the American's reflection in the grandfather clock as the man gazed down at his cards. He eased himself into a better vantage point, the better to study Prankman's tactics.

The grandfather clock chimed midnight as the game neared its end. The sharp-faced man had been forced to fold. Prankman slid his winnings towards him and stacked the chips into neat rows. Anton felt a dangerous current sweep through him.

'Changed your mind?' said Prankman as Anton approached.

Anton nodded. Out of the corner of his eye he saw Leo look up with interest. Two latecomers joined the game, one with a neat white beard, and another with a red face and gold spectacles.

The game was seven-card stud and continued long into the night. Hands were won and lost, though the man with the red face lost every hand and eventually left the table. As time passed the stakes increased.

Then it was three in the morning and the gaming room began to empty. Leo and several others remained to watch and drink at the bar. Presently the man with the white beard made his excuses. Only Anton and Prankman remained.

'You wish to continue?'

'Deal the cards,' said Anton lighting a cigarette.

Cards were dealt and hands played and the betting was getting aggressive. It appeared Prankman was going for a four of a kind, but if Anton could get a straight flush, that would beat Prankman's hand. The palms of Anton's hands were getting sticky, and he could sense Leo's discomfort behind him.

The final round of betting began. By now the pot stood at four hundred and eighty roubles. Anton looked at his final card and his stomach lurched. The ten of clubs. *What good fortune.* He waited for Prankman to lay down his cards: the ace, king and jack of hearts. Together with his queen and ten of hearts, Prankman had a royal flush: the highest poker hand. Anton's straight flush was a poor second.

There was silence.

Leo put a hand on his shoulder. 'Let's go home, Anton.'

'One moment,' said Anton, leaning over the table as Prankman brushed the chips towards him. He placed his hand over Prankman's wrist. 'I'm afraid you must forfeit these winnings.'

Prankman recoiled. 'And why is that?'

'Because you have been cheating.'

Everyone in the room seemed to freeze. Prankman tried to free himself from Anton's grip, but Anton pushed him back in the chair. 'Leo, summon the manager. These cards have been marked.'

Prankman cursed. 'Have you lost your wits, Sabroski?'

'Albert Prankman has marked these cards! Somebody examine them.'

Eager huddles of conversation erupted as other men returned to the gaming room with a look of excitement on their faces. A tall man with a black square beard and stiff way of walking approached the table. 'What is the problem, gentlemen?'

'This man has been cheating. He has been playing with marked cards.'

'He lies,' said Prankman. 'The man is drunk.'

'Accusing someone of cheating is a serious charge,' the manager told Anton. 'You'd better be right.' He turned and lowered his voice. 'Albert Prankman is a very influential man. Have you taken leave of your senses?'

'Examine his cards.'

The manager swivelled to face Prankman. 'I'm sorry, sir, but I must substantiate this.'

'If you insist,' said Prankman. 'But first tell this oaf to unhand me.'

Anton released his grip and Prankman pushed back his chair and stood up. With a quick movement the American swept up the cards and flung them at Anton. A decanter of wine toppled, leaking claret over the table. 'You've made a serious error, Sabroski.'

'Pay no heed to him,' said Anton. 'You'll find marks on all of the court cards.'

Leo and the manager bent down and picked up the cards, laying them face up on the table. Several were stained red with wine, others were bent and torn. The manager stared at them. 'I can't see anything wrong.'

'Look for a small, curved mark,' said Anton.

The manager screwed up his eyes. 'I can't see anything.'

'I told you so,' said Prankman. 'The man's unhinged.'

An embarrassed silence engulfed the room. Leo's mouth hung open in dismay.

'I think you owe Mr Prankman an apology,' said the manager.

'More than an apology.' Prankman sneered. 'I demand this man's membership be suspended.'

Anton picked up the cards and flipped them over. 'Please look again.'

The manager held up his hands. 'Mr Sabroski, please let us avoid any more unpleasantness.'

'Indulge me,' Anton insisted. 'Look carefully at the back of the cards.'

The manager hesitated and shot a look at Prankman, before picking up three of the court cards. He stared at the first card, turning it over and holding it to the light. He did the same for the second card, and finally the third. At last he cleared his throat. 'There does appear to be a small curve in some of the corners.'

'What does that prove?' said Prankman. 'How could I make such marks?'

'Mr Prankman has a point. These marks could have been made by anything.'

'Nobody else in this room wears a monocle,' said Anton. 'Take his monocle and press it onto a card. I'll wager the mark is identical.'

'That's a good point,' said the red-faced man. 'He's always taking his monocle out.' Other people muttered in agreement.

The manager held out his hand. 'Would you oblige, sir?'

Prankman waved his hand away. 'Certainly not. The accusation is absurd.'

'If that is your wish, sir, then we will have to take you at your word.' The manager's words sounded clipped as he linked his hands behind his back. 'Under the circumstances, and in order to avoid bad feeling, I insist on the return of all monies from games played this afternoon. My attendants will supervise.' His eyes swept over the room. 'Cheating at cards is a serious offence, gentlemen. I will not have the club's reputation tarnished. I suggest that in future gentlemen play with more caution to avoid misunderstandings. Let this be a warning to everyone. Cheating will not be tolerated in this club. Go to the saloon bars out of town if you wish for a more reckless experience.'

The room fell silent. Anton felt in his jacket for his revolver as Prankman turned to him with a glare.

'Well, Sabroski, that was a little unnecessary. I think we need a chat sometime to better understand each other.'

Chapter Forty-Five

Dawn had broken by the time Anton and Leo left the club. They sat in the park and watched the sun come up over the Caspian, then walked down the cobbled streets to the sea. Anton inhaled the sea air. He felt energised, even though he could sense Leo's concern.

'You've made a dangerous enemy,' said Leo.

'He was already my enemy. The man is loathsome. Somebody needed to put a stop to him.'

'Yes, but you exposed him. He won't forgive you for that.'

'So be it. John Seigenberg told me Prankman was cheating. I've been careful to avoid playing him until I could see the device he used.' Anton laughed. 'Let's go home. Come and have breakfast.'

When they got to the house the sun was up. Anton could smell freshly baked bread and syrupy pancakes and thick dark coffee. As they entered the hallway, the kitchen door opened, and Klara appeared. 'Anton! Oh... hello Leo...'

'Is anything wrong, Klara?' said Anton. He handed his hat and cane to the housekeeper. 'Olga, bring us some breakfast please. We'll take it in the library.'

Klara was holding the door to the kitchen.

'Is somebody here, Klara?'

'Only me,' called a familiar voice.

'Julia!' said Leo. He hurried across the hallway as Julia appeared in the kitchen doorway. She wore a cream day dress with a high lace collar which accentuated her paleness. Seed pearls decorated the front of her bodice. Leo took her hands and kissed them. 'How are you?'

Julia touched his face. 'Dear Leo. I'm just a little tired. How lovely to see you.'

'You are unwell?' Leo's face clouded. 'Why are you not at home?'

'I'm not unwell. Just a little weary.'

'Will you join us for breakfast, Julia?' said Anton.

'Maybe a little later.' Gently, she pulled her hand away and went back inside the kitchen. Leo watched the door close.

Anton led Leo into the library, opening the shutters and the courtyard doors so a breeze could ripple through. He pulled a fine hemp net across the door and secured it in place. Later the cook brought them a tray of blinis and a dish of eggs. Anton ate quickly, mopping up the yellow yolks with chunks of flatbread. Leo picked at his food and glanced at the door.

'Leave her to Klara,' said Anton watching Leo check his pocket watch for the tenth time. 'She'll join us when she's ready.'

'I didn't know Julia and Klara were friends.'

'Nor did I until a few weeks ago.'

Leo pushed his plate to one side. The high spirits which had buoyed him upon their arrival seem to have ebbed. Anton poured two glasses of tea. 'Here's to health and hope.'

Leo clinked the glass. 'And here's to new beginnings. I'm crossing my fingers for a good outcome for your court case.'

It was Anton's turn to smile. 'I hope you don't speak too soon.'

'And I hope so too,' said a voice.

Anton spun round. The hemp net snapped back, and Albert Prankman stood in the courtyard doorway. Anton felt for the gun in his jacket pocket, but Prankman was too quick for him.

'Too late, Sabroski.' A Smith 'n' Wesson revolver glared across the room. 'Don't look so smug now, do you?' Prankman smiled. 'I've come for a little chat.'

Anton bristled. 'Why would I talk to a cheat and a liar.'

'That's not very polite.' The American stepped into the room.

'What do you want?'

Prankman dragged the writing desk chair towards him and sat down. 'You know, you've been an irritation ever since you returned. Would have been better for everyone if you'd stayed away.'

'Better for you, you mean?'

'And people close to you, as you well know.'

An old ache grew inside Anton. 'Get out of here, Prankman.'

'I agree. We don't want your sort here,' said Leo.

Prankman swung the revolver towards Leo. 'Ah, who do we have here? Leo Rostov. In love with Seigenberg's daughter. Following her around like a puppy dog. But I hear you've wasted your time on spoiled goods.'

Leo rose to his feet. 'You bastard. Don't you dare speak of her like that.'

Anton put a restraining arm on Leo's shoulder.

Prankman laughed. 'Somebody got to her first. But you don't need to worry. Your rival is dead. Hasanov was a talented engineer. A shame he died in those tragic circumstances, but his death was your gain. Now you can have his girl.'

Anton stared at Leo. His face was grey as death. 'Fuck you, Prankman. Take your evil words elsewhere.'

'What is evil?' said Prankman spreading his hands. 'What does that word really mean? Is a man judged to be evil because his deeds are considered unacceptable, even though his intentions are good? And is a man judged to be good if he commits charitable acts even though he harbours evil thoughts? Don't ask me to believe that a little part of you wasn't pleased when Hasanov died?'

'It's not true,' said Leo. 'I wished him no ill.'

'What's the purpose of this?' said Anton.

'I'm coming to the purpose, but not yet.' Prankman sat back, resting his boots on the table, causing the cutlery lying across the egg-stained plates to fall to the floor. 'We never really know our friends. As you go through life, you realise you can trust very few people. Nobody is as they seem. All you see is the façade they choose to present. And you, Sabroski, you come back to Baku after many years and find old friends appear the same, but they are not. New friends appear helpful, but for what reason?'

'Is this nonsense leading somewhere?'

'Everybody has an agenda, and it is always self-interest. There are few people in this world without self-interest to promote. I've not met a single one.'

'Then I feel very sorry for you.'

He smirked at Anton. 'We live in a network of deceit. That servant girl of yours has an interesting past – you should watch your back. And then there's John Seigenberg, entrusted to look after you. He's repaid your father well, but maybe not in the way Nikolai would have expected. Ask Seigenberg about the *Pale of Settlement*. That will make him spin.'

'Get to the point,' Anton snapped.

'We were talking about Rafiq Hasanov. Why did he have to die?'

Ice began to fill Anton's chest. The dining room door creaked but didn't open.

'Your pathetic friend, Rostov, may have wished Hasanov dead, but he's the kind of man who wishes for things he has no business having. He strives to do deeds he is not capable of doing. It was no Rostov who murdered your friend. It was no ruffian from the mountains, well only in name. It was me.'

'What are you talking about?'

'Hasanov had something I wanted, or, more accurately, John Rockefeller wanted. But Hasanov died needlessly, because, as it turned out, I didn't get what I wanted. All the same, I'm glad he died, because it caused you pain.'

Anton jerked up and pulled out his gun. 'You vile bastard.'

Leo threw himself forward and caught Anton's arms. 'No. Not now.'

'I'll *kill* you for this, Prankman. I promise,' Anton spluttered as he struggled.

'Don't listen to him,' Leo shouted. 'There'll be another way.'

Prankman laughed as he backed towards the door. 'Listen to the soft words of caution. Inaction may seem like wise counsel for the present, but it won't bring you satisfaction.'

In the hallway, Julia listened. She pressed her forehead against the library door and closed her eyes. A hot mass filled her throat, expanding within her until her whole body was consumed.

Chapter Forty-Six

It had taken all of Leo and Klara's strength to prevent Anton from chasing after Prankman and shooting him dead. Klara confiscated Anton's revolver, emptied out the bullets and hid it. Leo locked the doors and shuttered the windows and poured brandies. Anton raved, filling himself with such venom he thought he'd drop down dead.

But, in the end, Anton saw sense. Killing Prankman would solve nothing and satisfaction would be short-lived. Much to Leo's disappointment, Julia had disappeared during the fray, but as soon as Anton had given his word not to do anything foolish, Leo set out to follow her.

Anton didn't know what he'd do if he laid eyes on Prankman again, so for the following week, he avoided the gentleman's club and drove himself hard on the oilfields. He imagined scenarios where he could dispose of the American without being arrested. Anton noticed that Klara appeared unsettled, but he doubted it had anything to do with the incident. She spent a lot of time away from the house and one evening she didn't come home at all.

A few days later, Anton noticed her slip out through the courtyard with a basket on her arm. He decided to follow her. She ran down the street towards the sea, stopping at a bakery and then reappearing minutes later, folding ovals of flatbread into her basket. She wove in and out of turbaned fruit sellers sitting on the ground with panniers of grapes. Then she vanished from view altogether.

Anton scanned the crowds and cursed. A child grabbed his hand, biting him when he tried to shake it off.

He made towards the docks. There were hundreds of vessels tied up along the wharves. Dark eyes peered out from makeshift shelters stinking of sweat and urine. An unending line of human traffic shouted and hammered. Stevedores bent double under crates twice the weight of a man and wharf labourers swung sacks onto decks, while others lashed down cargo. Boats knocked as they bumped against pontoons in the breeze.

Anton looked to the east to a line of mournful boats lying roped together. He saw Klara jump down onto the deck of one and duck inside.

The vessel was an old schooner. The hull was red and christened with the name *Daria* painted in curly Persian letters. The low mainsail was all that remained of its original three sails. The deck was strewn with matting, cooking materials, and rubbish. A blur of candlelight shone through a porthole.

Anton edged nearer and peered in. He could just make out three figures huddled together. A wave smacked against the hull, flinging droplets into the night air making the boat rock. Someone pulled the curtain back and the porthole snapped open. A gravelly voice filtered through. Anton ducked down.

'I don't reckon he'll last much longer.'

'Don't say that,' Anton heard Klara say. 'Make him drink more water.'

'It doesn't do any good. He can't keep anything down.'

Somebody else spoke but Anton couldn't make out what was said. He shifted closer, wrinkling his nose at the stench of faeces.

'You shouldn't keep coming here. The place is full of soldiers. If you get caught you know what will happen.'

'I won't get caught. Give me that cloth. Hold him still while I wipe his face. I'll see if he can drink.'

Anton heard water slosh into a vessel. A man coughed and spluttered and something smashed onto the floor. 'It's no good, he's too weak.'

'We need the doctor again. He needs to go to hospital.'

'You go, Rasoul. I'll stay here.'

Anton slipped back into the darkness and waited.

Rasoul returned with another man who bounced along the road, his black bag swinging at his side. Anton recognised him at once: it was Doctor Levon Kasparian, the Armenian doctor who was supplying his opium replacement leaves. The pair climbed aboard and entered the cabin.

On impulse, Anton followed.

Nobody noticed him enter at first, so focused were they on the dying man. The smell was overpowering. A pool of rice-watery stools and vomit soiled the floor. It was stifling hot and the air thick and dark. Doctor Levon examined the dying man. 'He has cholera. There is not much I can do except, if we get him to hospital, we can try to rehydrate him.' Doctor Levon lay a hand on Klara's arm. 'But I fear we may be too late.'

Presently, the doctor looked up and raised his dark eyebrows at Anton. 'Ah. We have a visitor.'

Rasoul's hand flew to his waistband and drew out a curved dagger.

'Stop,' Klara shouted. 'It's Anton Nikolayevich.' She glared at Anton. 'Why are you here?'

'I followed you. I wanted to see where you went.'

'Well, now you know,' Klara said sullenly. 'Looking after a dying friend.'

'Why didn't you tell me? I could have helped.'

'What could you have done?'

Anton spread his hands. 'Something more than this.'

Klara looked away. 'At least help me get Ivan to hospital.'

The words *Mikhailovsky Bolnitza* formed an iron arch above two high gates. The open ground beyond led to a three-storey building with rows of gridded windows.

A militia of white coats ran out as they lifted the dying man called Ivan out of the carriage and onto a stretcher. The attendants ferried him through the wide doors, past an open reception area, down a dark corridor and into a large ward. Doctor Levon led the way, his beak-like nose crowned with a pair of thick, black-rimmed spectacles. He had pulled on a white smock and cap and flapped his arms to indicate that Ivan was to be laid on an iron bedstead. 'Bring jugs of boiled water and a bucket,' he shouted at a nurse.

Anton stared down at the dying man's sunken eyes and wretchedly thin body. He had scars on his back and shoulders and his skin was grey and wrinkled.

'His fever is worse,' the doctor said. 'We must make him drink.'

The nurse appeared and set jugs of water beside the bed. The doctor opened his bag and extracted a large bottle.

'What's that?' said Klara.

'A salt tonic.'

'He can't drink that! Salt will make him vomit even more.'

'It's not just salt. It's a mixture of salts and sugar cane with some other ingredients. It will replace the goodness excreted by the body. It's essential he drink this with as much water as you can force down.'

Klara looked doubtful. Rasoul poured the water mixture from the jug into a cup and handed it to her.

Anton stepped back, feeling like an outsider. He recognised the disease – he'd seen it many times in the Orient but had never seen it treated with water and salts. Most people thought it came from bad air, and Baku was full of bad air.

'I am surprised to see you here, Anton Nikolayevich,' called Doctor Levon as he scrubbed his hands in a stone sink. 'This is a bad business. There are many ships impounded in the docks flying the yellow flag. The soldiers won't let any of them off. They lie dying in their dozens below decks. Is that poor wretch known to you?'

'No. Never seen him before. But Klara, as you know, lives in my house. She's my assistant,' he felt it necessary to add.

The doctor lowered his voice. 'The patient won't live much longer. He's too weak to survive. I can see he's been beaten badly in the past.'

'Have you treated him before?'

'I have no record of him, but I've seen wounds like this many times. A few years ago, during the tsar's visit, many young activists were beaten and tortured by the Okhrana.' The doctor sighed. 'It was supposed to be a festive time, a national holiday, full of celebration and fireworks.'

An hour later the doctor hurried over as Ivan was convulsing on the bed. His arms were thrashing about as Klara and Rasoul struggled to hold him. Then suddenly he stopped and went quiet. Anton moved closer and searched the man's face. The pain had vanished. His face, wet with sweat and vomit, had relaxed.

Doctor Levon felt for a pulse and then drew his hand over Ivan's eyes. 'I'm sorry,' he said to Klara.

Klara trembled and sank down to kiss Ivan's forehead. Rasoul and the other man took off their caps.

'I will prepare the death certificate and then we must move him to the mortuary,' said the doctor gently.

Anton followed Doctor Levon as he bobbed his way out of the ward and down the corridor, pushing through a pair of swing doors. The man turned right into another corridor, walked through an empty ward and then through another set of swing doors until they came to an office with a sign above saying *Birth and Death Registration*. A red-faced man with a broken nose sat at a desk piled with paperwork.

'Vosbigian,' said Dr Levon. 'Another death certificate, I'm afraid.'

'Name?' Vosbigian grabbed a packet of Duke's Cross-Cut that were lying on the table. A glass of brown tea, long cold, sat by his elbow stewing a cigarette end.

'Ivan Darkov.'

'Darkov?' said Anton, eyes widened. 'Did you say his name was Darkov?'

'Cause of death?' said Vosbigian.

'Cholera,' Doctor Levon said, opening a cabinet and extracting a large ledger.

Anton's thoughts were whirling. Was this Ivan Darkov a relative of Klara's? But then Darkov was a common enough name. He thought about what the doctor said about the young activists who were rounded up during the tsar's visit. Had Ivan Darkov been one of them, and if he was connected to Klara by name, was she an activist too?

Anton felt a sense of dread. The tsar's visit seemed so significant, so portentous, that it must mean something. He remembered the face in the coloured illustration of the newspaper: the court member who had accompanied the tsar at the Alexander Nevsky Cathedral foundation ceremony. The man was tall with sandy hair and a pince-nez with the features of someone familiar.

It was also the last time anyone had seen the accountant,

Dmitry Ivanovich – he too had disappeared during the tsar's visit, supposedly on a train to Odessa. But the letter he'd received from Dmitry's sister said her brother had never arrived. What if Dmitry never left Baku after all? Could he instead have been caught up in all of this? Anton felt a cold, hollow sensation.

'Doctor Levon,' Anton said. 'Those men who were beaten when the tsar visited – were they all activists, suspected by the Okhrana?'

The doctor considered the question. 'No. Not everyone. Why do you ask?'

'Can I see their death certificates?'

The doctor raised his eyebrows. 'There are a great many, but I don't see why not.' He turned to the clerk. 'Vosbigian, fetch the October eighty-eight ledger for the gentleman.'

Vosbigian dropped the end of his cigarette into the brown tea. It fizzed and then floated on the surface like a dead moth. He scraped his chair back and shuffled over to a wooden filing cabinet, pulling it open to lift out a ledger bulging with papers.

'What or who are you looking for, Anton Nikolayevich?' the doctor said as he opened the ledger. 'There were many hundreds of deaths over those three days. A total of…' – he pointed to some figures at the top of the title pages – 'three hundred and eighty-seven. Some were usual deaths – the sort that we expect – others were not so.' He swivelled the ledger round for Anton to see.

Anton scanned the list. He skipped over the women and children and examined the names of the dead men. Some of the entries had no names at all, just a description of their appearance and social status: *pauper, labourer, gentleman, young boy, old man…* He ran his eyes down the causes of death: *suffocation, fracture of skull, asphyxia, injuries to the head, drowning, old age, fracture to the skull, falling down the stairs, fright, bad teeth, growth in belly, infection…*

The doctor watched over his shoulder. 'Some bodies were

found on the roadside without any identification. Their bodies were taken straight to the mortuary. I recorded what I could. But you realise this is not a true list of those who died. Even now, many bodies never make it here. They are left to rot in unmarked graves outside the city.'

'If a man was held by the Okhrana, what was the most common cause of death?'

'Beatings usually.' Dr Levon pointed to several names on the lists.

Anton read aloud. 'Oil workers. Labourers. And young too: *eighteen, twenty-one, nineteen, seventeen*. Are they always this young?'

'Idealists are too young to know any better,' said Dr Levon. 'Many come from Kiev, St Petersburg and Moscow as they think the authorities won't know them. But the arm of the tsar is long, and the Okhrana's arm even longer.'

'Do you ever see female idealists? Does the Okhrana treat them the same way?'

'I don't see many women in these round-ups. Even the tsar balks at thrashing women. He doesn't think women capable of political opinions.'

Anton gave a grim smile as he imagined Klara's answer to that.

The door opened, and Klara herself walked in. Her eyes were red-rimmed and she was holding something in her hand. She glanced at Anton and sat down at the desk in front of Vosbigian. 'I'd like to keep this if I may.' She opened her hand and held out a golden ring.

'Are you his next of kin?'

She nodded. 'Yes… I am his wife. Klara Darkova.'

'His wife!' Anton exclaimed.

Anton stared down at the ledger, mechanically flipping over pages, reading names that blurred in front of him. He was aware that Klara had stood up and swept up her skirts and sped out of the room, and he could hear Vosbigian's pen scratching across the paperwork. He could hardly believe what he'd heard. *Why hadn't she told him? What more was she hiding?* He had never felt so confused. The girl whom his father had trusted, who seemed to know so much yet revealed so little, who had lived in his house for – what must it be now – eight months. Nine? She had hardly mentioned a single friend, let alone a husband. She never once talked about someone dear to her who was in trouble and in need of help.

Anton stared back at the ledger, his eyes barely focusing on the pages. If she had told him from the beginning, he could have arranged for her husband to be properly cared for. It saddened him to think Klara regarded him with such mistrust. He rubbed his eyes. Klara hadn't told him because she wanted her activities kept secret, which could mean only one thing. And, unfortunately, she was young enough and foolish enough to believe she was invincible, and that she could outwit the Okhrana. Anton knew from bitter experience that this was impossible.

He gazed at the ledger, seeing, yet not really seeing, turning pages, letting the names of the dead float past like inky wraiths. He wasn't sure what he was doing or what he was looking for any more. It was time to go home.

Anton was about to close the ledger when one of the entries came into focus. There was no name, but the dead man had been listed as a gentleman of middle age with thin red hair, and the cause of death recorded as: *severe head wounds consistent with a beating.*

Anton looked up at the doctor, who had steepled his fingers and was tapping them together in rhythm. 'Doctor Levon, do you see all the bodies that are brought in?'

'I try to. I ensure that the cause of death is recorded correctly.'

'Would you remember this one?' Anton showed him the ledger.

'No. But I can see that this man was an unusual victim. No money on him: no purse, watch, even a jacket. The deceased's belongings are listed here.' He tapped a column on the page.

'Do you think he was robbed?'

'Unlikely. He was still wearing an expensive pair of leather shoes and had a smart leather belt. A robber would surely have taken those.'

'What do you think happened to him?'

Doctor Levon shook his head. 'He doesn't look the type to be an activist. A bit too old to be one of their revolutionary targets. There's no way of telling, but it could be a deliberate attack made to look like a robbery – except they didn't carry it off very well. Many old scores were settled that week.'

Anton clicked his tongue. 'Too bad we don't have any papers to identify him.'

'There is something,' said the doctor pointing to the column marked *Other*. 'Engraved on the buckle of the belt was a set of initials: *D I R*.'

Anton's stomach fell away. Instinct told him who the belt belonged to.

Dmitry Ivanovich Rabinovich.

Chapter Forty-Seven

Anton left the hospital at sunrise. He breathed in crisp air and flushed out the putrid smells of the night. The city lay grey and silent.

He walked up through the park and sat on a bench overlooking an ornamental pond and lit a cigarette. If the dead man really was Dmitry Ivanovich, then he had been murdered, and even though Anton had entertained the idea for a while, it still came as a shock. The fraudulent accounts and the faked surveyors' reports were one thing, but he also had a priceless egg and a deceitful assistant to consider. The murders of both Frau Kalian and Dmitry Ivanovich set him thinking. Was it possible his father had been murdered as well?

He stood up and leaned over the side of the pond, staring into the water as golden fish swam through the reeds. He trailed his fingers over the surface watching them dart under the lily leaves and into the muddy depths. He tried to breathe calmly but a storm was gathering inside him.

Klara was waiting for him in the library when he returned to the house. Anton tried to keep the frustration out of his voice as he could see she was distressed.

'I'm sorry for your husband's death, Klara. Truly sorry. But why didn't you tell me?'

'Ivan was a dear friend. A man I needed to protect. I saw no reason to tell you about him. It made no difference who, or what I was to you, your father, or to Sabroski Oil.'

'He was a member of a political group, wasn't he?' said Anton. 'That's why the Okhrana are watching you and why you left Kiev. You escaped with him and fled to Baku.' Anton paced the room. 'You don't realise how dangerous this is. It's not a game. The Okhrana never forget.'

Klara pulled out a handkerchief and blew her nose. 'Ivan writes... wrote... for a newspaper. Pamphlets. I took them to the printers and got them distributed. The authorities didn't like his writings and destroyed any pamphlets they found. But they never knew who wrote them. Ivan was never a member of any political party.'

'Then why have the Okhrana been watching you? Why was Ivan living on that squalid little boat? Doctor Levon said he'd been badly beaten. I saw the scars. How did that happen?'

Klara paled. 'Ivan was a dear friend and he loved me and I believe I made him happy, for a while. I had to get away from Kiev. My mother died. I had nothing. Ivan asked me to marry him and come to Baku. There was work here, but...'

'But what?'

She sighed. 'Ivan was arrested as soon as we arrived. They accused him of stealing, but it wasn't true.'

'Was he convicted?'

'Yes. Imprisoned. But we bribed the guards and got him out.'

'How did you do that?'

'I had help... from your father.'

Anton stared in astonishment. 'My father?'

'Ivan was in prison for eighteen months. By the time we got him out, he was ill and very weak so he stayed here for a while. But by then it had become too dangerous, so he went back to Kiev. Ivan wanted to come back – he insisted, even though I tried to stop him, but he still came. We had to keep him hidden. He stayed on the Group Twenty oilfields when they closed down. The fields were quiet. Nobody went there.'

Anton blinked. 'He was there that day, wasn't he? The day I climbed over the gate.'

'Yes. That's why the men were so aggressive. They thought you were looking for him.'

'So, Ivan left the safety of Kiev to be with you?'

Klara fiddled with her sleeves. She looked back at Anton. 'Ivan was foolish. I'm not worth it. Nobody is.'

'And where does Rasoul fit in? I suppose he knew all about this?'

Klara nodded. 'Rasoul was Ivan's friend. Old school friends from Kiev.'

Anton lit a cigarette. 'What a curse secrets are.'

Klara's face hardened. 'Now it's your turn. Time to share your secrets. Why are *you* so worried about the Okhrana? What did you do in St Petersburg?'

'Nothing I want to talk about.'

'And you accuse me of keeping secrets! You must be honest with me.'

Anton looked away and finished his cigarette in silence. Then he went over to the French windows and stared out into the courtyard. 'I killed a member of the Okhrana. His name was Yuri Bulganin.' Now he'd said the words, it was easier than he thought to talk about it. 'I didn't know he was secret police. As far as we knew he was a student studying engineering. He was quiet. He never said very much. His girlfriend – her name was Maria – would cook supper every week and we'd go to his rooms and talk and drink. They were good times.' He turned back to Klara. 'I'm going to have a drink. Do you want one?'

She nodded. He poured two large vodkas.

'We were at Yuri's as usual when three men in uniform came. We were talking into the night as we always did. Maria opened the door, and they pushed past her demanding two of my friends be taken for questioning. We tried to stop them, but the men were armed and held a gun to Yuri's head and said they'd shoot him if we didn't cooperate.' Anton gave a wry laugh. 'Yuri fooled everyone. I always wonder what would have happened if we had called their bluff. They might have actually shot him and saved me the bother.'

'So how did you find out about Yuri?'

'About a week later. I wasn't going to let it go. The men they'd arrested were good friends of mine. I asked questions, went to the police, spoke to the university chancellor, created a fuss. I found out where they were being held and tried to see them, but was told you're not allowed to speak to political prisoners.' Anton downed his drink and refilled his glass. 'Then one night I came back early to my rooms. When I opened the door I found Yuri in my room, going through my things and reading my papers. I thought there had to be an explanation. Then the door opened, and a uniformed man came in. Yuri held up a warning hand and gave him a nod and the man left. When I confronted Yuri, he shrugged and said my friends had been members of Narodnaya Volya and that he'd been watching them for months.'

'Narodnaya Volya – The People's Will?' said Klara, her eyes wide. 'The group that assassinated the tsar.'

'I didn't believe it. And I still don't.'

'So why…?'

'Yuri intended to take me in for questioning. I knew what that meant. I had seen through his cover. Yuri pulled out his gun and I grabbed the first thing to hand and hit him with it. It was a huge glass paperweight.' Anton paused. 'Yuri's head split open.'

Klara gasped. 'How did you get away?'

'I locked the door. Turned out the lights. Cleaned up the room and put the body in my trunk. Then I found the others and told them what had happened. They helped me get the trunk out of the room and we dumped the body in the forest.'

'How did the Okhrana find out?'

'They didn't for a while. We all tried to act normally. I even went to see the tsar's parade.'

'You were there? On the actual day?'

'Yes, the very day of the assassination. I saw the bomb go off.'

Klara became very still. 'That must have been terrifying.'

'There was chaos. I knew I had to get away. If what Yuri had said was true, and the Okhrana suspected our engineering group had links to revolutionaries, we would be in terrible danger. I warned the others and got out of St Petersburg as quickly as I could.'

'And the others?'

'They were too slow. The Okhrana seized every member of every political group from every university. They arrested anyone who might have had a connection. There were thousands of trials. Eventually somebody talked and they found Yuri's body. They traced me to Baku. I knew I had to leave. I couldn't endanger my family. I joined the army and went to Vladivostok.'

'But you worked with the tsar's minister. Surely, he must have known. Your name must have been on the Okhrana's lists.'

'Yes, it was. Count Witte employed me after the Afghan war. He wanted me to work on the new railway project.'

'But he knew?'

'I told him my side of the story. He said that enough blood had been spilled and enough lives were rotting in Siberia. He needed me, used his influence to get my record erased. Except records are never completely erased.'

Klara frowned. 'Why did he care about you?'

'Witte is a liberal man. There are very few engineers with my level of training who wanted to work in Vladivostok and even less so in Shanghai. He'd seen some of my work from the army. The new Trans-Siberian Express railway was important to him.'

'So, are you safe from the Okhrana now?'

Anton shrugged. 'Who is safe? There are many lists. The count doesn't have universal influence. There are several members of the Okhrana who enjoy the chase and the suffering it brings.' Anton faltered. He knew he would have to tell her about Dmitry, and it grieved him to burden Klara with more bad news. 'There is something else. Concerning Dmitry.'

As Anton told the story, she folded her arms and paced the room.

'They murdered him to keep him quiet. They must have suspected he was collecting evidence.'

'The only person Dmitry confided in was Frau Kalian. My visit to her was fatal – they suspected she knew something.'

Klara threw out her arms. 'But who exactly are *they*?'

'David Cherlin... and his accomplices. Whoever they might be.'

CHAPTER FORTY-EIGHT

BAKU'S DISTRICT COURT ROOM WAS CROWDED AND NOISY. The alleged fraud of Sabroski Oil attracted many onlookers, a few who considered they had a claim and countless others who did not. Throughout the proceedings, Fabian Brakov sat granite-faced and motionless while John Seigenberg presented the facts to the panel of the Justices of the Peace. The men conferred, discussed, and absorbed the information for three days.

Following deliberations, the judge recalled everyone to the courtroom. He mopped his brow and adjusted the heavy gilt collar hanging round his neck which was decorated with two imperial eagle motifs. He popped a black-and-white humbug into his mouth and fanned his face with a thick vellum envelope. The heat was intense for August, worsened by the ceiling fans which mixed sweaty air with cigarette smoke. The judge pushed his spectacles back up his nose and banged the desk with his hammer. The room rippled and then fell quiet as he began to speak.

'It appears beyond doubt that Zenovitch Liquid Fuel was set up to defraud Sabroski Oil and the imperial government. At present, the whereabouts of the director of this company, David Cherlin, is unknown. However, the company's assets will be seized, and the perpetrator hunted down and punished. It is the decision of this tribunal that all Sabroski Oil company decisions and recommendations undertaken by Zenovitch Liquid Fuel are to be reversed. Where possible, monies are to be repaid, clients reimbursed, and company decisions overturned. I will appoint court administrators to oversee this.'

The judge continued with a long list of company names, persons, addresses and procedures, but to Anton, Sabroski Oil was the only name that mattered.

*

Albert Prankman left the court rooms and returned to his rooms. The fury inside him had swelled to dangerous levels, flooding his body with viciousness. He knew he would have to leave before he did or said something foolish. The loss of the fields and wealth was a blow, not that the decision was unexpected after Sabroski's discoveries, but it had severely interfered with his plans with John Rockefeller.

Prankman poured himself a glass of milk. He'd been foolish to expose himself to Sabroski after the poker game, but the venom in him had poisoned his reason. Now that his cover as an oil spy had been compromised, he'd have to dispose of Sabroski and his pathetic friend, Rostov. It was the only way he could continue to operate. The Pallid Harrier had a reputation and a network of agents to protect.

He decided that an accident on the oilfield would be the easiest solution. Sabroski's inexperience and lack of caution would make for a very plausible demise.

Prankman cursed out loud. No other opponent had managed to thwart him so relentlessly. The boy had unbelievable good luck. If Prankman could have known, he would have let Sabroski perish in the dungeons of the caravanserai long before Seigenberg came to the rescue. That damned lawyer had been nothing but trouble from the very beginning.

He cursed his fate. Rockefeller's displeasure at the loss of the tanker plans had been immediate. He'd turned down Prankman's request to be posted elsewhere, demanding he focus on the Rothschild refineries, ordering the destruction of the Baku-Batumi railway. These were impossibly difficult tasks.

Prankman fixed his monocle in place and picked up the paper in front of him. Already Rockefeller had moved his fight to the courts, instructing his solicitors Russell and Arnholz to arm themselves for a prolonged battle. Questions had been raised in the British Parliament about the proposed tank steamers and the passage through the Suez Canal. British ship owners had protested and the Welsh tin-plate manufacturers and coal-owners declared their interests would be threatened. Chemists and experts on oil were already compiling reports highlighting the dangers of an explosion.

It would not be long before Marcus Samuel's tanker plan coup was thwarted.

*

Julia Seigenberg climbed down the stone steps to the cupola-domed pharmacy. She pulled her shawl around her as, despite the humidity, she shivered; the place looked more like an underground vault than a pharmacy. Yellow lamplights streaked into the gloom revealing glistening concave walls with deep recesses storing a host of jars. The smell of ammonia, rotten eggs and putrid fish hung in the air.

Julia felt sick. Not just because she was pregnant, but because of the boasts she overheard Albert Prankman make outside Anton's dining room door.

On the other side of the room a short, lean man with dark curly hair and thick spectacles was busy examining bottles. He was wearing a white smock over a green check waistcoat and his shirt sleeves were rolled up. The man was muttering to himself, holding up a dark-coloured bottle, reading the label and writing in a book that lay open on the counter.

Julia folded her arms and felt for her locket. She needn't do this; she could turn round and go home. Nobody would have missed her this early in the morning. But it was too late, her distress had already escaped and alerted the man.

'Can I be of assistance, mademoiselle?' the short man said, looking up and wiping his hands.

She stepped forward. 'Good morning, sir. Are you Doctor Levon Kasparian?' Her voice was shaking, but he didn't seem to notice.

'Certainly, I am. What can I do for you?'

'I need a potion to make a man sleep.' She paused. 'My father has dreams that make him exhausted. They say you have such remedies.'

The doctor came out from behind the counter and scrutinised her. Julia felt he was trying to peer right inside her.

'I have several potions which can make a man sleep, but they must all be handled with great care. Let me show you.' He walked across the room, his shiny, pointed shoes clicking across the flagstones. There was a tall cupboard on the other side with deep shelves secured behind glass panels. He took a key from his belt and unlocked it. 'It depends on how deeply you wish your father to sleep. I assume you want him to wake up in the morning.'

'Indeed, I do, sir.' Her voice seemed magnified in this cavernous room and she imagined a thousand ears eavesdropping on their conversation. There were a variety of plants on the shelves lit by a bright lamp. A woody plant shaped like a parsnip lay on its side. It had long finger-like stems and dark green leaves which gave out a fetid odour. She wrinkled her nose and pointed. 'What is that?'

'It's a mandrake, but it is called Satan's Apple in these parts.

The root is scraped and mixed with opium and hemlock to cause unconsciousness. I use it before operations and mix it with milk to make a poultice.'

'Isn't that dangerous?'

'Not in small quantities,' the doctor said, 'and if heated, not at all. Most poisonous plants are rendered safe when cooked.' He returned to the cupboard and ran the tips of his fingers over a collection of glass vials, mumbling unfamiliar words. Then he stopped and selected a brown bottle and set it upon the counter. He turned to face her, placing his white freckly hands on the table, fingers splayed out like a starfish.

'I can make a sedative from mandrake and hemlock but you must use it with great care. Five drops in wine at night to disguise the bitter taste would do the trick. No more.'

Julia nodded. 'I understand.'

He pulled on a pair of India-rubber gloves and cut a section of root from the mandrake and mashed it in a heavy mortar bowl. Carefully he extracted the pulped juice, poured it into an alabaster dish and combined it with twenty drops from the brown bottle. He selected one of the empty vials from the wooden stand and decanted the solution into it. He shook the pale yellow mixture, one finger clamped on the cork stopper.

After half a minute he checked the contents. 'What I need now is a proper fitting cork. Could you bring one from over there?' He pointed to a cupboard on the other side of the room containing stacks of bungs, corks, glass stoppers and caps. She examined several for a few moments before selecting four different sizes and returning. He took the second largest and twisted the cork inside the vial.

'If you overdose by mistake, ensure your father takes a stimulant. Coffee or castor oil would reduce the effect. But be very careful.'

Julia nodded and he handed her the vial.

CHAPTER FORTY-NINE

WEEKS OF UNEASE HAD PASSED IN THE BRAKOV HOUSEHOLD. The discovery that Sabroski Oil had been defrauded had exacerbated the tension at home. Stefan's father became more demanding, insisting on Stefan's presence to run tedious errands. That very afternoon he had been ordered onto the Bibi-Eibat oilfield, one of the many that were to be returned to Anton. When Stefan arrived he could see his father talking to Albert Prankman.

They were standing next to a well that had been capped the previous year and talking to a couple of Armenian engineers. A blistering sun beat down on the forest of wooden derricks standing to attention like soldiers. Most of the operations were shutting down and equipment was being dismantled. All around him, a flurry of court administrators with thick ledgers and stained buttoned tunics were busily compiling inventories. Two weeks had passed since the tribunal and at midnight the fields would be returned to Anton.

Stefan lit a cigarette, fretting at the mud that stuck to his boots and the grease that spotted his morning coat. The field overlooked the Caspian, which glittered so brightly that when he looked away everything fell into shadow. His father beckoned him over with the same disdain he used when summoning a servant. 'I need you go to the office and fetch something for me,' he barked as Stefan approached. 'Don't look now, but the man to the right with the pockmarked face is a court informer.'

'What am I supposed to get?'

'There's an important package in the safe. Hide it in case you're searched. Here's the combination code.' He gave him a scrap of paper from his pocket

'You're a damn fool not to have remembered that earlier,' said Prankman dropping a cigarette end into the mud.

Fabian ignored him. 'Do what you can, Stefan, and make sure you leave the field before dusk.'

'Why?'

'Never you mind. Just do it.'

Stefan trudged down the hill towards a squat stone building near the waterfront. Everywhere, Tatars in flat caps and filthy tunics ferried equipment and supplies to wagons stationed next to administrators, who were counting, recording, measuring and inspecting.

He unlocked the office door and went to the desk and sat down. A row of empty cabinets lined the wall, and a large cupboard spilled its drawers onto the floor. An oil brazier, smeared with ash from the previous winter, stood in front of a disused fireplace.

Stefan lit another cigarette and leaned back in the chair. There was no rush. He had no desire to return to the company of his father. He wanted time to reflect. It was odd to think that by tomorrow Anton Sabroski would own the field. He couldn't work out whether he was annoyed or pleased; anything that frustrated his father brought him satisfaction.

Stefan took a deep drag and exhaled the smoke slowly. Things would be different now. The results of the court case had shown that his father wasn't infallible after all; his protective armour had been pierced.

It was eerily quiet. This was the first time he'd been on an oilfield and not heard the pounding of drills, the whistle of steam engines and the clank of tank cars. The whole orchestra had put down its instruments and stopped playing, almost as if the field had died. He took off his hat, put his feet on the table and closed his eyes.

When he awoke the sun had gone down. He rubbed his neck and pulled out his pocket watch. *Six o'clock. Shit!* He went over to the fireplace and heaved the fake fire-front away from the wall. Behind lay a steel door with a combination lock. Bending down, he took out the scrap of paper and read the code. He spun the dials and eased open the door.

A small box lay inside. Stefan took it, opening it to reveal its contents. It was a painted miniature of an old man with grey hair hanging in curls around his face, a prominent nose, and dark clever eyes. Stefan turned it over and read the inscription. He stared and laughed in surprise. Stefan secured the miniature inside his waistcoat, pushed the fireplace back into position and picked up his hat.

The ground beneath him trembled.

A few seconds later, a deafening roar shook the air and rattled the windows. Stefan was thrown backwards as the door smashed back on its hinges. Pulling himself up, Stefan staggered outside.

Up on the hill a well was spouting oil with such force that sections of the wooden derrick whirled in the air like a spinning top. Black oil spewed out, carried on the wind to neighbouring plots. Stefan watched in awe as the fountain stalk gained in ferocity, stretching its neck higher and higher like a straining black cobra.

Through the spray of sunlight and oil, Stefan saw two men lying on the ground: shiny black beetles with thrashing limbs.

*

Anton had spent the afternoon on the Group Nineteen oilfields with the oil baron Hajji Zeynalabdin Taghiyev. The old Tatar filled two glasses with tea and handed one to Anton. 'So, Anton Nikolayevich, we're about to become neighbours. I'm glad to see a Sabroski back in charge of these fields. Though I'm disappointed to lose such a good field, I'm delighted it's being returned to you. Tell me, what do you know about oil?'

'I'm still learning.'

Taghiyev laughed. 'I thought as much. I knew nothing when I started. And now look at me. A millionaire. And I can't even read or write.'

Anton laughed.

Taghiyev scratched his thick black beard. 'What you need, my boy, is to buy in some expertise and leave it to them. Find yourself a wife and start a family. A man like you needs sons. Do you have a sweetheart?'

Anton hesitated.

'Well then, that's your priority.'

'That's good advice, sir. I will certainly do what I can.' Anton sipped his tea.

The sun had started to fade, and a fresh breeze swept up from the sea. As the minutes passed, the dusk was deepening, pushing the sun down behind the hills. Anton never thought the Bibi-Eibat fields could seem beautiful, that it was possible to soften the edges of the stiff wooden derricks and cast shades of peach over the oil pools, but at that moment anything seemed possible.

Anton consulted his pocket watch. It was six fifteen. In the distance, the court administrators were packing up and leaving. He preferred to wait until the Brakovs had left as he did not relish an encounter. He had no desire to gloat or revel in their undoing. Whatever role the Brakovs had played in the matter would eventually become apparent.

A distant rumble shook away his thoughts. Taghiyev blanched, cursed and threw down his tea glass. 'A spouter!'

He opened the door and hurried out. Anton tore after him.

Outside, Taghiyev held onto his fez and stared up at the sky. 'It's coming from the Brakov fields – the ones they've returned to you. There won't be anyone there to stop it. We must act quickly!'

Taghiyev shouted orders to a gang of men who dropped their tools and ran towards the wagons. He turned to Anton. 'I'll send word to Emanuel Nobel. He has the best engineers in Baku.'

*

Stefan followed the railway tracks down to the sea. The mud paths had turned into rivers of oil and smoke clouds smarted his eyes. A ghostly figure appeared through the mist. Stefan stared and broke into a run. It was his father.

'How did this happen?' shouted Stefan.

Fabian Brakov grabbed his arm. 'You fool, Stefan. I told you to be gone by dusk.'

'*You* did this?'

Fabian's eyes gleamed. 'The damage caused by this spouter will be beyond Sabroski. I'd rather smash it to bits than give Nikolai back his field.'

'You mean Anton?'

'Nikolai. Anton. All Sabroskis. All the same to me.'

'Why? I don't understand.'

'The fools released the cap too quickly,' Fabian raved. 'I told them to ease the pressure off slowly and leave her to blow when we were out of the way. But the idiots didn't know what they were doing.'

'Where's Prankman?'

'I don't know. We were separated.'

A derrick cracked open nearby spitting charred wooden bullets in every direction. Stefan winced as a fragment pierced his cheek. His father's neck was bleeding and strands of his hair were clumped with blood.

'Did you get the package?'

'No,' lied Stefan.

'Damn you, Stefan. Why can't you do anything right?'

Stefan turned away. *Because you have a bloody useless son. You've said so enough times.*

Stefan led his father down to the beach. A thousand lights bobbed up and down in the breeze flowing across the crescent bay. A large steamer was approaching the harbour, funnelling waves that spiralled out from its wake. Several boats were tethered to a wooden pier jutting into the water.

Stefan climbed onto the jetty. 'Come on. We'll take a boat.'

His father hesitated and squinted out to sea with a frown. Stefan untied one of the boats from its moorings and climbed down into the hull. 'It won't take us long. We can row round to the harbour.'

His father growled a reply and sat on edge of the pier, easing himself carefully into the boat. Stefan held out an arm to help as Fabian heaved inside, clutching onto the sides.

Stefan pushed the boat away from the pier and rowed out into the gloom. He could see distant figures running onto the field as the alarm was raised. Soon they would bring in the engineers to cap the well. But it would probably be too late by then.

Stefan rowed towards the harbour. Fabian held onto the sides of the boat, his knuckles white. A sudden swirl of current made the boat lurch to one side. Stefan lost concentration for a second and one of the oars floated away. Cursing, he leaned over the side and made to grab it, but the oar spun out of reach.

'You fool,' Fabian cried, leaning over the stern as another wave hit the boat. Breathing fast, Stefan secured the second oar inside and stood up. The boat rocked and another wave from the steamer struck the boat again. Stefan felt the air being punched out of him as he fell back. He heard a cry and a splash, as his father pitched into the water.

Screaming, Fabian thrashed about, his head disappearing under the water. Stefan threw himself as close to the edge of the boat as he dared and leaned over the side. He thrust out his hand, but his father was too far away.

The errant oar floated past, and Stefan grabbed hold of it, but the oar was heavy and slippery. He gasped for breath as he tried to swing the oar towards his father.

Fabian was howling in fear, arms flailing as he grabbed the air. Stefan stared at the struggling man. He looked wild and brutal like some malevolent sea creature from the depths of the ocean.

Then, slowly, Stefan pulled the oar back.

Later, Stefan Brakov wasn't sure of the exact moment he decided to let his father die. As he crouched in the boat, watching his father surface, thrash about and then sink, he only knew he felt nothing.

At last, the sea was still. There was no sign of his father, just blue-black water reflecting fiery yellow from the field. Stefan lay flat in the boat and stared up at the pinpricked sky until the terror in his chest had calmed.

Then he picked up the oars and rowed home

Chapter Fifty

By the time Anton reached the field, the fountain was over two hundred feet high. An easterly wind had risen from the sea and a ridge of sand was piling up behind the remains of the derrick. Channels of oil gushed through and ran back down to the water.

'We'll need to block the pipe temporarily until the Nobels get here,' said Taghiyev, beckoning two men. 'Find something that will act as a mast.'

Anton led the men to a pile of felled trees by the side of the boiler room. 'Find some chains and pulleys,' he ordered, as he wiped his face with his sleeve. They loaded the logs into a cart and started down the hill. Anton cursed at the destruction. In less than twenty minutes the spouter had reached three hundred feet and was hurling boulders and sand in all directions. He shielded his face as a spray of oil rained down on him.

Anton approached the rim of the crater where the seventy-foot derrick once stood. Oil bubbled around the stalk of the fountain as a jet spurted up through the bore pipe. It shot hundreds of feet into the air, widening until it spread out like an umbrella.

Anton beckoned the men as they backed the terrified horse and wagon nearer. 'Hold her!' he shouted. The Kabardin black horse reared up, kicking and tugging at its reins, its jaw covered in spittle. Anton grabbed the reins but the sturdy horse from the Caucasus whinnied and wrenched free. It galloped away in terror.

Anton shouted orders and together they dragged the largest of the logs towards the crater. Two men stood ready with heavy clubs as Anton wiped the oil and sweat from his eyes. 'When I give the word... Now!'

In one swift motion they slammed the trunk down as hard as they could, crouching down to hold it in place while the two men whacked it with their clubs. Oil hissed in all directions. The trunk shook and tried to lift itself out.

'It's never going to hold!'

'Don't let go. Hold fast!'

Oil and sand broke free from the perimeter.

'Don't let go!'

The tree trunk fought like a wild creature. The men smashed harder with their clubs. On and on it went.

Until at last it stopped and became still.

The men staggered back. Anton's legs trembled and he coughed and collapsed to the ground taking huge gulps of air. Somebody grabbed his arm and helped him up. It was Emanuel Nobel. 'Good job, Sabroski, but it won't hold long. My engineers are here.'

Anton wiped his sleeve over his face and followed Nobel to a wagon where a crew of men stood next to a huge cast-iron plate. One of the engineers nodded at him. 'Don't you worry, sir. This cap will do the trick. It weights ten tons and can resist nine atmospheres.' He shouted to the gang of men who were digging channels in the sand trying to stem the flow of oil. 'Over here.' The men dropped their spades. But as they approached a rumbling started beneath their feet.

'She's going to blow again. Quick, get away!'

'Take cover,' shouted Nobel.

Anton watched in despair as the tree mast juddered. He knew what was going to happen. A tremendous roar blasted the mast high into the air and a shower of rocks burst out of the well. Within moments the fountain had reached hundreds of feet again. It was higher than before, almost as if the fury of it being contained had made it more ferocious.

Anton raced up the hill towards the cover of the boiler house and hurled himself inside.

At first, Anton thought the roof of the boiler house had collapsed. Something had struck him, but he couldn't see anything. He could smell burning flesh and the metallic reek of blood. Then he realised Prankman was standing over him. He had armed himself with a large piece of blackened wood. Its charred end was still burning, and red-hot nails protruded from the tip.

Anton forced open his eyes and gazed into a grimace of hatred. Prankman hit him again, tearing Anton's jacket and ripping through to his arm, but Anton hardly felt the pain. He charged forward and knocked Prankman to the ground.

Anton put his hands around Prankman's neck and squeezed, but his weakened arm betrayed him. Prankman prised his fingers away and Anton felt the American roll him round and try to gouge his eyes out. Anton jerked his knee up into the man's groin and threw him off. Prankman howled.

Panting, both men struggled to their feet. Anton wiped blood and dirt from his eyes and saw Prankman pull out a gun. Immediately, Anton dived to the right as the gun went off. He grabbed part of the broken cylinder casing and used it as a shield while bullets ricocheted round the room. The firing stopped, and Anton heard Prankman reload.

Anton propelled himself forward. He swung the cylinder casing up and brought it down hard.

Prankman fell backwards out of the door.

At that moment a tremendous crash shook the building. A gigantic rock had landed on the roof, causing the iron structure to collapse. Timbers and metal supports toppled in. The roof opened up to the sky and sand rained down.

Anton threw himself next to the cistern and crankshaft for protection and put his hands over his head. When the crashing stopped, all he could hear was an ominous hissing.

*

Prankman crawled away from the boiler house. The building had caved in and the roof was gone. He coughed in pain and struggled to stand. For several minutes he watched for movement, almost willing his adversary to rise up out of the ruins so that he could take one last shot. But all he could see was smoke and dust.

Prankman limped towards his gig. It was time to get away before anyone saw him. The pain in his chest was worsening and he knew where he needed to go.

CHAPTER FIFTY-ONE

JULIA HAD BEEN WAITING A LONG TIME. SHE WAS JUST ABOUT to give up, when she saw Prankman's gig tear round the corner, almost knocking down a group of sailors. The American had his hat pushed down over his face, his bloodied hands gripping the reins like a harness racer. Prankman's gig looked filthy and it was covered in oil and sand.

Julia ordered her carriage to follow, ducking back behind the window in case Prankman saw her. Not that he was likely to recognise her, because Julia hardly recognised herself. She had rouged her cheeks, painted her lips and borrowed a skirt and blouse from the housemaid. A large hat and an old cape had transformed her.

The girls at the opium den said that Prankman usually visited on a Thursday. So she waited, but he hadn't come. The hours passed and the sun started to sink so she concluded that this was the one week he had broken his habit. Frustrated, she had told the driver to drive back along the embankment. She would find somewhere to change and wash her face before returning home.

And then he came.

Driving like a madman.

And it was lucky that Julia knew where he was going because her carriage would never have been able to keep up.

She reached the railway station and jumped out and fixed her eyes on Prankman. She was shocked at his appearance. Blood streaked down one side of his face and his stained clothes were in tatters.

Julia made sure the carriage driver saw her walk through the main station entrance. She watched Prankman vanish down the basement steps as she darted into a doorway.

It was time.

Breathe. Be calm. This is for you, Rafiq, my love.

What she was about to do was irreversible. She had thought about it for days, weighing up the risk of discovery. Would she ever be able to absolve herself, knowing God was unlikely to forgive? Her faith, blindly accepted all her life, was now under attack.

Julia felt for the glass vial in her blue beaded purse. It lay on its side, corked, hard and smooth, a firm outline through the velvet casing. She slipped her hand inside and clasped it.

Sleep Bringer. Life Taker. Death Tempter.

The opium den was as Julia remembered: dim and foul with sweat and musk. Girls in silken gowns floated between bamboo dividers painted with geometric block-like symbols in red and black. A young girl approached. 'You new?'

Julia nodded, touching her hair. The girl surveyed her curiously. 'Haven't I seen you before?'

'Usually I have special clients.'

The girl grinned showing tiny yellow teeth. 'I remember. Good-looking man.' She jerked her head to one side. 'We have our usual horrors tonight.' The girl took her hand. 'Don't be nervous. This place isn't as bad as it looks. The men don't trouble you much. They just want to look at you and smoke.' She stroked Julia's face. 'But you're not dressed right.'

She hooked her arm through Julia's and pulled her behind a curtain. The area inside had a long mirror and a lantern suspended on a string stretched between two hooks. The girl picked up a box crammed with coloured implements and pots. 'Sit down and I'll fix you up. Your eyes need more kohl,' she said, pushing Julia into a chair. 'Men like big, dark eyes.'

She took a thin piece of horn and dipped it into a bottle of black powder, twisting it round to coat it. Then she tilted Julia's face upwards and pulled the stick across Julia's eyelids and into the crease of her eyes: a quick sharp movement. She dabbed spots of rouge onto Julia's cheeks and coloured her lips a brighter shade of red. Julia looked at herself in the mirror. It was like looking at a fairground doll.

'My name's Katherine. But everyone calls me Katie. What's yours?'

'Anna.'

'That's a pretty name. But one more thing. Take off your clothes. The men like to see your breasts.'

Julia froze. The girl laughed and pulled Julia's bodice open, staring at her breasts. She touched them; her hands were cool and soft. 'They'll like you,' the girl said, trailing her fingers across Julia's nipples. 'Just wear your corset and slip one of these gowns over your shoulders.' She unhooked a red satin gown from a peg on the wall and handed it to Julia. It smelled of musk.

Julia trembled as she unhooked her skirt and let it fall to the floor. The girl scooped it up and hung it over a chair. Then she held back the curtain and led the way. A new customer entered, prompting Julia to shrink back into the shadows. Katie hooked the customer's arm and took him behind one of the screens.

Julia pulled her gown closed and secured it with a silken tie as she stood breathing in the air of the drug-filled basement. Sweat gathered under her arms and ran down between her breasts. Low giggles and soft words floated from dark corners. *Please forgive me, Mama.* Julia's neck was clammy and cold and exposed without the locket, but this was no place for her mother to see.

She drifted along the aisles looking behind screens until she found him. He looked even more monstrous than she remembered. His face was bloodied and puffy. Red-stained cloths were strewn next to him where one of the girls had tried to clean him up. Prankman lay as still as death with his eyes closed.

A Chinese girl was sitting cross-legged on the floor, twisting the sticky substance around in the flame. The girl looked up at Julia. 'You want to take over?'

'He's a regular of mine.' Julia pressed her fingers to her lips.

'You're welcome to him. But be careful. He's in an evil mood tonight.' She handed Julia a long needle which was skewered onto a glistening brown substance. 'It's nearly done. He'll be ready for a new one soon. But don't give him too much, he's already had enough.'

'How many pipes has he had?'

'Two. This is his third.'

The girl slid away and Julia crouched down next to the oil lamp. Prankman sprawled on a dirty divan, shirt open, eyes closed, his tortoiseshell monocle attached by a black silken thread lying on his chest. A jug of iced tea sat on a low bamboo table beside him.

Julia looked around, her heart jumping with fright. She picked up the jug and filled a glass. Taking the vial out from her bag, she uncorked it and poured the solution into the tea.

Prankman stirred and opened his eyes. The whites of them were bloodshot, the pupils like pinpricks. 'I know you.' He levered himself up. 'Come here.'

Julia tensed.

Prankman pulled her towards him, probing his rough fingers into her silk gown and causing her to drop the empty vial. 'Finish making that pipe.'

'Would you like a glass of tea first?'

'No. I want another pipe.'

With trembling fingers, Julia relit the lamp and held the opium into the flame, trying to remember what she'd seen the girls do before. The drug cracked and glistened, and all the time she felt his eyes on her. 'Where do I know you from?'

'I was here a few months ago.'

'No. Somewhere else. You're not like the usual ones.' He kicked her. 'Pay attention to what you're doing. That must be done by now.'

She pulled the pill from the flame as he thrust the pipe towards her. Inside the bulb she could see flecks of ash. She pushed the opium into the bulb, kneading it down with her fingers.

Prankman grabbed her hand. 'You don't know what you're doing, do you?' He closed her fingers round the bulb and forced her hand into the flame. The pain was shocking, and she cried out.

Prankman whispered, clamping his free hand across her mouth. 'Who are you? A little spy?'

The skin across the back of her fingers blistered and the smell of burnt flesh filled her nostrils. 'I swear I'm no spy,' she gasped. 'This is my first time.'

Prankman released her and shouted over the bamboo screen. 'Mei-Hua! Come here?'

Julia nursed her hand and bent her head between her knees. She wanted to vomit.

'Hey, what's going on?' The Chinese girl had returned. She looked down at Julia in surprise. 'You all right?'

'Get her out of here.'

'I'm sorry, sir, but I thought you knew her.'

'No, I don't, and I don't want a beginner. Make me more pipes.'

'You've had several already, sir.'

'Do as I say.'

Prankman aimed a kick, but the girl dodged out of his way.

The girl threw Julia a questioning look as Prankman clutched his chest and manoeuvred himself into a sitting position. He was breathing heavily, sweat droplets forming across his forehead. He leaned across and picked up the glass of tea.

Julia slipped behind the screen, and through a vision of pain, watched him drink.

CHAPTER FIFTY-TWO

ANTON FOUGHT TO FREE HIMSELF FROM THE WRECKAGE OF the boiler room, forging a clearing before the men managed to reach him. Many of the engineers were bloodied and battered. One had been killed and several ferried to hospital with broken limbs. Someone checked over his injuries and declared his arm needed medical assistance. Anton waved him away and looked round for signs of the American.

Night had fallen and the field was bathed in moonlight. Anton searched his surroundings. Possibly Prankman had been so badly injured that he lay somewhere on the field. Or hopefully he had fallen into an oil well while he staggered about in the dark. That would be truly satisfying and Anton nurtured the thought for a while, examining any potential oil well that might have received such a worthy victim. But Prankman was nowhere to be seen.

Anton returned to the crater where scores of men sat on their haunches waiting for orders. Emanuel Nobel and Taghiyev stood with a group of engineers.

'My dear boy, we feared the worst!' Taghiyev gasped as he

looked him up and down. 'And you've been injured. Let's get you to a surgeon.'

It took three days before the fields were made safe. Anton didn't leave the fields until it was done. Luckily the bore casing of the well had not been ruined, which meant the iron plate cap could easily be fixed into place. Anton watched the engineers lower the cap into position and tighten the seal. Afterwards, one of the engineers pointed to the channel of oil running through a sandy ridge. 'If I were you, Sabroski, I'd run that lake of oil to a reserve. When the cap is fixed, this little spouter should bring you a tidy sum.'

It was on the fourth day while Anton was packing up and getting ready to return to the house that Klara arrived on the field. She looked horrified at his bandaged arm and battered face. She stood with her hands on her hips while he explained what had happened.

'Well, that might explain some of the mystery,' she said.

'What mystery?'

'Fabian Brakov is dead and Albert Prankman's gone missing.'

The next morning, Anton lay in bed deep in thought. It was hard to take in what had happened. A mysterious boating accident followed by the disappearance of Prankman. Had the American murdered Fabian as well? If so, where was the odious man? There had been no more bodies found on the field, he wasn't to be found at his rooms or usual haunts' rooms, and nobody had seen him at the club. It was possible he was recuperating quietly in an unknown clinic. Anton entertained the idea that he had already left Baku. After all, Prankman had been exposed as an oil spy as well as a cheat at the gentleman's club. He was also implicated in the Zenovitch Liquid Fuel fraud, and although nothing had been proved, in time evidence would be found.

And then there was David Cherlin. Perhaps Prankman *was* David Cherlin? He had posed as several different men, so why not another?

Anton rose from his bed, pulled on his dressing gown and went downstairs. The house was silent in the early morning. He picked up a cable from the hall table and went into the kitchen. He poured a glass of tea, cut some cheese, and tore off a chunk of bread as Klara appeared with Olga and a dead chicken. They disappeared down the scullery steps.

Anton opened the cable and read.

Marcus Samuel to Anton Nikolayevich Sabroski, August 28th 1891

Success! Lloyds of London classify Hasanov tanker as a Class 1 risk. Suez Canal Company to revise regulations. Ship builders to begin building tanker.

Anton had to read it twice before the cable's meaning sank in. His mind was clogged with thoughts of Prankman and the oilfields, but his head cleared, and he gave a whoop of delight. He punched the air and staggered down the scullery steps as fast as his injuries would permit. 'Klara!'

She looked up. 'What's the matter?' She was sitting at a scrubbed wooden table with a chicken flopped across her lap. Feathers lay about her feet.

Anton waved the cable in the air. 'It's from Marcus. The tanker's been accepted.' He grabbed the chicken and threw it onto the table. Then he lifted her up and twirled her about, ignoring the burning pain in his chest and arm.

'You seem to have recovered quickly!' Klara gasped. Two

hairpins fell out of her hair and a brown strand flopped down her back. 'Have you gone mad?'

'Rafiq's tanker is going to be built!'

'What? Put me down!'

'The Suez Canal have accepted Rafiq's tanker plans. We've won!'

Her eyes widened. 'Show me.' She grabbed the cable and read. 'Oh, my goodness, what marvellous news.' She stood on tiptoe and planted a kiss on his cheek. 'I am *so* pleased for you.'

Anton laughed as Klara dashed over to the sink and washed her hands. She recovered her hairpins from the floor and fixed them in her hair. Then she ran up the scullery steps and into the kitchen. Anton followed, watching as she snatched up her bonnet and shawl.

'Where are you going?'

'To tell Julia of course!'

CHAPTER FIFTY-THREE

AT THAT MOMENT, JULIA WAS SITTING IN HER BEDROOM with her eyes closed as dread consumed her.

I am a murderer.

She had seen Prankman drink the tea. He must be dead by now. Covering her head with her hands, she rocked herself as nausea swam up her throat.

Stop this! Stop this now!

She forced her eyes open, took a ruby glass bottle with a silver top from her purse and opened the lid. She inhaled the ammonia and felt her head reel as the smelling salts pounded the back of her nose.

She had executed Albert Prankman because he was guilty of the murder of Rafiq Hasanov. Prankman was the real murderer, not her. She had held the trial and played jury and pronounced judgement – she had merely carried out what the courts would have done. Surely God would see it like that?

She traced the outline of the owl on her blue beaded bag. Prankman was an American. She was a Russian Jew. He was an influential businessman. She was nobody, the daughter of a Jewish lawyer.

A stab of dread pierced her again.

I dropped the glass vial.

If anyone found it, they would know Prankman had been poisoned. The girls would know it was her, they would be able to recognise her, be able to point her out if they saw her again.

Julia stood up and paced the room. She must never go out. She would stay in the house for the next few months until the matter died away. The authorities had better things to do than spend months looking for Prankman's killer. Nobody would think her capable of such a crime. A woman with child wasn't likely to go around murdering businessmen. Daughters of respectable lawyers did not visit opium dens. She mustn't allow such fantasies to frighten her.

Her stepmother knocked on her door and made her jump. 'You have a visitor, Julia. It looks like that girl from Anton Nikolayevich's house.'

*

Stefan stood with his back to the window. Miranda was silent, encased in a black day dress. Olesia Brakov looked pale, dressed in a gown completely covered in black crepe. 'I don't understand it, Stefan. Why would Fabian get in a boat on his own? He was frightened of water. He never learned to swim.'

Stefan lit a cigarette. 'I don't understand it either, Mother. I was in the office. Father sent me to fetch some papers. I heard the explosion. I ran out and saw the well had blown. It was that dangerous one we'd had capped before.'

Miranda caught his eye, but Stefan looked away.

Olesia shook her head. 'And where is Albert Prankman? He hasn't even the decency to pay his respects.'

The deceit had been easier than Stefan thought. After his father had stopped moving, he rowed round to the harbour. Nobody took any notice of him as he pushed the boat back into the water and watched it float away. But then he hadn't looked much like a gentleman: soaking wet and oil spattered, no hat and a ripped jacket, bloodstained and stinking. Stefan had pushed through the crowds and hired a cab to take him home. Luckily, nobody saw him slip inside the back entrance of the house.

He wasn't sure what his mother felt; her spousal devotion had faded years ago. It had been a long time since she'd cried when his father took other women or had one of his rages. She hadn't shed a tear since hearing of his death, or else they'd been in private.

'Where is your father's body now?' said Miranda.

'In the city morgue. A fisherman pulled him from the water and alerted the soldiers.'

Olesia went to the window and turned her face to the sunlight. Stefan rarely saw beyond the maternal veil, but with the light on her face he could see her faded beauty: large violet eyes, thick greying hair and a wide mouth. But her summer was over; lines creased her skin and her mouth had puckered too many times in displeasure.

'From now on, Stefan, you are the head of the house.' Olesia glowered. 'But let us be rid of that American. This family does not need him.'

*

Two weeks later a body was found.

Stefan read about it in the Baku *Vedomosti* while eating breakfast, half an eye glancing at the daily news, the other skimming documents he had to sign. He wouldn't have noticed except for two things. Firstly, the man was a foreign gentleman as could be seen from the cut and style of his clothes, which clung to the decomposing corpse, and secondly, a list of objects belonging to the man accompanied the description.

The owners of a house near the railway station complained their water had an evil smell, and had paid a small boy to climb down. The poor child shrieked with fright when faced with such a ghoulish discovery. There followed a lurid description of what the body looked like, a full description of the well, interviews with the distraught owners followed by much speculation as to who the victim could be and why he had fallen down the well in the first place. Was it a gambling debt? A rival lover? A robbery? Perhaps the man had simply been drunk and lost his senses? Robbery was the probable motive, it reasoned. Baku had become a den of thieves with the influx of workers coming in from the countryside. The city had grown from a mere twenty thousand to over a hundred thousand within a few decades. It was no safe place for any respectable man or woman, and the mayor should do something about it!

Stefan put the paper down and spooned sugar into his tea. A list of objects had been found with the body and an invite was issued to anyone with information to present themselves to the chief of police.

Stefan hesitated.

A tortoiseshell-rimmed monocle with a black silk thread had been found tucked in the top pocket of the dead man's waistcoat.

CHAPTER FIFTY-FOUR

IT WAS JOHN SEIGENBERG WHO INFORMED ANTON THAT Prankman was dead. Anton conjured a gruesome image of the American's body bloody and battered at the bottom of a well. They proposed all sorts of scenarios as to how he met his end. Privately, Anton thought he knew: Prankman's injuries must have been worse than he thought. Perhaps he bled to death on the street or collapsed in the nearby opium den. But whatever the truth, he savoured the gratifying news.

Anton worked long days on the fields. The damage caused by the spouter was more extensive than he first realised, and he was grateful for the expertise lent to him by Taghiyev and the Nobel Brothers. Fifteen groups of fields were in the process of being returned to him, which meant a great deal of assessing, hiring and overseeing the transfer of equipment back to the company. Most of the money from Zenovitch Liquid Fuel was unaccounted for, despite the company's assets being frozen. It had undoubtedly been diverted to unknown pockets. Investigations were ongoing, but now that the main stakeholders were dead, Anton doubted the whole truth would emerge. Meanwhile, it would be a long time before the company was back on its feet. Anton hired a new accountant, charged Klara with being responsible for the workers' welfare, and Rasoul to run the Group Twenty fields. Anton also promised to discuss the formation of a cooperative. Following the news from Marcus of the tanker success, Anton felt that, at last, his fortunes were turning.

Except for the Fabergé egg.

Anton had pledged the egg in repayment for loans to buy back the fields. Now it was September and the agreed date was looming. The gentleman's agreement had been a gamble, and one that he'd sadly lost. Ironically, he would be a rich man someday, but it wouldn't be soon enough. De Boer had since reminded him of his commitment. The baron would arrive in Baku shortly and was very much looking forward to seeing one of Carl Fabergé's masterpieces.

One week before the Rothschild meeting, Anton received word from Melek, the Armenian silversmith, to visit him at his teahouse. When Anton arrived the place was heaving and thick with smoke. The sun blazed, and the shisha pipes uncoiled like sleepy pythons.

'I bring news of Katharine Lapinski,' said Melek.

'You know where she is?'

'No, but I know where she *was*.'

'Where?'

'The Grand Duke Konstantin installed her in a house in Kiev. If you remember, Konstantin had remarried, and the new wife did not approve of his liaison with Katharine.'

'He moved his mistress away?'

Melek nodded. 'He still visited, but as time passed, the visits became less frequent. Around eighty-six, the house in Kiev was sold and Katharine disappeared.'

'And that's when she came to Baku?'

'Maybe. But she may simply have died. Do you still believe those newspaper cuttings came from her?'

Anton frowned. 'I don't know. If they did come from her, I don't understand why she never wanted to meet.'

'Have you received any more cuttings?'

'No.'

'Melek scratched his nose with a long fingernail. 'A piece of Katharine's jewellery was found in Baku in eighty-seven – a very valuable ring given to her by the grand duke. According to accounts, it seems it was stolen.'

'Her ring? In Baku? Who stole it?'

'I don't know. All I do know is that the ring was returned to Konstantin.'

'So that proves Katharine Lapinski was in Baku in eighty-seven.'

'Possibly, but there are other implications. Katharine might have been robbed and murdered, here, or in Kiev. That would account for her disappearance.'

'Which means the person sending me those cuttings...' Anton said slowly, '... wants me to think she is still alive.'

*

The sea slapped against the wharf as Julia looked down at silver fish darting in and out of shadows.

Leo touched her arm. 'Julia, you know what I'm going to say.'

She watched fishermen pull their boat out of the water. 'I know you want a decision, Leo. But there's something you must know first. Let's walk a little.'

The wide embankment road followed the curve of the bay. A line of two-storey houses and shops with dirty awnings stood back from the water. There was an octagonal teahouse set in the middle of the embankment gardens.

The found a seat facing the quayside. Leo sat opposite Julia and clasped her gloved fingers, and immediately she withdrew them. Leo wasn't to know her burned hand still ached. 'I cannot marry you, Leo. I cannot marry anyone. I'm sorry.'

'Why do you want to make life so hard for yourself?'

'What do you mean?'

'I know of your condition, Julia. I know you are with child.'

Julia's heart thumped. 'How?'

'Miranda told me.'

'She had no right!'

'She's your friend and wants to do what's best for you. How much longer do you think you could have kept this secret?'

Julia couldn't look at him.

'I love you, Julia. It makes no difference. I've loved you all my life. I'm no one without you.'

'It's Rafiq's child.' The forbidden tears ran down Julia's face.

'I know.'

'I loved him. But that doesn't mean I don't love you.'

'I know that too.'

A steamer pulled into the harbour. People ran down the pier passing bags and trunks over the tops of heads.

'There's something else,' Julia said. A swell of nausea rose in her stomach. 'It's about Albert Prankman.'

Leo's face greyed. 'You overheard that night, didn't you?'

Julia nodded.

'I thought so. I heard something. I knew you were outside.'

'It's my fault he's dead.'

'How can it be your fault? Unless you pushed him down that well.'

Julia frowned. This was news to her. 'What do you mean?'

'Prankman's body was found down a well near the railway station. Stefan Brakov had to identify the remains.'

'How did his body get down a well?'

'Nobody knows. There's going to be a post-mortem.'

Julia tried to protest. 'But...'

Leo put his finger to her lips. 'Don't let's talk about this any more,' he said. 'You may have prayed for his death, but I assure you it wasn't anything divine that killed him. With your permission, I'd like to speak to your father tomorrow night. If he agrees we can book a wedding date.'

As they both got to their feet, Julia said nothing more.

CHAPTER FIFTY-FIVE

ANTON DIDN'T SLEEP MUCH ON THE EVE OF THE Rothschild meeting. He hated the idea of taking the Fabergé egg from its hidden compartment and surrendering it to the baron. But there was nothing more to be done: a promise was a promise.

Baron Alphonse Rothschild was every bit as impressive as he remembered: silver-white hair, the famous luxuriant moustache and long bushy sideburns framing a craggy face. The baron had been a handsome man in his younger days, but age had softened his features, causing him to appear like a benign old uncle instead of one of the richest men in Europe. The business manager, De Boer, had brought a stack of documents with him but it was obvious that they had not been talking business. Anton could tell by the awkward way De Boer shuffled the papers and the probing look on the baron's face. The room was scented with jasmine bunched in clusters around the walls and a huge chandelier caught the sunlight and sparkled overhead, but the perfume cloyed at the back of Anton's throat and the light hurt his eyes.

'Congratulations, Sabroski,' said the baron gripping his hand.

'You have your company back. Well done. You must feel very proud of yourself. I know I would be.'

'Thank you, sir.'

'And we have another success – Marcus Samuel's coup has paid off.' The baron chuckled and puffed on his cigar. 'I'd like to have seen Rockefeller's face when he heard that. De Boer has already prepared the contract for Marcus Samuel to sign. It appears he wishes to buy a great deal of oil from us. Since you are a part of this venture, perhaps you'd care to take a look?'

'I'd be delighted.' Secretly, Anton wasn't feeling at all delighted; he had no desire to read through a contract. The Fabergé egg seemed to burn against his breastbone, as if it were furious at being betrayed.

The baron smiled. 'But what we really want, Sabroski, is to see the Fabergé egg.'

Anton's pulse quickened as he retrieved it from his dinner jacket pocket. The baron took it, unwrapped it from its protective silk covering and held it between his forefinger and thumb.

There was a profound silence.

'It is far more beautiful than you described, De Boer.' The baron twisted it round, the light from the chandelier setting fire to the rose-red enamel, stars skipping off the encrusted diamonds. He trailed his fingers over the trellis of green-gold orchids. 'A princely gift indeed. And you say it was bequeathed to you by your father?'

'Yes, sir.'

'And how did he come by it, I wonder?' He looked at Anton quizzically.

'I don't know, sir.' Anton shifted his feet.

'And yet you pledged it for an oilfield. Even though it's probably not yours to sell.'

'It belonged to my father, and he passed it down to me. In that respect, it is rightfully mine.'

'Perhaps… but we shall see.' The baron placed the egg on the table. 'Your fields have had a bit of trouble, I hear.'

'The problem has been resolved.'

'But you still haven't met our bargain.'

Anton felt a flush of heat. 'With respect, sir, the field has a great deal of oil, but it was deliberately targeted by hired ruffians. I have a surveyor report that proves oil exists and I can organise another independent surveyor if you so wish. The field has rich potential for revenue.'

'I'm glad to hear it.'

'You know I can pay. It will just take time.'

'But that wasn't our agreement, Sabroski.'

'I understand that. But circumstances have changed. I hoped you would be more flexible.'

The baron raised his eyebrows. 'I'm afraid that's not possible, especially as your circumstances are about to change again.' He looked at his pocket watch and nodded at De Boer.

De Boer tucked his thumb into his waistcoat pocket. 'Sabroski, I have taken the liberty of sending a message to your assistant. The baron has a guest arriving who wishes to speak to her.'

Anton's heart thudded. 'Why? Is Klara in some kind of trouble?'

'I'm afraid I cannot say, but her presence is important.'

'Who wants to speak to her?'

'Do not concern yourself. I assure you she will come to no harm. However, I am aware that the lady can be somewhat wilful, so I asked that she fetch your cable from Marcus Samuel. I said that it was extremely important and that you had forgotten it. I pretended to be you. Please forgive my subterfuge.'

Anton frowned. 'I do not approve of this. I have no wish to deceive her.'

The baron placed a steadying hand on Anton's arm. 'I give

you my word that the girl will not be harmed. My guest would simply like to speak to you both.'

De Boer poured more drinks. 'There is just enough time to read the contract before he arrives.' The Rothschild manager passed Anton the thick document he'd been holding onto. Anton took it reluctantly, the dark type demanding attention: *BNITO – The Caspian and Black Sea Petroleum Company*: the Rothschild oil company. Waves of unease slammed into his chest.

He could not have been reading for more than ten minutes when he heard Klara's familiar spirited run and the rustle of her dress. Like a young colt, she bounded into the room. She was wearing her old-fashioned silk day dress, the one she wore on New Year's Day. It was edged with frilled lace on a blue background, embroidered with dark blue flowers. She had on her old, scuffed kid leather boots – he remembered they were also lined with pale blue silk.

Anton felt a lump in his throat. She hesitated when she saw them all sitting there, like crafty black spiders in a web. 'I brought you the cable.' She looked round the room and frowned.

'Thank you, Klara. I need it for... for confirmation,' Anton muttered, going over and taking it. He stood as close to her as he dared. Her hair was freshly washed and he detected a hint of violets.

The baron rose. 'So, this is Klara. I've heard so much about you.'

Klara took a step back, almost stepping on Anton's toes. 'From whom?'

'Klara, this is the Baron Rothschild,' said Anton, placing a warning hand into the small of her back.

'Don't be nervous, my dear. Would you like a little wine?' The baron signalled a footman.

'Why am I here?' she hissed at Anton, her eyes wide. 'You didn't really need that cable, did you?'

Anton lowered his voice. 'Somebody wants to speak to you.'

'Who?'

'I don't know.'

'You tricked me into coming here.'

'Trust me, I didn't know about this.'

The baron brought Klara a glass of wine. Reluctantly she took it, holding the base with one hand and wrapping her other hand around the stem as if the glass were about to explode.

Presently a carriage clattered to a halt outside. Horses whinnied and gravel crunched as servants ran to assist. Carriage doors opened and slammed shut.

Klara's eyes rounded on Anton: black, narrow and full of anger.

The baron put a hand on her shoulder as if to restrain any impulse to run. Her body seemed to slump into itself, but she said nothing and stared across the room with a fixed expression.

A mass filled Anton's chest and the back of his throat tasted bitter.

There was noise and activity as if a heavy weight were being brought into the hallway. A scraping sound advanced up the stairs along with a march of footsteps. Two men entered the room.

Anton reeled at the sight of blond hair and stooping shoulders and an array of lapels and tassels – the same military men he'd seen down at the embankment.

They regarded Klara and nodded at the baron.

A rush of nausea swept over Anton as he looked at her. All colour had left her face as she stood trembling. He hated himself. The Okhrana had used him to trap her.

Why did I trust the Baron Rothschild and De Boer. What a fool I've been!

He knew what would happen next. They would arrest her and put her in prison. He would never see her again.

Wildly, he looked around. He could take her hand and race down the stairs. He had his revolver. She could get on a steamer and escape. But even as he thought it, he knew it was folly.

The commotion on the stairs intensified until a group of porters entered carrying a wheelchair. It bore a man wearing an admiral's uniform decorated with golden epaulettes, a four-star insignia and a host of medals pinned to his chest. He had a sallow complexion fringed with a wispy beard and moustache. His sandy grey hair was swept back from his face and a pair of pince-nez sat on top of his long straight nose.

It was the man from the newspaper illustration.

Anton flashed a look at Klara and took her hand. He expected her to pull away, but instead she held onto him, fingers digging into his, as if she knew what was coming and was ready to face it.

The porters set the chair down and the blond man with the stooping shoulders went over and whispered in the admiral's ear. He adjusted his pince-nez and stared at Klara.

Klara held her head high, chin jutting out.

The baron bowed. 'Gentlemen, allow me to present to you the Grand Duke Konstantin Nikolayevich.'

Anton bowed, his knees trembling as thoughts crashed through his mind.

The grand duke signalled to the men. They hooked their arms under his shoulders and helped him to his feet, his medals clinking against each other. He took a slow breath, as if the effort of composing a sentence took all his strength. 'Hello, Klara. It's been a long time.'

There was a long silence. Anton felt as if everyone were moving and thinking in slow motion. The blond man and his military companion exchanged glances. The baron raised his eyebrows, and De Boer relit his cigar. Klara was as stone, hard and unmoving. It was a few moments before she answered, and when she did, she spoke in a slow, cold voice.

'Hello, Father.'

CHAPTER FIFTY-SIX

KLARA'S FIRST THOUGHT WAS TO RUN. SHE COULD PROBABLY dart round her father's henchman at the door, and for a moment she tensed, ready to spring. But then the desire suddenly drained away.

Four years of running and hiding had led to this.

If she ran now, it would mean leaving Baku and all she had worked for, leaving those who she cared for. And leaving Anton Nikolayevich.

It was too late. The bonds of life had got in the way.

Her father was staring at her. Not with one of his *Father-knows-best-for-you* looks, but with a degree of sadness. He was shaking, and even though the men were holding him up, he seemed shrunken and empty, as if he consisted of a grand uniform with shiny medals and nothing more. He was no longer the powerful man who had stolen her mother's heart.

The room was very hot, and she felt a prickling sensation in her head and her father's face started to blur. A strong hand grabbed hold of her arm and steadied her.

'Please come closer, Klara. I need to sit. My legs no longer take orders from me.'

The baron led her to her father. De Boer brought a chair and she sat down. The grand duke rested his hand on the sleeve of her blue silk dress. 'You are wearing one of your mother's dresses. You remind me so much of her.'

Klara shrunk back. 'Don't.'

He drew his hand away. 'I'm sorry. I know this is a shock. But I couldn't think of any other way of seeing you.'

Klara took a while to form words. 'Why do you care about seeing me?' She swallowed hard. 'You abandoned my mother. You left us and never came back. Mother died because of you.'

'Please forgive me, Klara. I know I wronged your mother, God bless her. But Katharine understood the situation. It is always the way with men in my position. I would have married her if it had been possible.'

'I don't believe you.' She stared at his face. His grey eyes were intense and watery and gleaming through his pince-nez. She wasn't sure whether the wetness was due to the condition of his age, or were tears.

The grand duke blinked. 'I loved Katharine very much. That is why we were separated. My wife wouldn't tolerate Katharine.' He sighed. 'I love you too, Klara. The day I left was the hardest of my life.'

'Even when she was dying you did not come. I sat by her bedside every day looking for a letter from you.'

The grand duke took her hand, and this time she did not pull away. 'You must believe me. I wanted to come, but the tsar summoned me to St Petersburg. I could not refuse him.'

'My mother died thinking you no longer cared for her.'

'That thought haunts me. I have never known happiness such as I had with your mother. I loved her as I have loved no other.'

Klara looked away. Words were easy, and they came naturally to a man like her father. And yet her mother had been happy. She remembered that now, but it all seemed so long ago. The bad memories had eclipsed the joy she once felt.

She turned to face him. 'How did you find me? I thought nobody would find me in Baku.'

The grand duke pulled a ring from his pocket and placed it in her open palm. It was a beautiful ring, dark blue enamel covered with gold latticework and encrusted with diamonds.

Klara closed her fingers around it. 'My mother's ring. The authorities accused Ivan of stealing it.'

'Ivan Darkov. I heard you'd married. Where is he?'

'Ivan is dead. He never recovered from being in prison.'

'I am sorry. I wish you had asked for my help.'

'And what would you have done?' Klara scoffed. 'Annulled this unsuitable marriage of mine? If I remember, you had other plans for me.'

The grand duke conceded. 'After your mother died, I thought it was for your own good. I would have placed you under the guardianship of a noble family. At least until you were eighteen. Married to a nobleman. You would have grown up to be a lady, been presented at court. Had anything you wanted.'

'Except my freedom. I didn't want that kind of life.'

'I understand that now, so do not be alarmed. My time is approaching. I am unwell. I wanted to see you one more time before it was too late. My men have been watching you for months, making sure it really was you and that you were in safe hands. You are my treasure, my beloved Klara Konstantinovna. Have you ever used your patronymic?'

'Never.'

The grand duke sighed. 'I hope you will one day. I knew you were in Baku, but I didn't know where, until the baron told me about the Fabergé egg. I knew it was the very egg I had presented to your mother.' The grand duke looked across at Anton. 'How did you come by it, sir?'

'It was my doing,' Klara interrupted. 'I gave it to Nikolai Sabroski, Anton's father. He promised to keep it safe. I didn't want to sell it – if I had done, it would have betrayed me. When

Nikolai Sabroski died, he left it to Anton.' She had to smile when she caught the look of astonishment on Anton's face.

'Why didn't you tell me it belonged to you?' Anton exclaimed.

'Would you have believed me? On that first day after the will was read?' Klara's gaze softened. 'After that, it didn't seem to matter. You kept it safe, you couldn't sell it, and besides, what would I have done with it? In some ways it was a curse – linking me to my past. I didn't want you or anyone else knowing who I really was.' She smiled mischievously. 'I rather liked the fact you had no idea.'

Anton frowned. 'Did you know I'd pledged it in return for that oilfield?'

'Not at first. but I thought it a good idea. A useless jewel in exchange for an oilfield to support men in need of work seemed a fair bargain to me.'

The grand duke squeezed her hand. 'Don't throw away your past, Klara. Don't think of the egg as a curse. That jewel has brought us back together again.' He looked across at Anton. 'I am grateful to you, sir. You've looked after my daughter as well as you've looked after the egg.'

Klara glanced across at Anton, but her smile quickly faded when she saw his expression.

He looked lost.

CHAPTER FIFTY-SEVEN

IT HAD BEEN TWO DAYS SINCE ANTON HAD DISCOVERED Klara's true identity. She hadn't come back to the house, and he didn't expect her to, well not permanently, but he hoped she might visit and explain. Except what was he hoping for? She was the daughter of the Grand Duke Konstantin Nikolayevich, a relation of the tsar. A Romanov. If he wasn't feeling so deflated, he could have laughed.

Klara.

The untrustworthy, scheming girl he'd wanted to ban from the house when he found her rummaging around his room. How long had it taken him to see her true worth, to appreciate her intelligence, her spirit, her kindness. *It serves me right.*

The revelation that afternoon had been such a shock that he'd found it impossible to say anything sensible. Apart from the spontaneous outburst he'd made when he'd heard those words – *Hello, Father* – he'd said very little that sounded coherent. He reran the scene in his mind: Klara standing stiff in that old silk dress, and the trembling sandy-haired admiral, supported by his henchmen in front of a wheelchair.

The baron had bidden him and De Boer to retire to the end

of the room, where De Boer had apologised once again. 'I'm sorry for the deception, Sabroski, but it was important that Klara wasn't told, else she may not have agreed to come. The grand duke does not have long to live. He had a stroke last year.'

Klara and her father talked for more than an hour. She had told him about the Fabergé egg and how his father had known all the time. And then there was Klara's mother, Katharine Lapinski, who had died a long time ago. She certainly hadn't been sending the mysterious notes.

Anton allowed himself one pipe that night. The following morning, he dressed in wool trousers and stout boots, pulled on his reefer overcoat and leather cap, and made his way to the Bibi-Eibat oilfields. The best thing he could do was to immerse himself in work. And indeed, the sight of the fields lifted his spirits.

Rasoul approached. 'Sir. We've run the oil from the spouter to a reserve. By my estimates we've collected about three thousand poods. Nobel's engineer was right – we'll probably get a thousand a day from her.'

Anton listened while Rasoul described the repairs, the condition of each well and their drilling prospects. He suggested new managers for the different fields along with a replacement for Klara. They hadn't discussed her much. Anton attempted to find out how much Rasoul had known, but the taciturn and monosyllabic replies deterred him from asking again. It was difficult to gauge the man's attitude to Klara and her change of circumstances, so Anton assumed that either he'd known all along, or simply didn't care.

Anton knew how much easier things would be if Klara was there. She knew the workers and understood the business, she knew how things were, and how things should be. He could see her scuffed boots and the hem of her skirt trailing in the mud, a hand holding onto her bonnet. Her shrewd mind and quick movements, her slender body full of energy and life. And her face.

A face he once saw as cunning and sharp, he now saw as compassionate and caring and beautiful.

He had squandered her, and now she had gone.

When he returned that evening a carriage waited outside the house. He didn't give it much thought as he was tired and just wanted to put a door between him and the dark. Olga, the housekeeper, flung open the front door with a smile that almost cracked her face. 'You have a visitor, sir.'

As he entered the hallway, the drawing room door opened. Anton stared in astonishment. In the doorway stood a version of Klara. Not the Klara he recognised. This Klara was encased in pale pink, framing her slimness like cherry blossom. She was wearing an astonishing hat, woven with what looked like green straw and chenille, the crown covered with ivory silk and some gold decorations. Ostrich tips arched across part of her face.

'Welcome, Klara Darkova,' he said as his spirits soared.

'Thank you.' Klara pulled out her hat pin and carefully removed her bonnet, self-consciously touching her hair.

Anton wasn't sure how to behave. His instinct was to embrace her, but he didn't think that appropriate. He had never bowed to her, never formally kissed her hand like gentlemen were meant to do in the presence of a lady. Maybe he should treat her like he did Julia, but that didn't seem to be right either. In the end he stood there unmoving and awkward like a schoolboy.

Klara laughed. 'So formal, Anton. I don't think I've ever seen you lost for words.'

'Would you like some tea?' he said, his voice catching in his throat.

In the end, Klara stayed for two hours, and after his initial discomfiture, they settled into their old ways of talking. She asked many questions about the oilfields and the men and Rasoul. She wanted to know his plans, his ideas on how to rebuild the company. She argued with him over who to put in each role, and became very defensive when discussing her replacement.

She said little about her father, only reiterating what the baron had said: the grand duke was ill and wanted to spend as much time with his daughter as possible. She played with her lace cuffs as she spoke and wouldn't meet Anton's eyes when he asked where she would go. The grand duke had palaces in Pavlovsk and Strelna, and Oreanda on the Crimea, as well as the Marble Palace in St Petersburg.

'Which one will you live in?' he said, trying to jest, but she became evasive and announced it was time for her to leave.

'I'll see you to your carriage,' Anton said.

She gathered up her skirts with care. There were so many unfamiliar silks and frills that slowed her down and she took great trouble to navigate the front steps of the house in a dignified manner. He helped her into the waiting brougham and blushed as she squeezed his hand and kissed his cheek. Then he watched until her carriage disappeared down the hill and she was gone.

CHAPTER FIFTY-EIGHT

THE WEEK FOLLOWING JULIA'S ENGAGEMENT TO LEO ROSTOV, Julia felt her spirits lift. The wedding was arranged, Leo sent their belongings to Moscow and her father rented a house for them with a view of the Moskva River. In less than a week, she would be married. She wondered if people suspected. She'd had several of her gowns altered and had bought two loose-fitting day dresses but luckily her weight gain wasn't that noticeable.

That evening her father invited people over for dinner. Anton had come looking preoccupied and tired, but since his world had turned upside down, she wasn't surprised. She had heard all about Klara. The gossip of the ragged street girl (as so many people saw her) turning into a princess was like something out of one of her novels. Miranda was proved wrong – fairy stories did come true, and it delighted her.

Julia had settled into her chair when something catastrophic happened. Her stepmother was taken ill, and the doctor called. Diane Seigenberg insisted she was well enough to join the dinner party, but had fainted an hour later. Her father insisted she lie down while he summoned the services of Doctor Levon and it was too late to retreat by then. All she could do was pray the doctor would visit and leave promptly afterwards. But her father offered the doctor some refreshment. To Julia's horror he accepted.

She stared down at her pink satin shoes and clasped her fingers together. A nervous sweat engulfed her, and she felt immobilised with fright. The moment the doctor entered the drawing room she knew he had recognised her. She caught him looking at her, peering over the top of his thick horn-rimmed spectacles, the light reflecting off the lenses, so it looked as if his eyes were constantly twinkling. He looked to Julia like a spider in his old black suit with arms that looked too long for him.

Julia could hear snatches of conversation. The doctor was talking about his work at the hospital. Anton was asking about the post-mortem of Albert Prankman; she almost laughed when she heard that. *What unbelievable bad luck.* The man who had given her the poison was the man asked to do the post-mortem on her victim. She trembled. As soon as he analysed the results, he'd know the American had been poisoned. He'd find traces of mandrake and remember he'd made that potion for her. In a matter of days he would alert the authorities. The girls would find the glass vial she'd dropped in the opium den and be able to identify her.

Even you won't be able to save me, Leo.

She looked up as the men laughed at some remark while her father replenished everyone's glasses. The doctor started to make his way towards her.

'Miss Seigenberg, let me offer you my congratulations,' he said sitting on the divan beside her. 'I understand you are to be married shortly.'

'Yes I am. Thank you, sir.' Her voice sounded like it belonged to somebody else.

The doctor took off his spectacles and polished them while looking at her. His eyes were sea-green like her own. An old silver cross hung around his neck with an engraving of three birds. 'Has your father had any more sleep problems?' he said conspiratorially, pushing his glasses to the end of his prominent nose.

Her stomach lurched. 'No.'

'Good. I assumed all must be well as you didn't return for a second bottle. I rather hoped you wouldn't need to... dangerous stuff, hemlock and mandrake. It's easy to overdose by mistake. Rather like the poor man I examined last week.'

'Who was that?' She thought she was going to pass out.

'An American who'd developed a taste for opium.'

'Was it an accident?'

'I expect so, although I did detect signs of violence on his body, but that could have been the result of his fall down the well shaft. Most men can tolerate six pipes or so, but more than that can be fatal.'

'I heard an American had fallen down a well. Is this the same man?' Her voice was barely audible so that he had to lean forward to listen to her.

'That's what the newspapers are saying. His body was found near a notorious opium den that caters for gentlemen. I imagine that if one of their clients was found to have overdosed, they wouldn't want to be associated with it. Bad for business.'

'So, you think...'

'I think the American died of opium and that the opium den owners disposed of the body.'

'But the newspapers said he'd been murdered.'

'Murders sell newspapers far more than accidental deaths.' He studied her face. 'Did you know this gentleman?'

'No. Not really. Yes. Well, a bit... I'd met him once or twice because he worked with Fabian Brakov. My father knows Mr Brakov and his son.' Her words were falling over themselves in an effort to line up in a proper sentence.

'I'm sorry if he was an associate of yours.'

She swallowed. 'I didn't tell my father about my visit to you.

He doesn't believe in talking medicines unless absolutely necessary. I didn't give him the potion after all.'

'Your secret is safe with me,' said Doctor Levon smiling. 'Not that the potion I gave you would have done him any harm.'

'I don't understand. You gave me hemlock.'

'Twenty drops of hemlock mixed with ten drops of mandrake was the exact formula. Highly poisonous and deadly in the wrong hands.'

Julia stared at him. Surely he was laughing at her – playing some monstrous trick. 'Please don't joke with me, sir.'

'Please forgive me. I meant no offence. The potion I gave you was harmless – a mixture of valerian and pomegranate.' He raised his hand to prevent her speaking. 'I always substitute a less potent remedy initially. If you had returned to complain that the administered dose had been ineffective I would have known that your intentions were serious.'

Thoughts clattered down the pathways of her brain like dominoes. 'And then what would you have done?'

'I would have told you that I was unable to supply you with a better-quality solution.'

For a few seconds she believed him and then she saw him smile. 'But I saw you grind the mandrake. I watched you pour in the hemlock.'

'You saw correctly, but I gave you something very different when you weren't looking.'

And then she remembered.

The cork.

He'd asked her to fetch one. It was on the other side of the room in the cupboard along with glass bungs and rubber stoppers. She'd had difficulty finding the correct size.

It had taken her quite a few moments.

CHAPTER FIFTY-NINE

THE HOUSE FELT PARCHED WITHOUT KLARA, AS IF SOME essence within its walls had dried up. For a few days Anton stayed home to deal with company paperwork and speak to John about his affairs, occasionally playing poker with Leo while listening to his wedding plans. Once he went to Klara's room. The whole time he'd known her, he'd never looked inside.

He stepped inside, feeling like an invader. The room was simply furnished with a brass bedstead, a few prints on the wall, and a round occasional table with barley-twisted legs that stood in the window. A bright rug covered the floor, and a row of serious-looking books lined a shelf. A pickle jar full of dried yellow daisies stood on a marble-topped washstand.

Over the fireplace hung a silver frame with a photograph. He took the frame down and smiled as he read the inscription: *Katharine Lapinski 1869.* He shook his head; he would never know who was behind the messages sent to him, but it didn't seem to matter now.

He spent his time overseeing repairs to the fields. It was early October when Stefan Brakov came to see him, dressed immaculately in mourning clothes: a black frock coat with a thick black band around his top hat.

They greeted each other awkwardly. They had not spoken properly since the fight in the Hotel Continental bar.

Stefan stared round the field watching the men replace the roof of the boiler shed and dismantle a burned-out derrick. 'Not as much damage as I thought,' he said, lighting a cigarette. 'You were fortunate.'

'Yes. Nobel brought in his engineers.'

'They probably saved you from ruin.'

'I'm very busy, Stefan. I assume this isn't a social call. What is it that you want?'

Stefan's cheer evaporated. He took another drag on his cigarette and produced a package from his pocket. 'I came to give you this. I think you'll find it instructive.'

'What is it?'

'Just something my father kept.'

Anton raised his eyebrows and then slipped the package into his own pocket.

Stefan kicked at a stone. 'I hear the Baron Rothschild has a distinguished guest staying. There are many rumours flying about.' He blew out a circle of smoke and looked down the field. 'Who would have thought that little housemaid of yours could be so well connected?'

'Nothing is ever as it seems.'

'Very true.'

Stefan finished his cigarette and dropped the butt into the mud. 'Well, I won't take up any more of your time.' Tentatively he held out his hand. 'I wish you luck, Anton.'

Anton hesitated and then shook Stefan's black-gloved hand.

Once Anton was certain Stefan had gone, he pulled out the package and opened it. The contents, wrapped in a silky material and bound with twine, revealed an oval-framed miniature surrounded with pearls, the entire painting fitting into the palm of his hand. A man with fierce curls swept under a brown hat stared up at him. He had calculating eyes and familiar shrewd features. Anton stared at it until he noticed a name painted inside the edge.

David Cherlin.

It was the name of the man who had signed the forged documents; the man responsible for the collapse of Sabroski Oil; the man who had ruined his father.

Why did you give me this, Stefan?

Anton turned the miniature over to read the inscription and his heart pitched into his stomach. Cramming the miniature inside his jacket, he sprinted across the field, jumped into his gig and tore down the Bailov road.

By the time he reached the house, Anton had worked himself into a frenzy. He felt for his revolver as he banged on the front door, trying to stem the wave of revulsion that crashed through him. He prayed he was wrong, that there'd been a mistake, or that someone was playing a cruel trick on him. It couldn't possibly be true. Because if it was, then everything he believed in was gone.

The door opened. Anton tugged at the kerchief around his neck to loosen it and ran his hands over his hair. Sveta, the housemaid, admitted him, saying the master was in his library and not expecting company.

John Seigenberg was sitting at his desk dressed in a red silk smoking jacket when Anton burst inside. The old lawyer looked up and blinked through his gold-rimmed spectacles. 'Anton. I wasn't expecting—'

'I think this belongs to you.' Anton thrust the miniature at him. The thunder in his chest made him feel sick.

John's eyes widened as he examined the miniature. He exhaled slowly. 'Where did you get this?'

'Stefan Brakov gave it to me.'

'I see.' John tugged at his hair.

'Why is your name on the back?'

'Because...' John paused and sighed. 'David Cherlin is my father.'

'Your father!'

Anton took a few deep breaths as fury surged through him. 'You knew *everything*. All the time!'

John took off his spectacles and rubbed his eyes. 'Yes, and for that, I'm sorry.'

It was too incredible to believe. It couldn't be true. 'Please tell me you weren't involved in any of this?'

John held his gaze. 'It's true, I'm afraid. I did help destroy your father. I hated myself for doing it. But it had to be done.'

Anton swore and pulled out his revolver. 'I should kill you now for what you've done. Why did you do it?'

'I had no choice. Fabian and Prankman forced my hand.'

Anton trembled. The gun shook in his hand. 'You *bastard*. All those lies you've told me. I *trusted* you. You were the one person I trusted in all of this.'

John made to stand, but Anton raised the gun. 'Don't you move. If you do, I'll put a bullet in you.'

John sank back down. 'I knew you'd find out. I wanted you to. I'm surprised you didn't guess when you found those papers.'

It took Anton a moment to understand what he was saying.

'You killed Dmitry?' said Anton hoarsely.

John shook his head. 'Prankman was having Dmitry watched. He suspected he was hoarding documents and learned Dmitry had a key. But Prankman assumed it was a safe deposit key, not a key to a safe in the office. The documents were right under his nose all the time.'

'Why should I believe you? All this time you've lied to me.'

'Because whatever I've done, I'm no murderer.'

'Then *why*?' Anton renewed his grip on the revolver. His palms were sweaty and he had to clutch the side of the desk to hold himself still.

John coughed. 'I wanted you to find out the truth. I tried to help you without anyone knowing. Prankman threatened Julia, Anton. He threatened my family. I couldn't have that. But what I should have done is had that foul American killed a long time ago.'

Anton smashed his fist on the desk. 'My father trusted you for years. He trusted you from the very beginning!'

John shrank back and held up his hands. 'Just hear me out. You can do what you like with me afterwards.'

'It was the money, wasn't it? They made so much.'

'I never touched any of it. Nikolai trusted me. Fabian knew that, which is why he made me destroy him.'

'Damn you,' Anton spat, and put the gun down. He lunged at John and punched him with such force that his hand cramped with pain.

John fell back in his chair and a glass smashed on the floor. Footsteps sounded in the hallway followed by a tap on the door.

'Sir, is there anything wrong?'

'No need to worry, Sveta. Just an accident. Leave us be,' John shouted breathlessly as he pulled himself up and massaged his jaw. His lip had split and he wiped away blood with the back of his hand. He coughed again. 'I need a whisky. Do you mind?'

Anton motioned to the decanter. John poured two glasses and pushed one towards Anton. It was a moment before he spoke. 'I met your father and Fabian twenty-five years ago. I helped them set up Sabroski Oil and put them in contact with the right officials. The imperial government kept a tight grip on the oil industry in those days, but I could see how the wind was blowing.'

'Get to the point.'

'Everything went well at first. They were great friends and business partners. But it was during that time that the trouble started, when—'

'What trouble?'

'Olesia Rosenbeck came to Baku.'

'Olesia? You mean Olesia Brakov?'

John nodded. 'Olesia was a very beautiful woman. Both men fell in love with her. Your father was already married and you had been born. But your father wanted Olesia. Nikolai was a very charismatic man, very witty and entertaining. Olesia fell in love with him too.'

Anton felt his heart pounding. 'They had an affair? Did my mother know of this?'

'I think she suspected.'

'But if Olesia loved my father, then why did she marry Fabian?'

'Fabian adored Olesia but she only had eyes for Nikolai. After a few months the affair ended. Olesia was a difficult woman and she made too many demands. Your father had no intention of abandoning your mother and your mother was becoming suspicious. Olesia flew into a temper and announced their liaison was over. Fabian saw his chance. He courted her and married her quickly.'

'Before she could change her mind?'

'Yes. Olesia married Fabian to spite your father.'

'What's this got to do with the company?'

John held up his hands. 'Listen. In seventy-three the government held the first public auction of the oilfields; your father and Fabian bought what they could… they made a fortune. Sabroski Oil became so successful; they built magnificent mansions, brought architects in from Italy.' His face softened. 'Those were such good years…'

'I don't want to hear your happy memories,' snarled Anton. The shadows in the room stretched black and a grandfather clock struck five. Even though he was sweating, Anton felt taut and cold, his hair sticking to the sides of his face. He wondered if anyone else was listening – the whole household must know that something was wrong now.

'It started when Fabian found out that Stefan wasn't his son.'

'What?' Anton almost stopped breathing. 'Who...?' He blanched. 'You mean... Olesia and my father...'

John held Anton's eyes. 'Yes... Stefan is your brother, Anton. Your half-brother.'

The shock swiped Anton like the slap of a wave. He turned away and looked out of the window. Across the street two sailors in white uniforms greeted each other laughing.

'Does Stefan know?'

'No.'

'So, Olesia was with child when she married Fabian?'

'No. Stefan wasn't born until after they'd been married a year.'

Anton spun round. 'Then how?'

'Olesia and Nikolai took up with each other again straight after she was married. All those protestations of dislike were for Fabian's benefit.' John touched his bruised chin. 'Fabian didn't suspect anything for years. But Olesia became indiscreet, and he became suspicious. He looked more closely at the time when Stefan had been born and calculated that Stefan had been conceived during a period when he'd been unwell, so knew the child could not have been his own.'

Anton felt a chill run through him. 'My father betrayed his best friend. No wonder Fabian hated him.'

'They betrayed each other. When Fabian found out he went crazy. He and Nikolai fought, and they would have killed each other if it wasn't for my intervention. Once Fabian calmed down, he decided on another way. A way, which he told me later, that would give him greater satisfaction.'

'So that was it. Fabian Brakov ruined my father all because of a woman.' Anton shook his head. 'But why *you*?'

'Fabian knew about my past. He knew about the Pale of Settlement.'

'The Pale of Settlement?' Something stirred in Anton's mind. It was something Albert Prankman had said to taunt him after Anton exposed him.

John spoke with a deadpan voice. 'The Pale of Settlement is a terrible place. It's where Jews are forced to live – that is, Jews without any influence. It's an area along the western borders of the Russian Empire, set up by Catherine the Great. The conditions are terrible: poverty, disease, torture. It's where I was born. But my father escaped and brought us to Baku fifty years ago. He changed our name and got us a special residence permit. If you could prove you were a local Jew and prove you were born in the region, you were allowed residency, but you had to pay a bribe each year.'

'And Fabian knew?'

'Oh yes. Fabian threatened to expose me. It would have meant losing everything. The business would have been confiscated and the family forced back into the Pale. I couldn't allow that to happen.'

'So, you decided to ruin my father instead.'

John met his eyes. 'I'm not proud of what I did. I was given the choice of saving my family or saving yours.'

Anton paused. 'How did you do it?'

'I set up fake companies and used my connections to get registration and contracts. We hired different surveyors, ones we could manipulate, and once Dmitry had disappeared, we put a new accountant in place – the rest you know.'

'But you weren't clever enough.'

John sighed. 'I hadn't spotted the design on the stamps. If it hadn't been for that…'

'And what about Prankman?' Anton said suddenly. 'Where did he fit into all of this?'

'Prankman supervised the supply companies, but he also had

384

another agenda that Fabian didn't know about. Prankman was a Standard Oil spy. I knew that, and he knew I knew. He found out about Nikolai's plan with Marcus Samuel – to split from Fabian and establish a new company outside of his control. He wasn't going to allow that to happen.'

Anton stared into space. He couldn't bear to look John in the eye. 'Prankman arranged to have Rafiq murdered. *He* hired those bandits and had him killed. He tried to kill me as well. He admitted as much to my face.'

'He wanted those tanker plans. New York would have paid handsomely for them. He threatened Julia and tried to demand I get them from you.'

'That's why he tried to beat it out of me in the caravanserai.' Anton looked up at John. The pieces were coming together. 'Why did you save me that day? If I'd died, no one would have known.'

'I never wanted you to come to harm. From the day you arrived from the Orient I tried to protect you. I was at the docks the night you came back. I sent that note to Klara so that she would find you in time. I helped you find out the truth. I'm the one who's been sending you those newspaper cuttings, Anton. After you'd told me about Katharine Lapinski, I knew you'd jump to that conclusion.'

Anton's eyes widened. 'The cuttings came from *you*.' He gave a sarcastic laugh. 'I knew it wasn't her in the end. But I couldn't see why anyone wanted me to think she was still alive.'

'It was the only way I could think of warning you and putting you on the right track. Anonymously. I couldn't let anyone know it was me. People had to think you'd worked it out for yourself.' John stood up, went over to a bureau and pulled out a bundle of letters. 'These are yours. They were written to you by your father. I'm afraid I kept them.'

'But Klara said she posted them.'

'She did, but I had them collected from the post office and brought here. I'm sorry.'

Anton took the letters and stared at John. The powerful image of the lawyer had been nothing but a façade. It was hard to believe that he had trusted the man so much. 'Does your son, Alfred, know the truth?'

'I think he suspected towards the end.'

'And Julia?'

A little of John's former strength returned. 'Julia knows nothing and never will. She and Leo will live in Moscow and be none the wiser.'

John took a step towards him, but Anton held up his hand in warning. 'Don't come near me. I have no desire to kill you… not any more… but when I leave this house, I will never come back. I don't ever want to see you again.'

John's shoulders sank. 'I understand. I am sorry, Anton. I am sorrier than you'll ever know.'

Anton hesitated. 'Did you get anything out of this? Apart from saving your family?'

John gave a small smile. 'Actually, I did. Fabian paid me a small… *compensation* he liked to call it. Fifty roubles every month. It mounted up while you were gone. Two thousand and seven hundred roubles, but I gave the money away.'

'Fifty roubles. Every month. The anonymous donation.'

'I told you I never touched any of the money,' said John sadly. 'I swore to Nikolai I'd look after you, Anton Nikolayevich. At least I managed to honour that.'

CHAPTER SIXTY

THE ROTHSCHILD HOUSE HAD SIXTEEN ROOMS ON THE ground floor all set around a central hallway with a marble staircase. Upstairs there were twelve bedrooms and two state rooms. Klara's bedroom faced the sea, looking down the cobbles of Sadovaya Street. She had hardly been out since that fateful day. The baron insisted she reside with her father in the mansion until 'arrangements' could be made.

The house was astonishing. It teemed with servants running to orders; it had rooms full of paintings and statues and ornaments; it had a library with hundreds of books and periodicals and journals. An inner courtyard cultivated rare blooms, and had grounds with trees and plants imported from Europe. It was as if another world existed inside the sandstone walls, one where real life with its dirt and disease had been banished.

The past two weeks felt like a dream. Klara had stepped into a world of new clothes, silky shoes and extravagant surroundings. Much against her nature, she had been persuaded to purchase a wardrobe of gowns and more hats than she'd ever owned in her life. Her father insisted on buying her the latest shell-bonnet in pink, which was shaped like a scallop trimmed with a feather at the back. Klara had never owned a parasol before. Now she had five with handles made of crystal and porcelain edged with lace. She never knew bodices could have so many names and now she had one in every style.

During the first week of October, Julia Seigenberg came to visit. Klara congratulated her.

'The wedding was very quiet. Just family. It's what Leo and I wanted,' Julia said. 'Tomorrow I leave for Moscow. Will you go to St Petersburg? If you live in a palace, promise you'll invite me to visit.'

Klara didn't answer. *So many questions and I have no answers.* This was a world she didn't know and didn't much like. She studied Julia's enthusiasm curiously. 'Don't you tire of this sort of life, Julia?'

'What do you mean?'

'All this dressing and undressing, fiddling with your hair and getting excited about jewellery, winding yourself into a corset and squeezing your feet into these shoes.'

Julia laughed. 'You'll get used to it.'

'I'm not sure that I will.' Klara watched Julia rummage through her wardrobe, holding up an ivory silk and trying on one of her new hats. In some ways it was an education, a glimpse into a world where there was no time to be a real person who could participate in anything, because you were training to be an ornament – a porcelain figurine, glossy and painted and fragile. Klara gazed down at her dress. It was made of a shining cloth of gold embroidery with patterns of overlapping peacock feathers. It had a low square neck, pleated puff sleeves and some sort of gauzy chiffon with a floating gold stole. When she whirled round, Julia said she looked like a twist of butterscotch.

'I went to see Anton Nikolayevich a while ago – just after he found out who I really was. Silly of me really.'

'Silly? In what way?'

'I wanted to know about everything. How he was, the oilfields and all that.' Klara looked away; it would be embarrassing if Julia guessed the truth. But secretly she had been desperate to see Anton Nikolayevich's face when she appeared in silks and frills, dressed in gowns of women he regarded as *properly* female. The sort of women he might have met through Count Witte during his time in the Orient.

'Why is that silly? I imagine he was delighted to see you.'

'Yes, he was.' *No, he wasn't.*

The visit had backfired. Anton behaved oddly, standing stiff and offering her tea as if she were John Seigenberg's wife, or some sort of distant acquaintance. He didn't say anything about how she looked, didn't compliment her gown or hat as other men did. It wasn't that she wanted compliments, she didn't care for them at all, so she wasn't exactly sure what she wanted him to say, except that saying nothing made her feel worse. She was so confused.

She supposed Anton was angry at her deception. Not that she had lied to him, more that there were things that she'd *not* told him. It must have exasperated Anton that she had confided in Nikolai yet not him. Anton's father had known everything from the very start. He knew who she was, and all about the Fabergé egg, and about Ivan, and her mother and father, but the moment Anton had climbed into the gig, that night down on the embankment, it had all gone wrong. She had been angry – unreasonably so she realised later – and he must have detected that. In return, he had a low opinion of her and a maddening disregard for her capabilities. And then there was the lack of trust which provoked them both to say unkind things and behave badly to each other. *It's all been a disaster.*

'Julia, do I look strange in these clothes? I'm not used to them. People might think I look…'

'You look beautiful and lovely and sophisticated. Stop doubting yourself, Klara.'

'Do I?' Julia was being kind. Anton hadn't bothered with such niceties. He must have thought she looked ridiculous. He'd only seen her in her mother's old clothes or cheap dresses she'd made herself. Why had she expected him to take her hand and tell her how enchanting she looked? It had been a foolish experiment, and even though she had covered her disquiet by laughing and asking him endless questions about the Bibi-Eibat fields, pretending to take an interest in who was going to replace her, she felt crushed by his lack of interest. When she told him it was time to leave, Anton didn't even ask when she would visit him again. He'd made a joke about her father's palaces and asked her which one she might live in.

'I can't believe you've kept these,' she heard Julia say as she pulled out Klara's faded blue silk and her battered straw hat with its strip of green ribbon. 'You should throw them away.'

For a moment, Klara thought she might cry. 'They're part of my past, Julia. Don't tell me to give it all up.'

Julia frowned. 'You're right. I don't know why I said that.' She hung the dress up carefully and sat down on Klara's bed. 'You know I've kept Rafiq's letters - Leo doesn't know. I also have a sash… saffron satin. He wore it a lot. It still smells of him.' She drew breath and placed her hand over her stomach. 'When *he* is born – because I know it will be a *he* – I will give him the sash and tell him it came from a dear friend. I want to see his child wearing it. Is that a bad thing? Do you think I'm betraying Leo?'

Klara shook her head. 'People don't have to know everything. Sometimes, not knowing things keeps them safe from the unexplained.'

'Thank you. You always make me feel stronger.'

Klara smiled. She had been glad to see Julia and glad to have made a friend of her.

Her father took up the rest of the weeks in her strange new world. The grand duke had been delighted at her 'conversion', as he saw it. And she was glad to make him happy, for a while. He was frail, became weary quickly, often nodding off after dinner. They spent the mornings talking until his strength failed, and he would sleep until the evening. That fateful afternoon had been so difficult, seeing her father for the first time in years. But she detected a genuine sadness in his eyes when he talked about her mother. It seemed the well of grief inside him had never fully emptied. It had quelled her anger and unleashed a different emotion, one that she hadn't known for a long time.

Peace.

The years of resentment and mistrust, which had knotted her insides, had slowly started to uncoil, giving her space to think about who she was and what she wanted. The solitude inside the grand house helped, and so, as the weeks passed, she began to understand who the girl everybody knew as Klara truly was.

*

The images from the confrontation with John Seigenberg haunted Anton. He read through his father's letters (the ones that had never been posted) and asked Rasoul to take charge at the oilfields while he took long walks and rode out into the desert and hired a man with a single-mast skiff to take him out on the Caspian. The sound of the waves slapping the sides of the boat brought comfort to him. The sea stretched out on all sides like a great silver cloak. He watched seagulls dive for fish and cry overhead, and the cool air helped clear his head.

Over the last few weeks Anton's world had dissolved into something he didn't recognise. It was as if he'd been living in a house that he thought strong and safe only to have it shudder and break, the floorboards beneath him splinter and gape wide to let him fall. There was nothing left of the old world he thought he knew. All loyalties were gone, their touchstones rendered meaningless.

Is this how his father had felt at the end?

Anton stared across the flat, grey water. He thought of Nikolai Mikhailovich Sabroski, his father, lying impotent and destroyed in a dishevelled, dirty bed. He thought of his late mother, and his father's treacherous business partner and lawyer, John Seigenberg. And he thought of himself, an absent son. What must have his father have thought as he lay dying, dictating letters to Klara which were never answered? Did he think it had all been for nothing? Did he realise that in the end the only thing that mattered was loyalty, and everything faltered without it?

Betrayal had destroyed all three men: his father, Fabian Brakov and John Seigenberg. Betrayal led to Dmitry's murder and caused Frau Kalian's death. The same betrayal had followed Rafiq onto the train to Tiflis, and betrayal had stalked Anton from the moment he set foot on the shores of Baku.

But now Anton hoped it had gone. Like a great black cloud, it had poisoned all those who breathed it. It had corrupted and contaminated and decayed what good there had been.

Despite John's treachery, Anton would miss his old guardian who'd been like a solid wall to lean against. He'd not seen Klara since the day she'd come to visit him, which meant that by now she must be on her way to St Petersburg with her father. He wished she had come to collect her belongings and say goodbye to him.

He thought about Stefan and wondered if Olesia would ever reveal the truth. He certainly wouldn't tell him. When he was younger, he'd always wanted a brother; Rafiq had become a surrogate brother to him, but he couldn't imagine Stefan filling that role.

Anton took a long, deep breath and filled his lungs with sea air. A spray of water splashed up and stung his eyes, prompting him to wipe the back of his hand across his face. He caught sight of the tattoo on his wrist: the Chinese symbol of eternity, a series of bold ink strokes which made up a single character. They had told him it meant *forever* and *perpetual*. The ones on his arms meant *strength* and *vigour*, and across his back the long lashes symbolised *endurance*. He would need these stamps of encouragement even more now.

He signalled the man to turn the boat around and take him back to shore.

Chapter Sixty-One

On October 22nd, Marcus Samuel arrived in Baku and took up residence at the Hotel Continental. Anton called on him the very next day. It bolstered Anton's spirits to see the merchant in happier times, as their previous meeting had been one of Anton's darkest moments. The audacious plan Marcus had devised with his father had worked, but it came at a very high price.

Some would have thought it a necessary sacrifice, but Anton would never willingly trade a life for prosperity. This, he reflected, meant he'd never make a truly successful businessman. Ruthlessness and hard-heartedness went hand in hand with victory – John Rockefeller was proof of that. Yet looking at Marcus that morning, as they shook hands and clapped each other on the back, he softened his cynical view. Marcus was the image of honesty and didn't appear to have a vindictive streak in him at all.

Marcus poured champagne. 'I cannot tell you, my friend, how delighted I am to see you with this news. Our coup has been successful. Rockefeller's lawyers have lost their appeal. Let us drink to our victory!' Marcus took a large sip, swallowed, and tapped the side of his nose. 'They tried their best, Messrs Russell and Arnholz, Rockefeller's lawyers, but they were not clever enough to outwit Marcus Samuel. The Suez Canal authorities have turned down every appeal and have upheld their decision. Rafiq Hasanov's tanker will pass through the Suez Canal next year.' Marcus beamed and drank the rest of his champagne.

Anton felt a rush. 'It is wonderful news. My father would have been delighted and so will Rafiq's family. A part of him lives on, which means a lot. More than you can imagine.'

'I understand completely, my dear fellow.'

'What are your plans now?'

'I shall meet with the Rothschilds this afternoon to sign the contract. Then in a few days I will make my way to Singapore to speak to my trading agents. Many are interested in backing our new company.'

'Who will manage the business from Singapore?'

'My nephews,' said Marcus. 'One of them is already there negotiating storage and shipping rights with the harbour authorities.' He smiled. 'The Samuels are well known in the Orient. My family have been merchants for twenty years.' He tinged the champagne glass with his finger. 'Shipping tankers of oil will make a big change from trading seashells.'

'Seashells?'

'That's what Samuel Samuel & Co have spent years trading, amongst other goods of course. But seashells have always been my favourite commodity. We make them into jewellery boxes for discerning young ladies. Didn't I tell you that?'

Anton smiled. 'I think you may have done.'

'We have a workshop in Wapping in East London which employs forty girls. They decorate all manner of boxes with shells for ladies to keep trinkets in. Some of the shells we collect are extremely rare and very beautiful. There is a high demand.' Marcus stuck his thumb into his waistcoat pocket. 'I shall name Hasanov's tanker the *Murex*.'

'*Murex*? That's a curious name.'

'It's the name of a seashell. A particularly beautiful one with sculpted spines. I think it will make a fitting tribute to my father's company.' Marcus placed his glass on a table and unscrewed the top of his fountain pen. He passed it to Anton and pulled a document towards him. 'Your signature is needed here.' He pointed to the dotted line and beamed. 'Congratulations, you are now a partner in my new company.' He paused. 'But managing the business from Baku will not be easy – the Rothschilds will drive a hard bargain. There will be rivals and many competitors who do not uphold the same ethics as we do, but I suspect you already know that.'

Anton gave a knowing nod. 'I understand.'

Marcus looked at him quizzically, but Anton decided to say no more. He would save his stories of treachery and corruption for another time, or he would never tell them at all. He held the pen tightly; his signature would signify the end of one part of his life and the start of another.

'What will you call the company?' he asked after a moment.

Marcus's eyes twinkled. 'I shall name it after my father's business. It was his idea to market trinkets from seashells thirty years ago.'

Anton bent down to sign his name.

Marcus smiled. 'The company will be called Shell Oil.'

CHAPTER SIXTY-TWO

WHEN ANTON RETURNED TO THE HOUSE, HE DISCOVERED A note had been delivered from Klara. Her father's health had worsened and he needed to see his physician urgently. Klara had decided to return to St Petersburg the next day. She wished Anton luck for the future and thanked him for all he had done for her.

He slumped into the library desk chair and stared at her handwriting: small slanting letters with curly 'y's and 'g's. He knew she would leave, it was inevitable, but he hoped she might come again, just one more time.

But then why should she? He had never been that nice to her and they had fought more times than collaborated. For a long moment he thought of Klara. Then he reached for a pen and paper and started to write.

Dear Klara, I am not very good at courtesies, but before you leave for St Petersburg, I would like you to know that…

He stopped. What did he want her to know? He stared at the nib as a blob of ink dripped onto the sheet. Cursing, he blotted it carefully and then continued.

... that I have great respect for your kindness and integrity...

He read the sentence, screwed the paper up and flung into onto the floor. It sounded as if he was writing to an aged aunt or a member of the clergy. He took a new sheet and started again.

Dear Klara, I am not very good at courtesies, but before you leave for St Petersburg, I would like you to know that I regret our past misunderstandings and greatly value all the advice you have given me. I am saddened that you will no longer...

He read it through and crumpled the paper into a ball. What was the matter with him? All he had to do was write a simple, honest letter, not a letter of condolence.

He closed his eyes and thought. What could he say to her that didn't sound pompous or formal or inappropriate? What could he say that was... nice? *Nice.* He didn't think he'd said much that was nice before – they had always been at war with each other.

He stared at the paper and then wrote the first thoughts that came into his head.

My dearest Klara, I wish you weren't leaving. I wish you were still here. I miss you so very much.

He put down the pen. That's what he really wanted to say, but he knew he couldn't send it. The grand duke would not appreciate a letter like that sent to his eligible daughter, whom no doubt he had ambitious plans for.

Anton pushed the paper aside.

*

Klara paced her room. Two trunks had been packed with her new clothes. She had crammed hats and shoes and gowns in a heap until her maid shrieked in horror. She had sent a note to Anton, hoping to receive an answer, but as the day progressed, none came. She sat on the edge of her bed and ran her hand across the ivory satin cover.

Her father had left the previous day. Arrangements had been made for him to travel in the royal carriage to Batumi and then across the Black Sea. But it was all too sudden for her to leave, she explained, and thus she would follow later. The grand duke had kissed her forehead and held her for a long time and said that she must do what she thought best.

*

Anton found it difficult to concentrate the next day. He had accounts to examine, contracts to read and equipment lists to check through, but he wasn't in the mood to deal with it. He rode over to the oilfields to inspect machinery and speak to Rasoul, and he even tried to re-read the Shell Oil contract Marcus Samuel had given him. By late afternoon, he gave up and returned home.

Once inside, he lit a cigarette and pulled out his pocket watch. *Seven fifteen.* The only train out of Baku was the one to Tiflis which left at eight o'clock that evening. The steamer to Astrakhan wouldn't depart until the next morning. If Klara was intending to leave by train, he could at least catch her and say goodbye. He folded the contract away, yanked open the door to the courtyard and shouted for his horse to be saddled.

A sandstone portal heralded the entrance to the railway station. Inside the station yard, the trains roared and clanked. Anton tied up his horse and raced to the ticket booth.

'Tickets over here,' shouted the man sitting behind the window.

Anton pushed to the front, ignoring indignant voices. 'Have

you seen a young Russian girl and her father today? He would have been in a wheelchair. Very well dressed and distinguished. A military man and would have had two or more attendants.' He paused. 'On the other hand, the girl might have been travelling by herself. Dressed in pink. With a hat. Lots of feathers.' Anton realised he was rambling. He slipped a few kopeks across the counter.

The man stared at him. 'A lot of ladies wear pink and most have hats with feathers.'

'I know. But these people are very grand and distinguished.'

The man spat out a globule of tobacco and scooped the money into his hand. 'Nobody like you describe. Nobody in a wheelchair. Platform Two if you want to check.'

Anton ran to the platform. A whistle shrieked across Platform Two and a steam engine creaked as it hoisted itself into its starting position. Doors slammed, people hung out of the windows and trunks and cases were piled into the luggage van.

Anton raced towards the first-class cars, pushing through crowds of bystanders and weaving past station officials, looking in every window, searching each face.

But Klara wasn't there.

With a tremendous shudder, the eight o'clock train heaved itself forward and pulled out of the station. A slow *chug chug* whipped the air as it gathered pace, a trail of smoke snaking back down the line. People brushed past Anton as they made their way out of the station. Thick hot smoke hung in the air and burned his nostrils.

Anton stood with his hands in his pockets as the dusk settled over the tracks. Crows started to chatter, their harsh conversations drifting into the hiatus.

She's gone. What was I expecting?

It had been a foolish fancy. The grand duke would have commandeered a royal carriage or some other kind of grand conveyance, not a common train car. No doubt they would travel by royal steamer up the Caspian to the Volga.

Outside the station Anton whipped up his horse and trotted down the road. The harvest moon hung in the night sky and glowered over the shadowy hills. He would watch the steamers tomorrow at first light.

The house on Nikolaevskaya Street was bathed in silver, and as Anton dismounted and led his horse through the gates into the courtyard, he realised how weary he was. His limbs felt as if heavy weights had been stitched onto them. The horse nuzzled his ear, its rubbery lips and hot breath nudging him forward. He handed the reins to the stable boy and turned to face the house.

The library light was on. He could see the outline of the floor globe through the French windowpanes, and it seemed to be spinning.

Anton's mood sank at the thought of having to entertain a guest. He would tell Olga not to let anyone in, to make an excuse to visitors. There wasn't a single person he wanted to speak to. All he wanted was a hot tub, a large whisky, and a long sleep.

He strode across and peered through the window. Someone was sitting in his favourite chair with their back to the window. Slim fingers on an outstretched arm walked across the surface of the floor globe. He recognised the sleeve of that faded blue silk dress with embroidered flowers. A warm rush sped through him.

Anton tapped on the window and Klara sprang out of the chair.

'I thought you'd gone,' he said as he pushed through the double doors. 'I went to the train station.'

'You got my note?'

'Yes.'

'But you didn't reply?'

'No.'

'Why?'

Anton hesitated. 'I don't know. I didn't know what to say.'

She raised her eyebrows. 'That's not your usual problem.'

They fell silent and contemplated each other. Klara seemed agitated and Anton felt extremely uncomfortable. He could feel his heart doing strange acrobatics.

'Are you going on the steamer tomorrow?' he said after a long moment.

'No.'

'Oh… Where's your father? Is he still…'

'Gone. Went already.'

'I see. And you?'

'What?'

'When are you going?'

Something crinkled in her hands. 'I'm not sure. Do you *want* me to go?'

'No! Certainly not… I mean I would rather you didn't, but you have to go. Your father's not well. He needs you.'

'I know. But my father's a survivor. He's survived without me for many years.'

Anton brightened. 'So you're not going?'

'I didn't say that, but my father knows that life is not for me and it never has been.'

They stared at each other again. Anton cleared his throat. 'Your mother's portrait. You left it behind.' *Why did I say that? She'll know I've looked in her bedroom.* He cleared his throat again. 'Did I ever tell you that I like that dress?'

She screwed up her face. 'I don't think you did. In fact, I don't recall you ever saying anything nice.'

'Really? That's not good, is it? I'd better do something about it.'

'It's about time.' Klara hesitated. 'Because I've become rather fond of this house, even though its occupant is so very grim.'

'I think I've grown a little less grim.'

402

She smiled and placed three crumpled sheets of paper on the table.

Anton glanced at them and felt himself redden. 'I would have missed you. Very much.'

'I think we've become rather used to each other.'

Anton nodded. 'Yes, we have.'

Klara bit her lip. 'Well, I'll organise some food and then we'd better talk. You've got a lot of work to do, and you're going to need my help.'

'I know,' he said.

Epilogue

Engagement Announcement in the Baku *Vedomosti*, February 17th 1892

Anton Nikolayevich Sabroski of Baku, son of the late Nikolai Mikhailovich Sabroski, has announced his engagement to Miss Klara Konstantinovna. Mr Sabroski is an enterprising young businessman and the director of Sabroski Oil. The enchanting bride-to-be comes from the noble Lapinski family of Kiev.

The *Murex* Sets Sail: *The Times*, July 26th 1892

Under the command of Captain Coundon, the Murex *sailed from West Hartlepool, England, on July 26th 1892. She stopped to fill her tanks with BNITO oil from the Rothschild refineries at Batumi and then passed through the Suez Canal on August 24th.*

Alderman Marcus Samuel, the private entrepreneur behind the scheme, attended with his wife and daughter. His new company, Shell Oil, has attracted a great deal of interest on the exchange.

Anton Nikolayevich Sabroski, Alderman Samuel's chief business partner, who had travelled all the way from Baku in Eastern Transcaucasia, caused great excitement when he arrived with his new bride, Klara Konstantinovna, who is rumoured to be related to the Romanov family. The story has been denied by Mr Sabroski and his wife, but it was noted that Mrs Sabroski was wearing a beautiful dark blue enamel ring covered with gold lattice work and encrusted with diamonds very similar to one worn by Tsarina Alexandra.

HISTORICAL NOTE

The main facts behind Marcus Samuel and the setting up of Shell Oil are true. Marcus obtained specifications from the Suez Canal authorities to build an oil tanker safe enough to take a short cut from Europe via the canal to the Orient. Marcus negotiated a contract with the Rothschilds to buy Baku oil, and the first tanker (the *Murex* – named after a seashell) set sail in 1892. It is also true that Marcus named the company, Shell Oil, to honour his father's seashell trading company, but the brand name of 'Shell' was not adopted for the actual oil until several years later. In 1897, to protect his interests, Marcus formally bound together the shareholders of Samuel Samuel & Co's *Tank Syndicate in a company called the 'Shell Transport and Trading Company'.

In the nineteenth century, the Samuel family were merchants trading in seashells collected from the Orient. Marcus Samuel's father visited Baku and was astonished by the amount of oil the region produced. His son Marcus further realised the potential of selling Rothschild oil to customers in the Orient as it was the only area in the world free from the dominance of John Rockefeller's Standard Oil company. Consequently, the project was shrouded in secrecy and undoubtedly dangerous, as oil spies, sabotage and violence were common practices.

Some spellings of Baku regions have changed over the years. I decided to use the spellings shown in the 1905 publication: *Baku – An Eventful History* by James Dobbs Henry, the 1970 edition of *BEARSTED: A Biography of Marcus Samuel* by Robert Henriques, and the 1961 edition of *BLACK GOLD* by Arthur Beeby Thompson. I used the Russian Julian calendar for dates 1890–1892.

I did take some historical licence – Rafiq Hasanov is a character from my imagination. The *Murex* tanker was actually designed by Sir James Fortescue Flannery. My version of the Grand Duke Konstantin Nikolayevich did not exist and thus his mistress Katharine Lapinski and daughter Klara are fictitious.

However, real historical characters who lived in Baku at the time and appear in the book are:

- Hajji Zeynalabdin Taghiyev – millionaire Tatar oil baron
- Emanuel Nobel – Swedish oil baron
- De Boer – Rothschild business manager

The Sabroski, Brakovs and Seigenbergs are all my creations, with one exception. Julia Seigenberg is the name of my great, great grandmother, whose ancestors were Jewish and originated from Russia. I wonder if she ever passed through Baku…

*The Tank Syndicate consisted of Marcus Samuels's associates who helped finance the 'coup' against John Rockefeller.

Further Information

The Baku Inheritance is the first novel in The City of Winds series set in Baku between the years 1890–1920.

For further information about forthcoming novels, please visit my website: www.thecityofwinds.com and sign up for my newsletter.

BV - #0088 - 081024 - C0 - 198/129/23 - PB - 9781068630200 - Gloss Lamination